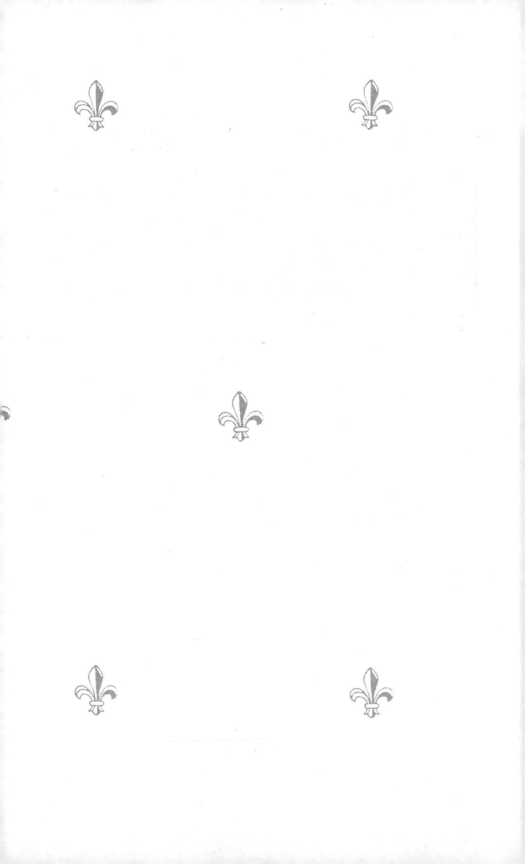

PROPHECIES
HELENA SOISTER

Bantam Books
New York • Toronto • London • Sydney • Auckland

PROPHECIES

A Bantam Book / July 1990

Library of Congress Cataloging-in-Publication Data

Soister, Helena.
    Prophecies / Helena Soister.
        p.   cm.
    ISBN 0-553-05878-9
    I. Title.
PS3569.044P7   1990
813'.54—dc20   89-18415
                                          CIP

Published simultaneously in the United States and Canada

Bantam Books are published by Bantam Books, a division of Bantam
Doubleday Dell Publishing Group, Inc. Its trademark, consisting of the words
"Bantam Books" and the portrayal of a rooster, is Registered in U.S. Patent
and Trademark Office and in other countries. Marca Registrada.
Bantam Books, 666 Fifth Avenue, New York, New York 10103.

PRINTED IN THE UNITED STATES OF AMERICA

DH   0   9   8   7   6   5   4   3   2   1

For my parents

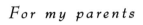

Charity never faileth:
But whether there be prophecies, they shall fail . . .
For we know in part, and we prophesy in part.
But when that which is perfect is come, then that which
*   is in part shall be done away.*

Corinthians I

♦ ♦ ♦

PROPHECIES

Two summers ago, when I was last at home, I was nigh killed by a madman. His attack put in me a foreboding that he was some sort of omen, but I paid no heed to this possibility. Now I know better. Had I stayed safe at home and not left London I would never have endured the fate that has just ended. Yet mayhap I was meant to go. Mayhap God had indeed intended that Bess and I go to Antwerp and to the fate that awaited us there.

I seem too insignificant to have a fate, though. I am only the widow and merchant Sara Lathbury. For most of my married life I lived in London, and there I chose to stay six years ago when my husband, Jonathan (God rest his soul), was lost at sea. He had been a member of the Merchant Adventurers, and as his widow I became as was my right an Adventurer in his stead and carried on our trade in cloths and divers goods that I had learned from him. He had been too for many years a partner in a company he shared with three other men. I replaced Jonathan in this partnership and with the others participate in joint ventures, or like them I perform my business independently when it pleases me. My sons, Matthew and Jeremy, have also become Adventurers and have joined my company as fellow partners.

Since the neither of them are yet married, my sons and I live together in some comfort near Ironmonger Lane, in a house connected to our countinghouse and warehouse. But not my sons nor my house have I seen in so very long a time. At last, in just o'er a day now, our ship will be in London. The winds have been stronger this last hour.

Had our company not become troubled, I would be in London still. Two summers past, howe'er, our factor in Antwerp became ill and scarce made it home to England and wife alive, so that old ventures sat there unfinished and new ones untried. His sickness caught him of such a sudden and his health waned so quickly that he had not been able to find another man to take his place. Since we Adventurers have by charter a monopoly on trade with the Lowlands, and trade with Ant-werp is of course essential to us, our man's illness was nigh more disastrous to us than to him; our company's business in that city could not be halted for e'en a few weeks. All the partners therefore decided that for at least a short while one of us must go to Antwerp, find another factor, put in order our trade there, and initiate new ventures. I was deemed the most fit. Of the lot of us, my Flemish, French, and Latin were the best, I was the most familiar with that city and, or so Matthew told me, I was the shrewdest judge of character; and withal, he added, our man had sent us a list of those merchants he most recommended to take his place. If several should prove capable of handling our business, then I had merely to choose from among them. Though I wasn't eager to sail anywhere, I made ready to go.

Two days before my departure, I said good-bye to Jeremy, who was off for Berkshire to barter with the clothiers there. Then I was busy with this errand and that, and not until the afternoon was ending could I finally make my way home. 'Twas in a marketplace along the way that I spotted Matthew. He was buying from an old woman some of the oranges piled into a basket at her feet.

"Buy one for me," said I when I reached his side.

"What? Ah, Mother—of course." He grinned and stooped to choose another. His long, sloping face had been reddened by the July sun and his honey-brown hair had glints of yellow burnt into it.

"You look like you've done all your work outside today."

"Aye, most of it." He put three oranges into the pouch at his side and tried to juggle the remaining two. In a trice one slipped past his catch and fell with a squash onto the street. He made a comical face, picked it up, and dropped it into the pouch, whence he then pulled a folded paper. "I nigh forgot—here's the list of men our factor thinks could replace him."

"Did any of our other partners recognize the names?"

"Not a one recognized a one. But that didn't stop Meric Dugdale from giving me advice on them anyway."

" 'Tis a bad habit he has."

"And too he said that if you wish, his wife will give Bess room and board, at a small price, till you return from Antwerp."

I began to wander among the booths and tables with him. "If she is foolish enough to come to London now." I had told my niece Bess that I would be in Antwerp for at least two months, belike longer, and that she should stay in Ipswich till I return. She had written me a letter in which she claimed that her late husband's family were trapping her in misery, fighting with her daily, and that she couldn't bear to live any longer under their roof. True to her fashion, she was dramatic in the telling. Though for six months now she was like me a widow and my sympathy for her was deep, I little doubted that she held her own in those fights. And too, her desire to strike out for London, with no mention of what she would do once there, certainly seemed no solution to her circumstances.

Matthew winked and prodded my shoulder. "Bess could stay with us if you but trusted your sons."

" 'Tis the gossip it would cause I distrust." I squeezed past a wheelbarrow and weaved in and out of the thickening traffic. "I'd rather plan for her to stay with Mistress Dugdale."

"Bess may already have a plan of her own."

I moaned at this. "She might, and if so there'll be no changing her mind on't."

Matthew drifted away to a table on the opposite side of the wide street, whilst I paused at a booth to buy a meat pie.

As we separated, shouts and the flurry of running feet rumbled down the street. Then a woman screamed and in that same sound came a horse's terrified neigh. Suddenly the people at that end of the market clambered frantically back and shoved tables out of their way and crushed the falling food under their feet. Scarcely had the hurly-burly begun when the waves of people parted and into the street bounded a huge snorting horse as white as winter, and on its back was a madman. He had the eyes of Lazarus and the cries of a raven, and his coiled strings of hair were flapping frantically against his head as if trying to escape from it.

"I am lost! I am lost!" he howled. With one hand he jerked the reins this way and that and with the other clawed his scarlet doublet so that shreds tore off like streams of blood.

The horse pranced insanely in a circle, snorting against the people who had unwillingly formed a trap around it. It tried to rear and buck and throw off its rider, but he held fast. The madman then pulled out a dagger and sliced the air with it and cried again, "I am lost!" like a forsaken soul flaying against a horror no one else could see.

I tried to get away, but my back was against the heavy booth and a broken table blocked my right side. I was about to rush off to my left when the horse stamped and leapt toward me. Suddenly the beast's heaving chest was mere inches away from my outstretched hand and the hot breath from its foaming mouth was shooting out at me. I could hear Matthew yelling desperately and I heard myself shouting for help. The horse pawed the ground and neighed like a wailing ghost. I could feel its violent strength which could pound me to death with one blow of its hooves. Then the beast reared and I looked up and saw that the madman's eyes were upon me and his arm was flung back and his hand and the knife it held were as high as a gallows.

The rearing horse came crashing back down and the madman's arm swooped at me. I pushed back hard—and the booth yielded. I fell back and out of the way and the flashing dagger just missed my throat but slashed in half the paper I was still holding in my frozen hands.

In moments it was over. The crowd closed in and the horse was snared in a bramble of hands. The raving madman was seized and dragged down and his skull was club-cracked. At last he lay still and senseless upon the ground.

At the same time Matthew had fought his way to the safe space beyond the booth where I had stumbled.

"I'm unharmed!" I panted when he called out and grasped me. "I don't think I was hurt."

"But I saw him stab at you!" He anxiously checked my arms for scratches.

"He missed me." I tried to catch my breath. " 'Twas only the list he cut."

"That was all?"

I nodded. "I'd forgotten I was holding it." I looked at the ground where I'd been standing. Trampled into the dirt were the two strips of paper where they had fallen like broken wings. I picked them up and turned to watch the horse being led off by someone, and the constable arrive to haul away the limp madman. "What a horrible sight that was. As baleful as an omen."

Matthew put his arm around me; only then did I realize how my limbs were trembling. "Well." He smiled and tried to jest. "Think you this was an omen of your trip?"

I folded the two soiled strips and with shaking hands put them in my pocket. "Nay, of course not." I sighed. " 'Twas only a madman on a horse."

He kept his arm around me as we walked home. Sunset had come by then; the air was streaked with violet, the shadows were spreading. All day the air hadn't moved, but now a dry wind whipped down abruptly over the rooftops and scattered dust around us. Some specks stung my cheek and startled me. Perchance because my nerves were still shaken, this swift change felt unnatural, and I hurried my steps so much that Matthew had to pull me back. Finally we turned down the street whereon was our house.

Few people were about, and no carts or animals, and so it seemed from nowhere that a horse and rider appeared at the other end of the street. Spurred by the wind, the horse was galloping wildly before it jerked to a stop at our house, nigh throwing the rider. Half-jumping, the rider was in a moment standing on the ground and pulling the reins to force the beast into control again. As if seeing again the madman and his blade tearing down at me, I recoiled. But 'twas only a woman. Her tawny and dandelion skirts were swirling in a dusty whirlwind, and her long hatless hair was undone and gathered together by a torn strip of lace wound down along it.

"By the holy rood, who's that on our doorstep?" asked Matthew.

Someone I didn't want to see. "First that madman," I muttered, "and now my mad niece."

II

When Bess threw her arms around me and let out a happy shriek and called my name, I quickly softened. How good it was to see her again, I said whilst she rattled the same to Matthew and me.

Matthew took the horse's reins. "Came you with no bags, and alone?"

"What? Ah, of course not. I traveled with a group of mercers—such a slow, dull lot. Once we reached London I was too eager to keep with them, so I rode on ahead. My trunks are on their wains still."

"Trunks?" I echoed.

She caught in her panting breath; a caution shot through her. "And a little more. All my movable possessions."

My smile faded, though I tried to prop it up. Matthew saw as much and, with the excuse that he would take her horse to our stables behind the warehouse, left us alone.

"Well," I stammered, knocking for the servant to let us in, "let's get you settled now."

"I can have the trunks delivered elsewhere if you wish, Aunt."

"Nay, I want you here with me. 'Tis only that you've clearly left the Marwicks' home for good then, and that I wasn't expecting. But I myself will be leaving for Antwerp in two days, and I told you as much in a letter. Did you not receive it?"

As she stepped inside with me, she grew quietly abashed. "Aye, just after my latest—and last—fight with Timothy's parents. I was packing to leave when it was handed me. If need be, I could stay elsewhere in London, I decided. And I still say that."

I shook my head. I also nigh asked her if she had walked out or been thrown out, but I held my tongue. "Nay, of course you'll stay here, at least till I leave. Then mayhap you can board with one of my partner's families."

Dust and dried sweat streaked her neck; I told her to go upstairs and wash herself and comb her hair. "A servant can fetch your trunks," I added.

In our enclosed garden I waited for Bess to come back down. Her arrival may have meant the annoyance of another matter to settle ere I left, but by then I minded not. Since the days when she was a child she had sometimes stayed with me, and since those days we had grown close. Now she was a widow, with no brothers or sisters, whose parents—my brother and his wife—had died of the sweating sickness soon after she was married. She was too much alone.

In a little while Bess came down into the garden. She apologized for so suddenly appearing at our door. I said something about her being always welcome. In the strain of not knowing what next to say, we fell silent. She wandered to a bush and pretended to examine its sparse blooms. There wasn't much more to the garden than a few bushes, a crooked tree, and a square of long grass.

I watched her as she moved. She had long since ceased to be the child I'd known and had become a woman past twenty-four years of age. Though not truly beautiful, she yet had a most peculiar loveliness, for I had never discovered its origin nor seen it in any other woman. Still there it was, lying somewhere in the proud brow and cheeks, in the faint colors of her skin made startling by her night-black hair and brown eyes, and in the intelligence and life sparking in her. Men usually found her fair, but most found far more fair any woman with sweetly pretty features and a girlish mind, none of which she had. Instead (and this she did even as a child) she sometimes seemed to look at the world as if at birth some knowledge not of this world had been given her. It was a look that could unsettle anyone.

She was lingering beside one of the high walls, where the moss had dried in the summer sun and clung crackly and dead to the stones. She looked for long seconds at the moss, at the violet and russet sky, and then at me. Only then did I notice that she had untied the top of her chemise so that it hung open above her small breasts.

"You'd best lace that up again before Matthew sees you."

"I shall. I shall." Her hand rose to the strings but did nothing else.

" 'Tis only that I want no"—the fingers tried to catch the words—"binding now. With the Marwicks I always felt as wound tight as their family clock."

I hesitated, but asked my question anyway. "You've written to me of your fights with them. Yet I never considered Timothy's parents to have much taste for arguments or anger."

A tension stiffened her shoulders. "True. They'd rather strike with a sullen and maddening coldness. 'Twas I who at last prodded them into fights, which you've already assumed, haven't you, Aunt?" She was regarding me as if she needed unquestioning loyalty and I had betrayed her.

"No, not at all." I tried to sound sincere. " 'Tis only that . . . I know not your circumstances."

"My circumstances?" Drops of bitterness were in this. Slowly she began to pace around the garden. "My circumstances are thus: The jointure given me by Marwick at my wedding, should Timothy die, is fifty pounds a year. I own sixty acres of good farmland I've rented out profitably. What my parents willed to me, their house and what filled it, have long since been sold and the money kept, save for those things I wish to keep for memories' sake. In all, I now have the handsome sum of over one hundred and eighty pounds, which I've put into bills of exchange to be honored here in London on the morrow."

I blinked. "I had no idea you had so much. You're a wealthy young woman."

"But not a wealthy merchant."

"A merchant?"

"Aye. I have more than enough to establish myself comfortably in the trade. And that is what I have—and want—to do now. Like you I am the widow of a Merchant Adventurer, and so can be one in Timothy's place."

I suppose I had been expecting as much. Certes this was the most logical step she could make. "That you could do, but you haven't all the training."

"I've most of it. Remember you I worked with my father at his trade, and then with Timothy and his father. God's wounds! I was better than Timothy. Sometimes in business he was like a poor dog trying to walk on its hind legs." As soon as she had said this, she was ashamed. "Nay, he wasn't so bad as that. And he did try. Some of his failed ventures—and he had more than his share—broke his heart." She stopped her pacing. "I should at least be kind to him."

I left the word-speckled air empty before asking, "And were you not kind to him whilst he was alive?"

"Not I to him or he to me for, oh, how long? Mayhap the last year of his life. When it appeared I wouldn't bear him another child soon, if ever."

I ached for her. "How sad it is to lose a child."

She was staring at the ground, at nothing. The white spidery seeds of ripened weeds drifted by her feet, weightless and aimless. "He was such a small babe, and he made no noise. He came into the world silently and died." She hugged herself as if holding together torn emotions. "My blood no longer comes each month. Sometimes there is no blood at all, and other times a little."

"Oh, but you can bear again. I've known many a woman who is the same, and then of a sudden finds herself with child, and gives birth to a healthy one to boot. The women in our family—your father's— tend not to bear frequently, and that can be a blessing, mind you. Too many mothers die from too many childbirths, or from but one."

She said nothing to this; I knew she had heard such hollow comfort too many times before. In that deep pause all I could think of was Bess as she had been only a few years ago, laughing and in love, and always with her chestnut-haired Timothy. Nothing that was good had lasted.

With brittle movements, Bess began to pace about again. "And so we both changed. He slapped me about till I struck him back hard. He lost more money in foolish ventures. And then at last he was unfaithful to me, and many times. And so when he caught a fever I was almost glad of it. Only when he wheezed and sweated and couldn't rise from his bed did I become worried. And then he died." She was fading to an end. "I never thought the fever would kill him."

"We can never know when the Lord will take us," I said uselessly.

"He had been the peacemaker betwixt his parents and me. But when he was gone they grew cold, and I grew nigh mad with frustration. I'd sooner have word-bloody battles than their awful coldness."

"Well." I cleared my throat. "Well, 'tis all behind you now. And about your becoming an Adventurer—I'd gladly help you with that. I can give you very good advice. Some of it, now, will have to wait till I return from Antwerp . . ."

"No, 'twould be much better if I went to Antwerp with you."

I gaped at her.

She stopped and faced me. "If I begin by buying and selling in Antwerp, and be there mine own factor, I'll have a firmer and sooner start than by staying here. I e'en have a buyer already. A cousin of Timothy's in Ipswich has told me he needs whatever fine foreign cloth I can send him. He also claims that he can find me other buyers."

"Marry. Well, mayhap you should go with me. That might do us both some good, and I confess I'd be glad of the company, and there I could better give you what training you lack."

"I'm not so lacking."

"How are your languages?"

"Flemish and French both are very good. I remember what I was taught and used them with the foreign merchants who came to the Marwicks' countinghouse in Ipswich."

"Latin?"

" 'Tis sufficient."

"And your money."

"I shall arrange to have my bills of exchange payable in Antwerp."

I whooshed away a night moth that had fluttered onto my sleeve. "Well, Antwerp might be a better place for you for the nonce. If you tire of it you can return to England, or if I tire of you I'll send you packing."

These last words, tossed off lightly, she took too seriously. "Do you regret my coming with you?"

"Nay. Instead, I don't want to regret leaving you behind."

No more was said. I rose and, brushing flecks of dirt and more fluttering moths from my clothes, turned to where she was standing beneath the tree. That too-knowledgeable look had crept into her brown eyes, luminous in the twilight. I disliked having them on me. Avoiding their gaze, I bid her come inside.

♦　♦　♦

Two days later Bess and I went to the docks. While our trunks were laded on a hoy, we said our good-byes to Matthew and too to our partner Meric Dugdale, who seemed to be there only to give me unneeded advice.

"Now make you certain, Sara, that you choose our factor with care. The failure or continued success of our company can depend upon him. I would help you myself if I could, but I'm too old for traveling." He smoothed back what graying hair was left on his age-spotted head.

"Sweet Jesus, Meric"—I leaned over his round belly and kissed his cheek—"you know I'll choose wisely."

"And a virtuous man. His name simply cannot be sullied."

We were being called to the ship. I hugged Matthew one last time. "I shall like enow see you in Antwerp if you don't return by October," said he. I told him to look after himself and his brother, and to run our business well. Then Bess and I boarded the hoy. There was shouting and hurrying, the anchor was hoisted, and the ship swayed and creaked and moved out into the waters.

"Free," said Bess. "Suddenly I feel free."

"That's just this sailing away from shore." I shrugged. " 'Tis an illusion I too sometimes have. But we'll both be home soon enow."

"You'll be going home, Aunt. Not I."

··⊱ III ⊰··

Our journey, thank the Lord, was blessed with no problems and fair winds. We sailed all day and night, and when I lay down to sleep I knew we'd belike arrive in Antwerp early on the morrow. Hours later I awoke, having felt in my sleep the ship shift its direction and the waters of the rough open sea beneath us become calmer. When Bess also stirred and like me was unable to fall back asleep, we rose, drew on cloaks, and went up to the deck.

It was no longer night, but that strange gray time betwixt dark and morning, made grayer still by clouds and an early mist floating through the thin half-light that appeared to come from nowhere, the dawn having not yet colored the east. There were nigh-hidden shores to either side of us, but I was familiar enough with the banks to know that we were on the Scheldt River and closer to Antwerp than I'd anticipated. I glanced about the ship; save for Bess and me there was only the coxswain on deck. He regarded us, nodded a greeting, then turned his eyes back to the bow and the river beyond, his arms slowly moving the steerage.

"How soon will we be there?" Bess was growing eager.

"Soon. This foggy air is too thick for me to calculate our bearings, but Antwerp is close by."

For a while we said nothing more. A fading wind whispered past our ears and made the sails slap against themselves. The rhythmic sound of low waves splashing upon the hull was nigh drowning the shadowed noises echoing from the banks. Gradually, there were more sounds: the stirrings below as the men awoke and readied for work, and the distant splash of another ship cutting through the water, and then another, and they came into view. A few men ascended to the deck and lolled about or found tasks that needed doing. A keel sailed nearby; we passed several barges; and before us appeared the small pilot boats, leading our ship and the others away from the sandy spots and up the river. The shrill cries of seagulls mixed with the rumbling shouts of men. The birds glided into sight, whipping in broad curves around the masts, diving with sudden speed as if to plunge into the watery depths, then curving again and soaring upward. I watched one gull as it dove, and when it slowly rose again it seemed to lift on its wide wings some of the mist, so that far beyond I espied the even lines of distant buildings.

"I can see it now!" With one hand I grasped Bess's arm and with the other pointed over the larboard bow. "There it is, that's Antwerp."

She escaped my grasp and pushed hard against the rail, bending dangerously over it.

At last the dawn broke, and as its light swam through the air the mist began to roll back, away from the land and onto the river, revealing as it retreated the scarlet, tattered band of light thrown long against the eastern horizon; and between that blood-bright ribbon and the gray moving waters could be seen Antwerp at last. It was a huge mass of buildings and houses and churches with squared or pointed or stair-shaped gables and roofs and spires which were pushing one upon the other and all upon the edge of the Scheldt, where it seemed hundreds of ships were sailing back and forth from its crowded quays.

"Dear God!" Bess was exhilarated. "What a sight it is! I should have come here long ago."

When our ship had docked at the English Quay, I talked with the captain, who oft interrupted me to bellow an order to a sailor, and arranged for him to hold our things till we had found lodging and could send for them. That much done, Bess and I made our way off the ship and through the wharf's traffic of packers and gaugers, overseers, collectors, and merchants.

I knew where the best lodgings could be had and so headed for the White Hound near Wool Straat, a place where I had boarded a few times before. The house, in Flemish fashion, was narrow and high, and scrubbed outside and in. We were greeted by old Vrouw Scinckaert, the ancient wrinkled owner of the Hound, who remembered me well. Thumping her cane at every step, she led us up a steep winding staircase to the top and third floor. It was of fair size, with a bed for two, a table, two backless chairs, and a window that looked out into the street. Vrouw Scinckaert thumped and shuffled her way from one end to the other, then bartered with me in Flemish until we arrived at the equivalent of six shillings a day for the two of us.

Bess sat on the bed, made a face, said naught.

"Are you disappointed with the room?" I asked.

"Oh no, I like it. But it comes at a dear price."

"For England it be dear, but fair for Antwerp. Your money will soon be gone in this city if it isn't replaced with profits."

"Then I'll begin turning profits all the sooner."

I spent that day and days more putting in order the company's business left unfinished by our factor. Some of my partners' and my goods had been left in our rented warehouse; I saw to their delivery. I sought buyers for other goods not yet sold and sent explanations to customers awaiting delayed goods. I called on debtors, paid creditors, took up or honored bills of exchange. Back and forth I went, from the Custom House at the English Quay to merchants' countinghouses, to shops and ships and home again to my office—our small room at the White Hound. And wherever I went so went Bess. Already she was carefully dividing and investing her capital by buying Turkish cloths, costly velvet from Genoa, and other such stuff and sending them as arranged to Timothy's cousin in Ipswich. Through letters she queried him and my sons for the names of more buyers, and too received from Matthew his shipped kerseys, which she sold. The profit she shared with him was soon invested again in ells of brocade. Through it all, she kept thorough ledgers, whether they were small daybooks for daily expenses or account books listing both debtors and creditors, and she dealt ably with the basic demands of purchases and sales. What things were unfamiliar to her she learned by observing me. She was soon proving to be a most able Adventurer.

In a fortnight my ventures and those of my partners were in order again, though most of them wouldn't be completed for a month or two more. Still, I finally had time to search for a factor. Two men were eliminated from my list since they were too busy to take on more work; another I scratched off when he proved to know little of the cloth trade. For this reason and that, others were marked off till only one man remained. I was to learn about him—and hear my first rumors of him—from Vrouw Scinckaert.

She told us on a muddy Sunday drizzled with rain. After hurrying back from church and changing into dry clothes, Bess and I came downstairs to the main chamber to have our breakfast. Vrouw Scinckaert was sitting alone at the fireside, wrapped in a smothering blanket and sipping posset. She let out a hoarse cough and wiped her nose to signal she had a cold, sufficient excuse for her absence from mass that day, and when we had settled at the long table, she moved her chair nearer us.

"Bring us some sack posset!" she called out to the maid, and turned back to us. "Your breakfast may take a little while. What my cook prepared this morning—enow to feed an army—was finished off by mine other boarders." Clucking her tongue, she complained about their appetites till our posset was brought. "This is very good for colds, you know."

"By the by, Vrouw Scinckaert"—I warmed my hands around my cup—"I was hoping you might give me your opinion on a man recommended to me as a factor."

"Aye, I will if I know him."

"He's an Englishman who lives in Antwerp. His name is Bartholomew Catlin."

She sniffed and coughed. "Catlin—aye, I've heard much of him, all right. He just might make you a right good factor indeed, oh yes. He's a wealthy merchant and clever as a fox. But honest. I've never heard anyone accuse him of dishonesty. He buys and sells, mostly in cloth. He factors. He has a money exchange. He speculates on the exchange rates of foreign currencies. And he lends."

"At a fair interest?"

"I can't say. I know worse can be had from other lenders."

"Many lenders are not liked."

"Oh, I never said he was liked. He's respected, but he's not much liked, especially by English merchants. I've heard some Adventurers complain he's more Flemish than English, or is too much of an ingezettenen."

That interested me more. So he was a settled foreigner in Antwerp who enjoyed most of the liberties of the city. "An ingezettenen could be very convenient for me and my partners."

Vrouw Scinckaert wouldn't let this practical observation interrupt her. "They don't like the way he hasn't been home to England in years, and goes only to the marts about the Lowlands. I think he has no need to travel, since he is wealthy enow to have his own factors or shipping agents do his foreign work. And too he spent some of his youth here—that was a lonely time for him, what with no mother and little time for friends. But he was at least here with his father, who came for long periods of business. You see, his father had a Flemish partner in Antwerp, and the two men shared the same countinghouse. But everything seemed to change when the partner, Martin van den Bist—was that his name? Aye, methinks it was—when van den Bist was killed."

"Killed?" I repeated.

"Murdered." Vrouw Scinckaert narrowed her eyes and let the word roll slowly out, savoring the years-old story. "Stabbed twice. And his murderer was never found."

Bess leaned forward. "No one knew who wanted him dead?"

"No one was charged. But there were suspects, plenty of them. He had his enemies. But Bartholomew wasn't one of them. No, the young Catlin and van den Bist had been quite close. So when the man died, Bartholomew grew strangely surly and angry. His father bade him to return to England, but he refused. I heard the two of them were nigh at each other's throats. And in another year his father died too."

"Murdered?" Bess asked.

"No." The old woman seemed disappointed. "Died in his bed. Drank himself to death, people say. And that was when this Bartholomew Catlin bought a large house here and set himself up in trade." Her voice fell to an eager hush. "But I must tell you, there are rumors about him, rumors of certain private sins . . ."

"Such rumors I like," Bess quipped. "A very good man is very boring."

"Aye, isn't that true!" Vrouw Scinckaert giggled. Suddenly the noise caught in her throat and she choked on it and stared past us at the other end of the room.

There stood a friar. He had entered without a sound, closed the door behind him, and like an owl was watching us. He was in the habit of a Dominican; his white tunic and scapular seemed repeatedly washed of any impurities and was fraying from the effort; and over them the somber black cape and hood hung emptily upon his lean frame. Young he was, only in his early or mid-twenties, yet no youth was in his face. His lips, nearly as bloodless as his skin, allowed for no curve, and between his sparse eyebrows a single scowling line cut into the pure brow. In contrast to all this was his blond hair, shorn in a monk's tonsure and worn like an unglimmering halo.

"No one should like such rumors." His voice wrapped around Bess like holy oil. He spoke in Flemish, as we had been, and turned now to Vrouw Scinckaert. "God bless you, Grandmother."

In an instant she was up and pulling over a chair. "Gerard, how good to see you! How unexpected a visit!" She bade him sit, called out to the maid for another cup of posset, sat again, and put on an abashed expression as if asking forgiveness for any sin she might commit in his presence. Finally she remembered Bess and me and introduced us. He gave us but a nod.

"And I pray all is well with you, Grandmother?"

At the word "pray" she trumpeted a hoarse cough. "Oh, Gerard, my dear, I trow I be well enow. Still I would that God would make me full well, since plagued with the ague I am. Not a terribly bad ague, mind you—I've had worse—but it makes me feel sickly."

"I grieve to hear that, Grandmother. You did not venture out in the rain today?"

"Oh, God forgive me, no, though I longed to hear my Sunday mass." She blew her nose, crumpled her shoulders, and grew pitifully frail.

"God will indeed forgive you. I shall pray for your health."

"I thank ye," she whimpered.

It was then I recalled of once being told that Vrouw Scinckaert had a grandson newly ordained in the Dominicans. Since the monastery was but a few minutes' walk from her house, he would sometimes stop by and ask after the old woman, though his visits seemed more like the hauntings of a grim confessor. "The legend of the White Hound's black friar," the lodgers dubbed them, as they would a ghostly myth.

All this time, Bess had been keeping her eyes upon him. "Why shouldn't I like the rumors about this Catlin?" Her question was a challenge.

Only his eyelids moved. "The rumors, mevrouw?"

"Aye. You heard our talk."

"Merely a few words of it."

I doubted that.

"But do you know aught of this Catlin that your grandmother does not?" she pressed.

"I know the secrets of men like him."

"As does God?"

At last his eyes slid around to Bess. Only then did I notice that his face was a handsome one, but rendered unappealing by his unearthly calm and the stern asceticism of his features. "Only God our Father is all-knowing. I am merely his humblest servant."

"Ah, but do you ever confuse the difference?"

"The difference?"

"Between you and God."

Brother Gerard's lips tightened. "That is blasphemy!"

Vrouw Scinckaert's eyes bulged and she drew her cloak about her as if to ward off the evil floating threateningly near. "Oh, God-a-mercy, she cannot mean blasphemy! No!"

"Of course I don't." Bess was looking hard at him and he at her as if a cold understanding was passing betwixt them. " 'Twas a poor jest I made, Brother. I meant only that I did not think this Catlin or his rumored secrets should be of any interest to you."

"He's of great interest when 'tis rumored that he favors heresy."

The very word "heresy" sent a nervous quiver through me. "I know nothing of that," I hurried to say.

"It is a heresy common among your more sinful countrymen." His eyes came now on me.

At last Vrouw Scinckaert rallied. Her grandson might float amidst severe angels, but she was an earthbound woman of business who could not afford to have her boarders frightened away. "Of course she knows nothing of that. We were merely discussing his trade and hers. Now let's speak of other matters."

His posset was finally brought, and he and his grandmother sank into boring talk of small and holy things. Bess and I tried to extricate ourselves from their conversation, but the black friar held us there with questions and suspicions. So until he himself left, we remained for a miserable hour caught within his claws.

God's blood, I swore to myself, I will see this Bartholomew Catlin, if only to spite this meddling monk. And spite him I did.

IV

On the morrow the sky was again heavy with clouds and a drizzle was ever sputtering. I wanted to stay within, warm and dry, but I couldn't put off meeting Bartholomew Catlin. So Bess and I walked to his countinghouse, which was nigh Kaiserstraat and in a costly part of town. 'Twas a three-storied house of somber stone and wood with stair-shaped gables, and fringing its door and window frames were carvings that may once have been brightly painted; but what paint there had been was scraped off years ago and the carvings were worn down into splinters. On the door was a plain sign with the words Bartholomew Catlin, Merchant Adventurer.

I opened the door, which creaked as it swung, and we stepped inside to a room as plain and dismal as the exterior. There were some shelves filled with parcels and such, and cupboards and benches were about, and before us at a table sat a beardless youth in apprentice garb. He was short and slight with orange-brown freckles that spotted his hands and face and vanished into his orange hair. He had been copying letters, but when we entered he stood and greeted us in Flemish. This man Catlin is surely more Flemish than English, I reflected, if he has not an English apprentice.

"I am here to see Bartholomew Catlin," said I in his tongue.

He heard my accent, so answered me in good English. "If you please to give me your name, I'll tell him you're here."

Another apprentice entered the room, this one tall and lumbering, with a mop of blond hair and an awkward jug of a face which was open and smiling.

"Be you both Master Catlin's apprentices?" I asked the orange-haired youth.

"We are." His efficient tone clipped off the edges of his words. "I am Michiel Mahieu, and this is Jan Spals." He gave the other fellow a grudging gesture.

The lumbering Jan, his arms full of papers, bobbed his head to us and clumsily dropped them onto the table. Like a peeved pet Michiel snapped a criticism at Jan's sloppiness.

In a minute there was the tinkle of a small bell. Michiel went into the room behind him. "Master Catlin will see you now," he said when he returned, and ushered us into the chamber.

Before us, seated behind a desk, was a dark man. He had black hair and a trimmed beard, was soberly dressed, and was scribbling into a ledger. The only sounds in the room were the scratchings of the quill and the fluttering of paper, and yet I heard—more with my mind than mine ears—a disquiet in him, a disturbed passion that ruptured the silence. There were two windows to his right and through them drifted the gray of the rainy morning. Away from the windows, away from the candle on his desk, were bleak shadows steeped-up in piles behind him, as if waiting for him to finish and depart that they might, as was their grim duty and his affliction, follow him.

He crossed out a line and looked up at us. He was mayhap in his middle thirties, but his features were strained as though he had, by much cleverness and plotting, lived too long past his allotted time and was weary from the effort. Yet despite this defect he was a somewhat handsome man, with eyes that were dark and intelligent and deep.

He rose, gestured for us to be seated, and sat again. I shot a glance about the room as I settled into a chair. Unlike the entrance chamber, it was elegantly furnished. On one wall were wall hangings, on another a sprawling map of Europe, in one corner stood a cold chimney and hearth. Leather-bound ledgers lay on a table, together with letters and keys, a standing-box for divers papers, a clock, a delicately strung balance scale and its weights, a touchstone to assess the fineness of gold, wax and a seal and a ring with a signet, and numerous other things.

"I may be of help to you, Mistress Lathbury?" His voice was like rich fur.

"That, sir, I do hope." I opened my surcoat. "I must need hire a factor for my company, which is of London, and am come from there to find a good man in this city. And this, sir, is my niece Bess Marwick, who is accompanying me during my stay in Antwerp."

He nodded to Bess but gave neither her nor me any idle pleasantries. I told him of my company, its members and trade, the amount of goods and money in which we dealt and other facts, in the end explaining what we needed in a factor. He in turn told me of his company, which consisted solely of himself and the two apprentices; he was an independent man who could work alone as he preferred and choose where, when, and with whom he might join in a deal. Indeed, the only times he agreed to work with someone over a long period was when he did factoring. "I am at present the agent for two other men, and they are the same for me; one lives in London, the other in Cologne." Finally he listed the remarkable variety of goods in which he dealt, adding that of course as a Merchant Adventurer he traded mostly in cloth.

"Can you send to England much good linen, or says from Haarlem and silk from Venice?" I asked.

"Certainly. I know where to obtain what I need or want."

"And can you sell here good English kerseys and broadcloths, or whatever else we might send you?"

"Cloths of good quality are seldom difficult to sell for a good price. I could also keep you informed on what is of late selling well or poorly in Antwerp. I or my apprentices would also oversee the packing and shipping of merchandise to you and your customers; if packers are not carefully chosen and watched, the goods may be damaged or not sent at all. Being an Adventurer, I oft use the English Quay and 'tis there your goods will arrive."

"I was told, sir, that you are a free man in this city."

"An ingezettenen. Aye, I am. I must still pay tolls and weighing dues at the docks, but withal I enjoy the liberties of a citizen."

"And that could be right convenient to us." I questioned him further, found him most knowledgeable, and perceived that he was probing me in turn and deciding whether or no it was worth his while to do business with my company. It seemed not to matter if I should choose him for a factor—he had more than enow money to do without me. Rather, he appeared to be considering if he should choose me; for he would be no servant to our company but an equal, if not a superior.

"I've also heard, Master Catlin," I continued, "that you deal in the money exchange. This could be convenient for us, as we'll not need to

seek that service elsewhere. I've heard too that you lend money. Make
you much profit in such loans?"

"Not really so much." On this subject he was taciturn.

"Aye, of course not." I understood why. English law, which had
once allowed for the taking of interest on loans, had some years ago
been changed again and now Englishmen couldn't take a penny in
interest. Most merchants avoided this restriction by hiding in different
ways the necessary profits on money lent. "I've made some money on
loans myself, save—and belike you do the same—when a debtor is
worthy of Christian charity."

He answered only with, "You're a kind woman, Mistress Lathbury."

"Oh, I thank ye. But what kindness I have is tempered by common
sense. Well, sir, I must say you keep yourself occupied with all your
work. I gather you've a wife who helps you?"

"I'm not married."

"Oh, a widower then, and not much different from the two of us."

"I've never taken a wife." He rested his firm gaze on me, ready to
be deaf to any similar questions about his private life. I was struck by his
dark blue eyes; they wove a boundless distance betwixt us.

I cleared my throat and tried to close the subject. "Ah, I see. Well,
I only meant 'tisn't common never to marry unless one is a nun or
priest."

"And thank God Master Catlin is not a priest," Bess suddenly
remarked.

A bare smile stirred his lips. "You don't like priests?"

"I don't like what they think of women. A priest once quoted me
the Bible and said that the head of every man is Christ, and the head of
the woman is the man. I told him I'd rather see his head cut off ere I'd
agree with him."

A small laugh escaped from him. I in turn became annoyed. Bess's
facetiousness was an interruption to our practical talk.

"Please you forgive my niece, sir," I hurried to say. "She is new to
our trade and . . ."

He paid me no heed. "Not only priests but nigh all men hold
themselves above women."

"But you aren't among them," said Bess.

"How know you that?"

"Because such men are fools, and you're clever."

His smile widened and hardened. "And so are you."

For a moment they shared a gaze that seemed to wrap around the two of them like a prickly touch. He appeared glad of the comical flattery she was giving him, as if he were too oft alone and serious with business. Still I tried to bring our talk back to that business.

"By the by, Master Catlin, this countinghouse is quite large. Be there sufficient warehouse space and workers to handle all the goods we would send you?"

"I have two apprentices and a manservant for my work here; I lack no help. And at most times I've more than enow space, though at other periods so many goods are stored here the house is like to overflow." He stated this only as fact; no boasting swelled in his voice. "If it pleases you, I'll show you some of the rooms."

I told him I'd like that, and so he ushered us back into the front chamber and down a hall leading to a large room in the back. 'Twas filled with boxes and packages and barrels, and vacant space was left only for a table and benches, a path to a wide door through which merchandise could be carried in and out, and a set of stairs. We went up them to the two rooms that took up the entire second floor. The smaller one was dark and cool and used for goods stored a long time.

"And the rooms above these," I asked him, "how are they used?"

"They're home for my apprentices and a housekeeper."

"Then you live elsewhere?"

"My house is near to here."

We went across the landing to the larger room. 'Twas half empty and over the front of the building. It greeted us with the swollen noise of our own entrance—echoes of footsteps, whispers tailing our words. Bess and I strolled to the two windows on the opposite wall and saw the drizzle outside brushing the panes with the frailest beads of rain. They sounded like a stealthy breath. 'Twas just then the only sound in the room, and I realized the silence was somehow, inexplicably, unsettling me. The gray air moved through the room like an unquiet spirit, folding its long fingers around me, drawing me deeper into itself, into something strange.

I shuddered, took hold of myself, turned about—and gasped. Out of the shadows lingering about the door were two eyes shimmering like burning coals. In a frightened spasm I hugged my arms around myself. Then I sighed. 'Twas only Master Catlin.

"Have you a chill, Mistress Lathbury?" His voice bulged in the shallow darkness.

"Oh . . . just a sudden one," I lied.

"Mayhap we should return to the warmth of my office."

"Aye, let's do." I quickly preceded him and Bess out and down the stairs.

He paused at the bottom and for a moment rested his eyes upon Bess. "Mistress Lathbury, you are yourself training your niece?"

"I am, sir. She is like me a Merchant Adventurer through her late husband. Though she's had already much training, she has seldom exercised her skills."

He briefly pondered this. "I have a factor in London, but 'twould benefit my business to work also with your company. Should we decide, mistress, to do business with each other, I shall also allow your niece to do some of her work in this my countinghouse. She could observe some of my apprentices' work or what passes here—though only those things I choose. I'll not have my clients' affairs prodded into."

"Then we have yet another reason to join in business."

"I myself would like that." Bess wanted to speak for herself.

I smiled as I realized that he knew this offer would appeal to me and yet not cost him a penny. You are a clever man, I said to myself.

"Please you," said he, "go into mine office and I'll join you in a moment."

"Sara," Bess spoke hesitantly, "have you ever dreamt that you've been in a place before?"

"What? Oh, sometimes."

"I feel as if I've been in this house before, mayhap in a dream. Have you?"

"Been here? Nay, but I must say this place . . . I don't know. I had a weird feeling upstairs, and just now as we came back. And Catlin himself—think you there's something a bit odd about him? I can't put my finger on't, yet there's something about him that bothers me."

"Is there?" Bess ran her fingers over the things on the shelf and tapped a brass string holder; it rolled away from her like a wary animal. "For me he's quite the opposite. I feel utterly at ease with him, as if I already knew him."

"And you spoke to him with gross familiarity. That jape about priests and men . . ."

"He laughed at it."

"Still it was unseemly because we scarce know him."

"I'd like to know him much better."

"Aye, I can see why. He is handsome, in a noble way, and he's wealthy and unmarried. If he's a kind man too, then he'd make a fine match for any woman."

"I've had my stomach full of marriage," she retorted. "If I have Master Catlin at all, 'twill only be for a brief folly."

"Oh, stop it, Bess! You're only trying to anger me with scandal." I pulled my surcoat back over my chilled shoulders. "Now, enough of this foolishness. We should both be considering him strictly in terms of trade, and I am indeed impressed with him and his countinghouse." He was also not only English and a Merchant Adventurer, but he had a money exchange and much space for storing our goods, which would eliminate my company's present custom of renting a warehouse in Antwerp. I now too had a selfish reason, since I liked the idea of Bess working in this place. Remembering the list of possible factors was in my daybook, I pulled it out, unfolded the two torn strips of paper, and read over the scratched-out names and advice. I put away the paper.

The door of the office creaked open and Catlin entered. "Your pardon for your wait, Mistress Lathbury." He sat down at his desk. "Shall we continue our discussion on our joining in business?"

"Indeed, Master Catlin, let us continue."

And so we reviewed what would be expected of him, what he would expect from us, and the amount of his commission. At last we came to an agreement, and I charged him with the business of my company.

"Now, mistress," said he, "I shall do my best to make you and your company wealthier than you had planned for."

I bristled a little at this. "Our purses are heavier than you assume, sir."

"Still I'll put more money in them."

And soon enow he kept his word.

V

From that day on, Bartholomew Catlin worked with Bess and me. Not only did he soon prove to be an excellent factor, but at his advice I and my partners began to deal heavily in goods we'd but dabbled in before. Now besides cloth we bought and sold spices, drugs, sugar, cotton, madder, hops, gum arabic, and countless other merchandise. When Catlin rightly foretold that excellent profits could be had with furs from the north countries, then I dealt too in sable, ermine, lynx, leopard, white fox, common fox, white wolf, common wolf, and the skins of sea beasts. I began to make much money. Catlin was right.

Yet the disquietness I'd felt when near him that first day, though it faded, never completely left me. At first I even paid heed to aught about him or his countinghouse that struck me as odd, such as the way all of the doors creaked, some with grating volume. I once mentioned to Michiel that their hinges should be oiled.

"Oh, the master wouldn't allow it."

"And why not?" I asked. "That squeaking is wretched."

"But Master Catlin wants every door in here to make noise. He says he cannot bear having a door open silently because then someone might sneak about secretly."

A twisted notion, I thought. But I grew accustomed to the sounds and soon scarce heard them. I even became something of a friend to Catlin (and called him simply that as he preferred), yet as he did with nigh everyone else he subtly kept me at a distance, as if wary of me. Still, with Bess he began to be different.

In contrast to me, Bess felt more comfortable with him and was so often at the countinghouse that it was becoming a home to her.

Sometimes she worked with the apprentices and learned from them, but it was Catlin she watched. Like him she was soon very busy and preferred to work independently, save when she joined in ventures with me. She was adapting to both the merchant's life and Antwerp so naturally that I had misgivings, for she never mentioned returning to London, never longed for England, never spoke of her future beyond her temporary stay in Antwerp. She even spoke little of the private hours she and Catlin were spending together in his office. I soon suspected they were sharing more than a mere friendship.

One afternoon, a few weeks after I'd hired Catlin, I stopped by his countinghouse to review with him my account books. Though no one was about, slipping beneath the closed door of his office were his and Bess's voices. I knocked and entered at the same time, then halted.

The two of them were close together, she sitting on a corner of the desk, he standing hard by her, and they were crooning low words and growling laughter as though wooing each other. A moment passed ere Bess saw me. Quickly she stiffened her body away from his whilst he, as though drawing a mask o'er his face, became again the solemn man I knew. I felt awkward.

"Sara—God keep you." Catlin bowed slightly. "How may I be of service?"

My wits had been briefly unsettled and I fumbled about for words. "Marry, sir . . . my account books. Might I work in them here today?"

"As you please. I'd offer you my office but . . ."

"Oh no no no," I fluttered. "The back room is better for me. So if you two are busy, or if Bess wants to join me . . ."

His smile was too knowing; it made me feel like the meddling fool. "Nay, I trust we're done. I was but showing her the value of foreign currencies. She learned them with speed."

His hand motioned toward his desktop where there was sprawled a mass of coins: ducats, francs, crowns of the sun, sous, crusadoes, hornadoes, philippus, and more. Just above them was Bess, her face as stony blank as a statue of the Virgin.

"I have a gift for money," she flatly stated.

"Well, that's good, that's good." Suddenly I wanted to get her away from him. "But I know your account book is like mine, so mayhap we should work together on them."

A moment of silence followed the sound of my forced cheer.

"It doesn't matter." Bess finally shrugged. "I'm finished in here."

"Then I'll see you both again later." Catlin began scooping the coins into a round money-box. "If you need aught, my apprentices will help you."

I thanked him and with Bess left his office.

"Well, you and Catlin have taken a fancy to each other," said I to her.

"I knew you'd have a comment."

"And why shouldn't I? I am your aunt and if aught is passing betwixt you and my factor that . . ."

Bess spun around. "And are we too your possessions that you can tell us what we may and may not do?"

I stepped back from her; my arguments shriveled. "Nay, Bess, of course not. In sooth, methinks I should be pleased. Marriages can be practical ties made in less time than you've known Catlin. I've seen good marriages founded with less lovemaking than I just saw. Aye, people e'en fall in love within hours."

"And out of love faster."

This made me pause. "Have you no love for him?"

She twisted under this. "My feelings are mine own."

"And marriage isn't your goal?"

"I am but playing with him and he with me."

The immodesty, the challenging boldness in her face struck me like a slap.

"Then you're a fool!" I spat, and turned my back on her and strode down the hallway to the back room.

There at the table I arranged my things and was already transferring the stuff from my daybook into my account book when she at last joined me and labored away. Within an hour, having grown tired of the tedium, she found some diversion in directing Jan and Michiel as they organized packages. She rained down on them japes for directions and teased them when she could. Sometimes they enjoyed the distraction from their routine work and sometimes they chafed as she played them off against each other.

"Truly, Michiel," she said to the fussy boy as he pulled at the folds of a bolt's wrapping. "You do keep great care of these goods. Perchance you're right claiming your work is better than Jan's."

Jan spun about and glared at his fellow apprentice. "Said you that?" he sputtered.

"I said nothing at all!" Michiel exclaimed, and waited for Bess's support.

She feigned innocence. "But you told me as much only this morning."

"I said nothing of the kind!"

"Nay, but you did, just after cursing the bolt you dropped."

"He has a quick temper." Jan eagerly nodded.

"Then I said something to the bolt, not you," Michiel insisted. "You were talking aplenty for the two of us."

"Od's my life, did you hear that, Jan?"

"He has a quick temper," Jan gladly repeated.

Unable to discover a way out of her jests, Michiel's face flushed darker than his orange hair. "I do not!" he returned.

"Nay, you do, but," she added, "you also have passing charm."

He made a grudging smile, as if he took her teasing and flattery both with doubt. Jan, however, was not so perceptive and huffed enviously at her sudden sweetness toward Michiel. Granted, he was yet a beardless youth, but still close enow to manhood that his envy did not strike me as innocuous. Even now he was frowning blackly as he heaved a package onto his shoulders and stamped to the other end of the room.

Then we heard the front door creak open. Michiel scurried to the front chamber and from the sound of it ushered a visitor into Catlin's office. When he returned, Bess seemed ready to tease them again. Enough of this, I resolved, and asked her to come up with me to one of the rooms above. "We need to separate my bundles of fur from yours, since mine will be shipped this week."

Once she was away from the apprentices and was pulling and pushing at the cotton-wrapped bundles, she ceased her useless chatter. She only commented on the furs and coughed after slapping them into another pile. The dust from their covers scattered up into a shaft of yellow sunlight.

At last I spoke to her. "You do tease those apprentices too much."

"They enjoy my teasing. I've become their good friend and e'en can make them do as I bid. Did you notice that? Michiel likes motherly pats on the shoulder whilst oxlike Jan wants flattery and flirting."

"You flirt too much with them both. They may be beardless, but they've enow manhood in them—especially Jan—to consider seriously your flirtations."

This only made her smile. "Methinks Jan has a fancy for me."

"And you're not lady or woman enough to discourage his boyish fancies. Isn't Catlin enough for you?"

Her eyes sparked. "Don't you speak of Catlin and me in that way."

I paid her no mind. "But Catlin at least is one thing, those boys another. If you can tease those two for your selfish pleasure, then that you'll do, and damn them and whatever they might come to feel for you."

As if I were merely wearying her, she dismissed our argument by sauntering to the other side of the room and there looked about for more bundles.

"How useless it is talking sense to you," I grumbled. She cut me short with a slash of her hand. She had pushed away a crate and was standing beside the wall and staring down at the point where it joined with the floor. Some seconds passed, and slowly, to make no noise on the creaking boards, she crouched down as if listening to something. I tiptoed over and stooped down beside her. Along the jointure ran a broad crack through which rose the words being said in Catlin's office below.

"But I'll ship only the two hundred pamphlets you can print," Catlin was saying, "and no more, lest we put ourselves in danger."

"God I pray will protect us," came a gravelly voice, "for our cause is His. He will see us to victory."

"Still we must not try our luck."

"Trust you not in God?" challenged the other man.

"I trust not the queen's searchers and spies," Catlin said, "nor that we'll be spared harsh punishment should we be caught."

My chest contracted painfully; I would listen to no more of this, I thought, yet still I did so.

"Be that as it may," the gravelly voice was turning coal-black, "as the printer of these pamphlets I can take no risks. I must be assured that you can ship them secretly into England."

"Think you I'm taking no chances? I'm hazarding much by spreading outlawed heresy."

"To you 'tis heresy."

"I'm calling it as the law does." Catlin sighed. "But if 'tis assurances you want, I'll give them you as best I can."

"Good, good." The man's emotions were rising. "Then when the pamphlets are ready, I'll hide them until you can ship them. And that will be?"

"As soon as 'tis safe."

"And there may my writings be a blow against papism, that monstrous abomination."

"As you say." Catlin's voice shared none of the other man's passion.

I'd listened to far too much. My heart was thumping against my chest and echoing in mine ears. I poked Bess in the back. She waved for me to be still. I poked her hard again and hastened to the other side of the room. She still had not moved when down the stairs came the scuffing of heavy feet.

"Someone's coming!" said I.

In a trice Bess was beside me, just before one last thump sounded on the landing beyond the door. Standing there looking at us was only Dorothea, the housekeeper for the apprentices in the rooms above. Her heavy body drooping in its crumpled clothes, her mouth hanging open, she gazed at us with dull cow eyes.

"Have you a question, Dorothea?" I finally asked.

"What? Oh no. I only thought 'twas the boys in here," she said.

"No, they are below."

"Those boys, those two boys." She shook her head. "I must go shop for them now. Not that it's worth the effort. They don't appreciate my cooking at all." She continued on down the stairs, complaining all the while.

"So . . ." I was trying to quiet my still-loud heart. "Catlin is an outlaw. Mine own factor is secretly shipping heresy."

Bess was watching me anxiously. "You will keep him as your factor?"

"How can I? I do want to, I do. Yet still . . ." I sighed and swallowed hard.

"But many merchants do the same with lawful goods. They must, what with all the tariffs and unfair taxes."

"And when they're caught are ofttimes reprimanded with a petty fine. But the spreading of heretical literature is a crime never treated lightly by our queen." And was treated harsher still in Flanders, I thought. Whilst Queen Mary ruled England, her husband, Philip of Spain, ruled here, and both were as fanatical about defending the Catholic faith as that man in Catlin's office seemed to be in spreading his own. "Even death could be the punishment for what Catlin is doing," I mumbled. A cold fear was sinking into me, and I tried to reason it away. "He's very careful, and he's shrewd. But oh, sweet Jesus, why is he shipping such things? I myself have unlawfully shipped only a handful of harmless goods, and that was years ago. I've not the heart for it at all."

Bess leaned closer to me. "Belike he believes in the purpose of the pamphlets. You yourself have some sympathy for the new faith."

"As do you, as do so many Merchant Adventurers. You and I are in widespread company. Aye, I admit there are many things in the new faith that I believe. I shall talk to God directly and not through a priest, and I shall read my Bible in English, not Latin. You're too young to remember when William Tyndale was burned at the stake for translating the Bible. Oh, how my heart went out to that good man."

"You go to the Roman mass."

"And so too must you. Not only is it safe for us to do so, but in it we pray to God."

"But believe you all the Church teaches, or would you, if it were safe, follow only the new faith? Despite what you claim, you seem oft to cling to the old religion."

"It comforts me." I shrugged. "And I've grown old with it. But what Catlin is doing, that I cannot tolerate, if only for mine own safety's sake."

"You will keep him as a factor?" she repeated, taking hold of my shoulder with tight fingers.

"And endanger too my partners' business?" My mind was clearing, a decision forming. "Nay, that I cannot do."

"But e'en if he's arrested his many clients won't fall under suspicion. You and all the rest will still be safe."

I studied her face; it was taut with a scratching worry. "And what of you, Bess—are you willing to fall with him?"

She let go my shoulder and wrapped her arms about herself. "I'll not take a fall for any man, and he himself won't fall. He's shrewder than e'en you think."

"If he were as shrewd as the devil, I still must find another factor."

Her lips paled. "I should never have let you overhear Catlin."

"That's all one. I'll certainly not tell him what I heard. I'll make mine excuses and find another factor."

I saw the anxiety trembling through her smoothed, and again she became the stony thing I had seen in his office.

"Do as you please. For mine own business, I am staying with Catlin."

"Bess, you cannot!"

"Oh, but I can."

For a moment we seemed to face each other down.

"So you do have some love for him."

"Think what you wish."

The room was becoming too close for me, the air too smothering. And too, my stomach was now bothering me, as it oft did when I was worried. "Let's both of us out of here," I said. "I have work to do now at the Bourse."

"And so too does Catlin. He wished to go with you today."

Ere I could protest, she was down the stairs and closing her account book. Then she headed for the front chamber and I did follow.

A man was emerging from the office, he whom we must have overheard from above. He was plainly dressed and had the sour face of a schoolmaster wasted away by too much fretting. As soon as his eyes alighted on us, they became hooded with suspicion. He but nodded and quickly walked outside. Ere I could do the same, Catlin appeared behind us.

"Ah, Sara, are you for the Bourse now?"

I edged away from him. "Aye, but I'll be a long time there, what with all the bills I have to settle."

"So too shall I. I can keep you ladies company."

I gave up any escape from him. He walked with Bess and me out of his countinghouse, down the streets, and toward the Bourse. His secret conversation was still hot in mine ears and I could think of little to say, yet Bess chatted with him in smooth familiarity as if naught had happened.

The Bourse was just ahead of us. 'Twas surrounded tightly by houses like a volcano by hills, and the low roar of a hundred and more voices was erupting out of its roofless center and its four entrances, one to each side. We entered through one such door. Men—and too some women—filled the open court or walked along the columned portico stretching around the rectangle, and in the shops above the portico. As was their custom, the English were keeping to the court's center, whilst the Walloons were to the left and the Venetians, Luccese, Neapolitans, French, Dutch, Germans, and others stood around them in their own favored spots.

We made our way over to the English. There at last I was able to shake myself free of Catlin and Bess both and lose my troubled mind in the comforts of business. And certes there was business. 'Twas now September and the time of the Bamas Mart, one of the four great Flemish fairs. Since Adventurers can fill orders for cloth and ship them to Flanders year round, yet accompany them only during the seasonal six-week-long marts, one of my sons or partners oft attended them for the company. But this time I was the only one who could go to the Bamas.

After a little I glanced about and saw Catlin. He was busy, I knew, with work for my company. The many bolts of cloth my partners had sent for the fair he'd sold easily and now was arranging payments for the stuff in bills payable in London. Within the last few weeks he had proven himself to be indeed an excellent factor, and as he had promised had given us great profits. Finding an equal to replace him would be nigh impossible, but replace him I must, for the safety of my company and to allay mine own fears.

"You'll not find another factor like him," Bess said o'er my shoulder, reading my mind as if it were housed in glass.

"No, I'll find none like him, but I will find one who is good enow for our company, and as soon as he has proven himself, then I'm for home."

"Home?"

"Aye, London. You remember it, don't you? Methinks in a week, a fortnight at most, we'll be gone."

"I shan't be with you."

I blinked in surprise. "What? Of course you shall be. You can't stay here alone, a young woman . . ."

"I'm a widow and a merchant." She was stiffening in her resolve. " 'Tis respectable enow."

". . . and 'play' with your Catlin."

"I'll do as I please."

"Well, do so!" I lowered my voice to a whisper. "Cause a scandal for aught I care!"

She smiled like a cat. "I myself don't care."

"Oh, you'll care, young mistress, when Catlin isn't harmed at all by your scandalous behavior but your clients shun you because of it, and you see your profits disappear so quickly you'll be bankrupt. Then you'll be the poor widow Bess, dependent upon the kindness of relatives."

The point drove into her as hard as a nail; I knew where to hurt her. Whatever she felt for Catlin, it couldn't compare to her fear of dependency and poverty, to her determination to control her life by buying as much freedom as she could.

She struggled for a reply. "Then I'll be as shrewd as Catlin—as wrapped in caution and secrets."

"Do as you please and you'll hang yourself yet."

I hotly turned away from her, drew a deep breath, and stopped suddenly. "God's blood, what is that?"

"What?"

"That wretched stench."

Bess sniffed and wrinkled her nose. "A sick dog, perchance. Aunt, list to me."

But I would not listen. With the stench came the sensation that we were being observed. I glanced about, and as I did saw the back of someone hurrying away. There was only a wrinkle of movement that stopped somewhere near Catlin before disappearing. "Sweet Jesus, Catlin is being watched," said I. " 'Tis because he's a monger of heresy and is so suspected."

"Nay, Aunt. You're only imagining that. All your fears . . ."

"Fears are reason enough."

"But, Aunt—"

"I said enough." And with that I snubbed her.

At first she tarried as if wanting to hear from me at least one relenting word, but I gave none. So she drifted away, and in a little I spotted her near Catlin. She was alone and, unbeknownst to him, watching his face, his movements, his laughter. In a blink I comprehended at last why she was so recklessly drawn to him. A loneliness was swelling in her, as painful as a disease and at present stronger e'en than the growing love she had for him. I should have seen it betimes. I should have seen it in her letters when Timothy died and she was abandoned. I should have reasoned that within the rigidly cosseted role of merchant she had exercised so much control, courtesy, and propriety that only with Catlin could she be her unfettered self.

For the first time that day I felt sorry for her. What I now had to do would only hurt her.

VI

Within the next week I passed my sparse free time secretly searching for another factor. My luck was poor: The few candidates who were trustworthy and skilled were too busy e'en to talk to me, and the lesser ones were not worthy of me and my partners. I began to despair. My reaction to Catlin's shipping of heresy now seemed extreme and the risk of doing business with him—from across the channel in England—a slight one. Still I looked.

I also longed for home. We had been in Antwerp since late July, September was now ending, and I missed my sons, friends, and home. Bess, in contrast, refused e'en to talk of leaving Antwerp and said nothing to Catlin of my factor hunting.

At the end of that week, she left the White Hound just after breakfast. I was about to depart myself and was reaching for the door when it swung open and struck my fingers, just missing my nose.

"Christ's blood!" I exclaimed.

"Is someone there? I cry you mercy" came a voice in English. Into the house stepped a young man who was only my height and so looked me straight in the eyes.

"Jeremy?" I gasped.

"Mother? Mother!" In a trice his arms were hugging the breath out of me.

"Jeremy!" was all I could repeat.

"Aye, Mother, I know. I've surprised you."

"Surprised me!"

"But there was not time to write you of my coming." He got a firmer grip on a leather bag under his arm. "I arrived just this morning. I set sail as soon as Matthew and I received your letter, the one telling us you would soon leave Antwerp. I prayed to catch you ere you could."

"Why? What's wrong?"

"Ah well." He took off his cap and glanced about. "Have you a room where we might talk?"

I had him follow me up to my room. There I sat on a stool and braced myself to hear the worst whilst he remained on his big feet and awkwardly shuffled about.

"Now what in God's name is wrong?" I asked.

He sighed and faced me. " 'Tisn't a disaster that's befallen us— Matthew and me. Not a true disaster. But still we need your help. If Matthew hadn't broken his leg . . ."

"Broken his leg?" I nigh fell off my stool.

Jeremy shrugged. "A barrel at Dugdale's warehouse fell on't. The doctor said it was a clean break and would soon mend."

"Well, I'll not dismiss such a break. I've seen men lose their legs o'er what started with a broken bone."

"Oh, he won't lose it." Jeremy never could be much bothered with his brother's well-being; of the two of them, he was the humorless merchant, leaving to the older Matthew the clowning and easy charm. And whilst Matthew was handsome, Jeremy's face was knobby and sloping like a sad turtle's. Sometimes, in compensating for these things, I had favored Jeremy a little, but now I was ready to strangle him for not getting to the heart of his story.

"And so you see," he was saying, "Matthew cannot yet e'en travel about London, so I must go everywhere for us. I scarce had time to leave for Antwerp, and I'll be here but one day. I leave tomorrow."

"But why are you here?" I howled.

He looked at me, then down at the bag in his hands, debating where to begin. "Well, first of all, to bring you this." He held out the bag to me and I took it.

"What's in it?"

"Several bills of exchange, names and addresses, instructions, letters, what have you. Altogether, they're better delivered in person than by the post. I accompanied too a shipment of sixty bolts of good kersey which must be sold with speed for Matthew and me before the Bamas Mart ends."

I felt a tightening around my heart.

"You see"—and here he stammered—"to be honest . . . to be honest . . . we have lost much money."

My heart rose to my throat.

"You might remember that this June last we ordered one hundred and fifty butts of Spanish wine. They were sent from Spain on two ships, one of which was set upon by Scots and plundered. The other ship arrived safely, but we discovered that our rogue shipping agent had packed the butts three deep, causing much leakage. From what wine was left and what paltry assurance payment we received, we made not enough money to cover our losses."

His brow was scowling and his eyes had changed from brown to grimly black; 'twas a face I'd ofttimes seen on him when circumstances forced him to be no longer his own master, but instead dependent upon me or Matthew or others, and this he could bitterly dislike.

"Well," I began, "well, such misfortunes happen. Your father had more than his share of them, as have I . . . So, how do things stand now with you and Matthew?"

He gave his stiff brown hair a raking and shifted his weight from this big foot to that, turned away, then back, would not be still and would not look directly at me. "Matthew and I must replace the money we've lost with speed, sith payments for the wine and other merchandise are soon due. Our reputations, his and mine both, could be shattered if we don't quit our debts soon. I fear we're desperate."

I put on my best soothing tone. " 'Twill not be so desperate if we help each other, and clearly you're here to ask for my help."

"Aye, yours and our factor's, if he can give it."

I hedged, not wanting yet to tell Jeremy of my search for another factor. "I can't answer for him. Catlin is a busy man and isn't bound to participate in your personal ventures not conducted through our company."

"Can we at least still ask him?"

"I suppose we can."

He looked about the room again. "This seems a comfortable place. Like you it?"

"It suffices."

"But I mean, will you mind living here for a few months more?"

Only now did he at last face me, and I gaped back.

He was becoming less chafed, less the merchant and more the troubled, pleading son. "Matthew can't travel with his leg, and I've so much work now in London—trying to restore the soundness of our partnership—that I've no spare time. And too, we desperately need more trade from Antwerp." He gestured with a splayed hand toward the bag. "We need someone in this city for some months more to look after that trade. What business you have in England I can handle for you. Can you"—his hand floated aimlessly—"if Master Catlin isn't able, can you handle ours here in Antwerp?"

I wanted to say no. I wanted gently but firmly to say no, that was impossible. I had to go home. I'd been here too long already. But their profits and losses were mine, I reminded myself, and mine theirs. They were my sons, so of course I would help them.

"Well. Well then. If it comes to that I suppose I must. But let's see first if Catlin can help." Or if anyone could, I thought.

I stood up on wobbly legs. Jeremy apologized for all that had passed but I hushed him and with him headed for the countinghouse. He was also meeting a client in Antwerp, I learned, and would sup and spend the night with the man and his family. I would have resented how he was passing his brief hours in Antwerp with someone other than me had he not also continued to tell me of the labor he and Matthew were pressing upon me. I was drowning under the needs of my sons.

At the countinghouse I once again found Bess and Catlin together in his office, though this time to my relief they were behaving like merchants, not lovers. Bess greeted her cousin, I introduced him to Catlin, and swiftly our conversation turned to the purpose of his visit. I summed up his news with a query to Catlin: Could he indeed take on the factoring work my sons needed done? For several moments, Catlin mulled over his reply.

"I'm most sorry, Sara, for your family's troubles," he said. "I would work for you in this case if I could . . ."

"We will pay you a good commission," Jeremy hurried to say.

"That doesn't matter. It's the Bamas Mart time and I'm nigh handling more work than I can bear. Then after this fair there's the winter mart in Bergen-op-Zoom, which will make heavier my trade here. Perchance another factor could be found . . ."

My heart skipped in guilt. "That I've considered, but truly 'tis best to hire someone already familiar with our trade. What Jeremy has proposed may be our solution after all. He believes—and I agree—that

I should remain in Antwerp for some months more, for my trade and theirs." I paused. "Well, what think you?"

Catlin glanced at Bess ere looking at me. "Remain in Antwerp to factor for them? Your sons' debts will indeed be diminished more rapidly."

"I was afraid that would be your answer," I grumbled.

"And, in sooth, I would enjoy having you near for howe'er long you stay."

"I thank ye." His remark seemed a truthful one; still most feelings he was keeping veiled from me. I turned to Bess. "And what of you, Bess? I know you're aught but eager to return to London, and you've trade that can keep you here. Wish you to stay or go?"

Her face was smooth with control, her emotions as hidden as Catlin's. "Staying in Antwerp would be best for me too."

I sighed. "Well, 'tis settled then."

A silence descended upon us, which Jeremy tried to dispel.

"Well then, Mother. The bag you're carrying—I must need review with you what's in it, but not till I've met with my client." He pushed himself up to his clumsy feet. "By your leave, Master Catlin."

I escorted him out to the front chamber and straightened the strings in his collar and brushed back his stiff mop of brown hair.

"So, that was a crisis soon patched," said I.

"It was, it was. But it should ne'er have happened at all. Matthew and I were fools to . . ."

"You're a fool to keep talking of it. What's done is done."

"Aye, aye." He nibbled on his lip whilst pondering. "I must say, I've scarce guilt for keeping Bess here with you. Do she and Catlin plan to wed?"

My stomach twinged. "Nay. Why do you ask?"

"Marry, there's clearly something betwixt them, and Bess is too clever and headstrong to become merely his mistress."

"Jeremy!" I snapped, but he only laughed at me.

"Ah, Mother—still easily shocked. Forget you what I said."

I told him I certainly would whilst keeping from him my fears that he was wrong about Bess. Then I saw him out the door before returning to the office, where I sat again and brooded, and tried to calm my stomach ere it would hurt and sting with worry.

"Well, so much for returning home," said I at last. "And now I'll have to turn a pretty penny for myself too, Antwerp being such a dear place to live in."

Catlin joined his hands in a prayerful slope, rested his lips on them, raised his head again. "Mayhap the commission your sons were willing to pay me they could render to you."

"They couldn't yet afford a commission for me. One always expects easier credit from one's mother. Mayhap I should instead leave the White Hound for cheaper lodgings."

"Cheaper lodgings?" Bess was dismayed. "But the room we're in now is already too small and humble."

After facing all the problems erupting that day, I had no patience for her whining. "It's good enough for us both," I snapped.

Catlin rose, paced about, then remarked, as if toying with the idea, "The two of you could live in my house."

I was speechless. I'd never e'en seen his house, nor had he ever invited Bess and me there for so much as a friendly tankard of ale. If the rumors were true, he scarce invited anyone into it. Yet now he was asking us (granted, without any enthusiasm) not only to his house but for a while to live with him. Why? Was Bess the cause? Or was there a kindness in him—and like Bess a loneliness—to which I'd been blind?

"I . . . I cannot accept, Catlin. No . . . I cannot," I stammered. "Though I'm beholden to you."

A mixture of relief and disappointed hopes clouded his face. "But your stay would cost me little. If you like, we could arrange a payment for your food and laundry and like things. Still you would save much and could remain in Antwerp for as long as you need."

"Which might be for a long time," Bess was eager to add.

"And 'tis quite common for one who's in another city to stay at the house of his—or her—principal or factor, or partner or what have you."

"True," said I. "But I feel uneasy . . ."

"I'm not so eager to say nay to his generous offer," Bess interrupted. "I myself will gladly accept it."

"You cannot!"

"I can do as I please."

"Nay, your aunt is right," Catlin said. "A woman alone could not stay in my house. But an aunt and her niece, both widows, both Merchant Adventurers who are doing much business with me, could do so and none would raise an eyebrow. In sooth," he said with a smile, "your presence might make me more respectable."

I felt myself succumbing to his arguments, and Bess was gazing at me with a terrible hope. But my doubts held me back. "Again, Catlin, I thank ye most kindly. But I must still say nay."

I was getting up from my chair and turning away when I saw from the corner of mine eye Bess giving Catlin a furtive look and a hushing gesture, as if she had a plan. Something was indeed afoot betwixt those two.

VII

Bess and I said little to each other that evening at the White Hound. During our supper she hinted often that we should after all stay with Catlin by complaining about the bed in our room, that she was tired of eating every night at a table crowded with strangers, that a change would be pleasing, that Catlin would be a pleasant companion to live with. I sharply rejected her every reference till finally she sulked into silence. Afterward we went to our room and prepared betimes for bed. I changed into my shift and began to brush my hair; there was ever more silver than auburn in it now. Bess sat beside the open window, smoothing rose water onto her face and hands. On the shadowy air seeped the clattering in the streets below and a thread of music was falling over the rooftops. A few musicians were in the Great Square, which wasn't far from our lodgings, and every evening during fair time they played upon their recorders and sackbuts and lutes. The sound was the very color of autumn.

Still it little soothed me. I had been unsettled during supper by Bess's comments and now by the disturbing depth of her silence. I began to doubt that Catlin's suggestion was no more than a generous offer. I had been hearing tales about him of late, rumors that he was a rake sometimes seen in the vilest taverns. Yet I watched him for proof of this and saw in the lines about his eyes and in the tired hollow of his cheeks not dissipation but signals of a private despair. But mayhap I was wrong. Mayhap too Bess had similar impulses and was bent toward sinful desires for him, and toward this end the two of them were conspiring. How ridiculous, I chided myself, for brooding on such queer ideas. I'd had too much posset after supper. Too much of Vrouw Scinckaert's brew at the wrong time always did give me weird fancies.

I slept soundly that night, not waking till early the next morning, and then was groggy and stirred only because Bess had risen. Grudgingly, my tired eyes opened but a crack, saw in the darkness her white shift as she moved across the room, and closed again. If she was restless that was her affair; I myself had no intention of getting up. The dawn had not yet broken and the room must have been too dark to allow her to dress, for I heard a scratch and smelled sulphur, and against my closed eyelids fluttered a faint glow; she had lighted a candle. Clothes ruffled. Then came silence. Just as I was drifting into sleep again, I heard indistinctly the latch falling away from the shutters and then a creak as they swung open. The sounds fell like dreams through my mind, heavy still with slumber. Then into sleep I slipped again, taking with me the annoying sensation of cold night-morning air chilling my neck.

I woke to a sharp cry. My mind was fogged—I knew not if I dreamt the sound. But another cry burst in my ears and I sat up with a bolt, my heart pounding. I was staring into a nightmare. The wall was alive, seething with flames. The window was gone and there instead was a sheet of fire. I saw Bess throwing water from a pitcher upon the flames and I heard myself screaming at her to throw a rug on it. I flew from the bed, frenzied by the horrifying sight and by the heat. She grabbed the rug ere I could and hurled it upon the blaze. I flung the blanket off the bed and up against the wall where the flames licked out past the rug. I pounded the wall and smothered the flames till the blanket too began to smolder, and I dropped it and crushed the sparks. A man rushed in with another pitcher of water and threw the stuff upon the scattered remnants of flames. He tore the rug away from Bess and fought the flames himself. She rushed to the wash pot and threw its water at them.

Cries of "Fire!" and screams and the sounds of panic shook through the Hound. People I saw only in flashes sped in, threw water on the wall and me and near any kind of flame. Not e'en a minute had passed, but somewhere in that time I perceived that the fire was not so bad as I thought. Already it was out. Sparks and glowing cinders were all that remained. Swiftly, fearfully, they were drowned or smothered. The smoke was still thick, though; it coiled blackly in the air and was waved out the window by frantic hands and swinging pillows. It stung my nostrils and seared my throat into parched rawness. I staggered back. Someone took hold of my shoulders and drew me away. I was drenched and shivering from the cold now, and from fear. Bess too moved away from the charred wall. A servant girl brushed flakes of cinder from her petticoat. People nervously shuffled in and out of the room.

About half the wall was charred. The window frame was a broken skeleton, the shutters collapsed bits of flinders. The ceiling near it was stained by smoke and the floor was damp with blackened water. There was the stench of things burnt.

I was still shivering badly within my wet shift. Bess pulled my fur-lined nightgown out of my trunk, draped it around me, and sat me down on the bed.

At last I saw Vrouw Scinckaert. She had reached our room just as the fire had been extinguished, settled herself at the stairs beyond our door, and told everyone about that all was well again, it had been but a small mishap. They could go back to their beds now. No, breakfast would not be served earlier this morn. Why should it be since naught was amiss? That much done, she came back into our room, looking frail in her pale nightgown yet exuding authority. A few men still with us told her no sparks were left to ignite the wall again. She thanked them profusely.

"But now, I pray you, sirs, these ladies are soaked through and must change into dry clothes ere catching their death of cold," she sniffled.

The men murmured of course and regarded us sympathetically as they filed out.

"Are you burnt at all? Are you hurt?" She pushed her wrinkled face close to us.

"I think not." Too dazed to feel pain, I examined my hands and naked feet. "Bess? Bess, are you hurt?"

"Nay, Sara, I'm not," she said.

"But your hand is burnt." Vrouw Scinckaert reached for Bess's left hand, which she was cradling tenderly in her other hand. On the back of it, near the outer edge, was a patch of seared, crimson and brown burnt flesh, painful just to look at.

Bess stared at it with numb amazement. "I can scarce feel the burn, truly," she stuttered. "I'm too cold to feel it."

The old woman held the hand and frowned at it. " 'Tis a bad one, but I've mine own remedy that might help it. Out of these clothes first, though, both of you."

Bess's petticoat and bodice were wet and her teeth were chattering. We undressed, dried ourselves, and quickly dressed again in warm clothes. Feeling was returning to the burnt flesh so when Bess brushed it 'gainst a sleeve she cried out in pain. Using her right hand only, she shook out her dank hair and asked me to braid it for her.

Vrouw Scinckaert helped us until distracted by the burnt wall. I pitied her; the damage wasn't great but 'twould cost a large sum to repair. She clucked her tongue and kept shaking her head, but did not yet remark to us about those repairs and who should pay for them. For that I was grateful.

She shuffled us down to the dining chamber where a warm fire was blazing in the hearth, and herself prepared for us some warm milk. Then she made a balm she applied to Bess's hand, and o'er that wrapped a bandage. When we both had stopped shivering and seemed ourselves again, she closed the kitchen and front hall doors, pulled up her chair, sat in it, and cleared her throat.

"You both are better? You're not cold? Good," she rasped. "God be praised. Now I must ask another question, and I do hope you've an answer. How did the fire start?"

I looked to Bess. She was holding her cup of milk to her lips and letting the steam soothe her mouth. A sob caught in her throat, she coughed it away, and with her uninjured hand wiped her face.

"I'm not sure," she answered weakly. "I rose early after a bad dream woke me. I wanted to dress, but since it was still dark I had to light a candle. Then I opened the window. I should never have opened it. The candle was on the table near the window." She struggled to put her words in a sensible order. "I sat back down on the bed and was brushing my hair when a cat came through the window. It must have been attracted by the light, mayhap by hope of food. I shooed it out, but it stayed on the ledge outside. Then I left the room to fetch more water from below so that I could wash. When I was in the hall there was a clatter—later I knew it was the candlestick—but I paid the noise no mind. By the time I returned the wall hanging beside the window had caught fire and so too had the window frame. I threw water on the wall and I screamed for help. That was when my aunt awoke and the other boarders came in." She turned her glistening eyes toward us and, miserable, waited for a response.

Vrouw Scinckaert shook her head in pity for herself and tapped the floor with her heels. "The damage isn't too bad. None of the structure was hurt. But the wall will cost a goodly sum to be fixed, and the window and shutters. And the table was burnt and must be replaced." She was leading up to the subject of who would pay for the damage.

"That cursed cat," Bess mumbled. "I hope 'tis dead by now. It was a striped, gangly thing. I should have thrown it to the street below. When I first saw it, I should have thrown it out."

The door to the hall must have opened, for though I heard naught I espied while reaching for my cup a flowing movement and sensed the presence that followed. I looked up to the black and white figure of Brother Gerard.

"Oh, dear Gerard!" The old woman half rose to meet him, but his hands gestured that she not, and she sat again. "My grandson," she explained to us, "has been in my private room waiting for me. He heard the commotion from the street and came in just when everyone was rushing about."

"I wanted to see what was amiss." His tranquil voice was an eerie contrast to our shaking ones.

"That was good of you," she said. "But I didn't want you hurt, and God knows we had enough people in there putting out the flames."

The friar sat down near her. "The maid told me you are not hurt. Please God she was right."

"Aye, aye, I'm not injured at all, the Virgin and saints be praised. But Mevrouw Marwick has burnt her hand. I have put mine own balm upon it."

He looked at Bess's cloth-wrapped hand lying on the table. "I pray the burn isn't severe?"

" 'Tis not. It will heal." Bess put the hand on her lap and out of his sight. With her other hand she pushed back under her bonnet some damp strands of hair; they had tumbled onto her cheeks and made her appear disheveled. "Well, Brother, we meet again whilst waiting for our breakfast," she said. " 'Tis yet early and the city is scarce stirring—but you're up and about already?"

"I have my tasks. I was told the fire was in your room."

Bess let her eyes rest on aught but him. "Aye. By a candle, an open window, and a cat."

"A cat?" His sparse eyebrows rose.

"The filthy thing got in through the window and knocked over the candle," the old woman replied for Bess.

He blinked in surprise—nothing more. "Does her room face the street?"

"It does." The old woman pointed with an age-bent finger.

"I was walking along the street." The friar's voice was hollow. I saw Bess's burnt hand flinch upon her lap. His gaze was like steel as he looked at her. "I was watching as I walked toward my grandmother's house. I heard the screams and so looked at the room whence they came . . ."

"And he rushed in to help, the dear saint," Vrouw Scinckaert peeped. "God bless him."

"You said a cat tipped over the candle?" Brother Gerard asked.

Bess gingerly touched her bandaged hand. "Aye, a cat. But I wasn't in the room when the candle fell and the fire started. A cat, a filthy cat."

His mind seemed to move around this like a claw. "So small an animal caused so much damage? Quite difficult to believe."

"Aye, isn't it though?" Vrouw Scinckaert clucked her tongue. "Now these two ladies will have to move out. Out of their room, out of this house. After all, 'tis full to the roof with other guests."

"I' faith, you are right," said I. "I had not e'en thought of that. We must now find other lodging."

"Oh, a difficult search that will be," said Vrouw Scinckaert. "And this is not a boast, but you'll not find lodgings and food as good as mine for less."

"But we must."

"During the Bamas Mart? Nay, there's not a spare room to be had."

Bess gave a wary glance at Brother Gerard ere saying to me, "There's our friend's offer."

"Eh?" croaked the old woman.

"A merchant friend," said I. Like Bess, I made no mention of Catlin's name in the suspicious monk's presence. "A good man with whom my company does business. He has invited us to be his guests."

"Ah, now that may do," Vrouw Scinckaert said. " 'Twill save you money, which, well . . . with these repairs to be made . . ."

As if cued, Brother Gerard stood to leave.

"You're going? So soon?" Affectionately, the old woman patted his arm. "Oh, Gerard, always you're in and out, in and out."

"I have my many tasks, Grandmother." He raised two thin fingers, made a cross over her head and murmured a benediction, and gave a shorter one for Bess and me sans the cross. Then he left the room, as before not seeming to disturb the air through which he moved.

Bess coughed hoarsely. "Vrouw Scinckaert, know you who could have owned the cat?"

"It was belike a stray. And a cat won't pay for the repairs." She was all business again now that her grandson was gone.

"And do you know of a good carpenter who will not charge too much?"

"I'm acquainted with two or three. I try to save money, but I do not cheat myself on workmanship."

"Well, have one in today and when he gives his price and says what must be done, let me bargain with him. I'll pay what we agree upon. I will also pay you the rent lost for that chamber whilst it goes empty because of the repairs."

I did not protest. I was speechless at Bess's steady grace, at the quiet strength in her reply. I would not discourage or hinder her, though I did think to myself she seemed to be feeling too much guilt for what was but an accident.

Vrouw Scinckaert was herself taken aback by this swift resolution to the problem. She melted into a smile. "You're a good woman, a Christian woman, Mevrouw Marwick. God bless ye. Well now, well . . . I'll get your breakfast. You both look so hungry."

She herself served us our meal, and as my stomach was by then churning painfully with worry, I drank only a little warm milk, but scarce kept e'en that down. When we had finished we could hear above us the other boarders moving about. Vrouw Scinckaert went off to ready her household for another day of work. Bess and I still sat, not yet wishing to return to our damaged room, not yet wanting to talk to each other.

Again the door to the front hall opened. Bess glanced up and smiled as if she saw what she'd been expecting. It was Catlin. He was hatless and his hair uncombed, and either he had spent a wakeful night in his clothes or had thrown them on in a hurry, for they were rumpled, his doublet was partly unlaced, and over them hung no sober surcoat but a long dusty cloak. I was amazed to behold the man I had always before seen as neat and dignified. He stood now in the hazy dawn like a dark and crumbling vision.

"I'd heard there was a fire here," he blurted.

"In our room," Bess said.

He saw her bandaged hand and in a moment was beside her. "You're injured?"

"A small burn. 'Twill heal." She pulled it away from his reach as if it were her guilt embodied and thrust it amongst the folds of her skirt.

"And you, Sara?"

"Unharmed."

"But where was the fire?" He raked his hand through his slovenly hair.

"In our room, which will not heal so quickly." Bess told him in brief all that had passed.

"You heard there was a fire?" I asked him when she had finished. "Has the news spread so rapidly that it roused you from your bed?"

"I wasn't in bed . . ." His mind drifted, then returned. "Sometimes I must keep late hours, or early ones. And news of fire travels fast in this city. I was in the streets when I heard there'd been a fire at a house in this lane."

"Well, Catlin, I must say you look as though you flew with the night owls," I jested.

He did not hear me. "Said you your room can't be used?"

"Not till the repairs be made," Bess answered. "And they won't be completed for a few days, I judge."

Catlin leaned his hips against the table and an arm upon it to balance his tired body. Softly he smiled. "My house is a large one and I've none but servants to keep me company there. You're still most welcome."

Bess turned to me. She knew I would have to accept. I remembered me mine odd musings of her and Catlin the night before. But now sunlight was sifting into the room. The images, the thoughts, what I'd felt the night before, what decisions I'd made the day before, were tumbling into a confused mass. They were making complex what was now simple: I was tired, we had no place to stay, our money was limited, his offer generous. The issue was settled for me.

"I thank ye, Catlin," said I, and glanced at Bess. She was smiling to herself in a way I did not understand and did not like at all.

A fter Catlin had left, I was enough myself that I could return
upstairs, wash and dress, and leave for the English Quay, because fire or
no I was still going to see my son ere he set sail for home. I found him
just as he was about to board a ship, told him of the fire and that Bess
and I would now be living with our factor. Of this he was wary.

" 'Tis one thing to join in business with this Catlin," Jeremy said
with a frown, "but to live under his roof, that's another."

"Oh hush, Jeremy. 'Twill only be temporary. We'll belike be back
in the White Hound as soon as the repairs are made."

" 'Tis what may happen afore then that I dislike. What know you of
the private man? Is his reputation unsullied? Could a young woman like
Bess be left alone with him, say, on some evening . . ."

"Of course she could," said I, though a little doubting this. "You
yourself said she wouldn't become his mistress because she's too
headstrong."

"Aye, but she's also impetuous and easily ridden by her emotions.
Mix that with temptation and she might prove to be trouble whilst in
his house."

He was right, but in my weariness and frustration I only wanted to
sting him for his truthfulness.

"That may be so, but what can I do about it? You and Matthew are
the ones who've trapped us into staying here."

He winced at this and guilt swept o'er him. Ere I could retract my
words the captain appeared on the ship's deck and waved to us.

"You must go aboard now." I studied Jeremy's face, for it would be
some time afore I'd see it again and would miss its awkward features.
How I hated farewells.

An hour later Catlin returned to the White Hound, now washed and properly dressed, whilst Bess and I were packed and ready to depart. Leaving behind our trunks to be later collected by one of his servants, we walked with Catlin to his house. We had not a long distance to go: He led us to the streets just south of the Bourse and finally to a house on a corner between Mier Straat and Crossbowmen's Garden. 'Twas a large, three-storied brick building with several gables and many windows for each floor, and was lined up with other houses that were much the same.

The woman who opened the door to us was introduced by Catlin as "Lijsken Boodt, my housekeeper and cook." I judged her to be of about mine own age, and she had a demeanor of busy rigor and a heavy jutting jaw.

Catlin gestured to a parlor just beyond the entrance hall, said the kitchen and servants' quarter were beyond, then led us up to our bedchambers. Along the way, I looked about. The place was not expansive or richly decorated; still the walls were lined with polished wainscoting and there were thick carpets and fine furniture and wide windows with circles of stained glass in their centers. Two staircases with an oak rail rose squarely to the second floor; Catlin only gestured again to a room on that level and continued up another staircase to the third floor and to two facing open doors.

Bess went into the chamber nearest her and I into the other. They were of goodly size—larger than the single room we'd shared at the Hound—and were similarly appointed: a four-poster bed with tester and curtains, a press for clothes, a few other pieces of furniture, the luxury of a chimney and hearth, and on the floor and bed a profusion of pillows. Yet hovering in my chamber was a stale mustiness and the furniture creaked with disuse as if left alone for years. Still, when I joined Catlin in Bess's chamber I much thanked him for my lovely new room.

"Do you indeed like it? Then I'm pleased." He was twisting his flat black cap in his hands and shifting his weight back and forth as if for once his control was slipping; clearly he was not accustomed to having lady guests. This I found charming.

Bess leaned out of her window. Before her was a scene of roofs, walls, and a modest garden belonging to another house. "Be there a rear door to this house? I see no garden."

"There's a rear door that opens only to the narrow passage you see below, which leads to the street and is shared by my neighbors." He stopped harming his cap. "But now, I must to work again. Forgive my sudden departure."

His housekeeper watched him leave, then waited for us to say something.

"Well, Lijsken." Bess emptied the contents of her bag. "Be there other servants in this house?"

Lijsken, who seemed to know only a few English words learned from Catlin, answered in Flemish. "Two others are here, my husband, Arnout, and the kitchen maid, Marie. I myself do all the cooking."

"Arnout we've met. He's oft at the countinghouse to help with the carting and carrying."

"Aye, that's him. There are only we three servants in this house. 'Tis quiet here. Now, wish you to see some other rooms?"

We followed her out and down the hall. Two other bedchambers were near ours: a small, stuffy, scarce-used one and Catlin's spacious own. The second floor consisted mostly of a large room, the entrance to which was doorless. I noted that immediately, for the rest of the doors in the house squeaked or crackled like those in the countinghouse. The open, handsome room stretched away from that corner entrance and was dominated by a massive stone chimney and long windows along two walls. Before the hearth and on a carpet sat a heavy table and chairs. When we walked on the naked floor beyond them our clacking heels resounded against the high-beamed ceiling. Away from the chimney, away from the table, the room felt half-empty.

Lijsken remarked that Master Catlin called this chamber the antler room. "For want of a better name," said she, pointing to the plain iron candle-branch hanging from the ceiling and the stag's antlers that curled around it.

At the far end of the room were a few stairs leading to a landing and a closed door. Bess ambled toward it. "And what's up there?"

"Mynheer Catlin's library. 'Tis very private. The door is to be kept shut."

"Ah, but I know he'd like me to see it."

Lijsken stiffened about the mouth as if the starch in her wimple was now also in her face. "I cannot be certain of that."

"Think you I'll tamper with secrets he keeps there?"

"He has no secrets."

"Then there's no harm in my seeing the room—though your fussing tells me differently."

The housekeeper grumbled something to herself and, relenting, went up the stairs and opened the door for us.

We stepped into a small chamber fitted with some wainscoting, but where the walls should have been there were shelves instead. They rose from our waists to the low ceiling and were heavy with books, most of them printed ones, but too a few aged ones that were hand-printed and illustrated. They were lined up against each other or laid out flat in spacious ease, two to a shelf, lest their weary old backs be broken. Little else was in the chamber: a table, a chair, a narrow cabinet, all huddled next to the only window and close to the stove. Scarce enough space was left for the three of us. Yet what truly struck me was the contrast in Catlin's habits here. Jumbled on the table were scribbled papers, an open inkpot, and much-used pens; and atop the cabinet were open and pushed-aside books. Absent was the tight control that marked his habits at the countinghouse. Instead here lay evidence of impatient and fervent study.

"What books he has!" Bess was more amazed than I. She reached for one but Lijsken intercepted her grasp.

"The master forbears no one to disturb his books. If you wish to have freedom in here, you must ask his leave." And with that she turned into a guard, watching our every move, waiting for us to leave.

We were crossing the antler room when I spied a waist-high cabinet stuck away in the small corner betwixt the entrance and outside wall. It jarred the room's spare harmony like an excrescence, an old, scratched, awkward thing with a drawer squatting atop four spindly legs.

Bess too noticed it crowded into the corner. "This thing seems shoved out of the way." Her fingers teased the knob of the drawer. "And what does Master Catlin keep in here—a secret, some guilt, or merely a small sin?"

Lijsken's face turned to stone. "Why don't you open it and see?"

Bess ceased her jesting. "Ah, Lijsken, I am sorry. Sometimes I do tease too much."

The housekeeper softened a bit. "Well, mevrouw, that's all one. I suppose curiosity can be strong in a young one like yourself. But now, mevrouws, shall we go below?"

Bess and I walked on, yet the both of us saw how Lijsken cast a chary glance at the closed drawer and then stepped backward and away from it, as if there were a dangerous animal therein.

We surveyed below the parlor and kitchen. In the hall betwixt those two rooms we met the maid, Marie. She looked to be sixteen years of age, with rough features marred the more by a birthmark splattered like an old purple stain across the full of one cheek, obliterating any claim to youthful prettiness she might else have had. The birthmark had also engrained in her a shyness.

We were in the hall still when Lijsken's husband, Arnout, arrived with our trunks. A taciturn bull of a man, he asked us only which trunk belonged where.

Bess and I settled our things during the afternoon. Then evening came, and shimmered with cordiality. After so many crowded meals in the White Hound, to sit down to an enormous supper with only Catlin for company was a blessing. And too, after the plates had been cleared away we didn't return to a small, shared bedchamber, but lazed still at the table, and drank sweet wine and jested and talked. 'Twas the first time, I realized, that I'd seen Catlin merry. He seemed nigh grateful for our presence. Not till that evening did I comprehend what a lonely man he was, and too that he wasn't really more Flemish than English as others had ofttimes remarked to me. Rather, he seemed to have no nation, no fellow race, no traditions, and hence to all men was a foreigner.

" 'Tis so good not to talk of business tonight." He leaned back in his chair and stretched his legs. "In truth, I have more than my fill of it at my countinghouse."

"As do I." Bess drained her glass.

"I grow too dizzy to sit sans swaying." My head seemed wrapped in soft silk from the wine. Rising carefully, I ambled to a window and opened a shutter so that I could look out into the dark. A fire in the hearth burned against the weak chill. "It's nigh October. 'Twill be cold ere long."

"You've never seen a winter in Flanders, have you, Bess?" asked Catlin. "Winters are cold here, colder than in London. But the Flemings make more sport in the cold. They skate more often upon ponds and some rivers, and in the country the children speed down hills on scraps of wood."

Bess sighed sleepily. "When were you last in England, Catlin?"

"A long time ago, and then just for a sennight."

"And in all this time you never desired to return to your native country?"

"I suppose not. Antwerp has become my home. I have only business acquaintances in London, no more."

"And no family"—Bess dizzily poured herself more wine—"there or here, what with your father and his partner long dead."

"Who told you of them?"

"Vrouw Scinckaert—the old woman who owns the White Hound."

"I know her not. Yet she knows about me?"

"She's an old gossip. Whate'er rumors and hearsay her boarders have to give she hoards like gold."

"And what did she say about me?"

"Oh, she served us some unsavory rumors, which she relished."

Catlin half smiled. "Of course."

"And she said that your father died years ago, and too did his partner, who was murdered."

"At least that much is true." He scraped his fingernail around the rim of his glass. "Did she know aught else about them?"

"A little," said Bess, "but hushed herself as soon as her nephew came in. He's a heretic-sniffing Dominican, and cold enough to silence e'en the patron saint of gossips."

"She did say, howe'er," I added, "that you were an excellent factor, Catlin, and with that I agree."

He raised his glass to me in thanks, and we all drank some more.

When at last we retired, the three of us walked upstairs together, and ere going to our separate chambers, lingered at the edge of the antler room.

"Lijsken showed all this to you?" asked Catlin.

"She did," said Bess, "and too your library, after I prodded her. I hope you mind not."

"Nay, I knew you'd want to see it, and that she wouldn't let you touch a single book."

"She would have bitten me if I had."

"She's a good dog for guarding."

"That she is, and I pushed her too far, methinks, when I jested about seeing what was in that drawer." Bess motioned to the spindly cabinet in the corner.

"And did you see what was in it?"

"Oh, and now you be annoyed with me too. I am sorry, Catlin."

This didn't satisfy him. "But did you see what was in it?"

"Nay. I was but teasing her."

Perchance it was the wine that moved me, but now I said something I should not. "I daresay it struck me as a little odd the way she treated this cabinet. You would think it was about to attack her."

" 'Tis true." Bess laughed.

Catlin moved his jaw back and forth. "Because of what is in it. Well, to prevent any mystery from brewing, I'll show you all."

With that, he opened the drawer and pulled from it a picture, which he handed to me. 'Twas a portrait less than eighteen inches across, and the person captured by its aging paints stirred something in me. Od's my life, I bethought me, what manner of man was this? He was about thirty-six years of age and shown only from the tip of his black flat cap to his velvet-covered chest, yet mine eyes were riveted to him. The painter had caught the smooth features and the color of flesh, yet no life was in him. The faint eyebrows faded lowly into colorless-seeming eyes, the nose was a sharp wedge, the mouth a thin line prone to a contemptuous frown. His left-leaning eyes were without warmth; they e'en seemed tinted with malevolence.

"Who's this?" Bess recoiled a little. "Whoever he be, his picture wants hanging. Was he hanged enough in life?"

Catlin smiled despite himself. "He wasn't hanged, but natheless died in a violent way. That's Martin van den Bist."

"Your father's partner?" I remembered me the name. "Sooth to say, and though one shouldn't speak ill of the dead, I care not for his face."

"No harm is in such talk. He's been dead for fifteen years."

"And have you a portrait of your father?" Bess asked.

"Nay, there's only that of his." He nodded toward the open drawer.

Therein sat a fat account book. The thing was old, worn, and bruised, but leather-bound, secured with leather straps, and clasped with a brass buckle.

"An old ledger?" I asked.

"It's all I have of him," said Catlin. "Look you at it too, if you wish."

"It must be years old." Bess pulled out the book, unclasped it, and, opening the creaking cover, flipped through the many folios within. The pages were filled only with common entries of debts and payments, names and amounts, and lines such as "duly repaid at divers times," and "as he doth owe me," and "for so much ready money lent to him." She closed the thing again and returned it to its place, and on top of it I laid the portrait.

"Two common things," she remarked. "What mystery is that?"

"There is none, as I've shown you. But still Lijsken is wary of this cabinet. It was kept, you see, near the servants' quarters in a room for storing old housekeeping stuff. But then the servants complained. Lijsken told me several stories: that there were noises coming from within that room, that the servants saw strange things, and what have you. So I took the thing out and put it up here."

Bess's eyes had grown large during his story. He laughed at her. "Pay no heed. Lijsken—well, she's ever the guarding dog. She hears sounds no other mortal can."

"Have you ever heard a ghost, Catlin?" I idly asked.

He hesitated. "I've never seen one, no."

"Or heard one?" I repeated.

He turned his back to me as he moved to shut the drawer. "Oh, methinks I've heard sometimes an odd noise that seems to come from nowhere. But then so does everyone."

He was hiding something, I suddenly believed. The way he avoided my face, the way his tone shifted, reminded me of my sons when they were young and in trouble, and too afraid to tell me the truth.

·- IX -·

Many other good evenings followed that one, so peaceful and spent happily over supper and talk. On other nights I'd write letters, there being so much business correspondence that needed doing, or sometimes I'd sew or the like. Bess herself now had to send out more letters, and ofttimes she'd write them at the table in the antler room. Catlin was usually in his library at such times, but ever and anon he'd bring a book down and sit with her. Yet when I was alone in that place and she was elsewhere in the house, he stayed in the library.

On one of those nights, after I'd gone to bed, I was awakened by muffled noises coming from below. I would have paid them no mind but for the sudden surmise that Bess and Catlin were their cause. So I rose, peeked into her bedchamber, and finding it vacant, descended to the antler room. There at the table sat Bess, clad in her nightgown, peering through candlelight and firelight into books and at papers spread before her. She was drawing lines and figures onto those papers; from their form, most like she was casting a horoscope. This was the first I knew that she was learning the science of astrology. I knew by then that Catlin cast horoscopes, which was yet another convenient skill a factor could have; when he wished to be reassured that a ship carrying goods would arrive safely, he could cast the stars himself rather than consult some other astrologer. If Catlin was teaching Bess about horoscopes, I thought, then that would be convenient for her too.

Just then her quill faltered, the ink blotted, and impatiently she crumpled up the paper and threw it into the fire beside her. She was alone, but I sensed that Catlin was nearby. Without stepping into the room, I bent in and saw that the library door was open, and from it came a light and the crackle of a book's stiff pages being turned. The both of them were up then, reading and scribbling. Of late, I bethought me, Bess had complained of sometimes being too restless to sleep the night through. Catlin appeared to be plagued in the same way, although his spurts of sleeplessness may have begun years ago for aught I knew. Well, let his books and her inky symbols replace Bess's slumber if she so desired. As long as she and Catlin were like this when together late at night and not like lovers, then I'd worry not. I went back to my bed.

On another evening I sat alone at my work in the parlor. Wanting some company whilst I wrote, I took my papers and ink, went up to the antler room, and there found Bess and Catlin. They were sitting on either side of the table's corner where the fire warmed their backs, and betwixt them were spread several books and papers. They were talking quietly and he was showing her how to draw some sort of figure.

I sat down at the opposite end and was arranging my letter-writing things when mine eyes were caught by one of the papers. On it was the ringed circle of a horoscope; in the outer ring were the names of the planets, in the ring within the planets' symbols, and in the circle's large center, drawn from this planet to that in every possible combination, a mass of crossing lines bearing in mathematically precise places tiny stars, squares, and triangles. A book near to it was open to a page with some of those same symbols and their names. The star was a sextile, the square a quadrat, the triangle a trine, and too there were the symbols for opposition, conjunctions, and those of the planets, all of them under the heading of "Here followeth the aspectes of the Planetes for the better judgement of Weather." Beside the book was a paper bearing yet another horoscope, this time a square within a square within a square, the middle one at odd angles to the other two and connected to the outermost one with lines, and along those lines and squares were again the planets' symbols and also many numbers. 'Twas as lacking in meaning to me as was the other horoscope, as were any of those papers and books.

" 'Twould mayhap have been a wise move if you'd consulted an astrologer afore you married Timothy," Catlin was saying to Bess.

She glanced at me; she disliked my presence but still talked on with him. "Any horoscope would have been a waste if it had failed to tell me what I wanted to hear."

"It may have told you what you wanted, that you were fated to marry him."

"Timothy, my fate? He was too insignificant for that. No, I chose him of mine own free will."

"Ah"—a mocking curdled Catlin's tone—"but how free is your will?"

"I like much what St. Bernard wrote: 'Where there is an act of will, there is freedom.' Well, I was most willful to marry Timothy, so I must have been very free. I wanted him for a husband, he wanted me for his wife, and spite my parents' threats it was my will we marry, and I won. My pretty little Timothy. Little in mind, soul, and heart. Ah well— God rest his soul."

"You sound the bitter woman." He smiled.

"I'm too young to be as bitter as I sound. You're hearing only the pretensions of youth. When I'm old, mayhap, I'll be truly bitter, though God forbid it."

"No, not God. 'Tis your free will that has already given you this much bitterness. You chose to marry Timothy and came to be unhappy in the end."

Bess's head rolled back, she let go a cynical laugh, and when she looked back at him her face was both glowing from the fire's heat and shadowed with melancholy. "Make not too much of that. My marriage lasted only five years, and in that time we were happy for a little. Then when he died he left me a widow of a Merchant Adventurer, which meant I could choose to be an Adventurer too. I could have kept myself safe at home in Ipswich or London. I have only a small jointure . . ."

"Not so small!" I scoffed.

"Small for my liking." Bess looked only at him. "Still I risked its loss by investing it. I could have clung to England, kept my dower stashed away, and used it to bait another husband. But that's the last fate I want."

"That's the last thing you could be," Catlin remarked dryly, "the humble housewife."

Bess smiled at him; it was a clever, seducing smile. Then, stretching like a cat, she slowly rose and half sat on the table's edge, her body curling around to him. "You were going to teach me more about casting a horoscope."

He reached out, lay fingers upon one of the open books, and drew it in to him as if luring her to follow it. "For what purpose now? You want no fate."

"Save the one I'll design myself."

"But fate is the will of God."

"How pious that sounds! You yourself seem to use astrology not to learn from God's stars what His will might be, but how to track an escape between them. I doubt much that you ever pray, 'Thy will be done,' but instead, 'How may I avoid it?'"

"Whilst you would pit your will against God's." His voice was like a soft tempting stroke.

"Well then, one thing is certain: We won't teach each other how to pray."

Soft laughter tumbled betwixt them. Catlin locked his eyes with hers.

"But as for astrology?"

She leaned yet closer to him. "Teach me!" she murmured.

I was stirred at last out of my silence. No more of these sorts of words, I decided, and I liked not the sinuous movements of their bodies. "You'll be taught none of that tonight," I said lightly to Bess. "You've yet to learn how to mark the time, for 'tis late enow that we should both be abed." I rose and gathered mine unused papers and inkpot and pen back into mine arms.

Bess herself stood still and glared at me from the corners of her eyes, silently telling me I was a trespasser. I looked to Catlin. Had I for an hour studied his face, half-lighted by candlelight and the glow from the fire, half-steeped in shadows, I could not have grasped what was passing in his mind; I saw only a vexation that flickered across his features ere sinking into concealment. For the first time I apprehended that I had blundered into something—a passion, I felt, and one tense with the desire of unquiet minds, as palpable as a loving touch. Tinglings of fear stiffened my back. They had gone beyond teasing, wooing words. Now they were hotly ready to bed each other, in that house and behind my back if need be.

I stared, then made as if I'd noticed naught. I fiddled with the inkpot. "What the dickens is wrong with this cap?" I muttered. "It does not fit the bottle anymore."

"Oh no, Sara, I pray you"—Bess's patience was breaking—"don't think I'm tired. I could be up for hours more."

"And be drowsy and churlish in the morning, and impossible to work with." I tried to be droll. In truth I didn't want to leave them alone together, not that night. "No, we must both bid good night to you, Catlin, and get to our beds and not keep you from yours."

"Then my good night to you both." He closed a book and opened another. "But I want to read a while more ere retiring."

He moved a little away from her and she from him, as if they'd been warned, and she followed me from the room. We were about to go up the stairs when from below there came the squeaking of the entrance door. Heavy boots thumped into the house, and the door was squeaking shut when it was stopped.

"What want you here?" came Arnout's voice. 'Twas he who had just come in, and it seemed he was now talking to someone at the door. A rough-scratched voice, its words indistinguishable to me, answered.

"What want you with Master Catlin?" Arnout asked suspiciously.

"I must give him a message." The voice was louder.

"You can give it to me."

"Nay!" The voice rose. "I must see him alone!"

I stepped back into the antler room. "Catlin, there seems to be a messenger at the door. He's giving Arnout some trouble."

Then we heard below the sounds of a scuffle. Arnout cried, "Stop! Stop you!" and pounded up the stairs after someone. Afore Bess and I could retreat a man hurled himself into the corner opposite us and there half crouched like a trapped animal. Arnout came after and almost jumped on the stranger, then quickly looked to Catlin for his orders. But Catlin, and too Bess and I, were frozen and staring at what was before us.

He was a small queer scarecrow of a man with blazing eyes that started from his head and were fixed unblinking upon us. His tangled dun hair and beard were mixed with yellow and his skin, spite where the sun and wind had mercilessly burned it, had a dead hue. Below his neck, hanging limply on his skinny, skittish body, were patched and frayed and filthy clothes. Just then, bubbling up out of his throat, came a strange sound like an animal's growl.

"Who are you?" Catlin demanded.

The man answered only with a hideous grin and rolled a dry tongue over his lips; around his mouth yawned sores and spots, signs that he was diseased.

Catlin recoiled—in fear and disgust, and too as if readying to spring into attack. "Who are you?"

"Thou art Bartholomew Catlin!"

"I need no rude and mad beggar to tell me who I am! Get out of this my house before I throw you out!"

"Do not smite me for I am sent to aid thee!" the stranger howled. His arm jabbed out, his skeletal fingers pointed to Catlin. "The Lord God knows of thy secret work and has made me thy guardian!"

The joints in Catlin's limbs abruptly bent and he fell back against the wall. With effort he rasped, "What are you talking about?"

The pointing hand rose higher as if the intruder were invoking God to be his witness. "Our King Christ Jesus hath led me to thee and revealed to me the work thou dost for the followers of His true faith. The sign came to me through the printed word. Christ's enemies cannot prevail against thee. Now I am come to keep thee safe against the papish idolaters, the Roman whore!"

Catlin blanched. "Get out!" he cried. "Get out, get away from me!"

"And thine eyes shalt be opened and thou shalt see! I shalt aid thee!"

"Get out!" Catlin threw himself forward and in a trice would have been on the man's throat had not the horrid creature swiftly, crablike, scuttled past Arnout's grabbing arms and down the stairs, out of our sight and out of the house. Catlin and Arnout raced after him, perchance even out into the street; I knew not since Bess and I could only remain fixed in our places. Moments later, we heard the door being shut and bolted, and Catlin murmur to Arnout ere walking up to us.

"By the holy rood, what was that?" I asked.

"A horrible madman," Bess declared.

"A beggar driven mad by his disease," Catlin said, "the French disease."

"He even had the stench of it."

Bess's words struck me and I sniffed the air. A foul odor hung yet in it.

"I know that stench," I mumbled. "I've smelled it before."

Catlin, who had sunk against the stair's rail, now leaned toward me. "You have? When?"

"At the Bourse, just some days ago. Remember you, Bess? I felt too we were being watched."

"The printed word," Bess whispered to herself, and glanced at me. I gathered her meaning. The madman might too have discovered that Catlin was secretly shipping heretical pamphlets. I hushed her with a shake of my head.

"He rattled in Flemish," I remarked, "and though I'm not a native, still I bethink me he had a foreign accent."

"He did, though I can't place it," Catlin said.

"But what was he raving about?" Bess gingerly prodded him. "How could he become your guardian?"

Catlin shrugged. "Speculations are useless. What he said was mere gibberish. 'Tis best we simply forget about him."

My stomach twisted with worry, making me weak and ill. I breathed deeply; I tried to let it settle, but it would not. Like the rest of me, my stomach was fretted with tension. Forget the madman? I could not forget what I'd overheard in the countinghouse and that mine instincts had told me to find another factor. Instead Bess and I were now living with a monger of heresy.

"But this, only this, I'll add." He looked hard at us. "Say nothing. Of that man, of what you have heard and seen tonight, say nothing to anyone."

My stomach twisted again. I felt as if I were at the steps of the gallows.

I **did not** question Catlin's insistence on silence. Though the intruder seemed but an outcast beggar ranting like a lost biblical prophet, yet as a virulent anti-Catholic in Catholic Flanders he could be dangerous. That this heretic might be shadowing Catlin as if in sympathetic collusion with him could only bode grave trouble. Certes his reason for doing so concerned Catlin's secret shipping, though how he was aware of this I knew not. I held my tongue, and as the days and weeks rolled by, we did not see him again and I began to hope that his single appearance had too been his last.

But then came a day when for only moments we saw him spying upon Catlin. 'Twas on a Sunday morning, just after mass at Our Lady's Church. When most of the crowd had shuffled out, Bess and I ambled down the aisle and outside into the Glove Market. There Catlin was waiting for us. He had not gone to mass (indeed, never had I seen him step inside a church) but he'd been taking a walk and was now ready to accompany us home. Then a foul stench drifted by me.

"God's wounds!" I gasped, grabbing Catlin by the elbow. "It's that mad beggar, Catlin—I smell him again!"

His face grew taut with fear and he jerked his head about. "Where? Can you see him?"

Bess peered across the Market. "There! Is that him?"

At the end of the open square, near a group of churchgoers, a ragged stick man skipped. It was the madman. His wild eyes were upon us, and when he saw us looking at him he arched his back as if a stake were being driven down through him, whipped around, and flickered in and out of sight, past people and doors, till he was gone.

"Damn him!" Catlin muttered.

I was opening my mouth to say the same when close behind me stirred the sound of moving robes. I glanced over my shoulder. The robes were white and black and above them I saw the mask-stiff face of Brother Gerard observing Catlin. He looked in the direction of the mad beggar now gone, then again toward Catlin.

"Who's that black friar?" Catlin whispered, uneasy.

"Brother Gerard," Bess said, "the one I've told you about."

Much as I disliked the friar, I nodded and smiled; I felt the need to be the friendly innocent with him. He nodded in turn, then, with his wan eyes lingering on Catlin, he at last moved away from us toward the corner around which the mad beggar had vanished.

"Think you he was drawing a connection betwixt you and the madman?" I asked.

"I know he was," said Catlin.

◆　◆　◆

On a day soon after, I accompanied Bess and Catlin to a cloth seller's countinghouse and there watched the two as they discussed a purchase. They seemed much like a man and wife, I bethought me, so familiarly did their words and movements weave together. Yet within that same hour I would be struck by the bitter irony of mine observation.

Their business done, we next headed for the English Quay, but were stopped by a broken stall blocking the corner. I stood amidst the small crowd whilst the thing was being cleared away, and Catlin and Bess chatted.

Mine own attention was drawn to a nearby lady who was talking with a laundress. Only by a glimpse from the corner of mine eye did I think she was a lady, for upon turning I realized she was something else. The gaudy frippery she was wearing, the saucy swaggering in her movements, the boldness in her very pretty but brittle face all betrayed that she was no more than a costly whore.

Bess too was watching her. Then another whore came by, a common street drab with painted cheeks like o'erripe apples and small, hard bird eyes. She spotted the wealthier whore and brushed back her rumpled orange skirt as if preening for a fight.

"Well, Yvette," she hooted, still some paces away, "take you your business to the street now?"

Yvette started and her face contracted sourly, then with false dignity she gossiped on with the laundress.

The drab's slash of a mouth twisted down. She shifted from foot to foot and ruffled back her skirt. "Well, Yvette?" she repeated.

Yvette mumbled to the laundress, and the two of them laughed shrilly. The sound was a slap to the drab.

"I expected to see you walking the streets," she said sharply. " 'Tis no secret your rich man no longer wants you."

At this the crowd looked around at the two whores and elbowed one another. I saw Catlin, though, give them only an uneasy glance and then step into the crowd as if to disappear.

Yvette's brittle face grew furious. She parted from the laundress and strutted too closely past the drab, brushing so hard 'gainst her that the drab nigh fell. Enraged, she dashed at Yvette, with a swoop of her arm ripped off her bonnet, and held it up like a trophy.

The crowd grinned with delight. Yvette grabbed for it but grasped the drab's face instead and had her fingers bitten. She shrieked, whipping her hand away so broadly that she nigh struck me. I let go a frightened cry and, as the whores flew at each other, I tried to vanish into the crowd as had Catlin. Then so too did the rich whore, breaking away from the drab. The watchers stepped away as she clambered among them and she fell against a man who had turned his back upon the fray. She clutched his arm, twittering her beseeches for help like a distressed lady seeking a gentleman's aid. But when he faced her, she blinked. "Bartholomew!" she stammered.

I looked at once at Bess. She was struck dumb.

Some people laughed, some giggled, some clucked their tongues and shook their heads. The drab hurled herself into the crowd and on Catlin and the whore. With a thrust of his arm, he tossed her off and she fell, cursing, at the feet of one whom with a sinking heart I recognized.

I looked up at the white and black robes and stark face of Brother Gerard. His eyes were fixed on Catlin.

In the sudden silence the two whores clattered off in opposite directions. Catlin returned the friar's gaze and then, not like an abashed man who had just been bedeviled by whores but like a proud arch-bishop, he went over to Brother Gerard and spoke with him.

Bess was staring at Catlin as if hearing still the whore calling him by name. I longed to tell her we were both deluded and had seen nothing.

But "What a ridiculous mess" was all I could think to say, "and to have this happen afore that accursed friar."

Bess was silent. "You know what we saw was naught," I said. She only shook her head. Then abruptly she went over to join Catlin, and I followed with dread anticipation.

". . . the humiliating assaults one can be victim to in these streets," Catlin was saying.

Brother Gerard's face was without expression; he seemed the stern confessor unwilling to grant absolution. "Indeed. Ironic, is it not, that we have seen each other before because of strangers."

Catlin's blank expression was well-feigned. "We have?"

"I believe, Mynheer Catlin . . ."

"Know you my name?"

"I do. I believe, mynheer, that like me you were standing in the Glove Market the Sunday afore last, where you were being closely watched and followed by a rogue."

"Ah, that Dominican was you then?" Catlin let a glimmer of recollection slip onto his face. "I remember me too some stranger was staring at me, but I paid him no mind. He seemed a madman."

"Damascus."

"What?"

"Damascus is his name, or that is what he calls himself."

"Then you know him also?"

"My brothers and I know that he must be . . . apprehended and his heretical calumny silenced. This, however, will be difficult. I regret to tell you he is a master of evasion."

Catlin was sympathetic. "Know you how to catch him still?"

"There is a way. He has been of late following another man, who in turn seems to be ignorant of him. Damascus sometimes follows select people about—all of them heretics like himself—in the deluded belief that it is his God-given mission to . . ."—he chose his words carefully—"protect them. If you mind not, Mynheer Catlin, in assisting me in trapping Damascus . . ."

'Twas Catlin who was being trapped, all mine instincts screamed. I looked at him. I knew the same warnings were ringing through him, but to avoid the friar's offer now could only incur suspicion.

"In whatever way I can, Brother . . ." Catlin bowed slightly.

"Gerard. My gratitude."

"But I fail to see how I can help."

"Do you?" He raised his eyebrows. "Damascus has been seen following you."

Catlin caught in his breath. "I am not a heretic!"

"I will accept your word—for the present. Still, it is what Damascus thinks that matters, and that will lead us to him. We plan to catch him by in turn shadowing the heretic he protects. Should we thus be able to lay a trap for him, your presence at a specified time may all the more lure him into it." At this point, at last and unwanted, Brother Gerard pinned Bess and me with his gaze. "Since Mevrouw Lathbury and her niece have been with you on those occasions when Damascus was watching you, then their presence with you would also be welcomed."

"No, not these ladies," Catlin answered too quickly, then again feigned cooperation. "Mine own participation I gladly give you, but to subject these ladies to a situation that might be harmful to them I could not forbear."

Brother Gerard was unmoved. "Naught shall happen to them."

"Or so say you," I bluntly countered. I had no desire to go anywhere with that friar, save to watch after Catlin's own safety. I looked to Bess for her protest, but she remained silent and kept her smoldering eyes on Catlin. She was thinking more of the whore than of Damascus, and for the nonce cared naught about any trap.

"Every caution for your safety will be given you," Brother Gerard said. "Of the place and time, I will send you word. And besides the capture of Damascus, all three of you will belike be proven innocent of heresy."

His face remained a mask and his voice flat, but we each of us, I knew, shuddered within at the threat of his words.

For hours after that encounter an apparition of Brother Gerard hung in my mind like a curse. Something dreadful will soon happen, I swore, and in response my stomach churned tight and sour and could not be calmed. Like Bess and Catlin I went about my work at the English Quay, but once we had returned to the countinghouse I could keep silent no longer. When we sat down in his office and the subject of yet another sale arose, I blustered out.

"Enough of this distracting stuff," said I. "We all three are thinking of the same thing—what Brother Gerard is planning to do to us."

Catlin's eyebrows rose, a sigh of exasperation slacked out. "He's planning to catch Damascus. If he suspects me too of heresy, no matter, sith I be innocent of . . ."

"No, Catlin, you are not."

He didn't move. His gaze was arrested by mine.

"I know of your secret." The words broke out of me with relief. "I know that you are shipping into England pamphlets praising the Protestant faith."

Catlin's shoulders contracted as if he were furtively withdrawing from my charge. "Nay, I am not . . ."

"You are."

"How know you that?"

"I overheard something I should have been deaf to, as did Bess. I' faith, this discovery so frighted me I began to hunt for another factor. I had no luck, so here we are together still."

"Then you disapprove of my actions."

"I disapprove of the danger, and with this madman and now a Dominican sniffing about you, there could be great danger."

"I can fool them."

"Can you? I hope so, but still I must think of Bess and myself. We live in your house, you are my factor, we have made investments and joined in ventures with you. There are too many links to allow us our innocence should you be caught, which God forbid."

"No harm will come to any of us." He sounded as though he were enveloping himself in stealth. "E'en if I must perforce forgo any such shipping."

At this Bess stirred. She had been sitting beside me in thorny brooding as if waiting for a moment to strike out. "But why are you spreading unlawful religion at all?" she challenged.

"I have my good reasons."

"Oh, do you indeed?" She was sour. "Just as you have reasons for doing other rogue mischief."

She was referring to the whore; we all knew this. But Catlin didn't grow angry; instead he seemed to break a little under the knowledge that what had happened in the street had hurt her. For Bess he now softened.

"Aye, I've done many foolish things. What do you wish of me, to ask your forgiveness?"

"What good would that do me?"

"Stop it!" said I. "This is no time for your silly vengeance. Whether or no we are willing to admit it, we are in danger. That is what should be concerning us. You are a dear friend, Catlin, and I couldn't bear to see you harmed, but . . ."

I gasped, clutched my belly, and bent over.

Catlin quickly reached for me. "Sara, what is it?"

"My stomach." I sighed. With effort, I straightened again. "It's been much bothering me of late, what with fear and then this arguing."

"Some hot milk will help you." Bess's worry was great.

"I've tried that before. 'Tis useless."

"Then you should see a doctor."

"I know of none in Antwerp."

"I do." Catlin closed up his desk, rose, and drew on his surcoat.

"We should out of here withal. Let us have you see a doctor—he's too a friend I met not long ago—and then we'll home."

"Aye, let's." I too drew on my cloak.

Catlin headed out of the office. "A moment whilst I tell Jan and Michiel to close up this house for the day."

As soon as he was gone, I turned to Bess. "God's wounds! Did you have to bring up that wretched whore? 'Tis the trouble we're in you should be thinking of."

"Do you expect me to forget her?" she grumbled.

"I expect more sense in you. How could you have been so surprised? Catlin is an unmarried man who goes never to church and about whom there are rumors of sinfulness. He's also been plainly lonely—mayhap more lonely than you."

" 'Twould serve him right."

"Oh stop all this feigning. 'Tis obvious that you love him."

Bess seemed to pull away from me as if I had discovered a weakness in her and she had to shield it. Then she made a cunning smile. " 'Tis also obvious that he left that whore for me."

"What a hollow boast."

The doctor's physic rooms were near the docks, Catlin told us, and so we three walked toward the Scheldt to Hoogstraat. We were in a place I didn't like. Granted, some handsome houses were about and close by stood the warehouses and countinghouses kept by many cloth-making towns. But nigh where we walked, just on the other side of the street, were the stews, or, as the area was known, the Street of the Stews, for crowded all about in a huddle of poor buildings were bath-houses and taverns known to be brothels as well. It was such an ugly place that I kept close to Catlin as we passed by the decaying buildings. I surveyed with disgust the drunken sailor who tumbled out of a door, the pig that grunted and munched upon a pile of garbage, the broken, jagged windows, the violence-ravaged corners, the grinning spider of a man with a deformed arm and one eye sewn shut who crept out of a bathhouse and fell to an insidious whistling, the spittle falling betwixt his rotting teeth. Everything was filthy, waste-yellow, and speckled with grit. The laughter and noise spilling from some of those houses were as hard as ice; the silence hovering around others put a shiver down my back.

In a minute we passed the stews, then the neighboring Pieter Pot Abbey, turned down a narrow street, and stopped at a door. A sign hung above and I took a step back to read it, squinting to do so, for the sun was clouded o'er and a long shadow stretched down the length of the passage. Painted in bold black letters were the words Doktor Nicolas van Wouwere, and below them a five-pointed yellow star to signify the doctor's knowledge of astrology, a useless symbol since every doctor of course needed to be skilled in the science. I glanced at the name of the house carved into the splintering wood above the door; 'twas Solomon's Wisdom. Paltry wisdom it must be, I thought, if these be the lodgings it brings Solomon.

We entered into a small chamber. On a stool at the far end sat an old man. His simple clothes and obsequious head bowing told us he was a servant. Only the thinnest handful of hair was left along his temples and the back of his head, where each white thread floated freely away from him and each other, making him look as if it were raveling apart.

Catlin gave the old servant his name. The man inclined his head again, then approached a closed door, knocked three times upon it, went in, and in a blink returned.

"You may enter," the servant said. "But I pray you remain silent till the doctor allows you to speak."

"A queer request," Bess remarked.

"Give it queer respect," murmured Catlin.

We found ourselves in a room full of shadows. On one wall were two windows, but their curtains were closed and only a bleak shaft of daylight fell below them. What other light there was came from the fire in the hearth and from a candle on a table. Seated at that table, the candle at his elbow, was a man. He looked more like a massive dark bundle. His thick figure was draped in a fur-lined, night-blue gown that parted to reveal an ebony doublet and a golden cross that hung shimmering on his chest. He'd a full brown beard salted with silver and half of his head was covered with a black undercap. Upon his hooked, looming nose perched a pair of spectacles, their black-wire frames threaded with the dangling hairs of his beetling eyebrows, their glass reflecting the candlelight so that his eyes were unseen and the direction of his gaze unknown; but the spectacles were aimed at a bottle clasped delicately in one hand. With his other hand he reached into a box, drew out a russet powder, dropped it into the clear liquid in the bottle, and for several moments watched intently for some mysterious transformation.

Other bottles were gathered about him on the table and scattered in profusion about the room. There were bottles and glasses and boxes marked with their contents: wormwood, camphor, gum seraphic, scammony, turbith, myrobalans, musk, and bloodroot. There was a celestial sphere painted with a map of the heavens, and bowls, porringers, ewers, books, papers, and skimble-skamble stuff. On a shelf betwixt the windows, alert atop two fat books with gilt-edged pages, was a human skull, its eyeless pits staring mockingly at us, its grinning teeth laughless. Beyond all those strange tools of the doctoring profession were the sooty wainscoting and low-beamed ceiling, a Turkey carpet, and slippery polished floor. Yet an ugly, fusty smell skulked in the place, and a foulness drifted about that night-blue bundle of a man motionless still at the table.

Then he moved. The light from the spectacles flickered away; sunken eyes wavered into view. A satisfied breath whistled out of the looming nose. The bearded head rolled up and the eyes fell upon us. A voice like remote thunder rumbled out.

"Ah, Bartholomew! How glad I am to see you." With heavy solemnity the bundle rose and took on the dimensions of a man. He proved to be tall and with a solid girth, made the more voluminous by his rich gown. He came around the table and smiled at Bess and me. "Thankful I am too," he continued to speak in his native Flemish, "that you've brought with you these ladies. I cry you mercy, good ladies, for had I known you were present I would have seen to your comfort immediately. Please you, be seated."

We did as he bid, whilst he went to the windows and drew back the curtains. The fading daylight sifted through the air.

"I pray we haven't disrupted your work," said Catlin.

The doctor pulled his chair around, lowered onto it his wide body, and let lie one arm upon the table, beside his bottles of unguents and herbs and liquids. "Nay, you have not. I merely didn't hear you enter. I but remember that my servant told me you'd arrived and that I told him to let you enter. I am, alas, too easily lost amidst the preparations of my medicines. The darkness of the room you must have found disconcerting. But now we've some light, so now I may better behold the ladies' fairness."

I made an obligatory smile to the flattery whilst Catlin introduced us. When his name was said—Doctor Nicolas van Wouwere—he bowed his head to Bess and me, his gaze lingering upon her face. She gazed back indifferently.

"So, Doctor, prepare you always your medicines in dark rooms?" she asked.

He took off his spectacles and lay them upon the table. Then he smiled at her, his teeth glimmering like his cross. "Not always. At times I need the brightest light that I may closely study what I mix. At other times, though, I prepare a potion, such as the one I just now was working with, so delicate in its balance that I must perforce shut myself into a closed-up room so no passerby may distract me."

"Nicolas studied physic at the University of Paris," Catlin told us. " 'Twas there he gained his license. Since then he's traveled the whole of Europe and has gone as far east as the Holy Land."

"My studies have taken me to many places." He was proud of himself. "The pursuit of knowledge can be difficult and costly."

"I envy you your astrology," said Catlin. " 'Tis brilliant."

The doctor nodded. "Precise astrological calculations make medicine the more potent. Therefore I must prepare some physic not only in the dark, but oft at night when the stars, moon, and planets are in the most propitious positions."

"Well then, Doctor," said I, "that I am glad to hear, as I have need of strong medicine."

He put on again his spectacles and squinted at me. "Be you ill, mevrouw?"

"My stomach doth bother me of late."

He rose, approached, and bent over me. "Pardon, Mevrouw Lathbury, but I must need feel your venter," said he as he lay his left hand on my belly. For a wordless minute he moved the hand around in circles. He asked me a few questions, I told him of my pains, and he returned to his table.

"Your complaint is a common one, a most common one. I believe I shall be able to prepare for you a good remedy."

Into a narrow phial he dropped the crushed leaves of herbs, poured in an eggshell-brown liquid he fetched from a shelf, added a pinch of fine powder, and stirred the lot of them. Then he capped the phial and handed it to me, along with a jar of ointment and his instructions on their use.

"Much thanks for this your physic." I put the two things into the pocket of my cape. "But doctors cannot live on thanks alone. I can pay you now for this, if you prefer."

He shook his head and sat down. "I want no payment now or later. You are a friend of my friend here; his company and yours are sufficient recompense."

"Marry, good words and physic both. For what more could I ask?"

Beside me, Bess stirred. By the way she was keeping her face empty, her body hard to herself, I could tell that for some reason she already disliked the man. "Aren't we blessed"—an irony cooled her tone—"that after all your wanderings you chose this city wherein to settle."

"Ah, Mevrouw Marwick, 'twas not truly my choice to live here." Van Wouwere heard only flattery. "I wanted to return to my native town of Ostend. But eleven- or twelvemonth ago I was visited by a series of most fantastic dreams, all telling me I should come here to Antwerp, and I have learned to heed the messages my dreams give me and the events they foresee. It was from my dreams I divined that there were certain people here whose lives I shall affect. Who was I to say nay to destiny?"

"You also consulted your stars and your numbers." Catlin much fancied this point.

Van Wouwere gave a single nod of his head.

"You don't mean those little games?" Bess looked at Catlin. "The ones you were showing me the other night."

" 'Tis a game only to the unlearned." Catlin was smiling but his words stung her. "Nicolas not only understands such means of divination, he is too marked with a sign."

Van Wouwere scowled and his beetling eyebrows joined into a long ledge. "There are things I've told you, Bartholomew, that you should hold private."

Bess squirmed at this intimation that Catlin was keeping secrets for a man who was yet a stranger to her.

"I'm sorry, Nicolas, but Sara's discretion you can well trust. I had hoped you could too trust Bess." He gave her a steely look.

A sigh heaved up through van Wouwere's bulky form. He pursed his lips, thought, and answered guardedly. "Perchance no harm is done in telling these ladies. But I must remember you, Bartholomew, that I desire few to know about my prophesying, as too oft are such things ascribed erroneous meanings by ignorant people, though these ladies I nothing doubt are themselves discreet and wise."

He paused, then talked on in a hushed voice. "When I was a student in Paris, I met a scholar. He was a strange man, a gelded man, and the hearsay was God had gifted him with the ability to read the future. Not only did he teach me many wise and mystical things, but he insisted that I too had a gift and could read the future. How? I asked him, fearing he had seen into mine own mind, for I had in truth queer premonitions and dreams. He took my left hand and held it open to me." At this, he unfolded his left hand upon the table and with the fingers of the other pointed to the palm. " 'Hast thou not noticed the mark God hast put upon thy hand?' he asked. I confessed I had, but to ease the trouble it gave my soul I'd turned a blind eye to it. 'A mistake,' he said to me, 'for this sign reveals thou hast great spiritual powers.' I have, you see, a star written into the palm of my left hand."

He took his hand off the table and, lowering it, held it ope before Bess and me. I leaned forward to better espy any pattern there might be among the wrinkles and lines filling his palm, and I found that a few of those lines overlapped and met in such a way that a crooked, five-pointed star could be discerned among them. One or two small lines that helped to form uneven points, howe'er, were somewhat unlike the others; in fact they could have been not natural lines but scars. I leaned forward the more to see them better in the poor light, but he pulled his hand away.

"Not only for the improvement of my physic but to understand this sign and what it means, I have pursued so much knowledge and so many sciences." He folded his hands upon his lap and the great fur-lined sleeves of his gown fell over them and they vanished. "You, too, I see, have a mark upon your hand," he said to Bess.

Quickly and uneasily she glanced at the scar from the burn upon her left hand and lay her right one o'er it to hide. "A marked hand? Such a poor thing to be compared with your portentous star!" Again the irony was in her voice. "I do hope you read your patients' stars more accurately than you read such supposed signs."

"I do not misread signs."

A movement in the near window diverted Bess's attention. A man was standing just outside and pressing his face 'gainst the panes to see into the room. I nigh gasped at the sight of the purple-edged skin of a nostril that had been slashed open and raggedly healed long ago.

After catching a glimpse of the doctor, the man moved out of sight. Seconds passed. Then we heard someone entering the other chamber and talking with the servant.

Van Wouwere frowned. "You can see now why I draw my curtains when I prepare my physics. Some people will pry into places where privacy is essential. I like not the way this house is so close to the docks and the riffraff working them. Still the area can be a fine one. Noticed you that there are rich men's houses but a short walk from mine? In one there is a family so wealthy they lend money to kings and queens."

From the chamber beyond came another voice rising above the servant's. "But the doctor will see me now. I have money now." There was the jangle of coins.

I coughed a little too loudly. "Aye, there are fine houses not far from here, but too other buildings of a different nature."

"Methinks too that some of the streets hard by are not very safe," Bess said.

"Alack, mevrouw, 'tis true," agreed van Wouwere, "but then even the best streets can hold danger in them."

"So right you are." She gave him too sweet a smile. "Know you what happened but this morning to us? A pair of fighting whores blocked our way and then one of them fell against Catlin!"

Van Wouwere shook his head. "A public insult!"

Catlin leaned against the back of his chair until its wood creaked.

"Ah"—Bess slyly winked at the doctor—"but the jest was that she knew him, called him," she squeaked in a broad imitation, "Bartholomew!"

Van Wouwere, uncertain how to act, tried to laugh with her. "Doubtless she was mistaken."

"Oh, no need to protect Catlin." Bess shrugged, all jolly. "It mattered not to me, save that she seemed a violent drab. 'Twould not surprise me at all if she has attacked him before."

"Indeed? Then I must say I may know her too—just by sight, of course." A bejeweled finger rose out of his sleeve and stroked his beard. He grinned at Catlin. "Was she the same who flew at you with a knife when you heard of some fire and rushed to leave her . . ."

He stopped himself too late and had revealed too much. His mouth shut tightly.

Bess smiled yet more sweetly. She had been told what she had somehow suspected.

For a moment we all sat in a silence prickled with unease. Then van Wouwere picked up a bottle. I coughed again, and Catlin rose.

"I fear we must leave now," said he.

"What, already?" van Wouwere put aside the bottle. "Ah, but then you're as busy as am I."

Bess drew on her gloves as if only too eager to leave. "Well, good morrow to you, Doctor."

"Oh no, Mevrouw Marwick, 'tis merely Nicolas for you."

"Merely Nicolas, then."

Van Wouwere smiled at her with an ill-fitting fatherliness, and bid us a farewell, and Bess and I then left. Catlin tarried behind to exchange with him some private communication and we waited in the other chamber. In that same room was the servant, who had upon his lap some silver he was polishing and his eyes upon the shaggy man standing nervously against a wall—the same man who had earlier peered in at us. He had started when the door to the doctor's chamber opened and we came out, and like a fly inched his way to one side that he could see past the open door behind us. Lest he not be granted the doctor's attention, he shoved his scaly hand into his pocket and jangled his purse again.

"This is what I fear the most about van Wouwere," Bess mumbled to me. "The way a man might be drawn to him."

"Why say you that? This is but one patient."

"I'm thinking too of Catlin. And van Wouwere knows just how to tempt him."

"Tempt him?" I scoffed. "How can he do that?"

"Catlin has his weaknesses, and astrology is one of them."

"You sound like a jealous lover."

"I'm nothing of the sort."

"Then don't talk like one. This doctor is not competing with you for Catlin."

Bess shrugged. "Aye, I know. Still there's something about him I distrust."

Though I felt the same, I kept my peace. At last Catlin came out but he said not a word to her, e'en when she asked as if in jest what in the world he had been talking about behind the closed door with van Wouwere.

·• XII •·

As **Brother Gerard** had blackly promised, word was indeed soon sent. Only two days later there was delivered to Catlin's counting-house a message from Brother Gerard that instructed us to meet with him that evening at about four of the clock before the gates of the monastery. No other information was given.

I tried to get on with my work, but my mind was ever on that dreaded appointment and mine eyes seemed to see only the hours slip away. When I wasn't near the clock in Catlin's office, I'd glance out a window to determine the time, but on that bleak November day a mass of low-hanging clouds had infused a gray sameness into everything so that even the shadows of moving hours were hidden. And a coldness was spreading. It threatened windows with the frost that would soon scratch them, buildings and streets with the snow that would bury them, the Scheldt with the ice that would make its waves crack and shiver. But no snow, no rain, no drops or flakes fell. Only the frozen promise stung an air barren and dry. Then, at just a little before four of the clock, Catlin and Bess and I stepped out of the countinghouse and into the cold.

"I had never wanted you to be in any part of this," said Catlin, as if asking our forgiveness.

"Aye, I know that," I answered. "And so you should bear in mind that Bess and I must consider ourselves first, whatever comes of this."

Bess drew her cloak tighter around her. "Nothing will happen to us, and we'll not have to abandon Catlin."

She did not look at him, and as we began to walk on they only drew a little close to each other. Still that was enough for me to understand that in the end that whore in the street had not split them apart.

Too soon we reached an open place where a few streets crossed and the Dominican monastery walled up one side. Standing before its closed double doors like an eerie sentinel was a black-hooded and caped reedlike figure. Instinctively, I slowed my steps. Only when we drew closer could I see what I already knew, that it was Brother Gerard, and only when we were nigh him did he speak.

"The place where we'll wait is not far from here."

That was all he said. He turned and moved on, with no invitation that we walk beside him or speak ourselves, leading us northward, down streets where the passersby dwindled into nothing and the mute buildings and leafless limbs of trees fell away behind us. By the time he stopped we were on the edge of the New Town, not where fresh structures were being raised and the old had been swept away, but near the canal, and before a long, crumbling warehouse, cinder-dark in the ash-colored air. Square holes gaped where windows had once been, and rusted nails rose like warts upon the splintered timber. For only a moment, the friar stood before the door, unlocked and crooked-hanging, then pushed it open. We followed him inside.

The warehouse was a deserted shell. Two stories above slanted the roof and where there had once been head-high, raised platforms now leaned only cracked poles linked by strips of wood and ropes dangling from pulleys. Just one, much higher platform remained, a kind of narrow stage that clung to the far wall and was connected to the ground by a ladder. Some water-eaten frozen scraps of boxes and barrels were strewn about, but naught else. All this I could see without much difficulty. On nearby buildings and along the canal torches burned, just beyond the windows and out of sight, so that ocher patches smudged our leaden surroundings. At a far corner, through a crack, came a thread of smoke from a close torch, like incense through a thurible. No heat from the flame drifted in though heat I wanted, so hellishly cold was that place.

The friar had again paused, but now his black form glided over the littered floor to a web of poles and ropes. When we joined him I perceived that with the dimness the web concealed us from whoe'er else might enter. Wordless moments passed.

"Are we simply to wait here alone with you?" Catlin asked at last.

"We are not alone." Brother Gerard's low voice was ghostlike; no human timbre pulsed in it. "There are city guards waiting just outside this building, on all its sides."

"But I saw no one out there."

"They were not meant to be seen."

Catlin studied the friar, who did not bother to look back. "You hid them well from me."

"You do not matter. It is from Damascus they are hidden since he must not be frightened away." Brother Gerard raised a bony finger to his lips to signal that we speak only in hushed tones.

Catlin lowered his voice. "Does that madman—Damascus—does he live here?"

"No one lives here, and where Damascus lives no one knows. But he will follow here someone who is steeped in heresy."

My skin prickled and beside me I could feel Bess grow rigid. Was it Catlin Damascus was trailing after? Was he bait and victim too, whom this calculating friar was using to entrap both men in one fell scene? Catlin, though I could feel his fear, kept his wits about him still.

"The heretic, then, you will also arrest?" he asked.

"If we can."

"And who would this other man be?"

Only now did Brother Gerard turn his eyes to Catlin. "I have not yet learned his name, but I know he will soon be here."

The muscles in my neck relaxed a whit. Still, a deeper meaning seemed buried in his reply; none of us was yet safe.

"And what of this Damascus?" Catlin continued. "What know you of him?"

"My knowledge is limited, but then no one knows much about him. Even what country he is from is a mystery, but he seems to live ofttimes in or near Antwerp. There are those who say he journeys at times to Rome, as if to the site of his conversion, for it was whilst there on a pilgrimage that he caught his disease from a harlot, the disease of lust, which you must have seen upon his face. He took it as a punishment from God, or if you will a sign, and so 'converted' to the heresy of Luther and Calvin. It was as if he saw himself as St. Paul on his way to Damascus to persecute the Christians until God struck him down and showed to him the truth. From that holy story Damascus has taken his name; what his true name was has long since been lost."

"And so he has joined with Protestants in Antwerp?"

"Not quite. Even though he shares with them the same beliefs, they have tried to renounce him just as sinners do with the devil."

Catlin considered all this, and then said, "He seems a dangerous fanatic."

"He is."

"And violent."

"As his emotions are violent, then so too must be his actions."

"Then these ladies should not be here." Catlin stepped between us and the friar as if to shield us. "Your assurances that they would be safe are baseless, and this you know."

Brother Gerard didn't so much as blink at this accusation. "No harm shall come to them."

"Will you swear to that?"

"No, for I might be forsworn should God Himself choose to strike down these ladies even as we speak."

"I'm not asking God to swear."

"Do you not trust Him?"

Catlin nigh answered no, that I could see, but he restrained himself and instead said only, "I do not trust you."

A strain raked through the three of us. To challenge this heartless Dominican was dangerous to Catlin and he knew it, but still he did so for Bess's sake and mine; and I was grateful.

"I wish to send these women home. With this Damascus and armed guards about, they cannot be safe."

"It might be dangerous for them also to walk back, alone and at twilight."

"They'll not be alone. I have a servant nearby with horses ready; he'll accompany them."

Brother Gerard made a wan smile. "You did not ride to the monastery."

"I instructed him to follow us from a distance, to aid the women if aught went wrong and"—he smiled back—"to watch our watchers."

Brother Gerard's face emerged a shade from out of the hood. "They'll not be harmed. They shall stay."

Catlin said nothing in return, but with a slight movement he seemed to draw Bess and me closer to his back, to protect us yet more. In a comparable gesture I put my hand upon his back, as did Bess. I was so ashamed at that moment of what I had said to him earlier that, in short, if pressed I would abandon him, for now I knew he would never have abandoned us. Now too, loyalty to him was surging in me. I had seen before the dedication his servants gave him, but this was something more, and shared by equal friends. Catlin wanted from Bess and me, and indeed was drawing, intense loyalty, whilst he in turn put faith in us, the way that friar would in God.

I could hear, just then, the movement of water in the canal beyond the warehouse, I could hear my breathing and my heart, but no other sounds. Small bumps were beginning to riddle my skin, from the cold or my fear.

"On that Sunday morning when Damascus followed you near Our Lady's"—Brother Gerard drifted a little away from us—"I wondered, Mynheer Catlin, about other men who may be drawn to you."

Catlin took on a perplexed look. "Other men?"

"Men who may, for example, be seen on occasion at your countinghouse."

"I did not know you liked to watch my countinghouse."

Brother Gerard's blond wisps of eyebrows stirred. "I don't. I was but wondering how well you know the men who come to it."

"Not well. In my trade I deal with many people with whom I talk only of goods, bills, tariffs, and other dry stuff, and nothing about ourselves."

"Or about religion?"

"Never. It doesn't touch upon my business."

"Then you may do business even with heretics."

Catlin stared in sudden discomfiture at him, as if through innocent bumbling he had admitted to a crime he'd never commit. "If I have e'er done so, then I've done it unknowingly. I am not privy to my clients' secrets."

Brother Gerard made no expression of either belief or unbelief. To me he looked as though he had just begun his testing of Catlin and would be patient.

Just then, out in the street, there came the softest tapping of shoes on stone. They stopped at the door. Immediately all our eyes were fixed there. I heard a thump and watched the door creep slowly, narrowly open. Like a furtive rat, a form slipped into the warehouse, and as it looked about and then began to creep along the wall, away from where we were hidden, the patches of light fell upon it and revealed it to be a man, slight, plainly dressed, and carrying a bundle. He stepped on a board and at its creak he swiftly recoiled, and again his eyes searched the room to ascertain no one was about. As his head moved, I recognized the face of the pamphlet printer. A moan rose in me but I suppressed it. This was the heretic and with him and his law-breaking Catlin was entangled.

Someone was passing noiselessly behind me. 'Twas Brother Gerard, making his way toward the door. Catlin too was moving, but deeper into the ruin of poles, as if to keep all the more out of the printer's sight.

"It is safer to keep those papers here, in a vacant building, than in your home, isn't it?"

'Twas the friar's voice, as hollow as that place and horribly composed, that rent the silence.

The printer wheeled around, gaped at the monk standing betwixt him and the door, faltered away, nigh dropped his bundle.

"There is no escape," Brother Gerard intoned.

Now indeed like a frantic rat, but ever clutching his bundle, the printer scrambled away, stumbled on scraps of wood, stared madly about at the platform-high windows, and espied the ladder and platform and a second-story window to which they led. He ran to the ladder and threw himself onto it. The first rung crackled and split in two and ripped open his thin boot. His foot too was cut; even from where I stood I could see blood. But to none of this did he pay any mind. In his terror he only jumped onto the second rung and began to climb.

All this while, in haunting counterpoint to the man's hot panting, Brother Gerard spoke on, as if reading a final judgment upon him.

"You are by trade a printer. With your full will and evil intent you used your trade to write and print heretical filth. You are trying also to disseminate it, and to this end you have brought it here that it may be hidden until then. Thus, in further covert and unlawful actions, you will send about your vile papers upon which are words offensive to God, His Church, and His truth."

The printer clambered onto the platform and reeled toward the window at the end looking over the canal when his bundle jerked him back. A sharp nail on the platform's rail had caught it. Though wheezing in terror, he would not let go of the bulky thing. Instead he clawed at the tearing cloth, slapped the bundle forward and back, and at last freed it.

"Oh yes, these things I know." Brother Gerard still was composed. "Just as I know that your printshop was closed by the authorities after you left it and all its papers were confiscated. Just as I know that you are trapped. There is no escape."

The printer was at the window hole. He threw the bundle over his shoulder and reached outside to the long joint of a pulley.

"There are a dozen men surrounding this building."

Even as the friar spoke, there rattled outside the chilling sound of boots and metal closing in upon the warehouse.

"They'll not enter unless I signal them to do so. But should you attempt to leave this building, then they shall set themselves upon you."

A wretched noise was now falling from out of the printer—maddened muttering or prayers or both. He shoved his head outside and as rapidly drew it in again, his eyes fixed upon what must have been the guards below.

"And so you shall lay down your bag and submit to an arrest."

The boots and metal had stilled; now there was only the wheezing of the printer. Suddenly, an unearthly howl burst out from above and wailed along the rafters and down the walls. For seconds, it stopped my heart. Even the implacable Brother Gerard was struck cold by it. The howl rose to a shriek. Then, up on the platform, near the printer and out of a hole or darkness or nowhere, stepped Damascus.

Had I never before envisioned the devil; had I never in nightmares witnessed the earthly appearances of Lucifer; had I never in my mind, through the influence of pictures or sermons on evil, seen demons, still I would have recognized what now stood before us. I knew him to be called Damascus, and I knew him to be the sticks-and-bones beggar who had invaded Catlin's house; still, at that moment, he seemed not of this world. His straw hair and shreds of beard were wildly matted, his ancient clothes clung to his frame, and around his mouth, more repulsively than ever, spotted the sores of his sinful disease. But, worst of all, his colorless-seeming eyes were starting starkly from his head and had in their scope the printer, Brother Gerard, and us three unwilling witnesses.

Slowly, his hands and arms began to rise from his sides, as if raising up his power. "Thou hast breathed threats of slaughter against the servant of the Lord!" he bellowed down upon the friar. Nigh immediately, against the roof and walls his voice rebounded, as if several voices rolled from his mouth. Turning his head, stretching out a hand, he cried to the printer, "Cleave to me and I shall save thee!"

But the printer only stared dumbly back as if confusion had struck him into paralysis. Then like sweat his terror broke out again. He stumbled back against the window frame, blindly felt for it, shook his head at Damascus's bony proffered hand, grabbed again the joint of the pulley, and flung a leg out the window.

"Throw thyself down, and I shall bear thee up again!" Damascus wailed to him in a voice like sulphur and smoke.

The printer lingered no longer. Heedless of the guards who were rumbling forward again, he heaved himself up and out the window. I had expected him to jump, but the canal was belike not close enow and the guards were just below him, for instead of jumping down he climbed upward. Out on the wall, then on the roof, we could hear his stumbling feet. He was climbing up one side of the peaked roof and down the other. All about the warehouse there flashed the lights from torches and the shouts of men, and around us fell, from along the printer's high path, splinters of wood shaken loose from the weak rafters.

But none of this distracted Brother Gerard. He was gazing solemnly up at Damascus, whose own gaze now was only for the monk.

"Damascus," said the monk.

"Brother Gerard," Damascus replied.

"Whence did you come?"

"From going to and fro on the earth and walking up and down upon it."

I thought how like God and Lucifer they sounded. But Brother Gerard made for an unfeeling, earthly lord, and Damascus a destructive, sickened devil.

Guards posted on the opposite sides of the warehouse seemed to have cut off the printer's escape, for we could hear him climbing back up the roof. Again splinters and dust fell about us, and then a board that would have hit Bess's head had it not been deflected by an overhanging rope. With that, Catlin pulled us away from there, out into the open and near the door through which we had entered. Only now were we plainly in Damascus's sight, yet he looked at Catlin as if he had known all along of our presence.

"Behold what this monk hath done!" Damascus cried suddenly to Catlin. "He hath led thee and brought thee into darkness, and not into light. But I will help thee. I will lead thee into the light and to refuge." As he spoke, he pointed out the window holes of the platform. Through the lower ones could now be seen the flames of torches. "Thou art a follower of the true Christ! Heed me!"

Brother Gerard turned also to Catlin, as an uncaring god watching a helpless mortal, waiting to see whether or no he would fall to the temptation.

Catlin shrunk from the beckoning Damascus. He could say no word, but over and over he shook his head.

A thump sounded upon the roof, as if the printer had lost his footing and fallen against the slope. We heard the scratching of his feet against the boards, a banging as the shouts of men were hurled at him. And then there came a cracking, quick and loud. The roof where the printer was struggling shattered open and with a scream he was pitched downward through the rafters and his body slammed against the floor.

He had struck the ground inches away from Brother Gerard. The friar had cringed at the falling man but now he was looking coldly down at the dead body, no trace of pity in his face. I had scarce drawn my breath from the horror when there came raining upon them both, and too hard by us, scores and scores of fluttering papers. From a jagged beam above hung the open, empty bag.

"Behold the word of the Lord!" cried Damascus triumphantly.

Now at last an anger shot through Brother Gerard. He spun around and pointed his finger at Damascus. "As there was no escape for him, so shall there be none for you!"

"Thou canst not touch me!"

"Ah, but I can!"

"Nay, nay! But though I be gone, still shall I guard him!" Damascus pointed also, but at Catlin. "I shall protect him too!"

"As you protected this man?" Brother Gerard gestured to the body of the printer.

Damascus stared at Catlin and leaned over the railing toward him. "I shall be with thee to the end of thy days!"

And then he was gone. Backward and into darkness, through what could have been a hole or door, he was gone. At once Brother Gerard hastened through the door beside us and shouted at the guards. There was the flashing of torches and the noise of running boots and clanging metal as the men hurried to the end of the warehouse where Damascus must have gone. Then, through a window, I could see them moving quickly along near buildings and away in pursuit of the unseen madman.

Bess linked her arm through Catlin's and hugged close to him. " 'Tis over now," she softly said. " 'Tis over. And I pray there's no evidence that can link you to this man?"

Catlin was looking at the dead printer, whose broken head was twisted half around and whose limbs were wide-splayed. "None. I was always careful."

"But has Brother Gerard seen a link?"

"I think not. It was belike only Damascus that made him suspicious of me."

Like a wraith Brother Gerard came back into the warehouse, walking calmly again and already deep in thought, halting only when he was beside the body.

"Damascus has not escaped, has he?" Catlin asked.

"He may have. But only for tonight. I will of course meet with him again."

He turned his gaze to Catlin. 'Twas then I knew that Brother Gerard absolved Catlin of nothing. But whether or no Catlin was his hunted prey I could not tell. Instead, it was as if Brother Gerard and Damascus both, like a god and a devil, were long involved in a hateful battle, and he was the sacrificial mortal through whom they were striking at each other. 'Twas the battle that mattered, not Catlin.

"Need you us any longer as your bait?" Bess bluntly asked him, and not without sarcasm.

"No, not tonight." Brother Gerard bowed his head to her. "I thank you for your presence. I would, however, wish to talk with you all but a little, merely to resolve some questions."

"Not here." Catlin slipped Bess's arm from his and went to the open door. "We shall talk at my house, where these ladies will be warm—and safe." He spoke as if now ordering the friar about. Then he stepped outside and made a sign, which was answered by the clattering of horses' hooves upon the street. Arnout was riding up with other mounts.

Bess had followed Catlin to the door. I lingered behind, my foot upon a pamphlet. When Brother Gerard's attention was elsewhere, I stooped down, picked it up, and curving my back away from him, quickly scanned it.

The thing proved to be only a single sheet of cheap paper folded to make four pages, and it was poorly printed. But the mean appearance was its least offense. Nowhere in it could I find one line of keen theological argument or the inspiration of faith. Certes the beliefs expressed were Protestant, but though I could count amongst them some of mine own, they were here so twisted I was ashamed to admit as much. Worse still was the writer's viciousness toward England's Queen Mary and the distorted deduction that it was unnatural for a woman to rule over men, for all women were feeble, weak, and foolish, and that since too she was a "worshipper of idols," then no obedience was due her. In all, it was a treatise corrupted and warped by hatred.

I was appalled. I dropped the paper and turned back around, only to see that Brother Gerard had been watching me. This time, I did not conceal my sentiments. That I had been ignorant of what was in those pamphlets, that my response to them was disgust, I wanted him to see. I believed that he did. But if he then concluded I was innocent it did not seem to matter. Instead, he was regarding me as if I was of no consequence.

He gestured toward the door. "Mynheer Catlin has a horse ready for you."

It was Catlin, I knew, who was of consequence.

⊶ XIII ⊶

We mounted our horses and began to ride homeward, leaving behind Brother Gerard. He had to instruct the guards on carrying away the dead man and gathering up the pamphlets ere he could join us. "Good," mumbled Catlin as the warehouse disappeared behind us, "let him walk to my house."

By the time we ourselves had reached it, the early winter darkness had fallen and our clothes were dank and stiff. We changed into warmer things and joined one another in the parlor, where much good food was now set out. Scarce had we sat down when Brother Gerard arrived. Lijsken led him into the room and took his black cloak. Beneath it, and beneath his black scapular, his white robe gleamed spotlessly as always, as if none of the day's violence had touched him.

"Your house is a fine one, Mynheer Catlin," said he.

"I thank you, Brother." Catlin pulled out for him a chair at the head of the table. "But doubtless you've visited yet finer houses."

"In truth, I seldom visit anyone. Hence I am most accustomed to my monastery, to its chapel and my cell."

A plague on his show of humbleness, I thought; I would to God he were back in his cell now. I hated having to look at his face. Pale though it always was, it had in the candlelight the color of a corpse.

"Well, Mevrouw Marwick," he continued, "you must be pleased to live now in this house after your small chamber at the White Hound."

"Oh, 'tis passing comfortable here, and I like it right well," said Bess.

"And like you well Mynheer Catlin's company?"

"Of course."

"So close together in this house—your friendship too must be close."

She studied him whilst deciding the intent of his question. "We are good friends and partners."

"And nothing more?"

"No. Does that disappoint you?"

"You must forgive me, mevrouw. I am perchance only too mindful of what the great theologians have taught us about women."

"And you accept their teachings with blind faith, for as a monk you can have no personal knowledge of women."

"Such knowledge can be dangerous."

"Dangerous?" Bess teased. "Can knowledge of me truly so threaten you with temptation, Brother?"

His mouth slid downward. "I was speaking of theology."

"Oh. I wonder how I mistook that."

"Women are the children of Eve, and as Tertullian taught, Eve was the door to the devil. In her person, a woman becomes an incitation to lust and concupiscence. Therefore men should shun women's company."

"Advice you have taken to heart in your vow of chastity," said Bess.

"I feel safe within its confines."

A clever smile played on Bess's lips. "Safe? Then you *are* threatened."

At last Catlin intervened. "Theology has naught to do with my friendship with Mevrouw Marwick and her aunt. It has instead much to do with business."

"Certainly." Brother Gerard glanced over the plate of mutton ere pushing it away. "You are all three, in short, partners."

With his suspicion of Catlin's link to the printed heresy, this remark had scant innocence to it. Had Brother Gerard's testing of us recommended already, wrapped up though it was in the woolly thickness of idle chatter? Through it all, Catlin had been pouring for us large cupfuls of malmsey, for which I was grateful. I took a strong gulp, whilst Catlin took on the friar's implications.

"I am Mevrouw Marwick's factor, and too join with her and Mevrouw Lathbury in ventures. Together, we do such business and more—all of it good, honest work."

Brother Gerard seemed to have felt the thrust of Catlin's last words. He regarded his cup and let his waxy hand glide over it ere lightly grasping the stem, as if consecrating his drink. His silence seemed as purposeful as his questions, and the pressure it might put on us much desired by him. Catlin's foot began to tap upon the carpet; his brow was pulling into a scowl, his fist was hiding his mouth. Then his fist lowered, grabbed his cup, and in a few gulps he finished off the drink and was pouring himself more. Bess, apparently sharing his feelings and knowing what to do, turned to Brother Gerard.

"Mynheer Catlin is e'en kindly teaching me a new business skill," said she.

"Indeed?"

"Astrology. I am learning to cast the stars myself."

Good, I sighed. Let us get on to a scientific subject so that this friar's sniffing about might be diverted.

"Judicial astrology, in fact," said Catlin.

"Use you it much in your business?" The friar became interested.

"Only as much as would any merchant," said I. "Being merchants, we wish to reassure ourselves as much as possible that a ship carrying our goods will arrive safely. Hence we consult an astrologer—or Catlin; he's a rare merchant who knows this science—to learn what weather our ship will have at sea, or if it will fall to pirates or sink. Mind you, though, I don't often consult astrologers, because they can be quite wrong. I remember me one I went to, said to be the best in London. I accepted his prognostication and sent my goods on the ship I'd asked after. The ship was lost in a storm and so I lost my money. Happily I'd bought assurance on them and so recovered some of my investment."

"The fool most likely read the stars improperly," Catlin remarked.

"As you say. But too bear in mind that storms and floods and all weather can be stirred up by God or the devil, not by the stars. I suppose, then, that it may be foolish of me when I go to an astrologer to learn too whether or no the ship will be captured by pirates, for how can one foresee events that are dependent upon the will of men?"

"How true." Brother Gerard's voice was like a chant. "Too often astrologers forget that the pirates who plunder a ship, who commit their sins, have chosen to do so. How can their sins be blamed on the stars? Sins should be fastened not on them, but on the sinner."

"But"—Catlin raised a pointing finger as if to an answer hanging nearby—"some say the stars influence the body, not the soul."

"But the soul can be tarnished and even damned by actions of the body," said Bess, "and such actions are the manifestations of the heart's and mind's will. And if our hearts and minds are influenced by the stars, then we are their hapless slaves, not God's children. No, that I don't believe. No one can foresee through the stars events dependent upon the wills of men, otherwise men would have no free will."

"Yet too there are learned men," Catlin countered, "who say the stars don't force but incline. Thus one could watch the stars and planets and declare that this kind of event may occur because the stars and planets are in a position to incline certain men to evil."

"Incline, but not force. The choice is still theirs."

"Which is why astrologers maintain that stars give them only conditional guesses and not precise facts."

"An argument that saves them from a red face when their prognostications come to naught." Bess was now debating only with him as was he with her; Brother Gerard seemed dismissed.

"That I don't deny." Catlin, nettled into movement, skimmed his finger along his bearded jaw. "But still you can't deny that the stars portend something. The Scriptures say, 'God made the sun, moon, and stars and appointed them for signs and for seasons and for days and for years.' Thus He has marked in the heavens not the future as He wills it but as man with his free will ordains it; and knowing all time and knowing man He knows what man will do, and all that will pass."

"But again you're taking man's will away from him and putting it in the heavens."

"Am I? I think not. Foreknowledge is not predestination."

"True," said Brother Gerard. "An eclipse will occur because of the natural movement of celestial bodies, not because astronomers predict it."

"And some foreknowledge we might have through astrology, I agree." Bess leaned toward Catlin. "But I will not like you read into the stars signs that don't exist. The great have their fates. Kings and queens and nations have their destinies. But who am I to find the borders of my small life strung across the heavens? Oh, I'll learn how to cast the stars because they can make me aware of general possibilities, but that is all."

"Don't underestimate your importance. Is it not true that God's eye is even on the sparrow? So even for you He has made signs and given you a purpose." Catlin spoke not with any reverence, but only as if he were reminding her of another astrological rule. He then took in his hands one of her own and laid it, palm upward, upon the table. " 'God caused signs or seals on the hands of men, that the sons of men might know their work.' "

Bess snapped away her hand. "There is nothing in my palm, and I'd sooner ignore the stars than heed them and you."

"*Vir sapiens dominabitur astris*," Catlin intoned, as if the words were an incantation. "The wise man is master of the stars."

"But can he master his own life?" she asked.

"You do both draw dangerously close to evil things," Brother Gerard warned blackly.

I grew anxious. What were Bess and Catlin trying to do, prove to this heretic hunter that they held forbidden beliefs?

"You talk about the stars," he continued, "yet say nothing about prayer or God's own decisions. Would not prayer render void any astral power? A beggar's prayer, if God listens to it, could cancel all the influence of Saturn and Mars. It is one thing to consult an astrologer about a ship's safety, but another to try to divine the future."

Too eager to agree with the friar, I cut him short. "I have heard tell that diviners and fortune-tellers are punished in hell by having their heads on backward, for as they sought to perceive the future, so they must look and move ever backward through eternity." There, I thought hopefully, mayhap Bess and Catlin will take that as a warning and cease such talk, but I was wrong.

"I am divining nothing!" Bess scoffed.

"But you are learning to cast the stars," Brother Gerard reminded her.

"Even the Holy Mother Church acknowledges the truths in astrology," said she, "and most of her theologians embrace its study."

"Especially for its symbol-rich meaning," he said firmly.

"And St. Augustine consulted astrologers and did not deny the accuracy of their predictions."

"Before his conversion, after which he taught that astrology led men to resign themselves to fate instead of struggling toward grace, that it appeared to deny free will . . ."

"Ah, with that I agree." Bess looked toward Catlin. "Free will . . ."

Catlin wouldn't let her win. "Which St. Augustine held to exist only when it grants man the freedom to choose or refuse salvation."

"There, when you quote the church fathers you are correct," Brother Gerard concluded like a pompous elder. "Cling to their teachings, else you fall beneath the errors of your prejudices."

"My prejudices?" Catlin asked.

"For predestination."

"And mine for unbridled free will." Bess looked at Catlin as if sharing a secret with him. Then suddenly she let fly a laugh. "And because both are heresies, you guided us away from them," she exclaimed to the friar.

His face contracted in sour anger. "That is a broad jest to you?"

Catlin was by then also laughing softly. "Our play for you was. This was but a game of ideas to entertain you. Tell me, were you amused?"

Now Brother Gerard's dignity was indeed affronted. He pulled his hands down into his lap, sat straight and still. "Why should I be amused?" His voice could put fear into a saint.

"Well, that silent mummery we were forced to give at the warehouse did not satisfy you, hence I was hoping this would." Catlin served himself some beef and poured himself more malmsey; his light manner grated against the friar's simmering one. "You suspected me of heresy but lost your false evidence of it, and so came here to ask me yet more questions in hope of finding more evidence." Self-pleased, he raised the beef to his lips and his eyes to the friar. "So we gave you a little heresy and let you think that through your wisdom we saw the error of our ways. Be you satisfied now?"

Brother Gerard's lips were quivering and his face was ghastly. "No, I am not."

"Then I must meet with your abbot about your undeserved persecution of me"—Catlin's voice was harsh, a sudden stab—"a most important ingezettenen of this city."

"He'll not believe you."

"Oh, but I think he might."

A silence followed this. I restrained myself from reaching for my cup and gulping it down for courage. What in God's name could Catlin and Bess hope to accomplish by taunting this Dominican? But mayhap their tactic was a brilliant one since our submissive behavior at the warehouse had in the end done us scant good; this would at least prove to him that we were not weak fools to be trifled with. Defiance might be our salvation.

Brother Gerard stood up. "I thank you, sir, for your wine and food." Beneath him, his filled cup and empty plate were nigh untouched. "The time grows late. I must leave."

Catlin almost rose to show him out, but I stopped him, fearing what he might further say to Brother Gerard betwixt that room and the street.

"Nay, please you, I'll show the good brother out," said I.

I opened the parlor door for Brother Gerard and closed it after us, there being a draught in the hall beyond. I assumed he would follow me wordlessly to the front door but when we were near it and he had drawn on his cloak, he turned and fastened on me his unshining eyes.

"Your niece was most eager to leave the White Hound and come to Mynheer Catlin's house," he said.

"Why say you that?" I asked, straining to be civil. "Surely you do not believe . . ."

"That only blameless ties bind them? You yourself must see that is aught but true. What is true is that she did fully intend to leave the White Hound and come here."

I tried to brush this off and open the door, but he pressed on. "There was a fire that forced you to leave that house."

"By the holy saints, I know that! I saw it only too well. But the damage was repaired and the repairs paid for. Why bring you up the subject again?"

"Because there was no cat that caused the fire."

Not only his words but their conviction stunned me; I struggled with what this revelation could mean.

"I was walking in the street just beyond your window when the fire began." His words came like incense, seeping through the air. "That you know. No cat entered or left through that window. No cat could have climbed to it. The wall is of brick and your window was too high. No cat could have even leapt from one window to another. These things you should have seen, just as I saw no cat."

I tried to scrabble together more facts and memories, not so much to argue with him but to deny to myself what he was implying: that Bess had set the fire deliberately. "Then there was some sort of accident," I stammered, "and my niece was too ashamed to tell me how it started. No more than a silly accident."

Unmoved, he looked still at me. Like Bess and Catlin, I was growing furious with him.

"The fire was stopped, the damages paid for, and your grandmother has her money"—I strained to keep my voice low—"so what do you plan to do with your presumed secret, use it as revenge against my niece and Catlin for their insult to you? Think you that a woman would set a fire in order to come here and argue heresy with a man?"

"No, not to argue heresy."

"Then to do what? Why do not you, the chaste monk who has no knowledge of women, tell me what she would do?"

"You have not the same suspicions?" For the first time, he proved he could be as cynical as they. "To become his unsanctified lover," he said flatly.

"Oh, was that her intent? And have you thought long and hard about their lovemaking too?"

"Such thoughts are sinful."

"Then you have sinned! So go—go and tell your precious secret to your abbot!" I was all uncontrolled. "And tell him your ridiculous conjectures about their heresy. And I'll tell your abbot that this is your revenge—for her rejection of you. For you sensually desire her. I've seen so myself."

A shiver of rage whipped through his spare frame. "That is an abominable lie!"

"Only in your eyes."

"The abbot will see it for the lie it is!"

"Will he?"

He said naught more. He but opened the door and, with his damnable eyes e'er upon me, walked out and away.

A nervous laugh escaped from me. After all mine amiability and dissembling, I had ended the evening by ripping apart that friar more than Bess and Catlin ever had. That was all I could think as with weak knees I returned to the parlor. There, the sight of their laughing cleared my head.

"Well," said I, "this be a merry sight to end a miserable evening."

Bess groaned and wiped her eyes. "The merriment of relief—how we need it."

"Mayhap. Still I feel none of your relief. He had his suspicions still when he left."

"Said he aught to you?" Catlin asked.

"Nothing of importance," I lied.

Bess laughed into her cup. "Oh, he has his suspicions still, of course. He suspects all men and women. He doubts not his God and never himself, but other men, lest they be dead and proven saints, he molds with his suspicions."

"Still, I trow he'll let us alone for a time now"—Catlin grew more sober—"not only because his evidence is now thin, but because he needs me to bait Damascus."

My knees were buckling and I sat down, and though the malmsey did not refresh me, still I sipped some. "Then perchance you and Bess were shrewd indeed to play with him as he had earlier played with us. He saw that you can fight him."

He had as well seen that something far from innocent lay betwixt Bess and Catlin. He had also seen, as had I, that whilst they claimed to argue astrology simply to entertain him, something again not innocent remained. I felt a fool for having assumed that the two of them had only been studying something harmless during their late-night sleepless hours together.

"Catlin . . ." I hesitated. "Your arguments on astrology, do you in sooth believe any of them?"

"All of them and more."

"He's more a believer in fate than e'en Brother Gerard thought," said Bess.

"And you?" I asked her.

"I spoke my true mind."

"And you both do far more than merely prognosticate the weather?"

"Aye."

She and Catlin then began again to make jests of Brother Gerard and to mock him, but I could not listen. My mind was lost in mine own thoughts and in the darkness that was creeping deeper into the room, like a curse against which the candles cast their glowing circles. Outside the wind was gathering, and it rattled the glass of the fragile windows like old bones.

"This is an ugly night," Catlin mumbled. He swung himself out of his chair, grasped the flagon of wine and his cup, swaggered into the hall, and called out to Lijsken to come carry the food from the table up to the antler room. "I'll sit better there than in here. So let's upstairs, fill ourselves with food and drink, and forget about that foul friar. Sweet Jesus, I'm glad to be done with him!"

Bess grabbed her cup. "First the mad Damascus and then Brother Gerard. What a plague of fools. I pray God there's no one else lurking about!"

They swept up the stairs whilst I trudged after them, sharing none of their cynical joy. In the antler room, Catlin fell into a chair, swung a leg over one of its arms, and nigh dropped the flagon onto the table. Bess sat down near him and began singing softly to herself a ditty she'd learned from one of the apprentices. It was not a lady's song but one a rude youth would sing. When I first heard her humming it some days earlier I had chided her, though that did no good; naught I said to her of late did she heed.

They ate and drank their fill whilst I swallowed not a thing. Nor did I sit at the table or near the hearth; instead I settled myself on the steps to the library and watched them.

Though they talked, 'twas the sound of the wind that filled mine ears. It had grown with unnatural speed. It spun itself into bursts of madness, crouched prowling, twisting, then soared and roared violently. In the street below the dead leaves, stiff and wrinkled, whirled on their breaking bellies and their brittle edges, cracked and broke upon the stones. Disturbed, I clasped mine arms about my knees and hugged myself. That accursed wind, I swore, is trying to come into this very room. It shoved some smoke back down the chimney. It wheezed into the corners of windows and threatened to break the panes. Throughout the house there was the clattering of windows being opened and closed as Lijsken and Marie reached out and shut tight the shutters, then folded over the panes the inner shutters too, to guard against the cold tempest night. I'll sprinkle my bed with holy water, I decided, afore I lay down to sleep; holy water to wash away what cried out there tonight. Lijsken came into the room, closed up the shutters, and left. When they were bolted tight, the place seemed a shade quieter. I sighed, relieved.

Bess and Catlin talked on and jested and drank. An hour slipped away, and another, yet when Bess began to grow drowsy from wine, the wind pricked awake her senses and prevented her from falling into a heavy-lidded, sleepy state. Catlin ever and anon listened to the hollow blasts as if he could hear in them a whisper. Then, in the distance, the hour bells in Our Lady's chimed nine times; the wind tossed the faint sound above the roofs and sent it racing over cobblestones. Her words came more seldom and his more slowly, until at last they both yielded to silence and only sat, smiling at each other, lost in thought. After a little while Catlin murmured a witty line; she finished it with the very words he would have used. She brushed her cheek, and when he a moment later brushed away a whiff of smoke, it was with the same tired grace that had marked her movements. His breath came calm and easy; her own breathing fell into the same rhythm. They were just then, I bethought me, much like a husband and wife long married. Mayhap they should marry. I could see Catlin living no longer alone. I could see Bess as mistress of that house.

Save for the wind outside, the house was now so very quiet, and quieter still were Bess and Catlin. A tranquility seemed to be weaving through them, braiding itself along their strange bond and drawing them yet closer together. I doubted that I had ever seen in Bess such a quietude, and I knew I'd never seen the like in Catlin. Yet probably they had shared such moments before. When Catlin was not at his work or in his countinghouse, when Bess's own work was finished, when they were alone together and had put aside their books and papers, they might indeed share such peace.

Then something in Catlin stirred. The corners of his mouth moved down. His eyes shifted their gaze away from Bess and the hearth to the other direction, as if toward someone else.

Bess saw this slightest of changes and roused out of her own tranquility. He threw his elbow onto the arm of the chair and his hand fingered his beard. There was a howl of wind and his eyes darted not toward the outside, but into the dark air in the middle of the room, as if trying to see and hear someone skulking there. Then he stared at a shadow in a corner, with such intense purpose it seemed he was trying to conjure it to life; but he failed, and his hand fell in frustration from his head to the table and clutched the edge as if to squeeze from himself a fear. Bess laid her hand on his to offer a confused comfort. Her touch gave him none.

"There's a quadrature of Jupiter with the sun," he mumbled, "that always causes great and vehement winds." He fell quiet again, and then without warning blurted, "What if I told you there is someone else lurking about?"

"What? Someone lurking?" Bess blinked.

Only then realizing his harshness, he tried to chuckle. "I was but wondering what you would think." He looked at her, looked away, knew not how to continue, and abruptly heaved himself out of his chair.

He strode to the cabinet. "But I know you haven't seen him yet," said he, pulling open the drawer. The corner was shadowed and the portrait within could probably be scarce seen, yet Catlin glared down at that face as if van den Bist was the man he meant.

"Not yet?" said Bess. "Then there is someone."

"But you may have heard him and not known it was him. I've heard him many a time and have felt him near." He pushed the drawer back in and strode away from the corner, only to stop as if not knowing where to go.

Bess was unsure of what to say. "What is he doing near you?"

"Watching me."

"But why?"

Catlin would not answer or look at her.

By now Bess was squirming in her chair. "But why? And who is this man?"

Suddenly his head gave a small jerk. He stared about. "Heard you something?" he whispered.

Bess looked around the room. "Nothing. The wind."

He did not believe her. Waiting for a sound, he searched the room with intent eyes: the door to the library, one wall, another, a crevice, a dark place beneath a window, the light that danced about on the floor. The fire was all that moved; its crackling and the moaning of the wind were the only sounds. Still Catlin listened, held his breath when it was too loud in his own ears, exhaled, and listened still until methought he became aware of something near, something or someone neither Bess nor I could sense.

I was frightened. My mouth had shut itself in confusion and I could say naught, but I too could no longer endure the growing torment in his face and his inexplicable acts. Slowly I stood, brushed smooth my skirt, and made to leave the room. Catlin spun around to me. Then he glanced at Bess, and at last seemed aware of how he had alarmed us.

"It is indeed an ugly night," said he, "the uglier for tricking me into speaking harshly to you."

"A night like this should be spent in bed," I stammered. I went to Bess's side. Her eyes were upon Catlin and flowing o'er with feelings: dismay, surprise, comprehension, confusion, tenderness. I took hold her shoulders and urged her up.

"The time is late and we're all tired," said I. "Bess and I will to our beds now."

Bess said nothing to him but good night and gazed at him still as we left the room, though he kept his back to us. I looked again as we turned in the door and saw him throw back his dark head as if he were in pain; then he leaned heavily upon the table and bowed his head.

⚔ XIV ⚔

A short while later, when I lay down to sleep, it was with a brain that was juggling all I had seen, heard, and felt that evening. I kept ope mine eyes for a little, for fear that should I fall asleep those images would turn to nightmares. I recited prayers and meditated on their words. Mine eyes closed and I grew rested, but then I was roused when I heard on the stairs the rapid steps of Catlin. They came up to our floor and went into his bedchamber, then of a sudden his steps hastened back down the hall.

"Where are you going?" Bess's voice shattered the air.

Only Catlin's steps racing down the stairs answered her.

"Where are you going?" she shouted after him.

I flew from my bed, threw on my nightgown, and in a trice was out of my chamber.

Bess, clad only in her shift, was standing in the dark hall and leaning down over the stairs. Two floors below the front door slammed shut, and she ran to Catlin's room. I quickly followed her.

But for the dying red embers glowing in the hearth no light was in the room. All I could see was Bess's white form tearing open the window and shutters. The wind blasted into the room, blowing away from her the flapping shift and her long, night-black hair. Feverishly she stared into the street below, and nigh cried out again, but the wind pushed her voice back down her throat and let it strangle there.

I grabbed her by the waist and pulled her back inside. Then I too looked down into the street and saw a figure in a cloak swirling about him.

In a blink, the sight vanished. Only the maddened dead leaves moved in the vacant street. Still Bess kept open with rigid arms the two casements. I wrested her fingers from off their latches and pulled in the shutters and closed the window.

"God-a-mercy, where was Catlin going?" I cried. "And at this late hour? Is something amiss? No one would go visiting or seeing to business now, and on such a night." I turned about. Bess was near the hearth, staring down at the embers and rubbing her hands together. "Well, you would have a chill now, wouldn't you? Letting the wind blow you like that."

She did not answer. Still her hands rubbed as if they were trying to put down a storm of emotions. Mine eyes were drawn to the bed but a few feet away from her. Unlike ours, it was not a separate piece but built into a corner. Its curtains were drawn, its blankets were thrown back and the sheet below wrinkled as if someone had been lying on it. Yet Catlin had not been in his room long enough even to undress. Then my heart jolted. A nightgown was lying across the bottom of the bed. 'Twas blood-red and too familiar to me. 'Twas Bess's.

"What is that?" I asked. "That's yours, Bess. That gown is yours." An anger rocked me. "You were in his bed!"

"I was not!" she spat. "I but threw it off me when I ran in here!"

"You were wearing only your shift in the hall!"

"Think what you like then, since you won't believe what I say!"

"I believe what I see."

Her eyes were like the embers and her teeth were beginning to gnaw so fiercely upon her lower lip that a spot of blood appeared. "Believe you I should do nothing in this house without your wishing it? Believe you Catlin needs your permission in his own house to be with me?"

"To be with you? In his bed? Then why did he leave so suddenly?"

Her breath was trembling. "You don't know him. You don't know him as I do."

"And how do you know him, Bess?" My voice was like a razor. "How many times have you waited till I was asleep before you crawled in here to his bed? Sweet Jesus! I'd thought Catlin was my friend. But behind my back, what has he been doing with my niece!"

"You have no say over me in this! And Catlin has had nothing to tell you!"

"Ere now?"

She didn't answer. Only then did I believe her. This was her first time in his bedchamber.

"Then thank God he left."

"I've no such thanks."

"You wouldn't say that if you found yourself unwed and with child."

Bess winced. I covered my mouth; I'd said too much. "Bess. Bess, I'm sorry . . ."

She left the room and went to her bedchamber. I followed. She was kneeling already before her own hearth and letting the heat warm her. Her nightgown, which I'd brought with me, I draped over her shoulders.

"Wish you to be something common and cheap?" I stood a little away from her, knowing she hated my presence and perchance was not listening to me. Still I talked, though gently. "That's all you'd be if you go to his room again. A common mistress. And I won't stand for it. Aye, 'tis your life. But I would refuse to live in this house if I knew what he and you were doing."

She said only, "Then I'll never let you know."

Nothing good was coming of this tonight, I decided. "No more such talk, Bess. To bed for the both of us for the nonce."

"I cannot sleep."

No suggestions, no orders or pleas would she brook now, that I perceived, and so I left her.

I returned to my bed but lay gazing into the darkness, my lips stumbling over prayers to make me drowsy. Mayhap a quarter of an hour had passed by when a light slid by the bottom of my door. A creak upon the stairs came like the whine of a cricket. Was that Bess roaming about? Once more I rose and drew on my nightgown.

Descending the stairs, a burning candle in one hand, was Bess. I followed her and watched the yellow glow of candlelight move below. It passed down to the front door and drifted back as she wandered again up the stairs. I retreated to the other flight of stairs, not wanting her to see me just yet. The candlelight cast upon the wall a crooked shadow of steps that jumped up and down and away into darkness as Bess came upon the landing. As she glided by into the antler room, she glanced at me when the light fell upon my figure, her face registering no surprise that I was there. I was chilled by the ghostly spectacle she made. Still I padded after her.

She lingered in the room's center. Holding her candle high, she studied the corners and shadows as Catlin had done earlier, but her gaze found nothing. In the frail glimmer, above the deep blood-red of her nightgown, her face was pale and haunted and that look of unearthly knowledge was upon it. She went up into the library, and there she sat at the table, examining papers. I sat down opposite her. The papers she held and the ones on the table were darkened with words, figures, numbers, lines, and triangles, with the squares within squares and circles within circles of horoscopes. For me that night such things had lost their harmlessness. Now they were signs of near-forbidden things into which Catlin had drawn Bess.

"Why are you here, Aunt? To keep your eye on me?"

"There's no need for that since Catlin was a gentleman and left you. But I like not this wandering about of yours."

She only mumbled to herself, "A gentleman."

The candle sputtered.

"He's with a whore tonight!" Bess spat out.

I was struck dumb.

"In a house somewhere. A house full of rogues and cozeners and cheats and drabs, that's where he is. He can't be in a tavern for 'tis past eleven of the clock now and they must be closed. He can't be out in the streets past that hour without a light, else the night-watch will arrest him. He's in a bawdy house."

"How know you this?"

She shrugged, frowned, knitted her brow. "How do you think?"

"Through that whore in the street." I sighed.

She glanced at another paper ere shoving it aside. "He's clever with all these figures. But I surprised him this week, I learned so much."

A clatter echoed in the house, and someone shuffled into the antler room. Bess grabbed up the candle and rushed out.

"God in heaven!" cried someone in Flemish. 'Twas Lijsken. "Oh, Mevrouw Marwick, you did frighten me!"

I joined Bess and saw at the door Lijsken, who with one hand was clutching a candle and with the other her chest.

"I hope we didn't wake you, Lijsken," said I.

"Nay, you didn't," she replied. "I thought I heard a shutter break open and rose to close it, but I knocked over a stool instead. No, I'm accustomed to the late hours my master can keep, so I paid no attention when I heard steps."

"Catlin isn't here," Bess blurted.

"Oh, isn't he?" she returned without feeling.

"No, he went out. Know you where he is?"

"I do not." She turned to leave.

"Lijsken, I prithee hold but a moment," Bess pleaded. She went to the woman, and too did I. "This much I should tell you. Tonight, whilst mine aunt and I were with Master Catlin in just this room, he began to talk and behave most strangely. He seemed to be listening or watching for something. He stared too at that portrait." Bess pointed to the cabinet just behind Lijsken. "Is there aught about that picture or ledger that can distress him? I thought those old things had been put there merely to please the servants."

Lijsken's eyebrows arched high. "None of the servants wanted that cabinet there. What does it have to do with us?"

"But Master Catlin told mine aunt and me that the thing had been in the housekeeper's storing room until the servants heard noises coming from there. So to put you all at ease he took the cabinet and placed it up here."

The eyebrows lowered into a scowl. "I'm not easily frightened. Oh, I was startled a moment ago by you, mevrouw. But I would never bid my master to do what I would wish with his possessions." She hesitated, gave us a doubtful perusal, then decided she could trust us enow. " 'Twas not the servants who were bothered by strange happenings. Marry, I'll admit we sometimes heard sounds. Sometimes we thought there were steps or that someone was watching us when we went into the housekeeping room where it was stored. But we paid scant attention to these things, we did. We would only cross ourselves and go on with our work. I still curse the day when I told Mynheer Catlin about it. I told him that when I was fetching a basin from that room, the cabinet had again been tampered with and the drawer was open.

" 'Again?' he said to me. 'What mean you "again"?' 'Why, we keep the drawer shut,' I answered. 'But no matter how many times we shut it, 'tis open when we next go into that room, which isn't often. I've e'en tied a string around that cabinet, from its front to its back. But the same thing happens. The string is soon untied and the drawer is hanging open again. You don't open it, sir?'

" 'I've ne'er looked at that portrait or ledger since they were stored,' said he. 'Well, sir,' I answered, 'we will try to keep those things from being damaged. But methinks that whatever poor soul is making noises in that room and seems to watch us when we enter is too the one that won't let alone that drawer.'

"He seemed to go deaf and his eyes had such a fear in them I can't tell you. 'Poor soul?' he said to me. 'What are you prating about, woman? And what noises?' I told him what I and Arnout and Marie had been hearing and feeling, that we only assumed some ghost, harmless to us, did reside in that room. But he left me like a man distracted. Then, soon thereafter, he began to go himself into that room. Once I passed him as he stood in its door and though I couldn't hear a peep, he had on his face the most wretched expression. 'Twas as if he alone could hear a voice from within, as if the ghost was talking to him. So I made some excuse and got him away from there—well, I couldn't stand to see the poor man be like that.

"Sometime after that he told me he had heard the ghost's footsteps. He made as if he didn't care. But then one night I was awakened by his hurrying past our servants' quarters. I could hear him storm into that room. Well, I quickly got up and had just reached it when Master Catlin came out—and he was carrying the cabinet! His face was all wild too. My God, what's wrong with the poor man, I wondered, and I followed him. He carried that cabinet up here and he dropped it down in this corner.

" 'There!' he cried. 'I've put this cabinet where anyone can look into it. Are you content now? Will you let me be? Walk here about your blasted portrait! Walk here for all eternity, for aught I care, and be forever without sleep as you would have me be!'

"Finally he saw me. 'He came too close tonight,' Mynheer Catlin said to me. 'He tried to come in whilst I was in my bed. He walked up and down the hall outside and then tried to come into my room.'

"I tried to tell him he'd been dreaming but he only shook his head. He left me then, went back upstairs. There were no other sounds that night, not from him or from aught else. Since that cabinet was put there—well, it's the portrait and ledger the thing holds that matters—

but since it's been put there, Mynheer Catlin has seemed a little more at peace. And he hasn't acted as strangely as he did that night."

Lijsken fell silent. By then I couldn't bear to look over her shoulder at the cabinet.

"If there is an unquiet spirit," Bess asked, "has it been laid to rest?"

"It seems not to be as restless as once it was. Certes we servants no longer hear or feel aught in the housekeeper's room. But the master says van den Bist is quieter now only because he is waiting, but for what I have no idea."

Bess paused, and then said, "Lijsken, did van den Bist deal in lawless shipping?"

The eyebrows arched again. "I knew not the man personally. He'd long been dead when Arnout and I came to work here. But I've heard it said that the man secretly shipped heretical pamphlets and the like."

"And did Catlin much like him? Did he admire van den Bist for his religious convictions?"

"They seemed to be friends, that's all. From what I've heard, van den Bist oft cheated his fellow merchants, so when he was killed no one was surprised save Mynheer Catlin. But if he hadn't been murdered he would likely have died of drink. Drank too much, people say."

"Van den Bist again," Bess whispered. She drew close to Lijsken and put her hand around the woman's arm. "Then it was van den Bist he thought he heard tonight?"

The housekeeper pulled her arm free and pushed her jutting jaw e'en farther out. "You must ask him that. The hour is late, and I must back to my bed."

"And too must we," I agreed.

Her jaw retracted a little. "You won't reveal to Mynheer Catlin what I've told you tonight?"

"Of course not," said I.

She bid us good night and left the room with a calm that helped to steady my nerves, and that I needed after hearing her fantastic tale.

"I can't sleep now," sighed Bess.

"Sleep or no, we'll out of here and to our bedchambers."

I took her into mine own chamber so that I could keep an eye on her and there'd be no more wandering about. I sat her down before the hearth, stirred its embers into a fire again and fed the flames some wood, and at last lay down upon my bed.

Outside the wind still shrilled and rattled the shutters. In one of its howls I heard the sound of Our Lady's hour bells; I couldn't discern how many times they chimed, or what hour it was. Bess moved a little when she heard the sound, then was still again. She had curled up on a cushion before the hearth and there hugged her knees to her chest.

My heart ached for her, she seemed so lonely, so hopelessly sad. It was as if, after the years since her parents' death, in the months since losing Timothy, Catlin had been her only comfort and cheer. Now, with his absence that night and after Lijsken's story, he too seemed to be slipping away from her. I felt useless.

A spark flew from the hearth; it fell and died near Bess's unmoving foot. I thought of the fire at the White Hound and what Brother Gerard had told me. No good would ever come from confronting Bess with his revelation; she would belike only lie to me or invent a new story. And I knew then that, though she never would have damaged aught more of the Hound, still she would have destroyed our room. She would have done so much simply to be with her Catlin.

I looked at the scar on her left hand. The burn had healed after all those weeks, but painfully so, and always would she bear that scar; the withered, ragged brown skin set like a mark of sin upon the back of her hand. Yet though it had once throbbed with pain and would always be ugly, still she had never complained, never e'en referred to it. No, I could not now berate her for what she had done.

I grew tired and mine eyes heavy. Still I watched her, fearful of where she might wander or what she might do if I did not. Still she might fly out the door after her Catlin. With all my power I would prevent that, if in truth I was able.

I was dreaming of my sons and of home when I awoke. The bells in Our Lady's chimed seven times, so it must have been early morn, yet no light was slipping past the shutters' cracks. Turning over in my bed, I saw Bess slumped still at the fireside. Clearly she had waited in vain all night for Catlin and hadn't slept at all. In her loneliness, she had e'en clung to my sleeping company rather than go back to her own chamber.

"Is it morning?" I grumbled, crawling out of bed and pulling on my gown.

Bess said nothing and averted her face. Still I saw it was haggard and her eyes were deep with dark circles. Yet it wasn't these things that arrested me. Rather, 'twas that the youthfulness that had always sparked alive her face was now gone, as if lost during the night. Nothing young remained. Aware of mine examination of her, she turned her face away yet more and rested it on her knees.

"We need some morning light in here." I yawned. I opened the inner shutters of one window, then the casements, and when I pushed back the outer shutters a bitter cold swarmed over me. Quickly I shut the panes again. A thin rag of frost lay in the streets and on the roofs, and downward through grayness fell thin snow, silently and with little movement in an air at last empty of wind. The dawn had arrived with a sun hidden by frozen clouds. Sadly I watched the flakes cling to the panes.

"I thought I'd be home again ere autumn." I sighed. "That certainly I'd not stay in this city beyond October. Now winter is come and I'm still here." The happy dream of my sons and home now made me melancholy.

I dressed and readied myself for another day of work. "You must ready anon to depart," I remarked to Bess. "I'll not tarry here this morning." When she gave no reply I continued. "For aught we know, Catlin may not return here first but go to his countinghouse. He may even have spent the night there."

"He wasn't there, and he'll return here first," Bess said flatly.

"Then do as you please and waste your time for him."

Though the two of us felt ill at ease with Catlin's unexplained absence, the servants behaved as if they were accustomed to his spending nights elsewhere. Marie served us breakfast with no inquisitive glances at Catlin's empty chair. Lijsken as usual inquired if we'd be home for dinner at noon.

After breakfast, Bess and I fetched our cloaks from our chambers, and when we again passed by the parlor, something creaked from within.

In his chair now sat Catlin. His face was sodden from too much drink and his clothes were wrinkled and muddy. One leg he'd thrown up onto the table, the other sprawled beneath it, whilst under his listless arms hung a dagger from one side, a sword from the other. Men in that city had need to go about armed; still Catlin was armed more than was his wont, as though wherever he'd been the night before required of him yet more weapons and wariness.

"Marry, a good morrow to you, Catlin," said I. "Bess and I were for your countinghouse. Wouldst you have us wait for you?"

A smudged hand rose and gestured a no. "Good morrow, good morrow," he mumbled. "Be off where you please and don't wait for me."

The relief in Bess's face gave way to pain. "It pleases us to be gone," she declared, and strode out of the house.

I myself sat down near Catlin. He wouldn't look at me.

"I pray you're not ill, Catlin. Your color is poor."

He mumbled that he was well.

I pressed on. "I was worried last night for you. You seemed so . . ." I let the sentence dangle. "I was worried, and so I asked Lijsken and she told me—and truly she didn't want to, so please you do not blame her—but she told me . . . that there might be something in this house. Something that haunts you. A ghost, if you will."

After long moments of brooding, Catlin spoke. "And you want to know if this be true?"

"You changed so abruptly last night, it would seem to be so."

"Ah. Well, if I should tell you yes, I do believe there is a most unnatural presence that at times draws near me, will your curiosity be satisfied?"

"No, methinks not."

At last he looked hard at me. Perchance he was trying to determine if I knew about Bess being in his bed and wished to fight him on't. "Then what else do you wish to know?"

I cleared my throat. I coughed. I looked at him and saw how achingly tired he was, how empty of any cheer. "What I want to know, Catlin," said I with a warmth rising from deep within, "is if there is any way I can . . . help you, or comfort you."

He hadn't been expecting this. "You are a kind woman, Sara."

"I am a mother, that's all, a protective mother. And in a fashion you and Bess have become my family and for the nonce this is my home. So I'll not stand by and watch you suffer or come to harm."

"I've nigh let you and Bess come to harm with this"—he flickered his fingers, trying in exhaustion to catch the right words—"this wretched trouble with Brother Gerard and Damascus. So I'm putting a stop to my pamphlet shipping. 'Tis far too perilous now withal, e'en for me."

I fiddled with my skirt. "I'd had some sympathy for you, Catlin, and e'en admiration when I learned you were moving Protestant tracts into England. You were risking much in order to act upon your beliefs, upon a faith I'd thought wasn't in you. But when I saw those pamphlets yesterday . . ."

"No, Sara, I knew not their contents. Nothing I've handled before has ever been like those hateful things. The man who died yesterday was a fanatic I should have avoided from the start. God forgive me, but when he was killed I was relieved. Not only was he willing to be a martyr to a cause, but he'd have gladly made me a martyr, too."

I pulled at loose threads in my skirt. "And Damascus and Brother Gerard have their own cause . . ."

"For which they're willing to destroy. But they're not the only danger. I've also been hearing that more English spies are of late slipping into Flanders. Since England and Flanders are in a way united through Queen Mary's marriage to Philip, who rules Flanders, those spies may work freely here. Happily for me, they're hunting mostly a few Protestant nobles who've fled England, or the busiest preachers. Still, they've already arrested and hauled back to London some commoners."

"Dear God."

"So 'tis the English spies I worry about since they could take me to a harsh punishment in England. Here, at least, 'tis the city's magistrates who prosecute heretics, and unlike the Dominicans—like Brother Gerard, who can only bring to the magistrates evidence and no more—they tend to be merciful with the accused should he recant."

"And if the accused is insincere?"

"It matters not; they have no jurisdiction to inquire into matters of conscience only."

"Aye," I sighed. "Then 'tis the English you must guard against."

E'en I myself knew how life in my country was becoming more parlous for many good Englishmen and women who were Protestants, and so they were leaving home for fear of what might come. They sailed here to Flanders or elsewhere, but Catholic Antwerp was not safe for them so they went on to Wittenburg or Geneva. Aid came not only from relatives but too from many English merchants, some of whom also dealt in forbidden Protestant literature; and for Catlin that could bode well, I realized. There's some safety in numbers. The queen's government had been able to catch only a handful of the Protestant helpers and mayhap some exiles, but more got away. Might Catlin be among the fortunate ones.

Catlin stretched his back and arms.

"You should go to bed now," said I.

"No, I must to work."

I rose, then paused. "Catlin, that printer who died, did you share at all his cause?"

"Not his ultimate cause, which you and I discovered too late from those pamphlets. But some of his beliefs, aye, and aye to much of Luther's writings, save for his rejection of the Virgin Mary."

"Yet even now you sound, as always (forgive me, Catlin), but you sound bereft of any passion in such beliefs."

With effort he rose slowly but did not yet reply.

I made my tone more gentle. "And if you have no passion for them, why risk your life with this law-breaking?"

"Risked, Sara. I'll no more of it now." He steadied his hip against the table. "An act of faith, that's the simplest reason I can give you. Or spiritual bribery, if you will. Upon a time, I went endlessly to masses and offered up the prayers of my youth, to no avail. They gave me no peace, and so I began to aid Protestants with whom I share many beliefs, though this too has done me scant good."

I shook my head. "In sooth, you have far more religious a nature than I'd e'er thought."

"I have a nature, God-given, that is always seeking God in hope, or evading Him in fear." He let roll a tired laugh. "What kind of God is He when the likes of Damascus and Brother Gerard are His faithful? All the better to evade Him."

"This fear of Him, this spiritual bribery . . ." I knew not what I meant to say.

"He also gave my nature its inclination toward predestination, and in my horoscopes I've sometimes read a fate that terrifies me. Thus the evasion. It is from that fate that I pray to be delivered. Thus the seeking." Seeing my widening eyes and flood of worry, he waved his hand. " 'Tis too long a story to tell just now. Another time, another time. Now we must both to work."

He began to walk past me. I put my hand on his arm—'twas trembling from too much drink—and held him back.

"Catlin, what you've just told me, has aught of it to do with this ghost you believe in, Martin van den Bist's ghost?"

"He is the cause of my fate. He is the punishment God has sent me."

⤙ XVI ⤚

By evening the snow had fallen ankle-deep. People hastened home and didn't drumble at shops or their work. Doors and windows were shut tightly against the stinging cold and the entire city fell quiet. Each sound, when there was a sound, was muffled by snow, and when a voice called out down the streets, its timbre crackled like shattering ice. Smoke from chimneys drifted upward. The air grew murky.

After supper, Catlin spent the evening at his desk in the library, scratching his pen over papers and looking through pages of piled-up books. I myself sat down with Bess in the antler room and there wrote letters. Then I looked up and saw she had joined Catlin, for I heard their low voices slipping by the open door of the library.

"You see now?" Catlin asked her, and a paper was ruffled.

"Aye," Bess replied, "but aren't these merely tricks with numbers?"

"They may seem so, but there's divining in them."

"Then I know what this is. 'Tis geomancy, isn't it? This is nigh the black art—and unlawful. You've not shown it me before."

"I learned it only recently."

"From Nicolas van Wouwere." It sounded an accusation.

"Why do you so dislike him?"

"Because I know what manner of friend he is to you."

This silenced them both. There were some whispers and the ruffle of more papers, and then nothing more.

The days that followed were as quiet as that evening. During them I seldom thought of Lijsken's story about Catlin. The few words he and I had exchanged on't helped to soothe my worry for him, and what unsettled feelings remained I kept to myself.

But Bess was different. The revelation that Catlin believed van den Bist haunted him seemed to wind its eeriness around her mind. On scattered occasions I saw her lingering in a room or hall as if she were listening to something, but then her expression of taut suspicion would sink into melancholy: The sound had escaped her. Once I found her standing before the open drawer of the cabinet and staring down at the portrait just as Catlin had. Still she could force no voice from that thin painted mouth. Still she could find no proof that a ghost walked that house.

Finally there came the day when I confronted her about this strange behavior. 'Twas on a Sunday, just after we'd returned from mass. We had our breakfast, which was small because van Wouwere had invited us to dinner, and when she finished she left the parlor. Some minutes later when I too was leaving I heard her voice drifting by the kitchen. If she's asking for more hot drink, I thought, then I'll join her, since I'd a chill in my bones. Upon going down the hall to the kitchen, howe'er, I saw only Lijsken standing in the doorway and looking farther down the hall.

"Methought my niece was here, Lijsken," said I. "Marry, how much warmer it is near the kitchen."

"You're cold, mevrouw?"

"A little, but 'twill pass with some hot cider."

"I could fill a glass for you. And Mevrouw Marwick was here, but she's just now gone to the housekeeping room."

"The housekeeping room? But what for?"

She gave me a steely look. "You don't know?"

"Oh, Lijsken, not because of what you'd told us!"

"I shouldn't have told the either of you a word about that cabinet." Her cheeks creased into lines as she dourly frowned. "Now she's prying, she is. Just now she asked me if aught has been amiss of late. I asked her what she meant. She said, 'The ghost you told us about—have you heard it of late?' I told her I've heard nothing of the kind but that she'd hear and see much if she lets her imagination run where it will. And that I told her."

I glanced over the woman's shoulder. Sitting nigh the kitchen hearth was Arnout and bent over the dishes she was washing was Marie. He had paused in his eating and she in her scrubbing to listen to what Lijsken was saying.

"I'm terribly sorry about that," I said, "and I'll see to it that she leaves the room alone."

I went down the hall, around the corner, and down another short hall that ended at a closed door. When I opened it the hinges squealed so loudly I jumped. Standing just beyond the swing of the door was Bess, whose head spun about at the noise and who, upon seeing me enter, shut her mouth tight in annoyance.

The room was scarce more than a closet lit by one window and was crowded with boxes, old napery, a broken stool, a shelf piled high with old pots and utensils, and other things seldom used. It was a closed-in cold place where no heat came or was needed, where the air was thick with dust and spiderwebs wagged from the broken shutters. My chill worsened and I shivered.

"Well, Bess," I sighed in exasperation, "Lijsken told me of your foolish prying. You've made her quite irritated."

"And silent. She answered none of my questions."

"And well she should not."

"Then I'll never ask her anything of the sort again."

"Good, do not." I brushed against a blanket whose cotton wrapping hadn't kept it safe from moths. As I was pushing the moldy things away, Bess ambled nearer the open door as if escaping from me.

"What, leaving already?" I asked scornfully. "But you've not yet found your ghost."

" 'Tis not my ghost."

"Continue to behave as you do, and if you die soon—God forbid—here should your own soul do penance for your foolishness."

"This house would be an apt purgatory," she mumbled. Again she tried to move past me but I blocked her.

"If this unquiet shade, real or not, and Catlin's belief in it so bothers you, why not ask him of it? I know he's told you more than he has me."

"Aye, but not as much as I want."

I shook my head. "You two do each other little good. Sometimes I think 'tis a mistake to let you be together."

"You cannot stop us."

"I can."

"Nay, you're too late. And we are good for each other."

"You're nothing of the sort. There's a wildness in Catlin, a secretive nature, and he's bringing out the same in you."

She turned on me as if cornered. "You make me sound like his pawn."

"Oh no, you're his equal. You sway him too, and also for the worse. These hints of yours that you want only a brief passion with him—that's provocation he doesn't need."

"How know you what he needs?"

"I know that like other men he needs a good sensible wife, not a hotspurred minx."

"But Catlin isn't like other men. You still don't realize that, do you? And what about my needs? Have you never thought that mayhap what I want of him fulfills a need in me?"

"If he fulfills you, you would not be in this room. If he fulfills you, you'd be happy and at peace with yourself. But you're not that at all, and nor is he."

She flung aside an old pot that had rolled off the shelf and clattered down in front of her. Then she stepped around me and gripped the door.

"Did I strike a nerve, Bess?" I said harshly.

She jerked around to me and her face, with its lovely cheeks, its soft curves, suddenly hardened like a man's. For a moment I feared she would strike me. But the moment passed.

"Let's out of here," she said. "Van den Bist is no longer in this room, that I can feel. Now 'tis the floors above he walks."

I left with a chill I couldn't rid myself of for hours.

In the early afternoon, we three wended our way to the doctor's house. The snow had begun to fall again, but I didn't mind our walk. The white-speckled air seemed all that moved in those Sunday streets empty of traffic, and it made gentle and quiet that small bit of world caught in winter's grasp.

By the time we walked down the narrow lane and knocked on the doctor's door, I was not only cold but damp around the edges. The old servant let us in (it being Sunday, the door was locked against the public), showed us through the front chamber, then through the door opposite and up a set of stairs.

I gaped at the rooms above. The furnishings, wainscotings, and carpets were all costly, and whatever could shine had been proudly polished—the wood, the silver and pewter, the brass and crystal. Everywhere there was gloss. Still something was lacking. 'Twas that none of his physic stuff, his herbs or bottles were about, though they were so abundant downstairs it seemed they should overflow. Instead only a man of pleasure lived here.

I passed the table laden with wine and sweetmeats and went straight to the fireside. There I stood next to the burning logs until the dampness left my hems and the shivering my bones.

I was by the fire still when the doctor swept in. This time he was not wearing an undercap, so that his naked head was revealed to be balding; his shiny, hairless brow stretched back so far that his skull seemed massive, and he had not his spectacles about him. He was wrapped up again in a fur-lined velvet gown, this one of verdant green that made him look like a moving mound of earth. The hands and arms swung out in welcome. As if suddenly confronted by the malevolent, by the unknown, I took a backward step.

"Ah, my friends, welcome!" His smile spread as widely as his arms. "Welcome to this my house—doubtless a humble one compared to your own, Bartholomew."

Catlin made the expected protests.

"Too kind of you, too generous." He took Bess's hand and kissed it. "And greetings to you, Mevrouw Marwick." He waited a moment. "So, you've taken on Flemish habits. Do not English women greet their men friends, e'en if they be scarce acquainted, with a kiss?"

"We be not in England." Bess smiled. "And what can be a good custom in one country may be laughable in another."

"Ah, mevrouw, I wouldn't laugh."

"But I might."

A cunning sparked their faces as they looked at each other. Van Wouwere then swung about to greet me; to my relief he didn't expect a kiss.

"What's this, Mevrouw Lathbury, be you cold? Here, sit you in this seat nearest the fire. Sit you all, please, as the food is hot and ready."

He shook a small bell and the old servant began to go in and out, bringing from the kitchen piles of beef, mutton, pork, coney, capon, wild fowl, and fish. I ate as heartily as Catlin and Bess, but by far most of the food disappeared into van Wouwere, and out of him came the most talk. He chattered on about himself, about his travels and the many cities he'd seen, about the learned men he'd met and their praises for him. Yet though his words flowed out of him as freely as the wine flowed in, still I felt he was a stranger.

After dinner we sweetened our tastes with marchpane and conserves of fruit whilst the dishes were cleared away. When the table was empty, van Wouwere gave the each of us an appraising glance. Delicately, with thumb and forefinger, he took hold of a few hairs on his beard, bent them around to his mouth, and chewed upon them. Only then did I notice that the hairs bordering his lips, from the sides of his mustache to his beard, had curled, broken edges from being ground by those topaz-bright teeth.

"I was thinking this morning of how I might entertain you," he rumbled. "I decided on a game of numbers, on a small game that will beguile you."

"Beguile?" Bess shrugged. "I'd prefer a sporting card game with wagers."

He inclined his head as if it were heavy with too much knowledge. "Oh, but I think you'll be natheless entertained by my game. It can be played in earnest, but today we'll play it to amuse ourselves. You see, its numbers will forespeak for you a little of your future."

"What if I don't believe that?"

"Your lack of faith can't affect it."

"Play the game." Catlin touched her elbow and his voice was like tempting fur. "I will."

She purred back at him. "You'll play it in earnest, but I'll play it in sport."

They all then looked to me, and I said I would join them.

The doctor rose and went to a nearby cupboard, whence he fetched some papers, a thin book, and a small blue silk bag, all of which he brought back to the table. He laid them out with reverent care, opened the book, and arranged the loose papers. Whilst he did all these things, he talked.

"Five or six years ago, when I was at the University of Heidelberg, I played this game for a gentleman. He wanted to learn if the venture into which he'd invested much money would be a success. He had seen too late how much of his fortune depended on't. So he sought me out, for though I'd been not long in Heidelberg, the precise figuring of my astrology and dream divinations had given me renown, I am proud to say. He told me of his situation and pleaded that I tell him what he might do to assure the venture's success. I charted for him his horoscope, and too I used this." He gestured at the things before him. "By those two means was I able to tell him that he would have ill fate by water for a fortnight to come. Ill fortune by water, I said to him. 'But,' he argued, 'most goods come into and leave this town by the river.' Avoid that river, I warned him, till the fortnight had passed. Then you would belike have success. He went away saying his business couldn't wait. So some of his goods he had laded onto a boat. Suddenly a storm broke, the laders took cover, and the river so swelled and the waves so rocked that the mooring came loose and the boat was swept down the river, where it sank. Finally the gentleman heeded my advice and stored his remaining goods till two weeks had passed. With what was left, at least, he had a good profit."

Everything was in order. He gestured for us to sit closer to him, and we found ourselves huddled over several spread-out papers. On each was a large circle, and in each of those circles was a design like a narrow-petaled flower; then in and in between the six petals was a word, each one different. The words varied greatly from circle to circle, page to page. Van Wouwere next took up the small bag and let roll out of it a pair of dice, their ivory old and yellowing, their dots coloring them like blackened age spots. Yet he picked up these old dice and handled them gently as if they were no ordinary pair, but sacred.

"I pray you, be silent for a little whilst I meditate," van Wouwere said. Holding the dice with his right hand, he placed them onto the wrinkled star of his left palm, closed his fingers over them, lowered his veined eyelids, and lost himself in a fervid meditation.

I grew disquiet sitting there, watching him aim all his mind at his left hand and its two paltry cubes. Suddenly I hated being there, in that room and with that man. With him even the wintry day I had earlier enjoyed turned sinister, and the white snow falling beyond the window became ashen and hoary.

Finally van Wouwere opened his eyes. He looked down at the book and papers as if he were their master, and then at us in the same way. "So, Mevrouw Marwick, on what matter would you like to hear a prediction? Sith you be a young and fair woman, I daresay you'd want to hear if marriage be in your future."

"I've sparse curiosity for that." She let her fingers play upon the exposed tops of her breasts; when his eyes also lingered there, she smiled as if having found his weakness. "In truth, I'm not sure what sort of prediction I'd like."

"Wish you to ask of travel?"

She shook her head.

"Of health?"

She gave no response.

"Money, then, and business."

He must have seen the faintest waver in her eyes. "Money and business, then, it shall be."

With his right hand, for his left still held the dice, he handed her the open book. "Find you the question you wish to ask, good lady. The ones dealing with money are on the first page."

I looked over Bess's shoulder at the book. On two pages were numbered questions and from them she chose one that asked if the reader's business would finish well in the next fortnight—the question the man in Heidelberg might well have asked. Van Wouwere matched the question's number to the corresponding circle and handed her the dice with instructions to throw them with a free cast into the circle. Bess rattled the cubes and dropped them onto the paper. They landed on the word "Sagittarius" and their dots numbered to eight.

"Number eight," the doctor remarked. "Look you now to the globes on the next page in the book."

Bess turned the page and found amidst the many small globes the one assigned to Sagittarius. Printed in it was Saturnus.

"Saturn, the planet of fate," van Wouwere said, as if discovering an illness he could do little for. "Turn now to the verses under the heading Saturnus and find the verse following the number eight." Bess did as he bade her, came across the verse, and read it aloud. Though in Flemish, when translated it read something like:

> This business is not like to be
> So prosperous in each degree;
> See that thou keep all things in frame
> To shun the danger of the same.

"Od's my life, what a gloomy presaging," said Bess.

"Ah . . ." Van Wouwere sucked in a heavy breath. "Thou must avoid completing any business in the last week of November then, and the first of December."

"I must? That's a jest. I can't stop work for a fortnight to follow the silly warnings of a game."

He smiled at her with his shiny yellow teeth. "Well then, cast the dice again if you like, and ask the game another question."

She perused the list of questions and read, " 'On what day should I not do business?' " Then she told van Wouwere the number of the question, he put before her the corresponding circle, and she cast the dice down on't. They fell on the word "Stars," and their dots added to four. The globe had in it the word "Luna" and under that title came the correct verse.

"This one's no less gloomy," Bess announced. " 'On any day that adds to eight, do not send thy goods, but wait.' "

"In the last week of any month is the twenty-sixth day." Van Wouwere made this sound profound. "The two and the six add up to eight. The next closest eight-numbered day would be the eighth of December. Therefore these two verses must mean (and I am most experienced in interpretation) that thou shouldst not ship anything or do any trade on the twenty-sixth of this month or on the eighth of December, for whatever thou deal in or send off on those days shall meet with misfortune."

Bess regarded the doctor with a mixture of doubt and belief. "I'll decide, I trow, what I'll do on any day."

"As you wish. But eight is also the number of Saturn and that planet can bode ill for many people. That your dice also led you to the verse under Saturnus I would take as a double warning."

"Then I'll doubly decide on the twenty-sixth and the eighth what to do," Bess said with a merriment that defied the man's gravity.

He nodded his massive head and laughed at her reply. He's too pliant for me, I thought; he too easily shifts his moods that he might match our own.

"As you please. Both the dices' foretelling and my interpretation may come to naught." Van Wouwere picked up the dice and held them out to Catlin. "And now, Bartholomew, 'tis your turn."

Catlin scanned the questions and read for us his choice: " 'Whether the person who gives me fair and good words will remain constant to me.' "

Though van Wouwere gave Bess a meaningful sidelong glance, I myself sensed that Catlin had aimed the question at the doctor.

Catlin let clatter down the rolling dice upon the circle given him. The words and numbers were consulted, he found the answer to his question, and his smile became a knowing one. " 'Tis an interesting reply," said he. "List to what it tells me:

> Fear not, my friend, be patient yet,
> And do not madly foam nor fret.
> For the one who took what was thine away
> Will, his own self, himself betray.

"Ah, Bartholomew, have you dangerous men about you?" Van Wouwere had a playfulness that was somehow menacing.

"Other than you?"

"Nay, this verse can't apply to me. Will himself betray? I'm too clever for that."

"And nothing of mine can you take away."

At this, the doctor let his eyes wander over Bess, and he grinned and chewed on more hairs. "Be not sure of that, my friend."

The dice were next given to me. I chose a few mundane questions, but each only led to a verse that had no answer. "I'm afraid e'en this game can't decide what my future is to be," I jested, and begged that I play it no more. Besides, I thought, the high clack of the tumbling dice was beginning to grate against me, as was the seducing mysticism with which van Wouwere veiled the proceedings. It was not such an innocent game after all; in his star-marked hand it bordered on the black art.

Van Wouwere returned the dice to their silk bag. "What fortunes this game did give, I wish could have been more favorable ones," said he.

"Do you really?" I mumbled.

He must have heard me, for he turned to me and held out the bag. "You are a cloth merchant, mevrouw. What think you of this fabric?"

I took the bag and felt it. 'Twas by appearance a fine velvet, yet as

I moved the stuff through my fingers, its touch seemed clammy and the dice shifted like bones 'neath old, cold skin. "A fine fabric indeed," I lied as I quickly gave it back to him.

My words were useless; he had perceived my true heart and was grinning at me. Suddenly I understood that I should fear him.

XVII

Two days after our visit with van Wouwere, Bess and I found ourselves with a free afternoon. We decided to spend it at the English House, where we could hear news of home and learn what goods in England were bringing high prices of late. Catlin too agreed to meet us in the main room there.

No sooner had we arrived at the English House, howe'er, when we regretted being there. Gathered in the main room were only a handful of merchants who were mumbling within their tight clusters, and when we entered they durst no more than skim us with wary glances. Still I felt hungry gazes upon us. My instincts sharpening, I looked about. Here and there, hovering in corners, filling up odd crannies, stood five or six men. Each was alone, each was standing in a different position, each was differently dressed; yet there was an ugly sameness about them all. They all also had their eyes upon Bess and me. Suddenly I wanted to check the door through which we had entered the room, as if needing to know whether we could make a hasty retreat. I turned about, and standing behind me was one of the men. From where he had come I had no idea, but he seemed to have guessed my thoughts and was blocking the way lest we leave before he wanted us to.

My nerves were set on edge by his face. His sunken cheeks were wrinkled like drippings of old wax and above them, in deep sockets circled with the purple tinge of sleeplessness, were burning eyes.

"I pray you, mistress," he said in English with an oily smile, "could you render me a small favor? I am new-come to Antwerp and in need of advice."

He asked me a harmless question about the inn wherein he was staying and if a better one could be had. I gave him my opinion, but ere I could excuse myself from his company he asked me another question, and another. Again I answered. Bess disliked being with him as much as did I, and both of us started inching away. Like a weasel he espied this. Ere we could move any farther he trapped us with a question touching upon religious questions in England. I had to answer him, or risk falling under his suspicion that I favored heresy. Again he asked more questions, and the slippery meaning of each dealt more and more with the Protestant exiles who were leaving England and coming to the Continent. When I found myself giving him cautious answers replete with sworn loyalty to the queen and Roman Church, I knew what he was: a government agent. A spy.

I glanced about the room. The lone men in the crannies and corners were probably also agents. They all shared that ravenous look, that furtive air of treachery. I felt as if Bess and I were in a den of weasels, each one eager for the taste of blood.

"I have friends here in Antwerp." The man scraped a pointed fingernail around and around one of his shirt's buttons. His clothes were handsome, yet so plain they helped him fade into the scenery. "But I've had difficulty finding them. Know you them, by any chance?"

He gave me several names, but I recognized none and told him so. I' faith, if I had known those people I would have lied and denied as much, for they were belike his hunted prey.

"A pity. I do hope I'll soon find them." He smiled and ran his tongue over his jagged teeth. "And I do thank ye for your advice about mine inn. Yes. I thank ye."

Bess and I retreated to a pair of stools at the fireside.

"Curse these queen's men," I said lowly to Bess. "I wish we hadn't come here."

"But now we must stay till Catlin arrives, else he'll walk alone into this lair of spies. Mayhap we should wait outside for him."

"No, no. If we end up standing about out there for very long, we might begin to look suspicious to these men."

"Well, we'll no good business talk here." Bess tugged her cloak around her shoulders against a chill sifting through the room. "And I wanted to ask about fish. This morning I was told salt fish are selling for a good price about Oxford."

I shrugged. "If there's money to be had in them, then we should buy a few barrels."

"I've already bought two today, though I've been warned not to."

"Been warned?"

"Forget you what day this is? 'Tis the twenty-sixth. Van Wouwere and his dice bade me do no business on this day."

"Aye, his queer prophecy."

"It meant naught to me. Isn't it enough that we read the stars in hope of reassuring ourselves a ship will arrive safely and the goods aboard will be unharmed? 'Tis for me. I'll not tether myself to prophecies, nor bind my will with fear. Besides, if van Wouwere truly knew the art of foretelling, if he could espy just hints of what is to come, as he claims to, think you he would live as he does now, and where he does? Granted, he has some wealth, but he only rents Solomon's Wisdom—I asked about and was told as much. And though certes his rent must be high, still he lacks the money to buy his own house and furnish it with as much luxury as he'd like."

"Mayhap he doesn't want great wealth," I argued, "but knowledge, as he says."

"He says!" she scoffed. "He's a sensualist, that one. Take away his noble mask and you'll see the face of avarice itself."

"You judge him harshly. I don't like the man, but I doubt he is as bad as you insist."

"You dislike him? I'm glad to hear that. I dislike him now and expect to detest him in time. That's mine own prophecy."

Someone entered the room. Before e'en looking around, I could feel those agents poise, peer sharply, sniff for the scent. Then I saw it was but another merchant. Already the weasels, seemingly familiar with him and knowing him to be useless, were turning their noses elsewhere.

He gave the agent who had talked with us a slap on the back and loudly asked, "Ah, sir, here again? No luck in finding your friends, eh?" The man grumbled a reply and the merchant, glad to have ruffled him, moved to a group of others near us. "God's blood!" he whispered too loudly. "These damned spies were here yesterday too, and the day before, hanging about like gloom itself."

"Then they must be determined to get what they want," Bess mumbled to me.

"Please God they fail."

Long minutes dwindled by. I sighed, moved about on my stool, and pulled from the pocket of my cassock a letter I'd received that morning. 'Twas from Matthew and I'd already read it, but to pass the time I perused it again. Both bad and good news were in it, along with assurances that his and Jeremy's present business (and hence mine too, especially because of my current joint ventures with them) was mending.

"My leg is healing well enow for me to go about the city more, and so I've oft been to Blackwell Hall, where usually I can find good cloths. Jeremy is therefore free to travel to towns not far from London, but still the neither of us can be long from here. We have another contract with a Winchombe clothier, who sends us his kersey before our payments, so thanks to him and a few others we've no need to travel."

He wrote also that winter had come cold and damp to London, and already the Thames had once frozen over. He thanked me heartily for a shipment of furs, for they had brought a great profit. Of course they had, I reflected, for Catlin had had his hand in the deal, and by my troth the man could conjure profits like the devil. Not e'en when my Jonathan was alive did I see in our account books the kinds of figures now writ in them. If only Catlin could now conjure himself into this place so that we could be gone.

More minutes passed, and in the hall beyond came the sound of approaching feet. Catlin walked into the room, and behind him, though obviously not with him, came another man. He was young and lank, with clothes too much lived-in and hair he seemed to have trimmed himself to save some precious pennies. I ignored this stranger and meant to wave to Catlin, but something held me back.

At the very moment of their entrance, the agents had grown taut. The one who had talked with us was baring his teeth and running his tongue over them, and his muscles were eager to spring. I could feel the hairs on the back of my neck rise in fear. Was it for Catlin these agents had been waiting? I could not discern if their greedy eyes were on him or the stranger. The stranger had strolled into the room before pausing, but Catlin stopped just beyond the door. He was sensing danger. He but glanced at us ere looking elsewhere; he knew that to recognize us could endanger us too if any mischief was afoot. Still I tried to warn him with my eyes, and beside me I could feel Bess's own body tightening as she readied herself to leap to his defense. But Catlin only looked about with a bored expression, as if the person he wanted to meet was not present. He came a little deeper into the room, sighed in exasperation, then turned to leave.

Just then the stranger's head jerked slightly—he seemed to sense his own doom. He took a step back, and another. The agents stirred. With the same painfully false casualness that he affected, they slowly moved toward him. I could almost hear them sniffing for blood. Now he was close to the door, but the circle of agents was closing around him.

Suddenly he ran out of the room and out of the English House and the agents tore after him. Before I could blink they were gone and Catlin was at our sides, and we three dashed to the window and peered out.

The stranger was in the middle of the street when a pursuing agent grabbed him. In a second the pack of spies were upon him and he was struggling madly. "What are you doing? Unhand me!" we heard him shout, his eyes starting from his head in terror. "What is this about? What are you doing? No!" He struggled still whilst they snapped insults back and began to drag him away.

Holding my breath, trying not to scream for someone to have pity and help him, I watched the poor wretch until he and his captors were gone from our sight. "God save the man," murmured Bess. She was as jolted as were all around us. Though there were mumblings and hushed asides and the shaking of heads, e'en then none dared to do more. The three of us remained silent for some minutes.

"I was terrified they wanted you," Bess said at last to Catlin.

"You knew they were agents," I added.

His long body was rigid, his breath shallow. "I could feel something was amiss as soon as I walked in."

Bess lay her hand on his arm. "One of the men had been asking us about religion. I doubt nothing that their victim was arrested because of it. His fate could have been yours."

"But not today."

"Well, no more of this." I pulled on my gloves. "Let's away from here. Should we home or to the countinghouse?"

Catlin gazed out the window as if searching for other lurking spies. "Nay, I don't want to go there. I don't want any walls about me just yet." He squeezed all his muscles, held them in, let them go. "The stables where I board my horses are close by my house. I'll ride, methinks. I'll ride outside Antwerp for a time."

"Shake off this trapped feeling?" said Bess. "Aye, I feel the same."

"Then ride with me. The stables will have a good horse to lend you." She readily agreed. Nothing was said to me though I wished also to go, to escape all those houses and men.

"How good riding sounds." I buttoned up my cassock. "And if you'd mind not my company . . ."

Bess's brow contracted in irritation but Catlin was kinder. "Please you, join us," said he.

And so I left with them. But no sooner had we stepped outside when of a sudden we halted and dumbly stared. At the corner of the English House, in a place blocked from our view at the window, stood Brother Gerard. He was looking down the street after the pack of spies and their quarry, who were now but a distant blot, then he turned his head and with the unchanging eyes of one who had been expecting our appearance, he surveyed us. I smelled at once his conspiracy in the scene we had just witnessed; for no other reason could he have been at that precise time in that street where no friarly duties could have taken him. More deductions were racing through my mind. Whether or no that arrest had been meant to take place only if Catlin were present I could but muddle over, yet certes Brother Gerard intended for us to see him now.

Even now he stood silent, as if he need do no more. And so it was; I understood. This was his machination to frighten and remind us he was watching us still, and too, as in the warehouse, that he could be the instigator of threatening situations in which he wished to place us. He knew that 'twould be far worse for Catlin to be hauled back to England and punished there for heresy than in Antwerp. This too he could arrange, and this too he was telling us.

The none of us said anything. We only looked at him and he at us. Then a hideous, cackling laugh burst out and we all spun around. On the other side of the street was Damascus.

He was sitting on a donkey and had fixed his eyes on Brother Gerard. Beneath a cheap woolen cloak, beneath the same filthy garments he always wore, his bony frame twitched whilst the donkey anxiously stamped its hooves.

"Was that one of thy victories?" he asked, his cackle clear to our ears as he leaned his head in the direction of the spies. "But that one didn't matter, nay!" His eyes rolled back and forth between Catlin and

Brother Gerard. "I am leaving now, I am leaving. But thou shalt see me again. Always I come back. I shall come back again and again!"

His last words rose in a screech like a swooping owl's. Then, with a thump of his legs and flapping of his arms, he beat the donkey into a frantic trot down the street and away, the meager traveling bag that was hanging across the animal's rump flopping up and down.

Brother Gerard lurched after him, ran a few paces, saw that pursuit was useless, and stopped.

"None of your city's guards be about this time, be they?" Catlin said.

The friar kept looking down the street after the vanished Damascus. "I nothing doubt that he is leaving Antwerp; only for a time, however. He will indeed be back."

"Will you miss him?"

He turned again to Catlin. "In time, he'll return to you. When he does, so too shall I." His voice was as smooth as holy oil, and so were his movements as he walked past us and away.

"Then we may be free of them both until then?" Bess wondered aloud.

"Please God," I muttered. And may Catlin and she and I ever be safe from them, I prayed, though I more fully apprehended than ever what he had already done might yet hang him.

Once more we headed for the stables, wordlessly at first, until Bess and Catlin began to make sport of what had just happened and then with effort talked of other things. The stables consisted of individual stalls lined around a cobblestone yard, and few horses were at the time in any of them; still two horses could be let. Catlin paid for their use and saddled his own horse whilst a stableboy and an old groom saddled ours.

I waited at the opposite end of the yard, beneath the roof of an empty stall where we were a little out of the cold. It was not a bitter cold, but a sharpness stung the air and the day was made yet bleaker by the grayness filtering down from the cloud-filled sky. Not the best day to go riding, I bethought me, but at least most of the ground was dry. In the yard, clots of muck and ice crouched betwixt the cobblestones, and a pile of straw lay damp and stained in a corner. A stench rose from the yellow stuff and traveled thinly in the chill.

Bess remained with Catlin while he readied his horse. She talked with him, she gestured in abrupt movements, she let fly a brittle laugh; she seemed feverish. Belike she is still only feeling the draining of that terror when Catlin was dangerously surrounded, I thought. I as well felt its effects. Now, protective and worried, Bess stayed by him.

The stableboy led into the yard a horse saddled for a woman. Not waiting for him to help her, Bess swung herself up into the saddle. Another horse was led out, I mounted it, and Catlin joined us on his own dun-colored horse.

We rode at a brisk walk through the streets jumbled thick with people, carts, dogs, and other horses, passed through St. George's Gate, and clattered across the bridge spanning the moat. The bridge yielded to open land, the clattering became muffled thumps, and with a cry Bess slapped her horse—the beast nigh reared in surprise—and set out at a gallop down the road. Catlin raced after her and called her name, but she only turned her horse off the road and onto the bordering farm fields, now lying fallow and patched with snow. I rode after them, but when the ground became too rough for me I only trotted my horse along the road. Bess was bent low over her horse's neck and guided it through crags of wet bogs, jutting mounds of earth, and tufts of frosted bushes. I thought her more feverish than ever, and now recklessly abandoned. Catlin caught up, laughed, saw something in her face that made him linger, then slapped his horse onward.

They rode for some time between bare orchards, past sleeping windmills. I soon tired of the sport and found my hands growing numb and my face raw. I called to Bess and Catlin.

" 'Tis too cold for me now!" I cried. "I'm going back."

They returned to the road and, for my safety's sake, watched me trot up between two farmers' wains that were rumbling along in the same direction; the men could give me escort to the city's wall. Seeing that I was protected and on my way, Bess and Catlin galloped off again.

The farmers did no more than glance at me nor I at them. For some minutes my horse walked along, though the skittish animal seemed to dislike having an ox and creaking wain to the front and rear. Then a noise cracked just behind us. My horse swung its rump away from it and I held the reins firmly to keep him under control. Looking over my shoulder, I saw that the noise had come from a spoke in one of the wain's wheels and that the farmer, while the wain kept rolling, was bending over to look at it.

Then came a louder crack and the spoke split in two. My horse swerved. I was thrown to the right and gripped the saddlebow to keep my seat, but as I was pulling myself upright the horse clambered down to the side of the road. In a jolt I was pitched out of my saddle and into the air, and then with a thump landed on my hip on a boggy mound. For seconds I could only blink and look about me. Then, groaning, I stood up. I was uninjured—aching and bruised but uninjured. My brainless horse was only steps away and looking at me. So too were the farmers. I tested my unsure legs, then took hold the dangling reins of my horse.

"Need you any help?" one of the men finally asked.

I shook my head. "Nay. I need none." I got my wits about me again but did not yet want to remount. "Please you, go on your way."

"You will be alone out here," said the man without expression.

"My friends are hard by." I waved them on.

And so they left me, and I looked about. Catlin and Bess were nowhere in sight. In fact no one was about, on the road or in the fields. I liked not being alone in that bleak landscape, in that swallowing emptiness. A dampness chilled my thighs and I looked down. My cassock and kirtle were stained with mud and my ankles were wet with cold. Certes I did not want to go riding back into town alone and looking so disheveled. Curse my coming on this riding today. I climbed back on my horse and with an impatient kick sent him off at a gallop across the fields in the direction where last I had seen the two of them. They must be near, I reasoned, and in that empty land I should be able to spot them. I rode to the top of a low hill. Just down the way, where the earth swirled up into high mounds, I could see the unmoving forms of two horses drawn against each other. I walked mine own mount toward them, then stopped.

Bess and Catlin were just beyond me. Leaning out of their saddles, their arms wrapped around each other, they were kissing long and passionately and over and over again. His arms moved down her back and drew her closer to him and nigh off her horse. She grew yet more fierce and lost in him.

Mine own horse stamped; they heard nothing. I could not watch them, yet could not look away. I didn't yet know how I felt about this. My heart and mind seemed as numb as my skin. At last I called out.

"Bess!"

She pushed quickly away from him and looked around. At the sight of me her arms contracted, but then with cool deliberation she left them lying on Catlin's shoulders, whilst he took his arms away—not as if in respect to me, but to wait till I was gone. Her gaze at me was accusing, Catlin's expectant, as if he, and not I, deserved an explanation.

I was hopelessly awkward. Whether I should be accusing in turn or beg their pardon I couldn't decide. "My clothes," I finally managed, gesturing at them. "I fell off my horse."

"Be you hurt?" Catlin's voice was a rumble.

"A few bruises. Naught more, methinks. But those farmers have left and no one else is on the road. I didn't want to ride back alone and like this."

He took a deep breath. It seemed he was grappling with storming emotions and tugging them back down deep into himself.

Mine own feelings for what I'd just witnessed were still wildly blowing about. I tried to jest. "I' faith, I can't decide if I should have indeed interrupted you both or let you be."

"Oh, Aunt," Bess said. "I should think you're glad you stopped us."

"That's all one," Catlin said to her, then turned back to me. "For the nonce, we cannot leave you here alone. 'Tis cold now withal, so we'll all go back."

He said nothing more to me. He and Bess took up their reins again and, looking only at the hard land, rode with me back to Antwerp.

XVIII

I said nothing to Bess or Catlin about what I had seen, but now whenever they were together I stayed close to them in a passive effort to keep them apart. They had frightened me with their embraces, as passionate as starved lovers'. Yet, mayhap hypocritically, I kept my fears to myself. Bess could remain in that house with Catlin only if I too were there, otherwise there'd be a scandal; this the three of us had always known. And if I discovered that Bess and Catlin had become naked bedfellows with no intention of soon marrying, then I could no longer remain under that roof with them but would need leave, which I didn't want. I was comfortable there and now dreaded the idea of ever moving back into hired lodgings. And so I was silent on the matter, and so too were they.

Our life together at least seemed to go on as before, save that Catlin was spending now more time not with Bess but with Nicolas van Wouwere, toward whom I felt an unshakable repugnance. Usually Catlin went to van Wouwere's house or somewhere about with him, but one evening, about a sennight after that scene in the frozen fields, 'twas van Wouwere who came home with Catlin.

Bess and I had arrived weary and hungry and were informed by Lijsken that we could begin to sup, for master had sent word he would be late. We ate and were finished and writing letters upstairs in the antler room when Catlin returned. The front door opened and there was the stamping of his snow-encrusted boots, but too the sound of someone else entering. Bess went to the landing and listened. She reported that van Wouwere was with him and they were sitting down to supper.

I fiddled unhappily with my pen. "Van Wouwere? I don't like that man being here."

"I hate it," she grumbled. "I'd rather sit through a score of pious visits from Brother Gerard than one with van Wouwere. Catlin has been seeing far too much of this damned doctor. And where do they oft meet? I can tell you because I know—in taverns."

"Well, Catlin has gone to taverns before with a client."

" 'Tis not the same at all. And Catlin does not even much like van Wouwere; he's only drawn to the man's astrology and supposed divinations."

She sounded more than ever like a jealous lover, I thought.

Since it was growing late, I presumed van Wouwere would sup and leave, but two hours passed and we could still hear the distant boom of his laughter. I was by then sleepy and so told Bess I would go below, say good night to Catlin, then go to bed. She claimed not to be sleepy herself and stayed behind, writing.

When I went below I heard their words drifting through the ajar door of the parlor. "Why don't we go out, Bartholomew?" van Wouwere was saying. "That's what both of us need to do, go out to a tavern, and mayhap another place or two afterward. You'd like that. I recommend it for our good health."

I stepped into the room. "Why, Nicolas!" I exclaimed. "Bless me, I didn't know you were here. I would have come down ere this to bid you hello. Instead I came to bid Catlin a good night."

Van Wouwere flung out his arms in greeting. They were long, swallowing arms, and when they reached the full length of their span they thumped onto the table before him and his fists pounded the wood, like a single boom of his laughter. The dishes and glasses rattled. "I am happy to see you, Mevrouw Lathbury, but I would you could dally here. Your health is now good?"

"It is, thank you. And I pray you be well? But I'll not keep you. I'll see you in the morning, Catlin."

I turned to him at last and was taken aback by his tired aspect; he looked readier for sleep than I. That van Wouwere wanted hours more of merriment for them both was selfish. "A good night to you, Catlin. I must say, you seem to have had as rough a day as did I and are as ready for sleep."

He smiled and bade me a good night.

Van Wouwere poured himself more wine. "Shall I walk with you to your bedchamber, Mevrouw Lathbury?" With his massive head bent still over his cup and inclined to one side, he looked up at me from the corners of his eyes. "I'll walk you well into it if you like."

"That is not necessary," I replied shortly.

"Ah, mevrouw, what a disappointment. I wouldn't mind at all seeing you to your bed, and being certain you're snug in it." He made a smug little smile that made me want to cuff him.

"No doubt, but I would greatly mind." I left without saying more. Jesus! Did he think his wanton jests were charming flattery? "That's a man who's too conceited," I muttered.

At the stairs was Bess, who waited until I was at her side to say in a sullen whisper, "Is our dear Nicolas leaving?"

"He and Catlin may go to a tavern now."

Just then the two men, their cloaks and hats thrown on, emerged from the parlor and van Wouwere boomed, "Ha! Mevrouw Marwick! Mevrouw Bess!" and again his arms swung wide.

She swept past him to Catlin.

His tired aspect was now mixed with feverishness. "I'm going out for a little, Bess," said he. As he walked past me, he briefly, comfortingly, put his hand upon my back as if in apology for van Wouwere's rude words to me. Then he opened the door.

Van Wouwere observed Bess and me with his deep-sunk eyes and, the pleased smile on him still, hurried outside.

Catlin took up the torch beside the entrance, lit it on a candle, and was hastening out when Bess grasped the edge of the door and would not let it shut.

"Stay here with me!" she urged.

Catlin looked back at her, then spun about and was gone.

She flung the door wide and flew outside, only to stumble to a stop just beyond the door. Down the street, into the haze of black cold, were the fast vanishing figures of Catlin and van Wouwere, glowing beneath the torch. Already I was at her side. "Good God! It's cold!" I exclaimed. "Get you back inside afore you catch your death!" At first she responded not. Then suddenly she turned on me like a dog.

" 'Twas you!" she spat. "That's why Catlin left. Now he'll go find some whores and with van Wouwere to help him. If you hadn't kept us apart, if you hadn't meddled, I could have taken him away from that damned astrologer!"

She was sparking with such wildness that I stepped back. "What? What are you talking about? Would you then be Catlin's whore?"

"He would never call me that!" she cried.

A while later I was in my bed. In her own chamber, Bess's slumber was unquiet, for she had a dream that made her cry out. It roused me, and I listened to learn if she had fallen asleep again or had risen, but I could hear nothing more. I listened too for Catlin, but he did not return till morning.

With that night I'd had my fill of Nicolas van Wouwere and wanted naught more to do with him; but some days later I was walking with Bess and Catlin when we came around a corner into the Glove Market and happened upon him. He looked quite the doctor again, in his undercap and spectacles and robes. He greeted Bess and me with haughty conceit but hailed Catlin and began to talk of business with him. He might join in a venture with a fellow physician who lived in Cologne, he said, a venture involving physic tools.

"I don't quite know, Bartholomew," said he, "how I should go about discharging for my Cologne friend his bill of exchange or how to draw up one here to be discharged there."

Catlin seemed distracted by the joint presence of the doctor and Bess. It was as if he knew how to behave when alone with van Wouwere, or how to be himself with Bess, but not when they were together; he was becoming too different a man for each of them to be only himself with them both. His answer was detached, his manner constrained.

Sometimes whilst talking, van Wouwere's glance followed several comely housewives or girl servants who passed by, and once he leered and licked his lips. I fought to keep out of my mind the repugnant images of the man fondling any woman.

The doctor said he would walk with us toward Catlin's counting-house and we crossed the muck and snow of the Glove Market. Along the walk to either side of us were lined three- and four-storied buildings, all of them dwarfs beside the tremendous front and high towers of Our Lady's Church that rose at the far end. We paused on its steps when we reached there to kick the snow from our feet. As I was thumping a foot 'gainst the stones, I heard the tinkling of a leper's bell and looked up to see a bony form moving out of the shadow beside Our Lady's. He was swathed in rags, his half-covered face hidden the more by the blinding

sun and shadows; and in one hand he held a staff from which hung his
bell, required by law to give warning of his presence. In the other he
held out a beggar's cup, and perforce I stepped back from his diseased
presence and closer to Catlin and Bess. Catlin was stooped to help her
clear the snow from her shoes so the leper turned to van Wouwere. The
doctor let his glance only skim toward the poor beggar and then shift
elsewhere. In that moment when he beheld his suffering fellow man, I
saw the quintessence of indifference.

For some seconds more the leper held his cup toward van Wouwere,
then leaned on his staff toward me. I dropped a few coins into it and he
mumbled a blessing and moved wearily on.

Catlin had seen none of this. He straightened up. "Shall we go?"

I shook my head and drew back. I wanted to be alone, and far from
van Wouwere. "No, I have somewhere else to go, I just now remember
me. When will you be at the English Quay, Bess?"

"At half past one of the clock. We won't be long at the countinghouse, and Catlin said he'll accompany me."

"Have you a shipment to oversee?" van Wouwere asked.

Bess gave him a sour smile. "A small shipment. Merely two barrels
of fish."

"But today is the eighth of December." He was solemn.

"I know what day it is, and I arranged for these fish on the
twenty-sixth of November."

"You may do as you please," he intoned, "but I must still warn you
that, having been bothered by what my game of dice had told you, I
decided to cast for you your horoscope. It could not be exact, of course,
for I don't know the exact hour of your birth, only your birthday. So I
cast a horoscope and to my great dismay discovered that the direction of
Saturn was to the moon's evil aspect. This signified damage to partner-
ships and beasts, and too, other goods; it signifies certain losses. The
angles of the *figura caeli* did as well bode ill for you."

Bess's tone was cold. "I hope you did not waste too much time
upon my horoscope."

"None of the time spent was wasted, mevrouw." His voice was as
bitter as wormwood. "I was thinking only of your welfare."

"And I was thinking of my profits."

I bid them be off lest Bess be late for the docks, and I watched
them go. Damn the doctor and his game and his astrology; damn mine
own unease.

I went into the church. I needed to seek sanctuary, to banish a malevolence I felt at the borders of my life. Only a few men and women were kneeling or standing about, and those who were selling things or striking bargains or meeting for one reason or another kept in the entrance that day, and away from the center of the church. I went on until I came to the statue of Our Lady, and there I stood, and knelt, then stood again. I gazed at the statue and at the serenity with which the face was composed. Beneath her were shining candles, burning with sinners' contrition, with hopes of intercession: shriving flames, soft-fleeting, sending sparks into eternity. *Ave Maria. Miserere mei Deus.* For whom was I praying, myself? And whose sins must I ask be forgiven? I wanted the forgiveness of van Wouwere and all men like him, lest their sins touch me.

I let no more words disturb my mind, and prayed without any, and then sat down in a nearby spot where I could see above the altar screen the great bronze crucifix and at its sides the crosses on which hung the bad and good thieves. I waited till a quietude had settled again upon my soul. The church was peaceful, and now when there was any sound it echoed up into the expanse of air ribbed with stone arches so high that I soon grew dizzy when I tipped back my head to look at them. My soul moved, broke from the constrictions of uncertainty, and rose out of myself and into that high air. I had sought respite from malevolence and indifference, from obsessions and mysteries, and had found it. I felt the fool for having been so unsettled by the warnings of horoscopes and by van Wouwere, such a ridiculous man. Should I find myself so disturbed again, I resolved I but needed to reason with myself or to come here and pray, and then go on, guarded by benisons and orisons.

Only when the clock had struck the quarter hour did I realize how long I'd been there. I had to leave if I wished to meet Bess at the dock. Now too I could do so, with my tranquility having been restored to me, and being no longer shaken by what must have been only fears stirred up by mine imagination. When I stepped outside, even the harsh glare seemed to have waned and the shadows were too shallow to have hidden in them anything strange.

The docks were not as busy as usual. Though there was not much ice in the Scheldt, enough floated in the water to keep away smaller sailing vessels. Still there were several large ships being laded or un-laded, and men were busy with the towing to and fro and the lifting of this and that. Near one of the ships in the English Quay I spotted Catlin, and close to him was Bess, who was investigating her merchant's mark upon the bungs of two large barrels. Moving slowly above her was the slack rope of the dock's crane, which had just unloaded from its net into the depths of a dromond some unwieldy casks. A sailor stood on the deck of the ship trumpeting directions to the men operating the crane. Into the net they rolled two hogsheads, secured the rope, then worked the crane and watched the hogsheads begin to rise.

I could see no sign of van Wouwere, and was relieved. Of course he would not be here now, I thought, since here was Bess flouting his gloomy prophecies. He was a proud man accustomed to having people treat with respect his attempt at foretelling; he did not like being challenged by this laughing young woman.

I asked Bess where the doctor had gone to. "To hell, for aught I care," she answered.

The taut rope of the crane, straining with its load, moved along on its wheels and made them creak. The creaking mixed with the bangs and shouts of the dock. Bess and I walked idly mayhap fifteen feet away from the barrels and were about to walk back when we heard the wheels squeal out suddenly and the net filled with hogsheads swung dangerously back and forth just above Bess's barrels. There was a snap of breaking rope as part of the net gave way. It swung back and forth whilst shouts of warning flew all around us. In a second the net snapped again and again the hogsheads teetered, then tumbled over the edge and crashed down upon Bess's barrels, bursting them and themselves violently open and spewing out their contents. Wine had been in the hogsheads, and it mixed red and running with the silvery, blank-eyed lifeless fish that slithered over one another.

I stared at those fish, bloodied with wine, and a quiver of fear shot through me. In those few moments my trust in mine own perception of what was real and what wasn't died.

W e were able to save half of the fish. A few empty firkins were rolled out and the laders quickly threw into them the sprawled-out mess. Some of the fish were riddled with slivers of wood; a few were smashed and slimy with organs; a few were cut clean apart. Some of the ruined ones were tossed in with the good and others into a sickly pile of waste. The wine of course no one could do aught about, and it flowed down the dock in every direction whilst its owner, a portly Englishman yelling oaths, stood rooted in its midst and bewailed his loss. Not Bess, Catlin, nor I, howe'er, so much as raised our voices. When the tossing and piling were complete, Catlin approached the other men to discuss what might now be done. Bess was about to join him when I pulled her away.

"We'll not tarry here any longer," said I. "We'll to the counting-house and there wait for Catlin. By God, the neither of us will do more business today!"

"But my fish—I must see . . ."

"You saw your blasted fish! There's naught else you can do."

She was silent all the way to the countinghouse and intolerable once there. She paced into Catlin's office, where I had settled myself, and paced to the back room and to the front again, shoving things out of her way and arguing with Jan and Michiel. After half of an hour of this she announced that she was going to nearby shops.

"And why?" I demanded. "Was not what just betided your fish sufficient business for you today? Oh no, you must need conduct more."

"Go to! I'll do as I please, not what you or van Wouwere would like." She crossed her arms and smiled scornfully at me. "My my, Aunt, how you've changed your tune. Don't you remember the time you chided Catlin for his astrology? A little astrology to reassure you of your goods' safety on ships, that was all you needed. To peer any more into the future was wrong. But let a rogue like van Wouwere perform a clever trick and tell so broad a prediction that it ensnares in its meaning any mischance, and you become the hypocrite."

"I am a woman who has lived in this world twice longer than have you," I scolded. "I do not disclaim what I once avowed. I only listen to mine own feelings when they urge caution. What has happened I don't understand, and I will not tempt evil to visit me again by biting my thumb at it, and neither so should you. For aught you know, van Wouwere could be in league with the devil."

"For aught the either of us knows, he could be a master of tricks."

She reached for her cape and I grasped her wrist. "What's this? Your hands are shaking! You've more lost your nerves than have I, and you call me hypocrite!"

The office door creaked open. Bess wrenched her wrist away from me and stopped. 'Twas Catlin who had entered. With quick control she joined her hands, emptied her face of emotion, and faced him. Either she was more a hypocrite than I had trowed or stronger than anyone suspected.

Catlin, in contrast, seemed all furrowed. He half sat on the edge of his desk, sagging with weariness. "Mayhap half of your fish can be sold. The other half is so damaged it could only be given away in charity. So I directed the lot of them to an honest fishmonger I know. He'll sell the one half and give the other to poor families living near his stall."

"My profit on them is of course lost," Bess said flatly. "But will I recover half the money I spent on them?"

"No more than that. The fishmonger will of course have his usual profit."

"Well"—she took a deep breath—"happily this misfortune doesn't lighten my purse too much."

"A brave showing, Bess," I said gently.

A hard smile curved her mouth. "Think you I'm being brave? Oh no, Sara. Now I be merely honest. What I've lost today I've spent before on a pretty kirtle with a gown and sleeves, and that I could well afford. Of late all my ventures have been quite profitable. Catlin, show her if you would what we've recorded of late for our joint ventures."

Catlin leaned over and drew from one of the desk's drawers a book marked "Joint Accounts," opened and handed it to me. Scattered over some pages was entry after entry with her name and his and the money they were earning. I had of course been familiar with most of her business, as was she with mine, but I hadn't e'en suspected that she was doing so very well. She'd become already, with astonishing speed, the skilled merchant and diligent worker she'd sworn she would be. In time she might e'en be wealthy.

Bess's quiet hands began to twist. "Catlin, what about the broken crane rope?"

"The crane is part of the English Quay." He returned the account book to his desk. "Who would be responsible to pay for the damage done by it will be very difficult to establish, especially since you alone sustained a loss: The man whose wine was destroyed had taken out assurance on his hogsheads."

Her knuckles crackled under the twisting. "But why did the rope break?"

" 'Twas an accident. I investigated but found no foul play, and witnesses swear the same."

"It could have been a trick."

"And what if it was not?"

"If not, it doesn't matter"—she grew yet more sullen—"save that your friend Nicolas will be more puffed up with pride."

Catlin grew stern. "He foresaw your troubles and gave you fair warning. Can't you admit that?"

"Nay. He foresaw nothing."

He sighed at this and was rising from his desk when Arnout passed through the front chamber. "Arnout, go home to Lijsken," he called out, "and tell her I am having Doctor van Wouwere to supper tonight. I'll send Dorothea to the market to buy her and Marie more food."

Arnout gave his master a tip of his hat as he left.

" 'I'm having Doctor van Wouwere to supper tonight!' " Bess mocked. "Of all nights, why must you have him visit us tonight?"

"I'd asked him ere we parted today—you were there. We could not know what would happen afterward."

"Oh, but dear Nicolas claims he knew. And tonight I must sit by and watch him revel in satisfaction."

"Then don't sit with us and don't watch him."

"Oh, I'll sit with him and look him straight in his eyes. I'll never let him assume I'm awed by his supposed prophecies."

"Think what you will. I think he may be a true diviner."

Here I piped in weakly, "And I think he may complot with the devil."

"Nay," said Bess, "he merely consorted with some men at the dock."

That finished our wrangling. We were all divided and all out of words. Bess drew on her cape.

"Enough of van Wouwere. I'm for home now. This arguing over him does us little good."

By then the afternoon was darkening. Clouds had been tumbling up over the horizon and into the sky till at last they hid the heavens. We had not long been home when snow began to fall. Bess sat beside a window in her bedchamber and watched the flakes as they drifted around and down on the weak wind. Then she rose to change her clothes and after that was restless and could sit no more. She stalked out of her room and through the house, searching for something that would feed a sudden hunger in her. Catlin had closed himself away into his library but she wouldn't have him there; she wanted his company, and not whilst being again bent over books with him.

"In God's name, I cannot sit idle now!" said she, pacing into my bedchamber. I had just lain down to drowse, tired more by my nerves than lack of sleep. " 'Tis like a cage, this house. Of a sudden it keeps me too confined. I wanted to escape from here and go riding, but Catlin wouldn't hear of it."

"As well he should not, nor should you." I rolled over toward her. "Ride about in this weather, and for sport? You must be mad."

To this she gave me an impatient groan and paced back out.

I fell to drowsing again until in a little I heard her laughter and Catlin's rising from below. Amongst its sounds there came too directions that Catlin was calling out to her, and the clash and clanging of metal, like fighting swords. Perturbed by this unfamiliar heap of noises, I rose and followed them down to the antler room.

I stopped in the door. Catlin and Bess were each grasping a long, thin sword and cutting and slashing. They were flushed and hot-breathing and flying about in the pale light, and off them were hurled their mad-dancing shadows, like scarce-seen shades flickering out of hell. Bess cut too wide a swath and Catlin, lightning-quick, saw his chance and stabbed at her, his sword's point stopping inches from her chest. 'Twould have been his killing thrust had the fight been real.

"Ha!" he bellowed. "Again I win. E'en for a man long out of practice with his sword, you're no match."

She sliced at him and they began anew to fence. "But mark you," she cried out between gasps, "that I'm only a novice with a sword. Don't I fight well in spite of that?"

"You fight like a woman who's never held a blade."

She slashed at him for that. The near blow caught him unaware and he jumped back. She laughed at his retreat and fought on, clumsy and untrained against his skill.

I wanted to shout a stop to their dangerous sporting, to the strange sight of a woman with a sword, but they would never heed me. Though they caught glimpses of me in their spinning, they wasted on me neither attention nor words. Now their passion was bared. Now their play was as violent as their emotions for each other, as afflicted as their souls. Better that Bess should slip into Catlin's bed than this. I could watch them no longer. I turned and left.

The smell of meat and poultry being cooked for dinner was wafting through the house, but I had no appetite and was about to go back to my bedchamber when there came a knock at the front entrance. I looked down from a window at the door below, where stood Jan and Michiel, their arms full of food freshly bought. None of the servants hastened to open the door so I went down the stairs and let them in myself.

Jan easily carried his load of nuts, dried fruit, mustard sauce, and boxes of comfits, but Michiel huffed under a firkin of ale.

"What's this?" I asked. "I've ne'er seen you do a chore like buying and delivering."

"Dorothea went to the shops," Michiel wheezed. "Master Catlin wanted us to but deliver what she bought. We'll share tonight's good supper with the servants in compensation."

They took the food to the kitchen whilst I fetched some sewing from my bedchamber and went to sit in the parlor. There I could hear the voices of the servants and the clatterings of dishes and pots and pans and other everyday noises, rather than the sounds that were swirling above.

Jan was coming in with more candles when Bess and Catlin, both lively and sweaty, bounded into the room behind him.

"Marry, what a good fight that was!" she exclaimed. "What's this?

Have you come to play servant to us, Jan? If you were my servant—or my apprentice—I'd give you much better orders." She plucked a stray hair off his collar. "Think you that you could rise to my commands?"

Jan shuffled from one foot to the other. "Aye, I could rise indeed." He grinned, then glanced at his master and became proper again. "I'm simply carrying these in for Lijsken and Marie."

"Oh, so 'tis Marie now, and here I thought I was your secret love. How faithless you are."

"I'm not at all."

"And neither are you doing your work." Catlin dropped into a chair. "So be off with you and no more of this vain flirting."

"Did you hear that, Jan?" Bess raised her eyebrows. "He thinks my flirting is in vain. Mayhap some day we'll prove him wrong."

"Aye, we could, we could." An odd giggle broke out of him. At first the poor boy actually seemed to think that she was sincere. Then he realized that as usual she was only teasing, and he grew all awkward and red. A knock came at the entrance door and he hurried to answer it as if glad to escape from us all.

" 'Tis Nicolas, I trow," said Catlin.

Van Wouwere entered the room, his arms spread in magnanimous greeting, his teeth glittering in a smile, his face ruddy from the frosty evening air, his spectacles of course missing. Again, I sighed, again.

The dinner was served and we had only begun to eat when van Wouwere coughed a little on some hot meat, cleared his throat, and turned to Bess.

"I am sorry, mevrouw, of the most unwelcome mischance that befell you today," said he gravely.

Bess finished her bite of duck and remarked to Catlin on its flavor, but she spoke in English, a language van Wouwere didn't know. He looked on, puzzled.

"Oh, I do forget," Bess said airily. "You speak no English, do you, sir? Well, it matters not. I was only saying how rich the duck is."

"All the food is delicious," van Wouwere agreed. "But what happened to you today, Mevrouw Marwick—I wish to express my hope that it did not in any way harm you."

She was seething 'neath her pleasant aspect; I feared she might even throw a plate or two at him.

"Oh no, sir, it didn't harm me at all. A little profit was lost, and a little more beyond that. Be bothered not about it, Nicolas, since I am not."

His eyes dug into her to detect if she were being truthful, but she only gazed back proudly.

"That I'm very glad to hear, indeed I am." He paused to belch. "But I must say, I do feel a part of this misfortune since I did predict this day's bad luck."

"A prediction? From a game and then a horoscope that you said couldn't be exact? Oh, how silly of me. I simply paid no heed to your game of dice, just as I do your game of flirting."

He raised his tangled eyebrows. "My game of what?"

"Of flirting."

"Mevrouw, you be mistaken." Now his voice trickled with venom.

She busied herself with slicing the roast lamb. "Oh, not at all, sir. You tried to play a bit amorously with me."

"Perchance I did," he conceded, as if only to please her rather than admit she was right. "But that was to make merry, and too because you are a fair woman."

"Aye, I know. I also know why you quit that game: because I wouldn't play, and because I proved too intelligent and strong for you, so you must move on to easier prey."

"You do wrong me, mevrouw, and you make me seem the heartless hunter."

"Heartless is your own word, and why wrangle with you there? But hunter? We're all hunters in our own way. Tell me, sir, what are you yourself hunting for?"

He regarded her with caution. "For knowledge and contentment."

Her sidelong glance at him was cynical. "Oh, of course, Nicolas, of course. And for grace in the sight of God, as are we all."

"Do you doubt me?"

"Doubt you? I've no doubt at all about you."

Catlin could see that she was now really warming for a fight, but that he would not tolerate. "Go to! No more of this talk of God and doubts," he exclaimed. Then he told us a bawdy jest, at which the doctor roared and slapped the table. I myself was grateful for this change of conversation.

There were more jests and easy talk, and so much wine disappeared into van Wouwere that for the first time I saw him become bousy. He leered, he swayed, he talked on and on. By supper's end I'd had enough of him. I had to get away. I was rising to excuse myself when he interrupted me.

"What ho! This woman has the good sense to stand ere becoming fixed to her chair. I should do the same and clear my head. But, in sooth, I could drink a gallon more and yet be sober."

"I myself have no more need of drink," said Bess with disdain, and rose too. "Were you leaving, Sara?"

"I pray you pardon me, Catlin, and too, Nicolas," said I, "but I have letters to write . . ."

"Of course, Sara," Catlin waved us away. "We'll not keep you here. And for you, Nicolas, I'll go choose us some more wine."

He left the room, and I mumbled an awkward good night to van Wouwere. Bess was close behind me when van Wouwere wrapped his large hand around her arm and pulled her close to him.

"Why go you so soon, sweet chuck?" He winked and gave her a lubricious grin. "I'd much rather you would dally with me instead."

Bess's eyes narrowed. "If I remain here, 'twould be only to give you more insults."

"Ah, but that I like. A woman's resistance can be her allure."

"Then you must find all women alluring."

He ran his tongue along his lower lip whilst his free hand rose toward her breasts. "Ah, Mevrouw Bess, what hot humors you stir in me."

"Hot humors?" With a sharp twisting back of his fingers, she peeled her arm away from him. "You mean ugly spite."

With that, she left the room and nigh walked into Jan and Michiel. They had been coming down the hall, each carrying a pot belike filled with meat given them from the supper.

"Mistress Marwick!" Jan sputtered, steadying his pot.

"Oh, Jan, I pray your pardon!" A shadow just then fell over us. Van Wouwere's broad frame filled the open door.

She studied him, then gave Jan a coy expression. "If I dally at all, Doctor, 'twill be with young Jan. His sweet youth is alluring, and never so the fumbling of old men."

Jan at first was happily docile under her honey words and the soft stroke she gave his hair. Then his dull mind comprehended that she was teasing again, and like a betrayed pup he pouted and lurched backward into Michiel.

"Watch out!" Michiel barked and nigh dropped his pot. "Mistress Marwick"—he sighed, all proper business—"we truly must be on our way."

And so they left. Bess went to the library, and I myself to my bedchamber. I fetched my pen, papers, and inkpot and went down to sit with her. She was bent over a book and staring at its pages, her eyes unmoving.

"What a vile man that doctor is," I said. "Methinks you should tell Catlin of what he did."

Bess scarce stirred. "Nay, not yet."

I sat down and proceeded to write. An hour later the quiet was broken by loud laughter from below. 'Twas the sound of men with too much drink in them.

Suddenly Bess lifted her head, puzzled and disturbed. She looked around the room, then stood at the steps beyond, searching and listening for something. When she returned her eyes were wide and her lips tight shut.

"Bess, good niece, what is it?"

She stared at me. Her hands were on the table and she squeezed them together, as if forcing out a surging fright. "Did you not feel someone walk by?"

"Someone walk by? No, not at all. No one is here save us."

"But for a minute there was someone else here. I could feel someone near me. Someone walked by me."

Her face froze me. I leaned forward and took her hands in mine. "No one was here. You felt nothing but the movement of your own imagination. 'Tis rattled after the end of this trying day and evening. Come, we'll to bed now, that's all we both need."

Weakly she took up a candle and with me left the library. As we were passing out of the antler room, another burst of laughter rolled up the stairs.

"We should bid them good night," said I.

"Nay, I don't want to."

"Then I'll say good night for us both."

I went below and stopped outside the parlor when I heard a giggling within—'twas Marie's laugh, and she was being answered by van Wouwere.

"You should believe me," he was saying. "I could cure that mark upon your face. I can erase it, and then you'll be the fairest maid in Antwerp. What? You laugh at me?"

Beshrew the scoundrel! I thought, for so lying to a silly, credulous girl. He couldn't possibly have in his bag of physic tricks a cure for a birthmark.

I stepped into the room with a deliberate thump. Marie was sitting in van Wouwere's lap. He had one arm around her hips, whilst his free hand pulled her cap farther away from the stained side of her face. At my entrance, she jumped up and cowered in a corner. For me 'twas van Wouwere who was the truly guilty one, but he was regarding me with indifference, his eyes rimmed red and his head swaying.

"Do you desire to join us again, Mevrouw Lathbury?" he cackled.

I said nothing to him. I only turned and, seeing Catlin near the kitchen, went to his side. He was trying not to stagger and when I drew near he rested his back against the wall to steady himself.

"I came to say good night, Catlin."

"Aye . . . aye." His tongue was stumbling. "Nicolas and I shall soon retire."

"He'll be sleeping here?"

Catlin nodded and rested his head too against the wall. "He should stay the night. I told Lijsken to make up the small bed in the spare bedchamber. Too much snow is in the streets now, and he's drunk so much he'd fall into a snowdrift and ne'er climb out of it."

"As you wish, Catlin. Good night."

In a little I was in my bed and reading a book by candlelight. Someone, probably Lijsken, soon came up and into the empty bedchamber, and shortly afterward left it. At last I heard Catlin climb up the stairs whilst beside him sounded the drunken steps of the doctor. Eventually they settled into their separate bedchambers and their thumps and mumblings ceased.

I read on. Around me the house fell still and hushed. Suddenly a wail tore me off of my pillows. I whipped forward and half off my bed. It was Catlin, I swore it was Catlin who had cried. He must have had a nightmare, that was all. A door squealed open and swiftly I ran to mine own door and peered out. 'Twas Bess's that had screeched upon its hinges. She was standing in the hall, barefoot and wearing only her shift, as was I, and staring down the hall at Catlin's chamber.

Scarce could we move again when his door was flung open and he flew out, a candle in his hand and his eyes bulging, beads of sweat on his brow. His foot caught on nothing and he fell against the rail of the stair, and there he half crouched whilst the candle sputtered wax onto his unfeeling hand.

"Leave me alone!" he cried. "For God's sake can't you leave me alone! I'm already haunted more than enough!" He weakened, fell lower, wheezed.

Bess ran to him and threw her arms about him. "Catlin! What is it? God-a-mercy, how you're shaking!" When she pulled him closer he let go the rail and grabbed her arm. "No, no—you've nothing to fear now. You're safe."

" 'Twas a nightmare, that's all." I hurried to take away his candle, for he seemed ready to drop it in his trembling. "Now you're awake and safe."

"Oh, Sara, I was awake when my nightmare came to me!"

Bess pulled him up. "Come, we'll back to my chamber if you'll not back to yours."

"I'll not go back in there!" He violently gestured at his own bedchamber, which gaped dark and ope behind him.

"Then you'll sleep in my room," said Bess, "and I'll sit with you till you sleep again."

Bess and I walked him to her bed. He lay down, she sat beside him, and he calmed a little, as if knowing that as long as he was with her he was safe. I too sat with him till some time had passed and I could see that he wanted to tell her of his nightmare, or of something else. I'll leave them alone, I decided, and let the poor man unburden himself to Bess. I whispered to her that when he at last fell asleep she could come to sleep with me.

I was crossing the hall when I remembered me van Wouwere. God forbid that he'd heard any of that scene; it had revealed a part of Catlin I nothing doubted that doctor would exploit. I went to his door but all I could hear beyond it was snoring. He was too drunk to awaken.

I put more coals in my warming pan, curled up in my blankets, and waited for Bess to come to bed. The chimes in Our Lady's struck twice ere at last she came in. She sat down on my bed, wakeful and somber.

"What is it, Bess?" I asked softly.

She stirred. "What Catlin told me. What I had suspected: that he was only waiting. He had only for a little withdrawn, but now he's back. I sensed as much in the library. I told you I felt someone was present."

"What mean you? No one was there, and Catlin was below."

Bess rubbed her fretted brow. "Ah, Sara. Bless God for keeping him from you. You couldn't feel him as I could. You warned me not to pursue what haunted Catlin. But we're now too close and too much alike, so I knew that whatever haunted him might in time haunt me. It was a damned soul. That's what I felt in the library. It was him. I could feel his evil."

"Who do you mean?" A cold shudder moved up through my spine. "You say over and over 'he'."

She looked at me curiously. "Have you never suspected that a man's ghost does indeed walk this house? And one does walk, Sara. 'Tis the soul of the dead partner, Martin van den Bist."

I stared at her. "I'd thought that man's ghost walked only in Catlin's fevered mind. No. No, I don't want to believe it, and it sickens me to hear you talk so. I had thought sometimes that Catlin was now and again a little mad. Now I'm as fearful for you."

Bess gazed in the direction of her bechamber as if Catlin were calling her back. "Better to believe van den Bist walks than to think of me or Catlin as mad."

I could listen no more to such talk. I drew her down and told her to sleep, and then lay near her. The candle beside my bed I let burn, the black night being now too eerie for me. Again, all grew quiet. Somehow I slept, but only for a while. Then I oped my eyes, rolled to my other side, and realized slowly I was alone. "Bess?" I asked. She was gone. A knowledge creeped through my clearing mind. Slipping out of bed and pulling on my nightgown, I padded out of my room and across the hall to Bess's chamber. With stealth I turned the knob and swung slightly back the creaking door.

There lay Bess and Catlin, gently naked 'neath the half cast-off bedclothes. His breath was entwined in her hair, beside his chest her head rested, and around each other their limbs had fallen, exhausted and pale in the darkness. And in this way the two slept as if after a long, unnatural separation. I closed the door again and went back into mine own chamber.

A**fter a time** I opened my shutters to the dawn's light and sat on my bed. 'Twas not such a bad thing, what Bess and Catlin had done. Mayhap she had given some peace to him; mayhap this was indeed as I'd thought better than their swordplay. And withal, when I was young and ere I was married to my Jonathan, I had slept naked betwixt sheets with him. Of course when my mother discovered this she beat and scolded me, but still I would not regret what I'd done. Now Catlin and Bess had done the same.

No, not quite the same. Jonathan and I slept together only after our banns had been posted, as had many of our friends. Catlin and Bess had still not even spoken of marriage. And too again, they were not like other men and women. Catlin might be haunted by a ghost, as Bess had told me, but if not, then his mind was gravely afflicted, and though he was my friend and I loved him as such, something in me was still distressed when I saw my niece with him. What did Bess feel in herself, what disquieted her soul and made her such a preternatural companion to this man?

The light thickened; the day was here. A creak sounded out in the hall, and then my door squeaked open. Into the room stepped Bess, wearing only her shift and with her hair falling over her shoulders.

"Coming back to my bed ere I awake, Bess?" I said smoothly. "Too late for that. I know where you've been."

Wordlessly, she looked long at me. Then, putting on a serene air, she ambled to the window.

"I said, I know where you've been. I saw you with him."

"Then you know." She shrugged. "Should that matter to me?"

I laughed under my breath. "Oh, ever bold. You know how it matters to me!"

"Matters to you? Bold?" she scoffed, but like me she kept her voice low. "Forget you I'm a widow, a grown woman, and not a child you can rule? 'Tis my life, Sara. You have no say in it."

"I don't want to fight you, I truly don't. But I can't stand by and watch you become a lover to Catlin. 'Tis so sinful, Bess, so mortally wrong. If you and he were going to marry, well, I grant you that would be different."

She turned her face back to the window and closed her eyes.

"And that is all I'm asking."

She shook her head. Her feigned serenity was already gone and she was wringing the sides of her shift. "Marriage. There is so much to consider in marriage."

"You two have considered it?"

Her voice weakened. "I am so in love with him, Sara. So much in love that I ache."

"And he loves you?"

"Oh yes."

"Then you'll marry . . ."

"No, not yet, not that." The soft white linen was nigh tearing under her fingers. "The time will come, I hope—it will, and soon."

"But not now?"

"Now . . . No, he's not at peace."

I groaned. "How well I know that."

"Then you know . . ."

"I know you can't cure him of his ghost. You can't love away his obsessions. And he cannot cure your unquiet spirit either, Bess."

"And neither will marriage cure us, both he and I know that."

I shook my head. "I cannot live in this house if you become his lover. And if I leave, so too must you since e'en Catlin won't forbear a scandal."

"There'll be no scandal. No one else but you will know."

"Isn't it enough that I know?"

She was panting to hold back tears. She raked her hand through her hair, pulled at the open neck of her shift. "Stay here!" she both demanded and pleaded. "Stay in your bed at night. Perchance we'll not sleep together again for a time."

"And if you do?"

"You'll not know of it!"

"Sweet Jesus!" I gripped my head and tried not to scream at her. "How can I consent to that, Bess? I've already felt the hypocrite with what I've seen 'twixt you and him."

She reached out to grasp me but I whirled away from her. "Then we'll talk of marriage!" she cried. "Catlin and I will talk of it."

"That alone won't do. I must know."

"Can you not wait a little while? Only a month?"

I sank against my bedpost. All my thoughts and feelings were jumbling in too much confusion for me to fight her longer.

"A little time, Sara."

"After the New Year. Just after the New Year. And then we'll see."

She sighed and nodded. We remained now on opposite sides of the room, she staring out the window at nothing, I looking at her. Our emotions echoed so harshly in that tender morning air.

"I'm not e'en sure I should press so for marriage," I said dismally. "What will you be living with? A man who's left you before to go to a whore."

The words pained her. " 'Tis different now."

"Is it?"

That unearthly look came into her pale face. "You don't understand."

With that she left me. She stole back into her bedchamber, sat beside the fire, and waited for Catlin to awaken. Soon I could hear him rising and returning to his bedchamber.

An hour later, Bess and I were at the countinghouse, straining to behave as if naught had happened. We'd been in the back room some time when Jan entered.

"Put you my crate in the room above, Jan, as I wanted?" she asked.

He did not reply or look at her. Though doubtless he was pouting from her teasing the night before, she did not perceive this; she only loudly repeated her question. His head whipped around and his face swelled with peevishness. But a moment passed and he only grumbled, "Aye."

Bess recoiled. Finally she saw the damage she had done, that at present he needed to be left alone. She went upstairs and I with her.

"I bought my first glass from Venice," she told me proudly. " 'Twas dear, but worth the price." She found her crate, sat on another one, and with a bar began to loosen the nailed-down lid. Catlin entered the room. His walk was weary and his color was bleak 'neath his black hair and beard. With sad eyes Bess watched him approach before turning back to her crate. I myself now looked at him differently; for me he had changed because he had slept with my niece. By still being his warm and silent friend, I felt as if I were betraying my conscience.

"What have you there, Bess?" he asked.

"I'll show you." She laid the top aside. "I gather our friend Nicolas left when you did?"

"Aye. He also told me o'er breakfast that he foresees good health and business for me this month."

"God grant you that for many years," said I.

"Did he use his dice or astrology, or mayhap geomancy?" Bess asked. "I know he has many games and tricks."

"Not dice, yes to astrology, and yes to other means." He blinked as if his reddened eyes had a stinging in them. "I know you jeer his foretelling . . ."

"I do desire your good fortune!" she interrupted.

"But you've doubted him too much. In sooth, he's made for me other predictions I've never told you of because you'd only scoff. I lost a small item; he told me where to find it. I've had dreams potent with meaning; he read their symbols and what he explained would happen did indeed come to pass. In all, his advice has helped me."

Bess studied him. "Did you tell him of what passed last night, of Martin van den Bist?"

As if wine were still weakening his knees, Catlin sat down on a firkin. "Nay, not a word. But he talked of you. I must confess—and for this I'm sorry—but when we went into my library this morning he chanced upon your horoscope, that one you did yourself. In the margin he read the note of your hour and place of birth."

"Chanced upon?" she retorted. "I doubt that. He's long wanted to cast my horoscope."

"Well, he told me he thinks he will within the month and give it to you as a New Year's gift."

She leaned over her open crate and raked away the packing straw. "What a strange feeling that gives me, as if he were trapping me."

"A horoscope for a few months' time—what harm can it do?" Catlin sighed in exasperation.

"I want only my will to determine my future, not his figuring."

"Oh, Bess! He'll merely say which days are good for business, when to ship, when not to—the sort of advice any merchant seeks."

"That's not what he's seeking for me! What he wants to see in my stars is my whole future and all bad fortune that will strike me!"

"You seem convinced of his ill will toward you."

"Aye, of course I am. E'en you're aware of the evil in him and the ugly sporting that ties you two."

Catlin nigh squirmed. "He merely foretells things for me!"

"And that's his control o'er you—your obsession with fate and future gazing. He knows your weaknesses!"

"I'm not a fool, Bess. I confess I've suspected as much. Sometimes I've felt tainted merely by being with him. But he's fulfilled a need in me these past months."

"And what is that need? To drink—another of your weaknesses. To spend long hours where? With common drabs?"

He winced as if she had slapped him. "Think what you will. But for myself, there are times when I am so tightly wound I feel like to shatter into pieces. So he helps to ease my mind."

"He's helping you to destroy yourself. And by casting my horoscope, he hopes to do the same to me."

Catlin gave up and said naught.

As if to brush off the quarreling, Bess made a show of digging into the straw and pulling from the depths a cloth-covered bundle. Out of the cloth she then took a glass goblet with gold powdering that sparkled in the sunlight. "My first Venice glass." She held the thing up. "There be five more in here like this one. I'll wager they'll bring me a handsome profit in London."

Catlin cast an expert eye o'er the thing. "Aye, they must have cost you a pretty penny. I myself will soon be investing, by the by, in a tapestry bound for Cologne. A friend of Nicolas in that city has requested him to find him a good one."

"So the doctor has turned merchant for you now. All the easier to squeeze his claws around you."

"He has naught to do with this venture," said Catlin. "He told me his friend will pay well for good Flemish tapestry, so I'll send as much to him. I have a man in Cologne; he's my factor there and I am his in

Antwerp. I'll send the tapestry to him. He'll oversee the payment and assure its safe delivery. Nicolas has nothing to gain in any of this."

"But a deeper hold on you?" Bess quietly challenged.

"Nay, Bess. He doesn't know this yet, but this venture may be his last tie with me. When it ends, so too will our friendship."

Bess gazed at him and slowly smiled.

I seldom saw van Wouwere during the remainder of December, thank God, and in that time Bess seldom referred to him or the horoscope he was casting for her, but I could tell it was preying on her mind and setting her more and more on edge. He didn't visit Catlin's house again, though Catlin several times went to Solomon's Wisdom or somewhere else with him, and twice did not return till it was nigh dawn. When he then came home, he'd again too much wine on his breath, and a weary cynicism was lining his face. But come home at least he did, and if to Bess instead of a whore I didn't know and wouldn't ask. And too, as Bess had said, she seemed indeed to be taking him away from that astrologer. Bess was winning.

Christmas came and went, and the month and year were almost at an end. Two days before the New Year, when the short winter afternoon was dying, Bess and Catlin and I finished our tasks and made to go home. Erewhile we left, howe'er, one of Catlin's clients stopped by the countinghouse and invited him to supper. Catlin accepted, but first he accompanied us home.

As soon as he was gone Bess hurried to her bedchamber and pulled on a thick dark huke.

"Why are you wearing that?" I asked. "You don't mean to go out again?"

"Oh, but I do, Sara, and in this plain thing I'll pass for only a common Flemish woman and not a merchant with a purse full of money. And where I'm going there might be too many thieves who need no tempting."

"But where are you going?"

"To visit our dear Nicolas, of course."

"Aye, I've been expecting as much. You can no longer wait to hear your fortune."

"To hear what fate that lying, stargazing empiric has mixed for me. Whatever it is, he won't tell me about it freely so long as Catlin is present. So I'll go to him alone."

"But 'tis evening. 'Tis not safe for you to be out alone, not near the houses and streets where he lives."

"I'll be going by horseback since that is safer, and I'll pay for a groom to accompany me." She pulled on her gloves. "I'll be safer still, Sara, if you wish to come with me; and you do desire to come."

"Nay, not really." Indeed, I would as lief not see the man ever again. "I'm only too much of a worrying mother to you."

She smiled. "Well, then—you have a huke. Put it on."

Put it on I did, and left the house with her.

At the stables we secured two horses and on a third a groom to accompany us. He was a large, burly man, and too a silent one who seemed accustomed to being paid more for a tightly shut mouth than an open one. He kept close behind us, one hand on the knife at his waist, whilst at a brisk walk we set out toward Hoogstraat. About us was the thin traffic of people tramping through the snow, hugging their parcels or empty arms to warm themselves, or pushing carts with ice-hindered wheels. Shadows were crawling everywhere and turning as dark as the sky, and in windows candles took up their stations, like weak atomies bravely blinking against the immense evening beyond their walls of glass.

In good time we came to Hoogstraat; van Wouwere's house was around the corner. Just down the way, about the stews and taverns, there hung in the air laughter and loud talk and the sound of a night's revels beginning. We slowed our horses and turned down the narrow passage, but Bess didn't pull up before the door; instead she stopped in the shadow of a neighboring house.

"Why are we dismounting here, Bess?" I said whilst the groom helped me off my horse. " 'Tis so clandestine."

"That's how I want it. I want no familiar passersby—be they clients or apprentices or whoever—to see us at this place. Let's tarry a moment till all's clear."

So there in pitchy obscurity we stood, the groom holding the horses' reins, and Bess and I in our hooded robes. We were so wrapped up in their depths that I felt as though we had almost disappeared and only our white smoky breaths held us within the visible world.

Our wait was brief. Some drunken sailors tumbled by in the street beyond and vanished, and then a young man emerged from the doctor's house. He had a twitch in his neck and a palsy in his hands and he was grasping a bottle. As if the thing were filled with gold, he hurried away with it, nigh tripping someone coming toward the door. This second man was a short creature with a tumid chest balanced atop legs too small and thin not to buckle a bit under the weight they bore. He was like a wounded beetle, its limbs clambering forward 'neath its painfully rigid back. He glanced into our darkness, saw possible harm in our presence, and looked away as if afraid his eyes would draw as much to him. He opened the door and hobbled quickly inside.

"God's blood," Bess murmured. "What desperate people are drawn to this doctor."

At last we entered too. The servant glanced at us, by our hukes judging us to be not worth rising for, and only gestured that we seat ourselves on the bench. Bess tossed back her hood and opened her huke, and he perceived his error. Muttering apologies, he followed us to the bench with servile bows ere returning to his stool.

Two people besides us were waiting, as if accustomed oft to sitting in that chamber: the wounded beetle man and a lady's maid.

Our own short wait was stifling. The room seemed stuffed with the inhabitants' unhappiness, so that when laughter from a tavern once reached our ears ours was a shared unease for having heard so ill-fitting a sound within these walls.

The laughter had just flitted in again when the door to the doctor's chamber opened and out stepped a shy lady of mayhap thirty years of age. Her poor face was marred by dark hairs above her lips and a mole on the bridge of her nose. Her eyes wandered too much and she walked as if she were about to break. As would a babe to its mother, she went straight to her maid, who linked arms with her as together they left the house.

The old servant shuffled into the doctor's chamber, came out again, and bent down to the beetle man to plead with him to wait but a little more whilst the doctor saw these ladies. Then the servant showed Bess and me into the chamber beyond.

The same night-crawling shadows we had hidden in outside the house were in that room also. They were lying as if in unholy vigilance in the corners, along the beams of the ceiling and the edges of the floor. In the midst of the room, in the orange-yellow light thrown by candles and the high-crackling flames in the hearth, stood the commanding shape of the doctor. The light wavered over the silver-streaked hairs in his beard and bounded glimmering off his rings and his cross. Suddenly, horribly, I felt as if I were not merely in a physician's chamber but in some supernatural realm, filled as it was with so many queer things, herbs and strange powders and liquids, books and parchments, their uses, effects, and natures known to him alone, their minister.

Van Wouwere was holding his spectacles in one hand. He laid them on the table, grinned, and gestured for us to be seated. We both remained standing.

"I pray you ladies are well?" he asked.

"Oh, most well," Bess replied. "So you may wonder why we're visiting a physician."

He feigned to be disappointed. "You're not visiting me as a friend?"

"I have no friend here, though Catlin thinks he does. He told me too that you planned to give me my horoscope at the New Year."

Van Wouwere's grin became narrow and subtle, scarce there. "You've come early for your gift. Couldn't you wait any longer? You need not plan your days by it just yet, mevrouw."

"I've never planned my days or circumscribed my acts to follow your games."

"Then you've come to disparage your horoscope."

"Ah, you're closer, sir. I've come to disparage your interpretation of my horoscope and your prognostications."

His smile spread again in contempt. He moved a little, and in doing so stirred up the room's pungent smells of smoke and wax and herbs.

"Bartholomew doesn't know you're here with me now, at this hour and dressed as you are in common Flemish garb," van Wouwere said. "He'd have come with you had he known. Well, a sudden and secret visit from you then, and merely to scorn what you've not yet heard? I don't believe you, Mevrouw Marwick. In your heart, you urgently wish to hear what your future holds."

"I alone know what lies in my heart," Bess retorted.

"No, God alone knows. You, like all others, know yourself less than you think."

With a bored face she looked about the room. "I trow this be the first time I've heard you refer to God. In truth, of late I've wondered if you're in league with the devil. Certes you can have only evil purposes for attempting to read my future, since we are by unspoken agreement rivals for Catlin. Your horoscopes may lure him into a friendship with you, but not me."

"Ah, but my casting your stars lured you here, didn't it?" he replied. "And now you'll stay when I tell you that I had very disturbing forebodings and dreams about you. They moved me to look into your future. You'll of course wish to know how . . ."

"I know already," Bess interrupted. "You think you read my stars."

"I read them and more. I'm an astrologer, and a better one than any physician you're like to meet, and a geomancer and diviner of dreams, and more. By these means, and by mine own gift"—slowly he opened his star-palmed hand and held it beside his dark face like an ominous sign—"I searched and discovered that you have a most marked fate." He walked to the shelf whereon sat the death's head and the books beneath it, and with the same hand held down the skull that it would not topple off, and with the other fingered through the pages of a book; from it he drew a few papers. He unfolded them upon the table, laid side by side, looked at them, up at her, and in dramatic mummery said nothing.

It was then I perceived that one paper was filled with a horoscope and symbols and words in an unfamiliar hand, belike his own, and that the other had on it a similar chart writ in a hand I knew.

"That paper was written by Bess," said I, pointing to the second sheet.

"Is it?" Bess stepped closer to the table. "In sooth, it is. 'Tis an old horoscope of mine I scribbled out one day." She swelled with anger. "How came you by it? Why do you have it?"

"I found it at Bartholomew's house," he replied, "and thought it might be useful to me."

"So you stole it!" she accused.

"I borrowed it. You may have it back if you like."

"Nay. 'Tis as worthless as you."

I didn't like this at all. I wanted to take her paper away from him, for such a thing in his possession could become malignant. But Bess was too angry to perceive this.

"What manner of doctor are you," she exclaimed, "that you more oft spend your time on such arts—forbidden arts—than on healing or pain-soothing physic?"

"I will give you a twofold answer," he replied. "The first part of mine answer is that I am a skilled physician who must study at least the art of astrology if my physic is to be efficacious. The second part is that these arts help me to descry the natural state of my patients' health. For example, Mevrouw Marwick, you have no child, or none that has lived, and you fear you never will, do you not? I believe you are barren."

Bess did not flinch, though the words were a hard blow. I was aghast at the doctor's cruelty, at the disdain with which he dismissed her womb's disorder. Furious, I lashed back.

"Is this how you treat your patients' ills, by such vicious bluntness? And think you that I believe 'tis by your arts alone you could have known she is childless? Catlin or someone else could have told you that she'd never borne a child that lived—I know Catlin would have told you nothing more—and from that common fact you rashly concluded, to your delight, that she is barren. Whether or no she is I can't know. But neither can you, since you're no true doctor. 'Tis a physician's trade to heal, not to inflict wounds."

"If that is what I do," he said, and pointed to the chamber beyond, "then why do so many patients come to me?"

"I've seen your patients!" Bess snapped. "They come to you who would come to any doctor: the sick, the maimed, the deformed, the ugly and pathetic; and if they have money you will look to their complaints. Many a doctor would be honest and tell them not only what he can do for them but what he cannot do. But you offer cures where there can be none. You measure out with your drams and scruples and mix up in your bottles a useless potion, which the poor sots quaff with vain hope and undeserved faith in you. Not when they're cured, but when they have no more money, then you are done with them!"

"You are rattling ignorant falsehoods!" Van Wouwere did not shout, yet his voice shook my bones. "Only licensed physicians are allowed to practice in Antwerp, and I am not only licensed but have studied at more universities than any other physician in this city. Ask about and people will tell you I have effected many cures, and have eased much pain, and have reversed the malignant progression of many a disease. You speak of people who come to me with a sick heart and soul. Those same people take such illnesses first to their confessors and the saints, and to God. They pray to God from every church. When the saints do not intercede, when God does not answer, when the priests give them only comforting words and holy relics, which ofttimes these patients must pay for, then they come to me. I give them no unseen, spiritual hope. Nay, the hope I give them I embody with paper, with charms and amulets, with numbers and words they can read, balms they can feel, medicines they can drink. When they come to me their hopes have been beaten ragged and they've too little faith left to squander."

"Still they squander it on you!" Bess hurled back at him.

"How can you claim that? Are you a learned physician? Tell me, prithee, all you know of the Doctrine of Signatures, of logic and physiology, of the letting of blood and of purging . . ."

"Oh, Doctor," Bess cried, "I know full well how you should be purged. You give hope? Is that what you gave that woman who was in here ere us? The one with the weak mind and plain face? I trust you gave her hope in the form of medicinal trinkets that cost her dearly."

His arm shot out and pointed at the bottles, boxes, and things covering his table. "I give her love philters, for which she asks. If I don't give them to her, she'll go elsewhere for them, and to those men who have not my knowledge in the arts, nor my powers. Even my love philters have in them an efficacy. With them, she will attract to her a man."

"Marry, how easy it must be to convince such a woman that your potions work. You merely have to display yourself the effect her philter has on you."

"My physic and philters are potent! I know the astrological signs well. Only when the stars are propitious do I make my physic and gather my herbs. I e'en dig for herbs at night if the planets bid me to."

"And so too does any doctor. But what doctor works with charms and amulets and claims to have power in the magic of a star-marked hand? What other doctors go from the necessary astrology into the divining kind? You are naught but a sorcerer! A necromancer! 'Tis black magic that you practice!"

His face swelled with such a scarlet-burning fury that he seemed about to burst. For a moment his hands quivered, almost swung as if to strike Bess down, but the next moment an eerie control came over him again, and he only laid his hand upon his spectacles and put them on, their circles of glass, like the bottles about him, flashing reflections of light. Then he took up one of the papers. "Such passion isn't good for you, mevrouw, as you should have learned by now. *Passiones animi* is caused by the uterus, which in turn can render the uterus barren. Yet even after such damage, still your female organs can give a woman's thinking strange perturbations. Should I calm you now with mine own masculine science?" He made an ugly smile. Then, as if announcing an irrevocable decree, his voice rumbled forth.

"This year is ending, the next is coming. Before the next year is three-quarters spent, thou wilt have suffered injustices and hardships. Thy money thou wilt lose, thy wealth vanish. Thou shalt be forced to go a-begging amongst those who will only harm thee. In this chapter of thy fate I see a whore and a cleric, a whore and a cleric who shall be the agents of thy fate. But poverty thou shalt not suffer long, for ere the eleventh month ends, thou shalt die a bloody woman's death. I see, too, thou shalt die a lonely death."

Bess turned as white as a dying night moth. Her breath came in short and shallow pants. The desperate need to disbelieve crossed her eyes and she grasped at it frantically. Suddenly I saw a rage in her. Her body shuddered and her face dreadful and her eyes wild.

"The devil take your hide to hell where it belongs!" she cried. "By God, you are cursed! You are in league with the devil, and for teaching you some paltry tricks he'll carry you down into the pit! Damn your pride and arrogance! Do you truly believe you can usurp God's powers and have of my life as you please, decide my fate as it amuses you? Oh, and it amuses you. These vain prophecies are only manifestations of your hatred for me, and that's why I came here tonight: Because I know you want your revenge. I've slighted you. I've laughed at you and all your pretensions. I've scoffed at you with Catlin when you're not about. All these things have stung your pride. So you trundle out your games and proclaim your hollow prophecies and savor the revenge. But I've foiled you! I knew what the nature of your 'gift' would be, so I came to receive it now, before the revelry of the New Year, without Catlin about, with no one about whom you could impress. So your revenge is as hollow as your prophecies. Go on, Doctor—practice your tricks and recite your predictions, but I'll none of them!"

She flung on her huke and spun about as if to fly out of that damned place, but ere she could, van Wouwere spoke one more time.

"You can run from me. You can try to leave behind my prophecies. But still your fate is in you. For as it is with everyone, you are fated to be yourself, and that is a fate you can never escape."

Bess rushed from the room, and I with her. But as we fled out of the house and into the night, and e'en as her bold words rang in mine ears, I could not hold them to heart. We were running only into the illusion of escape, I feared, and before us were dangers we were blind to, dangers e'en more dreadful than the ones van Wouwere had just laid upon Bess.

XXI

On the Eve of the New Year, Catlin and Bess and I took to the streets and joined with the throngs of strangers in their boisterous festivities. All over the city people roamed, tucked into fantastic clothes and beaked and horned masks, glittering the black night with laughter and mischance and mischief. We felt as if we were sweeping headlong into a parade of dream stuff, of odd angels and motley beasts and the unreal creatures of half-enchanting, half-terrifying tales. The music of singing and bellowing and rattling was everywhere. Everywhere too in that haze of velvet darkness was the lace of luminous snow, bejeweled with the amber of burning torches and flashes of color.

I wore no costume and neither did Catlin, but in a dare with him Bess had donned one of his hats and pulled on over her clothes a doublet, jerkin, and cloak of his, and hanging from her waist, as from his, was a rapier. Then, swaggering like a youth, she wandered the streets with us.

"God's blood!" she yelped just as we were entering a crosspath, and she whipped out her sword and spun about. Trotting hastily away from her was a man dressed as a blue monster.

"What's wrong?" cried Catlin.

"That man!" Bess sputtered.

I laughed at her frustration. "Did he pinch your bottom?"

"Oh!" Bess shouted.

"Put back that sword!" Catlin laughed. "Wouldst run a man through because of a pinch?"

Bess lowered the rapier. "Nay, just frighten him," she said gleefully.

"And put it back in its sheath," said he, "lest a night-watch arrests you."

"I'll not be arrested. Clearly I'm but a jesting woman playing in part a man." She tipped up the blade again and looked around as if for a target, but all that was near her was a house, stiff in its glassy coat, its icicles pointing downward like disapproving fingers. With a swift cry she sliced at a window, and a handful of icicles cracked and fell tinkling into the snow.

"Fence with me, Catlin!" she demanded exuberantly. "A game of swords would be marvelous good now."

"Are you mad? Then indeed we would both be arrested."

"No we won't! Not on this night and with me in my skirts. Any night-watch could see we are but playing."

He studied her face, which was impassioned and eager with life, and as if knowing she would not be denied, he whipped out his own rapier. "Then fence it is!" he cried. He moved into the middle of the crosspath, raised his blade, and with eyes as glistering as hers, wordlessly challenged her to take him.

A laugh tumbled out of Bess and she approached him cautiously. Her wrist moved slowly around so that her blade carved hoops in the air. A streak! and her sword had slashed at his and he had pushed off the blow.

The swords did not stop but poked and sliced and clanged. Catlin called out an instruction and she nimbly responded. He stumbled and she paused ere moving again at him. I could see at once that they'd played at swords more oft than I had thought, and though they were but playing, a fervor was swelling in Bess. Her eyes were ever on Catlin's sword, and she was striking at it again and again—as if at van Wouwere, methought. In minutes she was panting, a smoky vapor swirling from her mouth and into the night. All about us silver reflections from the blades darted across the snow and ice. Still she swung her rapier.

The people near us on the street had laughed upon first seeing their sporting, but now they avoided them and moved away, as if warned off. I called out to Bess to stop her fighting. She would not or could not hear me. I shouted to Catlin, "Enough of this!" He slowed, gasped for breath, held up his hand for Bess to stop. Only then did she do so.

I smiled with strained mirth. "Marry, your fencing may keep you warm, but I'm close to freezing from standing here and watching you."

"Some hot drink would do us all good," Catlin suggested.

"Posset," panted Bess as she slid her rapier back into its sheath. "Methinks I saw somewhere about here a man selling hot posset."

"Please, Catlin, see for us where he is," said I.

He gave us a comical bow and went down the street, leaving Bess and me with the revelers who were already dancing near us again.

"Well," said I, "I pray you've finished with this fighting."

She shrugged. "Aye, for tonight."

" 'Tis not a womanly pastime. 'Tis not e'en a good pastime for many men."

"But a good one for me."

"There is danger in it."

"Ah." She tipped back her head and smiled up at the cloudy half-moon. "Bloody danger, and bloody death. But since this isn't a woman's pastime, Sara, it cannot be a woman's death. Still I am flirting with danger, you think, because of that cursed empiric's windy prophecies. He spun them out of empty air."

"You have no faith in them? By all that is holy, I'm trying to forget them."

"Good. Do so. For myself—I have faith in me, not in van Wouwere."

"I know of your faith," I reminded her. "It has frayed holes wherein creep many a doubt."

"Then perchance I can weave a stronger faith. Sweet Jesus!" She laughed and swirled about. "What airy talk is this, full of allegory. I've had today my stomach full of allegories and symbols. We went to the Tapestry Pand today, you know—Catlin and I. He was searching for a tapestry for van Wouwere's friend. A group of master weavers showed him their best one, which of course had a scene full of allegory, and 'twas that one he seeks. 'Tis huge and beautiful, but the price!"

"Is it dear?"

"Dear! It isn't at all like the tapestries you and I have dealt with, at a few shillings an ell. This one is fit for a king and shot through with gold and silver threads."

"Then it must indeed be costly."

"Aye—seven hundred Flemish pounds."

I was astonished. "Seven hundred? That is nigh the same in English sterling. 'Tis three times what my home and countinghouse in London are worth."

"And with the cost of duties and shipping the thing, he'll be spending more than that ere he sees his money back, let alone his profit, which I daresay will be an admirable one." The warmth stirred in her by the fencing was ebbing, and she opened her cloak to draw the doublet closer around her. Its deep seawater green was a sparkle of brightness 'gainst her loose black hair.

"Have you told Catlin yet of van Wouwere's prophecies?" I asked.

She tied shut her cloak, so that like a candle the doublet was snuffed out. "Not yet. You and I might proclaim our unbelief in them but Catlin has a queer faith in that man's horoscopes and tricks, and he may believe those false prophecies and fear for me. Too, he may become furious with van Wouwere and confront him, or e'en attack him. Then van Wouwere would want revenge on Catlin, too. No, I'll not have that. And he knows how Catlin would act, so he'll keep his silence. I can tell Catlin of what van Wouwere told us when their friendship is ended, and it will end soon. Catlin praises him not at all now and e'en makes fun of him with me. 'Tis the doctor's arts he clings to, and the doctor's role of a drinking companion." She smiled to herself. "But no longer a whoring companion."

The very thought of that was ugly to me. "That he ever was—'tis why I still sometimes wonder if you should marry him."

"But that is my decision to make, not yours."

"And his, too."

She lowered her sword and began to scrape a pattern into the snow. Though she dislike to speak of this, I still pressed her.

" 'Tis only just now the New Year, I know. But mayhap you should tell me now, Bess. Will you marry him?"

She looked down at the pattern she had scraped, through a nearby window at the revelers on its other side, at aught but me. "I will marry him, Sara." Her soft answer was nigh lost in her white breath. "That I know."

"You know? Oh Jesus, I gather your meaning. He hasn't yet asked you."

"We both avoid the matter. 'Tis still too soon and van Wouwere is yet between us. But in this new year"—she smiled and spread her arms as if gathering it to herself—"I know we'll marry."

"Oh, Bess. To me that answer smacks of folly."

She turned back to me. "Haven't I known rightly many things

before! I understood Catlin's friendship with van Wouwere from the start. I was right that I could take Catlin away from him. And I know I could give Catlin some peace."

"What peace? E'er since we moved into his house, you two seem to have made each other only sleepless with obsessions. You've fevered each other, what with all your endless book reading and star casting and so on, and late into the night."

"But we haven't been like that these last weeks, have we, Sara? Catlin retires now with us and sleeps the night through. Now, since I have been with him . . ."

"Slept with him."

". . . he's been changing."

"And all because of one night, Bess? Or have there been other nights?"

At first she wouldn't answer, then said, "What should matter to you is that he has now some tranquility."

"Does he? Is he truly laying his ghost to rest—whether in reality or in his mind—or is his present state only the calm before the storm?"

Her lips parted, closed, as if I had struck too near her heart. Long seconds passed.

"I don't know. I don't know." Her remark seemed almost a lamentation. "You are right to speak of storms. I am so afraid, so wretchedly afraid that there is a storm in him that may yet break out, and I might lose him in it."

"Lose him to the storm of his obsessions." I sighed. "And you're so close to him, and have your own obsessions, that he may drag you in with him."

Unwilling to believe this, she shook her head. She slid the sword back into its sheath and with her foot rubbed away the snowy pattern. Then Catlin emerged from the shadows and called to us he had found the posset vendor. With sudden joy Bess ran to his side and in a trice both were swallowed up in a crowd of gamboling, carousing revelers. I heard Bess scream with delight and her scream then buckle into laughter. I hurried to join them.

During January Catlin wrote to van Wouwere's friend, who wrote back that the tapestry was precisely what he wanted. He instructed Catlin to buy it, and buy it Catlin did.

I saw it when it was delivered to the countinghouse a week or so after the purchase. I arrived there alone, having left Bess at a nearby shop, and came upon the spread-out tapestry in the back room. On either side of it were Jan and Michiel, who were about to roll it up into the protective wrapping of the canvas lying beneath it. 'Twas a beautiful work, with gold and silver and silk threads woven into a picture of rich-colored trees and flowers, horses and hunters. As Bess had said, there was allegory in it, and every man was within his predestined, measured-out place.

"Your master chose well," said I to the apprentices. Then I went to Catlin's office, desiring his advice about some matter, but found the door closed and heard within the muffled sound of conversation. So I sat down to work in my ledger until he was free, and looked up only when came the sound of the entrance door opening.

Into the room stepped a man and a woman. Apparently they were husband and wife, and more apparently they were not merchants, for by their clothes I judged them to be an English gentleman and his lady. Their deliberate air told that they meant to conduct business, yet 'neath that was a wariness; they cast too many glances about them and the husband looked back out into the street ere closing the door behind them. Upon seeing me the wife smiled quickly, and as quickly turned to her husband in expectation that he speak to me.

He hesitated, then said with effort, "*Je veux voir Monsieur Catlin.*"

"Master Catlin is in," I replied. "I believe you are English, as am I."

He smiled with relief, but the feeling vanished swiftly behind his caution. "Aye, my wife and I are both English. Be you Master Catlin's wife?"

"Oh no, not at all. He is my factor. I too am waiting for him. He is for the nonce with someone else."

"I see. Well, mistress, if we may, we will wait with you."

The two of them sat down on the stools near a window. She kept her hands buried in her lap; he kept his clasped to his knees; and a worrying held still their tongues. I pitied them, so ill at ease did they seem. Neither appeared accustomed to Antwerp or to winter traveling, and they struck me as being somewhat dazed and lost and meek and their middle-aged faces, soft and kind, too easily beaten raw by the cold. They should be back in England and in their house and beside the fire, I thought.

"Are you newly come to Antwerp?" I asked.

"We are, aye, we are." The man cleared his throat. "Our ship docked just this morning. What a great city this is. I had been told of its grand size, but the telling did not ready me for the seeing of it. Is much French spoken here?"

"Flemish is of course the language of Antwerp, but French after that. Save for the English merchants here, almost no one speaks our language. German and Italian are common. Speak you those tongues?"

"Some German," the wife replied, then seemed to regret that much.

"We've come to Antwerp only for a few weeks, just for a while," her husband said, and added, "We came for business purposes." Then he glanced at his wife as if uncertain how to explain her. "My wife wished to see the things that can be bought here. I fear she might spend all my money if I watch her not."

Both of them laughed too much at this small jest. As we talked on, I perceived that the man did not seem to have any real business with Catlin and would not say why he wished to meet with him. I mentioned the English House, and he said he and his wife would frequent it whilst in the city. Still I deducted, not so much by his words as by his manner, that the two of them knew more of the English House than they claimed and in fear would avoid it. A suspicion was forming in me. More and more Protestants were of late exiling themselves from England and the harsh laws there that threatened them. This couple could be amongst those exiles, and could have been told to seek out Catlin for help.

He had abandoned his secret shipping of Protestant pamphlets but I had not thought whether or no he was beginning to offer aid to such people, like many Englishmen living abroad. But sans doubt, if my suspicion was correct 'twas unwise to leave them sitting long by the window, where the wrong passerby might see them and in whose house they were being sheltered.

"Master Catlin should be finished soon," said I. "Perchance I should inform him that you are waiting for him."

I knocked on the office door, aware that both of them were anxiously watching me. Catlin was behind his desk, and sitting opposite was Nicolas van Wouwere. I was startled, and when he looked up and his eyes met mine, the message I had prepared to give Catlin fled my mind.

"Doctor van Wouwere," said I awkwardly.

"Mevrouw Lathbury."

"Your pardon for interrupting, but I need only to tell Mynheer Catlin that I must see him soon. Oh," I added, as if remembering something, and spoke in English to Catlin, "there is an English couple here to visit you. I believe you'd wish to see them soon."

No questioning was in Catlin's face as he acknowledged this; he had gathered my meaning. "We're nigh done," said he in Flemish.

"Aye, we are," agreed van Wouwere. He had been holding a letter which I could see was in Catlin's hand and was now folding it and slipping it into his doublet. "An excellent letter is this. I thank you for making this copy for me yourself."

That I at once disliked. First he had a paper written by Bess and now one by Catlin. I was certain no good could come from his possession of such things, he with his black art and mysteries; they were like small pieces of them both over which van Wouwere had control.

"Sith you've already read it through three times, a copy was scarcely necessary," said Catlin as he folded and sealed the original for posting.

"Forgive me, my friend, but I am so unfamiliar with the many parts of merchants' work, and it doth interest me." He picked up the ring with a signet with which Catlin sealed all his letters and idly studied it; this too I disliked. "Your agent in Cologne seems most capable. Mine own friend there will be pleased with the efficient fulfillment of this deal, and too with the tapestry you chose. But I'll not keep you any longer, Bartholomew, for I know you're as busy a man as am I."

They rose and followed me from the room.

"And the tapestry you mean to ship on the morrow?" van Wouwere asked.

"On the morrow," said Catlin. "It will leave for Cologne in the care of a transporting firm to which I ofttimes entrust my goods."

"Excellent."

In the outer chamber Catlin glanced at the couple, who at his and the doctor's entrance had risen a whit too hastily. Van Wouwere seemed intent on lingering.

"I pray you pardon me, Nicolas, but I must no longer keep these good people waiting," said Catlin.

"Of course." He pushed his hand into a glove. "Oh, whilst I think on't—I shall not be able to see you tonight, nor tomorrow. Too many of my patients are sick with agues and fevers—common winter illnesses—that need attending. The next day, mayhap?"

"Mayhap." Catlin was not disappointed. He directed the couple into his office and shut himself away with them.

Unhappily, I was left alone with van Wouwere, for still was he drawing on his gloves and examining their fit. I returned to my ledger with the intention of fetching it and going to the back room, but he spoke ere I lifted the book.

"I pray Mevrouw Marwick is well."

I wanted to feign deafness but did not. "She is well, 'spite your worthless prayers, if indeed you pray at all."

"Oh, we all have our prayers, but only saints dare utter theirs. Mevrouw Marwick, I daresay, has prayers in her that are best left unsaid."

"What prayers she has she says to a different God from the one to whom you pray."

"Ah, but we all have a different God. Or, I should say, everyone has the one God, but each gives Him a different face. Your niece, howe'er, is afraid to look upon the face she has created."

"You touch on blasphemy," I retorted.

"No, I touch on that which few men will admit, that is all. Good morrow to you, mevrouw." He gave me a mocking bow, and I watched his broad form stride away down the street whilst cursing him under my breath and entertaining a wish to do him violence.

"Is the doctor gone?" Michiel's voice broke in upon my thoughts.

"He is."

"I saw the doctor in a silversmith's shop yesterday," said he, as if reporting on a venture. "He'd several vessels of silver before him, and I assumed he was buying them—or perchance was selling them."

"And did you watch him for very long?"

"Only when I realized the dealing would involve much money. My master might have had need to know whether or no someone with whom he deals is secure or insecure in his affairs of finance." He was crisp and proper.

"Happily, your master does not have aught to do with van Wouwere's money, much of it, I trow, ill-gotten from patients who should never seek his help."

Michiel nodded. "I heard him boasting only this morning of the large fees his richest patients have paid him of late and the jewels he'll buy with them."

"What a vain villain," said I.

I did not see van Wouwere, nor did Bess, for nigh the rest of January. Then we went one day to the cloth-selling houses close upon where he lived, and needing then to go to the English Quay, had to pass near the Street of the Stews. In a muddy lane we came upon a common tavern, out of which was spewing the hard noise of drunken men, and we quickened our steps. But a bundle of a man staggered out and almost fell upon us as we were hastening by the open door. It was van Wouwere.

His bousy eyes wandered, then sharpened on us, and a glint came into them and a grin across his face. For only a startled second did I look at him. Then without saying a word we stepped around him.

"Why, Mevrouw Marwick," he exclaimed, "such a grim face!"

I could feel the hairs bristling up and down my neck. We had taken only a few steps when he spoke again, this time in a tone scraping with disdain. "I do pray, Mevrouw Marwick, that what I told you when last we met is not the cause of such grimness."

Bess stopped and snapped over her shoulder, "The only thing you have cause for in me is disgust."

"Oh, not true, not true at all! My foretelling has affected you far more than that."

Bess spun around. "You've no effect on me. I will not let you."

Van Wouwere's grin twisted at the edges, and he moved his heavy shoulders so that the abundant fur on his cloak shifted like an animal coming back alive. A dread of impending danger stole through me. I wanted Bess to say no more to him. I pulled on her elbow, but she shifted away from me.

"My prophecies will not wait for you to 'let' them come to pass!" he scoffed.

"They're as absurd as you!" A rage was growing in her, but 'neath it I could indeed hear the fear she had of his prophecies. "You're naught but a drunken scoundrel!"

"Do not insult me!" he shouted. He moved toward her menacingly. "Did you not learn the last time that I'll not forbear your insults?"

I wanted to grab Bess and run. But she was several feet away from me by then and as I moved toward her I slipped on a patch of ice and fell hard against a wall. As I gasped for the air knocked out of me, van Wouwere threw his bulk upon Bess and pinned her against the opposite wall, his hands holding fast both her arms.

"For I'll thus do with you what I please!" he cried. Then—all in seconds—he tried to press his open mouth to hers, let go one of her hands so he could grope for her breasts, and pushed his body against hers. But he had scarce touched her when a wild savagery burst out of Bess, and with her free hand she clawed his cheek and from it grabbed a handful of beard and ripped it out. He yelped in pain. Both his hands flew to his cheek and the blood spurting from it. She did not stop. As he staggered away she lurched toward his throat with her hands curled like claws. He lifted his cumbrous load and scuttled away down the street.

Mine arms flew around Bess to keep her from pursuing him. She was straining against me and panting, and her fury still was unleashed. I looked about us. No one else had been in the lane, but in the street beyond some people were passing by.

"What in God's name was he trying to do to you?" I exclaimed. "And where people could have seen him!"

"To humiliate me!"

"Well, you more than struck him back."

Her face was a dreadful thing. "I'm not done with him yet!" she cried.

I was trying to think. "We must go to the city sheriff."

"No! Catlin would become involved, and authorities and van Wouwere both might bode ill for him. No, 'tis only Catlin now who must be told of this."

We knew that Catlin was elsewhere that morning but would be returning home at noon, and so home we went and there waited for him. Two hours dragged by, during which Bess not only tamed her fury but became almost cheerful. "What van Wouwere did will finally destroy what remains of his friendship with Catlin," she said.

"That I'll welcome," I rejoined. "But Catlin will also want to attack van Wouwere, and God knows in what way."

She was not much troubled by this. "Oh, he'll try to give van Wouwere a deserved beating, but for his own sake I'll restrain him."

"Restrain him?" I scoffed. "You cannot control him, just as he cannot control you."

Finally Catlin came home. He plodded up the stairs, grumbling under his breath about the incompetent merchants with whom he had dealt that morning and the shifty ones he would wrangle with in the afternoon.

Bess greeted him in the entrance to the antler room. "I met van Wouwere this morning," said she.

"And little enjoyed the encounter, I can tell." He gave her not a glance but only walked past her into the room. "Well, I saw him too. But you'll be pleased to know that we'll not see him again for at least a fortnight."

"We won't?"

He dropped into a chair and heaved a leg up onto the table beside him. What little patience was in him was already draining away with every word he spoke. "He's just left for Brussels. I saw him an hour ago, and he told me he was leaving immediately to tend a sick friend there."

"That such a friend e'en exists I doubt." With her hands on her hips, Bess sauntered over to Catlin. "But I do believe he's left Antwerp, and I know why. When you saw him, had he a bald, bloody patch on his cheek?"

Catlin looked up at her. "How knew you that?"

"Because I put it there when he attacked me."

His leg crashed onto the floor. "Attacked you?" he repeated.

"Aye, because I angered him." Her own anger was rising again. "So in the street he forced me against a wall and tried to kiss me and feel me with his hands."

With a jolt Catlin was on his feet.

"But I paid him back, Catlin!" she cried ere he could speak. "Ere he could harm or humiliate me, I bloodied him and sent him running!"

"He touched you in that way!" Catlin was enraged.

"And I stopped him and ripped out his beard! Aye! Now at last will you have done with him?"

As Bess had looked when van Wouwere assaulted her, so now Catlin looked; his burning face was frightful. Then in the next second he was before Bess and his hands were holding her face. "You are not harmed?" he asked her softly. "He did not hurt you?"

"He tried to but failed. I am well."

"I will not let you be harmed." His eyes were locked with hers, then he stepped back, rage again surging. "He dared to touch you!" His shout shattered against the walls. "I will not forbear it! He will suffer for what he did!" He spun about and strode quickly to the wall whereon hung the two sheathed rapiers.

"But you will not!" cried Bess, flinging herself upon him. "I will not let you suffer!"

"He is no match for a fight, Bess! And when I'm done with him he'll not dare tell anyone who thrashed him!"

Bess grabbed Catlin's arm, but still he pulled down a sword and held it away from her grasp.

"But he's left Antwerp!"

"I'm riding after him!" He jerked his arm free from her, shoved the sheathed rapier beneath his belt, next to the shorter sword already hanging there. He looked into her eyes, and again his hands rose and held her face and he kissed her long and violently. In the next moment he was running out of the room and down the stairs.

"Catlin!" Bess called after him. But I too had by then reached the landing, and clasped her to hold her back.

"Let him go, Bess!" I urged, wrestling to restrain her. "There's naught else you can do."

"I'm going with him!"

"No, you are not! You know he doesn't want you to follow him."

For a moment she struggled still, and then at last relented.

We spent the rest of the day only waiting since the neither of us could fix our thoughts on any work. I let the hours shrivel away whilst I drifted from one distraction to the next. I knitted half a mitten and sewed up a torn hem. I tried fitfully to read from a scattering of books. I wrote a letter to my sons, but it sounded so melancholy that I threw it onto the hearth. I talked with Lijsken, sorted through the clothes in my bedchamber, took a long bath. Still I found myself, time and again, sitting down in the antler room and only waiting. Bess did nothing much more than wait too, pace the room, watch the traffic in the street below. In tiny, endless pieces the day dwindled away, and nigh imperceptibly twilight crawled into the house and into the room, implanting shadows that grew long about us till I felt lost in them. I lit some candles and watched their flames. In the distance the hour bell clanged. In another hour the city gates would be closed against the night, and Catlin could not get into Antwerp till morning. The heavy air of waiting that was stifling us now became veined with tension. Bess and I began to give sudden head turns at every noise.

Again I raised my knitting needles; my hands would not lie still and needed purpose. But after only four more rows my ball of yarn had rolled to its end and so I rose and went up toward my bedchamber to fetch some more. Since my mind was still wandering elsewhere I had not thought to bring with me a candle, but the edges of the stairs were dimly outlined and the fire in my hearth would doubtless cast light enow for me to find my yarn. I reached the top of the stairs and found the latch of my door.

A thump at the bottom of the stairs startled me. 'Twas a heavy footstep. Then there was another and another; someone was walking up the stairs. I turned to see who it was. Shafts of orange light sifted up from the antler room. I could see the stairs and to my horror no one was on them—but still those unseen feet thumped up the stairs, one by one, louder and louder. I faced untenanted air. Out of terror my eyes could no longer move but only stare wildly down the stairs. One final footstep came upon the landing and toward me, and then two more. Then they stopped.

I could not breathe. I had no voice and could not scream. Whatever insubstantial, unhuman thing there was was but inches away and looking at me and I was too terrified e'en to raise my eyes to where its eyes might be. I could see nothing. I wanted to see nothing. I wanted to pray silently but could not.

A whishing suddenly sounded upon the floor—an unseen foot was turning—and the steps began again, thumping around and down the hall toward Catlin's bedchamber. Shafts of light fell between the railings and across the hall, but no body, no form, or aught that was quick and palpable disturbed them. Only those echoing steps gave signal that something was there still, walking now away from me.

My heart burst and my breath wheezed out in a voiceless cry and at last my wooden limbs broke and I hurtled myself down the stairs and away from those damned ghostly footsteps. On the landing below I nigh fell against the doorframe.

Bess had jumped to her feet and was looking anxiously at me. "Did you hear something?" she asked.

"What?"

"Is Catlin back? Is that why you ran down the stairs?"

"No, I . . . I . . . ." My heart was hammering so painfully that 'twas all I could do to get my wits about me. "I thought I heard him below but I was wrong."

I looked out a window as if in search for him. Then I turned about, surrounded by misty light and in Bess's company, to face the open door. No one was there; the footsteps were no more, and the house was quiet once again. Crouching down nearer the embers of the fire, throwing a log on them to stir up more light, I tried to warm my shaking hands and burn out of my face the horror that must still have been upon it. Should I tell Bess about the footsteps? And if I told her? She would say they belonged to Martin van den Bist, that his sleepless soul was walking the house in search of Catlin. I did not wish to believe that. When I had turned around only to see those empty stairs below me, I had wanted to see Catlin. I had wanted to think that it was Catlin come home. At that a new fear streaked through me. What if it had been Catlin? Mayhap he had come to harm somewhere. Mayhap he had been killed in his hotspurred pursuit and that which I had heard was his soul come home. No, oh no. Far better to believe it was van den Bist who had come so near to me, and that whilst his ghost walked the house Catlin was safe; this was my bleak solace.

I was calming and I pulled away from the stinging heat. How much time had passed I could not judge, yet it seemed that far too soon the hour bell was ringing again. The dull sound pierced our ears as sharply as a needle. Bess went yet again to a window, gazed below, sighed, moved away. Then came the trotting of a horse. The hooves clacked down the street and stopped outside the door.

"Catlin!" Bess's cry was like thunder in the subdued house. She sped down the stairs whilst I went hurrying behind her, relief breaking out on me like a sweat.

She flung open the front door. On the step stood Catlin, weary, mud-beslubbered, squinting against the light falling out on him. He shuffled inside, and Bess wrapped her arms around him and helped him to the parlor. There she took off his damp cape and he dropped into the chair beside the fire and turned his face toward its warmth. Bess pulled the gloves from his stiff hands. Whilst he held his fingers near the flames, she waited for him to speak.

Long minutes dragged by before we heard his voice.

"I never found him." He sounded hoarse and tired. "I galloped for miles along the road to Brussels. I stopped at posthouses to get fresh horses, and none of the hostlers said they'd seen a man like van Wouwere. He could not have taken the road to Brussels."

"I doubt he's gone there," said Bess.

His fingers began to twinge as feeling stole back into them. "That's what I discovered. So I headed out on the high road east, and then north, and asked questions where I could, and told hostlers and travelers alike that I was looking for him. Perchance some news will be sent back to us. Certes he'll have to come back here. His home is here, and all his possessions."

Clumps of snow fell from the soles of Catlin's boots. With my foot I pushed them into the hearth where they hissed as they melted.

"Oh, he'll be back," I rejoined. "Like an unrepented sin, he'll probably be back to plague us."

"Good," said Catlin. "Then I will have my chance to kill him."

"You cannot!" said I. "You'll be arrested."

Bess agreed. "We can have van Wouwere arrested," she argued. "And if I must, I will give testimony against him that will hang him."

She spoke with such hatred that I was startled, and could say naught as she began to plot against him in turn, and with Catlin relished the vengeance they could wreak if all went right. Their minds were becoming clouded, I realized, by a rage that could cause them to make grave errors. I tried to speak soothingly; I offered calm reason. But by then they did not hear me, nor did wish to.

XXII

Where Doctor van Wouwere disappeared to, we did not discover. But when he was gone a pressure seemed lifted off Bess, as if he had taken with him his woeful prophecies and they could weigh no longer upon her. True, she had not seen him betwixt the night he had told them to her and the day of his departure from Antwerp, but the knowledge that he was always near and still in his way her rival for Catlin reminded her of his prophecies—or so I thought. But now he was out of the city, hence they would soon be out of her mind. My cheer dissolved, however, when one night soon after van Wouwere had left, Catlin made a remark to me.

"Bess ever and anon doth take on strange ideas, doesn't she?" he said whilst we were playing a game of chess.

"What mean you by that?" I moved a pawn.

"Sometimes she might pay sudden heed to that which before she cared little about. For example, I know she's ever wary of Brother Gerard, but not of any other cleric. Yet today when a humble Franciscan crossed our path twice or thrice, she watched him as if he were about to attack her."

My stomach tightened. "A Franciscan?"

"And a gentle-seeming one at that. She had no more benevolent an attitude toward an old priest who for a little stood near us in the marketplace."

My stomach now pushed up toward my heart. "A flight of fancy for her, Catlin, that's all. Pay it no mind."

Early on the morrow, I set out with Bess for the English Quay. We'd only a short distance to go when she turned down a street I had never taken before. I said naught, and soon we came to an open place where a few streets crossed. Bess headed directly for a well that marked its center and lingered there. My stomach churned when I saw where we were, as it had whilst talking with Catlin: just across from the Dominican monastery.

"Let's on," said I. "There is no use in standing here and getting befouled with mud from the passing carts."

"Hold for a moment," said she. "I have some purpose here."

"Nay, Bess. I know what you're about, and 'tis foolish. You're letting van Wouwere's vengeful words frighten you."

"Frighten? No, he but reminded me to be wary. There is a cleric about, after all, who poses a threat to me and you and Catlin. I do believe that since Damascus left Antwerp, Brother Gerard seems to be letting us be; but for aught we know he might still be spying upon us, and so may know of our supposed friendship with van Wouwere."

"And why should that matter?"

"What if he knows of van Wouwere's divinations? Of his black art? Then by oft being with him, we too might be suspected of practicing such crimes. So I will bear witness against van Wouwere to Brother Gerard. That will make me—and you and Catlin—appear innocent, and foil any plot this monk may be planning."

"Mayhap. Or mayhap you're tossing a bone to a mad dog." Thoughts of Brother Gerard were spreading through my mind, and with them a secret I'd been carrying around for too many weeks; 'twas time Bess heard it.

"Brother Gerard too can bear witness. He told me something when he was at Catlin's house. He told me he saw the fire when it started in our room at the White Hound."

Almost imperceptibly, a shadow flickered across her eyes.

I went on. "Remember you he was in the street below."

"So he claims."

I paused. "He said there was no cat. He believes you set the fire deliberately, that you could be with Catlin."

The skin on her face grew so taut it seemed like to tear. "He told you that?"

"And that it was impossible for any cat to have entered our window."

Her teeth bit down, grinded. "If you believe him . . ."

"I don't know what to believe! Certainly when it comes to your Catlin you've never hesitated to deceive me!"

She averted her face, and when she looked back at me, her expression was one of disdain. "You can believe the monk or me. I care not a whit." Then she turned her gaze to the monastery.

"And how long do you intend to wait here?" I asked.

"Not long. This is the time and place I appointed."

"What? You've arranged to meet with him?"

"Aye."

"Well, I want none of this." I was sharp with her. "Why did you trick me into coming with you?"

"I didn't mean it as a trick, Sara. 'Tis only that . . ." she hesitated.

" 'Tis only that you are not as brave as you think and needed my company to steel your resolve. For that I should leave you here alone." I sighed. "But—God forgive me—I'll stay."

For some minutes more we stood at the well. Then one of the two wide doors of the monastery opened and out stepped a thin figure narrowly clad in a dark cape, beneath which moved the spotless white tunic of a Dominican friar. 'Twas difficult to catch sight of his face through the traffic but the faded yellow hair and stiffly held body were disagreeably familiar. He walked toward us. It was indeed Brother Gerard.

"God give ye good den, Brother," said Bess.

"And to you." He was oil-smooth.

"We have not seen each other for some weeks."

"Indeed we have not."

They had the unreal civility of enemies between whom a temporary truce had been called. Even then Bess shifted into a position more directly facing him, as if mindful she might yet be attacked.

"I was thinking erewhile of Damascus," said she. "Is he gone still from Antwerp?"

"He is. If he left for Rome, then he may yet be gone for some time."

"I pray God that such an evil man be always gone from us."

He made a wan little smile. Behind his calm I swore I could see his mind calculating with fearful speed. "Damascus is not the reason you have sought to meet with me, mevrouw."

"True. There is someone else who has committed crimes against God. Belike you know of him already."

"Do I?"

"Aye, because belike you have had us watched, hence you know of him. He is a physician. Nicolas van Wouwere by name."

"I know of him, and how you and Mynheer Catlin have oft been seen with him."

Bess was all steel and ice. "Still, you saw naught but innocent acts on Mynheer Catlin's part."

"Not so. There is merely no evidence of guilt."

"You sound disappointed."

He made no reaction to her cutting words. "Nicolas van Wouwere, however, is suspected of committing unlawful acts, and as his friends you may have known of them and kept silent."

"Nay. We have only just learned of them and without delay I have arranged this meeting that I may report my suspicions to you. Hence 'twould be difficult to find me—or mine aunt or Mynheer Catlin—guilty of silent duplicity with van Wouwere."

Brother Gerard's smile fell away. "That may be true. Still Mynheer Catlin might need to answer many questions—though not to me. Nicolas van Wouwere is being investigated by appointed fellow physicians."

"By *physicians?*" I repeated.

"It is considered most necessary. Suspicions about van Wouwere were first put forward by one of our Dominican brothers, the apothecary for our monastery. His services were requested by a former patient of van Wouwere's. Our brother, after treating this patient, sought out others and found that in their cases also salves and potions ofttimes prescribed them by this doctor were unsuitable for their injuries or complaints. He also concluded that van Wouwere relied too much upon water casting, sith the lack of balance among the humors cannot always be discerned only by looking at a flask of the patient's urine. What is worst of all, our brother discovered much evidence that Nicolas van Wouwere practices the black art."

"Holy Mother, protect us all!" I crossed myself.

"We have suspected as much too," said Bess, "and 'tis on this matter we are willing to testify. But methought the city magistrates or the bishop would be the investigators."

"No, the physicians first. Because medical science must perforce at times rely upon such related knowledge as astrology, they would be the best judges to decide whether or no van Wouwere crossed over the

border from the legitimate application of that knowledge into blasphemous divination. I must add, however, that there are indeed witnesses
who have already stepped forward and charged that van Wouwere not
only tried to divine the future but claimed certainty for his predictions.
Such prognostications *pro certo* are heresy, for an astrologer can never
infallibly tell how men, from whom those events may come, will
behave, because their will and intellect must remain free. Such heresy
and our brother's evidence that van Wouwere practiced such black
magic as necromancy and the making and selling of spells and amulets
indicates that the magistrates will most like be ultimately involved."

"Then he is guiltier than e'en I thought," said Bess. "And I'll be
glad of his arrest when he returns."

"Returns?"

"Aye. But a few days past, he left for Brussels."

I was relieved that Bess said nothing of van Wouwere's assault on
her or Catlin's pursuit of him, for the less Brother Gerard knew of us all,
the safer we belike were.

"Van Wouwere told you he was leaving for Brussels?"

"He told Mynheer Catlin he was going to see a sick friend there,"
she replied. "But none of us cared where he was going so long as he
went away from us."

"It is good you do not care, for he may not have gone to Brussels.
He knew most likely he was under investigation and so thought it
expedient to leave Antwerp."

"Then Catlin is well rid of him."

In one spare movement, the friar let nod his head, yet his face
revealed nothing. Bess in turn looked boldly in his eyes. 'Spite their
differences—their stations in life, manner of living, gender, actions, and
thoughts—they made for strange equals, both being nigh the same age,
yet utterly bereft of any youth.

"It may be wise of you," said he, "to warn Mynheer Catlin that
though you have given testimony to me, he may still be questioned by
the investigating physicians."

"Much thanks, Brother Gerard," said I with feigned sincerity, "for
this warning. 'Tis given, I know, in Christian charity."

The faintest apparition of mirth—the only true mirth or good cheer
I had ever seen in him—and with it a melancholy knowingness, wavered over his face. Then a hand emerged from beneath his cape, not to

sign a blessing but as if to snuff out our discourse. "And now, mevrouws, I must take my leave of you."

His bony figure glided away. "Damn van Wouwere!" Bess muttered.

We were quick to tell Catlin of Brother Gerard's news. We found him at the Custom House at the English Quay, where Bess took him aside and repeated to him all the friar had imparted to us.

"I told Brother Gerard," said Bess, "that you and van Wouwere are enemies now, and that you wish never to see him again."

"Not see him again? Perchance it's also his decision not to see me. And now an investigation—damn!" Catlin sounded fretful. "But go you please about your work again. I myself must investigate something that of a sudden bothers me."

He had earlier told us he would have much to keep him busy that day, yet he returned home ere did we and settled in the parlor with a glass and a bottle of wine that was about empty by the time we joined him. He poured for us the remainder when more glasses were brought, but he remained pensive and distant and did not speak until we too had begun to drink.

"I decided to go to van Wouwere's house," he finally said. One of his feet tapped out a muffled beat upon the carpet. "I needed to discover whether or no he would return to Antwerp; that he would not is a suspicion that has crossed our minds. So to his house I went and found his old servant there, and some patients who were asking when van Wouwere would be back. Though he tried to stop me, I forced my way into van Wouwere's doctoring room. His precious physic stuff was still there. He boasted so oft to me of it that I trust he will return to fetch it." He said this with more desire than conviction, then added, "If I e'er set eyes on him again, I'll give him a fierce beating. Aye, at least that. Still, whether or no he will return I had a pressing need to know. I queerly feel more unsafe with him gone than if he were here."

More days passed and in them we said nothing of the doctor, though our avoidance of his name sometimes knitted knots of strain into our hours together. The middle day of February came and went; it was now exactly a fortnight since he had left. He had not yet returned; nothing was yet said.

On a morning in the third week of his absence, I went with Bess and Catlin to the countinghouse, where we closed ourselves away in the office and there reviewed our accounts. After a while Michiel came into the room with a bucket of coal; he tossed some coals onto the hearth and poked them about until the fire was crackling. Unlike Jan's, Michiel's smaller limbs were prickly with chill whenever the house grew too cool, which it did ofttimes during these winter months; and when it was so, we could hear him padding from one pan of burning coals to the next, upstairs and down, and we could smell the whiffs of smoke that were soon floating through the rooms. Even now he was lingering before the warmth of the fireside. Then he cleared his throat.

"Master Catlin?"

Catlin looked up.

"I've heard of late some news of your friend, Doctor van Wouwere. I paid some heed to it sith you have indirectly done business through him."

"Is this news I should hear?"

"Methinks so," said Michiel. "Yesterday when I was near Hoogstraat, I overheard in the street the talk betwixt two men. One was a tapster at a nearby tavern, and he was saying that a wealthy physician, van Wouwere by name, had left unpaid a large bill, and that it is commonly noised about he has fled Antwerp. Hearing this, I returned to the silversmith's shop wherein sometime in January I saw your friend van Wouwere. 'Twas a trifling incident I mentioned in passing to Mistress Lathbury."

His repeated use of the term "your friend" for van Wouwere was not welcomed by Catlin. A thin cloud of humiliation was moving over the three of us. Ignorant of this, Michiel continued like a scrivener, dry and precise.

"When I espied van Wouwere in the silversmith's, I had assumed he was purchasing several vessels of silver. But the smith this time told me that van Wouwere had not been buying but selling his own vessels, and too seemed in a hurried need for money." Michiel paused and summed up his account. "That is all I have to say. I thought you might wish to know the finances and trade of anyone with whom you do business."

"Indeed I do," said Catlin. "I have trained you well."

Satisfied with himself, the apprentice left us.

"Well, little by little the truth will out"—Catlin's efforts to talk lightly failed—"and we'll soon discover if our very excellent friend Nicolas will or will not return to the many people who await him here."

Uneasily, we proceeded with our business deliberations, wanting not to speak of what was troubling us. Then Jan entered with a letter in his big hand.

When Catlin saw the sender's seal he broke the wax and opened the letter. We watched as his eyes sped across line after line, stopped, stared in unbelief, returned, and read them once more. A trembling moved through him. He stared wildly at Bess. Then he seemed to go mad.

"Damn him!" he bellowed. "Jesus Christ! Damn that lying thief! What a fool, what a cursed lack-brain and knave Schorer was for believing him! I sent no such letter. God curse that Judas van Wouwere!"

His fury had lifted him out of his seat but then he fell back into it, his hands squeezing his temples and hiding his eyes.

Bess and I held our breaths. We durst not yet ask him what was so horribly wrong. At last he spoke.

"I have been deceived." His voice sputtered, failed, then came again. "I have been cozened, cheated, swindled, fobbed. There aren't enough words for it."

Bess gasped, grabbed up the letter, and began reading it.

"And I'm the victim. I'm the fool of a victim in a fraud. Our good friend Nicolas, smiling Nicolas, has stolen from me the payment I was to receive for his friend's tapestry."

"Sweet Jesus, no!" I cried.

"Over seven hundred pounds," he whispered, "seven hundred pounds."

"But how could it have happened?" I blurted. "How could he have gotten the money?"

Catlin rose and began to pace this way and that as if looking for an escape. "My factor, Helmut Schorer, received the tapestry within a week of its leaving Antwerp." He sounded as though he himself were trying to sort through the facts. "Before it arrived, he had my letter directing him to sell the tapestry to a man named Mueller, who had word from van Wouwere to contact Schorer. I instructed Schorer on what price to demand for the tapestry, from the payment he could deduct his usual commission, and then send me my money by a bill of exchange. Yet this is what he writes." He took the letter from Bess and read aloud, " 'I did follow, as you may note, the instructions of your second letter.' My second letter? I wrote no such letter!"

"But who could have written it?" I exclaimed.

"Who but van Wouwere?" Bess's tone stabbed at the name.

"Oh, van Wouwere knew most thoroughly the contents of that second letter!" Catlin was now half shouting. "Schorer writes that in it I instructed him to make the bill of exchange payable to van Wouwere, or to directly give him the money when van Wouwere arrived in Cologne, for the letter also said I had trusted van Wouwere with other business he was to see to there. Van Wouwere of course would need money for it. Of course. He says that Nicolas was a most worthy gentleman, and so courteous, and most concerned that Schorer received his full commission. Schorer says that the doctor 'gave himself most truly as a man who could be trusted with your business.' That blasted fool! As big a fool as am I!"

"More than seven hundred Flemish pounds!" Bess groaned.

Quickly Catlin returned to his desk, flipped open his account book, and counted up his losses. "The seven hundred pounds for the tapestry, plus the one percent *toule* for exporting it from Flanders, plus the cost of its preparation for shipping, plus the cost of shipping it to Cologne. Oh, and the cost to me."

"But van Wouwere," said I, "if he be still in Cologne . . ."

"He may not be there. Schorer writes that van Wouwere hoped to arrange my business quickly 'ere he left Cologne."

"But still you might catch him!" Bess declared.

He jumped on this with only some hope. "I myself cannot leave Antwerp for weeks to come. I have too much business that cannot be trusted to anyone else."

"Then *I* will leave!"

"Ridiculous!" he shot back at her. "I'll not let you go, and you cannot travel there alone. No, I'll send there a man to search for van Wouwere. That I can do. I would to God I could do more. I would to God I could kill that accursed van Wouwere!" A thought stopped him. "But won't he need to come back to Antwerp? When I was last at his house much of his costly possessions were yet there. Was his flight so hurried that he'd not the time to sell all he couldn't bring with him?"

"You could claim his things! That would be some small recompense." Bess was on her feet in a trice, as if ready herself to snatch up the claim for him.

"I could, I could. And I must go there now." He threw the letter into his standing-box, locked it, and was ready.

"I'll go with you," said I, eager to help him in any way I could.

"Yes, Sara, go you with him," Bess murmured to me. "I'll elsewhere; there's something touching on this theft that I must look to."

We threw on cloaks, hats, and gloves and Bess was off in one direction, Catlin and I in another. I ran to keep up with him, so rapidly did he walk. I said little, for his eyes were always straight ahead, his face stiff with worry, so that whatever words I spoke were met only by distracted answers when he heard me, silence when he did not.

"The letter," I panted, "how could van Wouwere write so well a letter that fooled your own factor?"

"He had a copy of my letter to Schorer, which I myself had written. He could see my hand, study it, copy it."

I tried to keep closer to him. "And he could so write in a style that Schorer knew it to be yours?"

"In style and content. By his copy, he saw how I addressed Schorer, gave him instructions, signed my name."

"And he studied your seal." That I remembered. I tightened my cloak against the cold. "So this theft is yet another reason van Wouwere invented that patient in Brussels."

"Where he never went."

We reached the street wherein was the doctor's house. Now Solomon's Wisdom seemed locked up; the star-marked sign was gone, the shutters at the street level were closed. Catlin knocked hard on the door; no answer came. He rapped several times more, and still the house was mute; but down the narrow lane, so empty of traffic or passersby, the door of another house opened and out bent a woman with a hard face that was splintered into wrinkles and framed harshly by black hair pushing stiffly out of a wimple.

"Why are you pounding away there? There's no one to answer," she barked, her voice as hard as her face.

"No one here at all?" asked Catlin.

"So I've just said."

"Was not a Doctor Nicolas van Wouwere and his servant residing here of late?"

"That doctor—Satan keep him—has been gone for nigh on three weeks. His servant ran off two days ago. Satan keep them both. Know you the doctor? Tell me where he is if you know. He owes me money, the bastard does. This month's rent he's left unpaid."

In his anguish, Catlin I knew was ready to demand of the woman if the doctor's possessions were still in the house, but I spoke ere could he.

"This place, then, is to let again?" I asked her.

"Of course it is," the woman snapped. "I want tenants in there 'fore the month is out. The less time lost, the less money. Know you the doctor?"

"Only as a patient knows his physician," I replied. "Certes we cannot answer for his whereabouts. But I saw his rooms here, and thought them comfortable and to my taste. If this house is to let again, then I would greatly like to see the rooms once more. I am, you see, in present need of a good house."

She bent farther out and peered at me, her mouth jutting downward into a frown whilst she considered whether or no to believe me.

"Want you to see the rooms, do you?" she barked.

"If you but let me into the house, I'll bother you no more till I've finished my perusal of it."

"None of that going about it as you please. I'll let you in and let you out, and when you're there inside you'll be with me."

"Agreed."

"Wait you there, then," she demanded, and disappeared for several moments. She emerged again, like a short bull from a shed, with a huke thrown slovenly about her and a ring of keys grasped in both her thick hands. With no pardons or courtesies she brushed abruptly past us, shoved a key into the lock, turned it fast and hard, opened the door, and stepped in, impatient for us to follow, doubtful still of mine interest in the place. I composed my face with a concern that the house might indeed be just what I wanted and as we followed her I asked divers practical questions on the number of rooms and the amount of rent. She in turn began to hide the blatant distrust she bore toward us.

The front chamber had in it only a bench; the chair and stools were gone. I moved toward the door of the doctor's room, but the woman opened it and went in first. Catlin and I stopped and stared. The chamber was empty. There was only the shelf against the wall and the table that had once been crowded with bottles and boxes and strange physic things. Now all was gone, belike packed off to van Wouwere by the servant, or sold. Even the foulness seemed to have fled.

We were led upstairs. It had been in the rooms above that Catlin had wordlessly put his hope, for there had the handsome furniture and other valuables been kept. But the sound of our feet stepping from stairs to the upper floor made my heart fast sink, for it echoed in rooms too empty to diminish the noise. Catlin hurried ahead of me, blind to the woman, deaf to the inane chatter and questions I kept inventing. The distrust she had been harboring broke out like a boil on her leathery face, and she heaved her squat body after him and like a pestilent insect followed him from room to room. Being at last alone, I myself hastened into the chambers nearest me and sadly surveyed each one. They were all empty, save for two or three pieces of furniture that might bring a few pounds. That bullish woman too was owed money by the doctor, I thought. But surely she could not claim everything he had left behind; surely something Catlin might have.

I turned around and nigh fell upon her as she stood glaring at me.

"Only a few odd pieces of furniture are about," I stuttered. "I'd thought the rooms would be better furnished. Are these the doctor's?"

"They're mine!" she snapped. "They're all mine, every one of them. They were put in here for that thief but he's gone now, so I'll have them back. A tenant in this house provides for himself. If you rent this house, I'll be taking them back."

Of that I'd no doubt, nor did I doubt that she was lying, as I had been.

Catlin stepped into the room. I looked beyond the woman, who glared still at me as if poised to slap down any claim contrary to her own, and saw the resignation with which he looked back at me. Slowly, he shook his head and I knew there was no hope for our purpose in that house; to pursue it any further would only render him another indignity. Well then, I sighed, let the hag keep what little there was; it will make her no more content than it would us. Still I played out my game, for I sensed that my civil questions were all that were keeping her from having a fit of fury. Finally I told her that I needed a more furnished place, and so talked my way out of her clinging company and out of her house.

When she'd slammed shut and locked the door, we bid her thanks and began to go on our way. She gave us no good morrow and I was expecting her to yell curses after us when instead she called out, as if just remembering something, "Be you Bess Marwick?"

Catlin and I stopped abruptly.

"Nay, I'm not," I replied, and nigh added that she was my niece when I paused. "Why do you ask?"

"You sound English, and that's an English name. Know you her?"

"Only a little," I lied.

The shrew fumbled about in her huke and drew out what looked like a letter. "The doctor left this for her, right on a table. She must be one of his whores, and he knew she'd come to see him again and find it. You give it to her if you want. I'll have naught to do with it." With that, she tossed the thing at us and plodded away.

It wavered through the air and fell onto the ground just below my outreached hands. Picking it up, I saw that it was indeed a letter, addressed to Bess in van Wouwere's hand and sealed with a lump of red wax that looked to have been broken and then sealed again. "I nothing doubt that woman opened it to see if there was money inside," I grumbled.

"And if there were information on van Wouwere's whereabouts," Catlin said. "Know you why he would write to Bess?"

An ugly feeling rose in me. "Nay, nay, save for a vengeful purpose."

With heavy steps, we headed back to the countinghouse. But scarce had we walked two streets when a hissing noise crept up behind us. Half behind the corner of a house stood van Wouwere's servant. He was crooking a finger at us to come near and when we charily did so, he hurried us around on bent legs into the house. With Catlin preceding me, we stepped past the open door and into a dim hallway. From somewhere above drifted a baby's cry, and thumps and voices echoed along the walls. 'Twas a rotting old house divided into rooms, the type inhabited by the poor and drunk. But what held mine attention was the servant hard against the wall. His feet were nervously shifting back and forth, his white hair looked like a spiderweb in the shadows, and his old shoulders were stooped over his hands, which were tapping and squeezing a folded paper with a broken seal.

"Mynheer Catlin?" he asked.

"Aye. And you're van Wouwere's servant," Catlin said accusingly.

"I am. I was. He's gone now."

"God's blood, I know that."

"And I have no master. But I have something he sent me."

Catlin glanced at the paper in the old man's hands. "And what is that?"

He held the paper up before clasping it again to his chest, fearful that Catlin would snatch it away. " 'Tis a letter from him. And 'twould be worth much to you."

"Does it tell me where he is?"

"Nay."

"Does it say where he's going?"

"Nay, it doesn't."

"Then 'tis useless to me." Catlin turned to leave.

"Hold, mynheer—it is worth much. 'Tis about your lady friend."

"Which friend?" I quickly asked.

"Mevrouw Marwick. He is conspiring 'gainst her through this letter. He sent me instructions about it." He fumbled beneath his shirt and pulled forth a small slip of paper. "He tells me in this what to do."

Catlin was suspicious. "How can he conspire against her when he's gone from the country?"

"His letter will show you how." We could hear the tempting in his voice.

"And how know you this? Can you e'en read it?"

"I can. I can read."

"Then let me read it too."

"Nay." He slapped the letter harder to his chest. "But I'll read to you his instructions. He says"—he glanced down at the slip of paper and read awkwardly—" 'You must deliver this to the clerks in the Vierschare. Tell them it must be given to the magistrates.' "

I was piecing together his story. "Why would van Wouwere expect you to do something for him when he is long gone, and you have not a spot of loyalty to him?"

"Because he sent me money and said he will send more. He will, I know, to keep me quiet. But I can get more money from you." His eyes went back and forth from me to Catlin. "He had so much learning he thought of me only as the foolish servant. 'Tis a little error, but he made it."

"And you are also much in error," said Catlin, "if you think I will give you a groat for that paper ere I've seen a word on it."

The old man stared, blinked, and tapped the letter as he thought. Then he twisted about, unfolded it, and carefully tore it in half. With a thrust he gave the bottom half to Catlin.

I leaned over Catlin's arm and with him read the torn piece.

". . . saw with mine own eyes the mark of the devil upon Mevrouw Marwick and read her plots for her evil spells and how she did lewdly disport with other witches on Allhallow even. Of all this will I send you proof written in her hand. I had hoped to secure and send it together with these accusations, but for fear of my safety I must speak now. Word has reached me, through travelers who have spoken with hostlers along the roads near Antwerp, that an Englishman is looking for me. I fear it is her lover, who desires my death. I beg of you to arrest them both now, lest I be killed and the proof destroyed." And so the letter ended, not signed but for "No Name, for Safety's Sake."

"Sweet Mother of God," I mumbled. "He means to have Bess accused of witchery—and he traps you too!"

Catlin became all cold business. "Have you any other such letter from van Wouwere?"

"Nay, only this one," said the servant.

"Then give me the other half of it, and I will pay you for it."

"I want much money."

"You'll have what we can give you now and no more, or I'll run you through your rotten heart." Catlin laid his hand on the sheathed dagger at his side.

The man cringed. "I'm only asking for what's right, by the saints I am. I'll take what you can give me—but you must be fair."

Catlin took from beneath his cloak a capcase heavy with money. "You're in luck, you old thief. I settled a loan today and have on me more money than I should. Now give me your piece of this letter."

With one hand Catlin held out the capcase and with the other reached for the torn paper. The servant nervously shifted his weight and with his eyes ever on Catlin's hands, grabbed the capcase and quickly shoved the paper at him. Scarce had Catlin grasped it when the servant tried to rush out the door. But Catlin blocked his way and glowered down at him.

"And what of this 'proof' van Wouwere will send you?"

"He won't send it now, at least not to me"—the servant was withering in fear—"for I won't write him back. I'll be leaving Antwerp myself now. This is too dangerous for me, this treachery."

Catlin bent closer, all threat and anger. "Leave today, for if I see you again, I will kill you."

A strangled cry broke within the man's throat and he hurried his ancient body past Catlin and out of the house.

"What does the rest of the letter say?" I asked.

Catlin read it o'er and then handed it to me. It contained only more scurrilous lies about Bess and not a word that could help us track down van Wouwere.

"Why did he not name you?" I wondered aloud. "He only called you her lover."

"Belike because I am too respected a merchant to be brought down by a nameless letter—only strong proof could do that. But Bess, being a woman and having much less wealth, is more like to fall victim to such lies. So the clever villain did not weaken his attack on her by naming me."

"Having her arrested would be enough!" The more I thought out his evil plan, the more furious I became. "That would keep you from pursuing him because you would be too busy trying to help Bess."

Both mine anger and Catlin's only grew when we returned home. There he sat down with a pitcher of ale and drank too much, and I matched him glass for glass. I felt ugly with hatred and bitter with frustration. Still I thought aloud of what we might do, whilst Catlin grew darkly silent.

It was evening when Bess arrived home, looking all worn out and cold. She said naught until she had drunk some ale and pulled off her shoes, and when she asked what we found at van Wouwere's house, we gave her only a brief answer. I was about to tell her of the letter we had bought but she interrupted me.

"I've been going about to the transporting companies, asking about van Wouwere and if any of their workers had done trade with him." She rubbed her sore toes. "Most could not help, but in time I found the company van Wouwere used; it was the Italian company of Mattia Greco. Oh, our friend planned his departure most thoroughly, hurried though he was. The day he is said to have left for Brussels he gave to Greco's company several large trunks filled with his most costly possessions, I trow. All were bound for Cologne."

"I always knew he was a clever rogue," said I.

"Catlin"—Bess touched his arm—"there's a chance van Wouwere is still in Cologne. He can be caught."

Catlin spoke through clenched teeth. "There's an equal chance he'll be gone by the time any man I send can arrive there. He knows he cannot stay long in Cologne, so he'll arrange to go elsewhere."

"But it's winter and such preparations are not quickly made. He belike rode post-horse all the way, but slowly since he's not hardy enow to travel swiftly over such a distance. A sturdier man could pursue and catch him."

"Aye, I'll send a man. What you learned today will aid him in his hunt. But in the meantime you must think not of me but of yourself. Van Wouwere has also set afoot much evil mischief for you."

"What mean you?"

I gave her the torn letter. "We bought this from his old thief of a servant."

As she held the two pieces together and her eyes went down them, she began to pale. "Well, Catlin," said she too flatly, "I now have mine own reason for wanting van Wouwere caught."

"We have at least discovered his plans!" I tried to be encouraging. "And we intercepted this letter."

"Still he can send the proof directly to the magistrates," added Catlin, "or have it delivered by someone else. He belike was only sending the letter through the servant to further cover his tracks. So she is not yet safe."

"A witch." Bess trembled and tried to steady herself. "The villain will have me accused of being a witch."

I hated what I had next to do. "And this too, Bess." I handed her the other letter, still sealed. "Van Wouwere's landlady gave this to us to deliver to you. 'Tis from him."

She opened and read it, and a harsh laugh fell out of her. "Oh, what a vengeful devil. This is his revenge for mine attack on him!"

"He cursed you with his wretched predictions! Wasn't that enough for him?" I burst out, and realizing too late what I may have revealed, I looked to Catlin.

" 'Tis all one, Sara," said Bess. "I've told Catlin already of van Wouwere's predictions for me."

"And what is he telling you now?" asked Catlin.

Bess propped her elbows on the table whilst she read. " 'You drew my blood, now I'll draw yours. It will be you who are arrested and you who are charged with ministering the black arts and divining by geomancy and, too, witching means. The truth will out, and you will burn.' "

None of us said a word. After all the overwhelming emotions we had endured that day we were now strangely numb, unable to bear yet another wave of rage and frustration. Yet I did feel fear, at least, and understood how it would soon grow to terror for what could happen to her.

"He's so sure of himself and his proof," said Catlin at last. "But how could it be in your hand?"

"That paper of yours, Bess." I remembered me the night at van Wouwere's house. "That's how he knows your hand and can copy it. I should have taken it from him. The moment I saw it, I should have grabbed it away from him."

"What paper?" Catlin asked.

" 'Twas a horoscope for myself that I'd written out," said Bess. "He stole it from your library."

Catlin closed his eyes. "God's blood, the rogue! Oh, Bess, I was such a fool!"

"Nay, think not that way, Catlin." Her eyes were filling with tears. "You could not have foreseen this, just as I did not."

"We can fight his false proof!" I tried to cheer us.

"And hazard all," said Bess. "And be burned to death as a witch or sorcerer."

"Nay," I insisted. "You can return to England and there be safe."

This idea, given too quickly, was met with only silence. Bess leave her Catlin? That she could not do.

"That letter we can show to the magistrates," Catlin thought aloud. "Van Wouwere was a dunce to have sent a message of his conspiracy 'gainst you."

"He was no dunce." Bess pushed the letter toward him. "He frames every word with the implication that the proof is real, not forged, and not that this is vengeance but the truth. I will be guilty ere proven innocent."

"Aye, if you're accused of being a witch," said I. "That must be why the landlady gave us this letter—which I doubt nothing she read—and feigned ignorance of its contents. She wants naught to do with so dangerous a charge."

"But why leave you any letter?" asked Catlin.

"To make me—and you—wait in fear till his proof is sent, after which I could be burned. He would take much pleasure in such fear."

"But you won't be burned!" I insisted. "I know, I know how! We can forge a letter of our own, write again this one in his hand."

"I've not a scrap of paper with his own writing on't." Catlin sighed but brightened a whit when an idea came to him. "Yet at least I may be able to learn when that proof arrives at the Court House, the Vierschare, and perchance intercept it there. 'Tis well-known among the wealthy of this city that the magistrates' servants at that place can be bribed."

I jumped eagerly on this. "That is some hope."

"Not a surety," said Bess.

Catlin seemed to be growing blacker with each passing moment, more outraged, more silently murderous. "I will send a man after van Wouwere," he said as if swearing a death threat.

"Aye," Bess swore in turn.

I had by then too much drink and was showing the effects far more than was Catlin. Mine eyes were now bleary and my mood disconsolately miserable. "I'm so sorry for you both." I sniffed into my cup. "So very sorry, for this great danger that may befall you, Bess. And for you, Catlin—to lose so much money and in such a damnable way is tragedy indeed. Least, though, 'twas your money that was lost, my friend, and that can be had again. Better to lose that than to have any harm come to you yourself."

"Like poor Bess," he said, sighing.

I sniffed again and wiped away a tear. "I could not bear to lose the either of you."

He smiled and pushed the ale out of my reach. "I may have lost more than a great deal of money, Sara. Because of this cozening, I may lose much of my reputation and be regarded as a fool, should word get out of what has happened. And if I lose my reputation, then I shall lose my business as well."

For a moment we sat all in silence, then he rose and left the room.

XXIII

I happened to see briefly the man he sent on the journey. In the morning I paused on the landing and through the window saw in the street, just beyond the front door, Catlin talking with a burly, bearded man. He was the groom from the stables who had accompanied Bess and me to van Wouwere's house that ill-fortuned night. How ironic, I thought, that he was now being sent on a journey in pursuit of the doctor. Though it did not matter, I wondered if Catlin had learned from him of our visit, but I doubted this sith the groom seemed the kind of discreet man sent on many a secret task for other men and women.

The groom pushed some papers farther into his jerkin and out of sight. I deduced they were from Catlin and had on them addresses, names, instructions, and descriptions, for he had spent much of the night bent over papers and inkpot, writing away. The groom bowed his head, mounted his horse, and rode off.

Catlin had also written several letters, and those he posted himself that same morning ere joining Bess and me at his countinghouse. There he closed himself away in his office, where I disturbed him only once and found him huddled over account books studying their entries, calculating and scribbling out sum after sum, figuring into them the amount he had just lost and scraping together sources of immediate money. The night before, I had offered to lend him however much he needed and I could afford, and so too did Bess, but he would not hear of it. Granted, he was a wealthy man and could belike muster enough money together to hide from others the theft done him; but the loss of seven hundred Flemish pounds would still hurt even him.

He finished with his calculations in the afternoon and at last came out of his office, ready to accompany Bess and me to the Bourse, where each of us had business to conduct. Ere we left the countinghouse, though, he took us aside.

"There are two matters of which I must tell you," said he. "The first is that I've already been to the Vierschare and am paying a clerk there to hold secretly for me any letter mentioning Bess Marwick. The second matter is that an English couple will also be at the Bourse today. I did not want to meet them there, but 'twas they who sent note of the appointment and I have been unable to get word back to them that we should meet elsewhere. And so, though we'll look as if we're only conducting business, the two of you must keep your distance from us."

"What is all this about?" asked Bess.

"The couple are Protestant exiles from England."

I moaned. "Oh, Catlin, has this to do with more law-breaking?"

"I'll merely be giving them this, which because of van Wouwere's theft I've had to claw about for." He pulled half out of his jerkin pocket and then dropped back in a small bag tinkling with coins. "I'll only be honoring their bill of exchange. Still, sith they are exiles there may be eyes upon them; because of this they've had to move frequently whilst in Antwerp and have been only once to my countinghouse; for my sake they won't come again. If I could help it I would not honor their bill, for I cannot now afford to. But from what I've heard they are desperate and I trust I can collect on the bill soon enow."

"But is there danger for you in helping them today?" I asked.

"I was more like to be caught whilst shipping heresy. Few Adventurers deal in Protestant pamphlets but many of them do this much. So like them I feign ignorance for safety's sake, while knowing full well that by such bills of exchange these Protestants carry with them their wealth, or their families and friends at home send them outlawed aid."

"Outlawed?" Bess repeated. "So 'tis the same as your unlawful shipping."

"Nay, this is different. This is an act of charity."

At the crowded Bourse we made our way to the English section in the middle of the courtyard. Bess soon found the man with whom she had made an appointment and for a little stood with him. Catlin and I continued to talk with each other until he saw in a nearby huddle a man he knew. He went toward the stately old gentleman with the intent of a few friendly words. The man, who like others had been looking about occasionally for people with whom he might meet, was doing so again when he turned toward Catlin. His face became stiff with disdain. When Catlin reached out his hand in greeting, the old gentleman turned his back on him whilst his companions looked with curiosity on the man he had just silently rebuked.

Astounded, Catlin stared at the man's back, then recovered himself and began to walk back to me with a determined show of dignity. But someone off to his side made a remark, and the words slapped him hard and he winced. When he reached my side, I smiled and began to talk to him of this or that and made as if naught had happened. Just then a Fleming near us declared a little too loudly, "His physician friend has been denounced as a liar and villain. One wonders if he be the same."

His companions leered, the Fleming's voice fell into a mumble I could not make out, and all laughed. Neither Catlin nor I looked at them; rather I moved away as though to protect Catlin and keep him from such humiliation. But there was no cease to this; an English voice just ahead of us barked scornfully, "Only a fool or a villain would have been friend to such a doctor."

I uttered a jape, made myself laugh, and in other ways tried to act unmindful to what was happening around us. Catlin only half heard me. He was listening to all being said by everyone, rummaging through the several languages to catch any more talk of him. He heard his name and the stews spoken of in the same breath, and the two together scraped him like a knife. A cruel remark was thrown. All about us I kept hearing van Wouwere's name. Rumors and hearsay and news of investigations and the doctor's sullied reputation were spreading amongst the merchants like the plague. Thank God, I thought, these people did not know also that Catlin had been defrauded by van Wouwere; with such information they would be truly vicious.

It took Catlin several minutes ere he could raise in himself enough serenity to fight the growing humiliation. He pulled up his frame till it was regally tall and tilted back his head a degree too high in an effort to appear imperturbable. I wanted desperately to stop this torturing of him and hated myself that I could not.

Bess too had borne painful witness to what was happening. Quickly she joined us. "Have you spotted yet that couple?" she asked him.

He answered her with stoic calm. "Not yet, but 'tis only just now our appointed time to meet."

"Don't meet with them. Get you out of here and away from all these hateful hypocrites."

"No, Bess. Then they will have won and I shall be the coward."

"To hell with them and what they think." A thought struck her. "And now you cannot remain. Too many eyes are upon you. You cannot now honor that unlawful bill unnoticed."

As Bess was saying this I looked warily about. Through one of the entrances came a man and woman and stood on the steps whilst studying the crowd. With a start I recognized them. They were the English exiles I had met in Catlin's countinghouse, the soft and fretful middle-aged husband and wife. In a moment the husband espied Catlin. With a feeble smile of relief, though still with worry shrinking his movements, he put his hand protectively against his wife's back and began to walk with her down the steps and toward Catlin.

"They're here," I whispered, and slipped mine arm around Bess's. "Let's busy ourselves elsewhere, Niece."

Whilst Bess and I ambled away, Catlin drifted toward the couple and the German area of the Bourse, and away from the scandal-mongering English and Flemish merchants. For a few minutes the three exchanged wooden smiles, talk no one else could hear, and money and paper. During it all, thank God, Catlin seemed unnoticed by anyone else. Only Bess and I, whilst pretending to be busy, had our eyes on him.

Then it was over. The couple walked away through the crowd, out the doors, and were gone. Catlin returned to the English section, glancing about for us. Again we saw him wince and heard the barbs being thrown at him.

"I myself have heard that his friendship with the doctor was a most unnatural and unmanly one."

Low laughs and a few gasps followed this, and then a quieting as the merchants looked at the speaker. 'Twas a young man, short and puffed with pride, with a leer on his spotty face and a haughtiness in his stance. His eyes were shifting back and forth from his companions to Catlin, but when Catlin stared hard back and then strode over to him as if to strike him down, the crowd hushed. One step away, and with his hand on his dagger, Catlin stopped. The young man stiffened and laid nervous fingers on his sword. His leer had shrunk but yet remained, like a dare.

"Only a coward would repeat such a lie," Catlin charged.

The young man withered a little, then feigned indifference. "Ah—a double lie! I'm no coward and 'tis no lie."

"You're yellow with cowardice and have not the courage to tell me who gave you this falsehood."

"I've no reason to tell you."

"Was it an English merchant?"

"It doesn't matter who gave me mine information . . ."

"But it does matter if it be the merchant I speak of." This Catlin announced loudly. "He swore he would revenge himself on me. You're his instrument for that. He has lied to you and sullied my good name."

Bess and I glanced at each other. We knew Catlin's story to be a trick, but it worked. People were mumbling and nodding. They liked this twist, especially since revenge over matters of finance was familiar to them. The young man surveyed the crowd; he could feel his audience turning against him.

"Tell that rogue merchant to come forward," Catlin demanded, "and I will prove him false."

The young man scratched his nails up and down on his chest. His voice was a snarl. "He is not here."

"Aye, of course. He's such a coward himself he'll send another to spread his lying filth."

The young man grew red. "I warn you—insult me no more."

"Insult you? But I be merely speaking the truth."

The young man grasped more firmly his sword. His companions were inching away. "Nay, you are doing me a gross wrong. And now you mean to run me through with your blade."

To this Catlin only smiled.

"You will be arrested if you dare draw your sword in here," the young man sputtered.

"Why be you so unmanly timid?" Catlin asked, all innocent. "Think you I will spank your bottom?"

The crowd laughed. The young man pulled his sword halfway from its sheath and was stepping toward Catlin. But ere more could happen his companions had their hands on him and were pulling him away and out of the Bourse. Safely distant from Catlin, he was now blustering, "I will fight you! I will!" but his empty threats only garnered more laughs from those looking on.

At last the young man was gone and Catlin stood alone. The show being over, the merchants gave him scarce another glance but turned back into their huddles.

Bess went to Catlin's side. Slipping her hand through the crook of his arm, heedless to all about them, she proceeded to walk with him out of the Bourse. I followed close behind, but unlike them, kept looking all about, praying that no one would look back. Catlin's life now seemed surrounded by enemies.

XXIV

Catlin withdrew into himself as if into an uncertain refuge. The hours were added to hours, became days, and at the end of each he shut himself away all the more from his common pattern of work, his habits of daily living, his business acquaintances, his servants and apprentices, all save Bess. She alone was allowed to be near him, unless to the both of them I could sometimes be a companion. But little more. To me he said nothing of the Bourse and what had happened there, nor did he speak to me of how deeply he had been wounded. But he was watchful, so watchful, and Bess too became like him, and I in a faded way like them both.

The investigation, Catlin had discovered, was not so near its ending as he had hoped, and too he was hearing more rumors about van Wouwere, and lies and false stories—and some true ones—of his friendship with the man. There was a notification sent to him, on the evening after our ill-fated visit to the Bourse, in which Catlin was told that in three days' time, on the coming Friday, he would be visited by important physicians who had been chosen to pursue the allegations against their fellow doctor. And in those days when he waited for them, and for God knows whom else and what else, he watched. He and Bess both claimed that there were strange, furtive men, caught with only a glimpse ere escaping their sight, who followed them about and kept their eyes upon them, at uneven times, in obscure places, without continuity of manner or length of vigil. I too soon saw a man crookedly studying Catlin's house from just around the corner of the street; his neck was strained in too uncomfortable a position and his head bent around too long to make his gaze wholly innocent, or so I decided.

Then I too watched. In only a short while the dividing line of reality blurred betwixt such seen figures and insubstantial shades. Strangers' faces were changed by memories I no longer trusted and became dreadfully familiar, glancing too oft from behind clouded windows and within deep doors. Disfigurements of shadow and movement along the streets held suggestions of someone following too closely upon our heels, and tight-mouthed, glowing-eyed men crept from my imagination and into the night, disturbing the quiet flow of darkness. I grew worried, I grew frightened. I reasoned with myself and fettered with some determination these loose-roaming apparitions. Yet even after that much was done and I felt more myself and less the presence of unseen threats, I sensed inexorably, and with dread, that there was indeed a most dangerous reality that was crouched somewhere in Catlin's future, waiting.

Like grim bodies of darkness, four dignified men appeared, silent and stiff, at Catlin's door precisely at the appointed hour on the fog-wrapped Friday afternoon. I heard their knock and looked from the window above down on to them; I saw their different shapes, two with white beards frosting their faces, two without any beards, and save for their faces naught could be seen from that angle but their black-caped, black-capped shapes, eerie in the pale street. Lijsken had been told of their coming, and so when she opened the door little was spoken; one of the men only said that Mynheer Catlin had been expecting them, and after the resonance of his voice had risen and fallen, and with whishing sounds and muffled steps, the four physicians entered the parlor and in that chamber were closed away. I heard no more.

All the time they spent in there Bess spent in the antler room, and in the library, and on the stairs' landing, pensive and hushed. No criminal allegations, we knew, could be charged Catlin, but implications could be made and damage done to his good name. Already there had clearly been some damage. Thus Catlin could even gain some benefit from this solemn inquiry, for if before those men he could loose himself from his past friendship with van Wouwere and make of it no more than a passing acquaintance, or if he could at least destroy the ugliest rumors those four physicians were certain to lay before him, and aid himself their investigation as best he could, then a few good words about Catlin might be spread. Methought their meeting with him did seem to be proceeding in Catlin's favor: No angry denials or accusations rose from below, no loud voices. Only quiet, only order.

An hour came and went, and Bess spoke at last, though only to say that she was thirsty and was going down to the kitchen to get herself some ale. I felt the same thirst, and too the same worry that tortured her, so I went down with her.

I had hoped that as we passed the parlor door we would hear a little of what was occurring therein. But before we even reached there, the door creaked open, and one after the other in solemn succession, the four physicians emerged. We therefore stood nearby and wordlessly nodded our heads in brief respect. The first of the four, answering for them all, accepted our gesture as if it were their due, scarce bowed his own head in return, and did not pause but moved on with a slow and steady gait. I went before them to the entrance door and opened it; again there was the slight movement of the same head. One by one they passed outside, and in the chilled street they gathered together, their black forms blending into the gray foggy air. A thin snow was falling, as bleak and white as shards of bone, and it curled around their dark figures like threads of a winding sheet whilst the four moved on and away, their shapes obscured, until at last they disappeared.

Catlin came out of the parlor and leaned wearily against the wall. He smiled at Bess and me in a knowing, pleased way. "Well"—he loosened his jerkin and untied at his neck the strings of his shirt—"I trust that is the last we shall all see of those gentlemen. No more will my name be mentioned in their investigation."

Bess groaned with relief, then let tumble out a tired laugh whilst she put her arm about him and he put his around her shoulder and they walked upstairs to the antler room.

Yet the end of his involvement in that affair was the end only of one small worry. Still there were the furtive men who ever and anon were spotted, their eyes upon him. Still he was watchful and even more distant, irregular in his hours of work, sinking lower into long stretches of melancholy, and rising in bursts of feverish restlessness. The days passed and another worry, though not entirely dissipating, at least waned; no word, it seemed, had gotten out of the fraud or of the money Catlin had lost to the thieving van Wouwere. With difficulty, he had hidden his loss. But this too was of small comfort to him.

I came upon him one evening in the antler room when he was deeply buried in his sadness. He was sitting on the carpet before the fire, his legs stretched out long before him, his back against a chair, and one of his hands held by Bess, who sat beside him on a low stool. She held his hand, tenderly, unmoving, in both of hers. As if too disturbed to be reposed, Catlin stared vaguely into the fire, exhausted by yet another day of struggle with himself, and undone by the ache of it. Bess herself sat wakeful, infused with a willfulness, her own disquiet hushed for the present; and for his sake she forgot her own weariness, as if she were his protector who must needs keep him safe, and too for her own sake, that she might brood the more upon deep thoughts. As I had learned to do on so many other times like this one, I left them alone and went away.

Then there came a day, somewhere in the midst of all those days, that broke and spread bleakly and remained throughout its allotted hours the very color of dying winter. It was a Sunday, and after returning with Bess from an early mass, I'd no need or desire to go out again. I'd no one to visit, no letters to write, no work to do. I had breakfast with Catlin and Bess and afterward went to my bedchamber and sat before my stove and sewed. The morning had passed away when I heard Bess come up the stairs and go into her bedchamber, and for a while after that there were thumps up and down the hall and in and out of rooms as Maria set about her cleaning. Eventually she departed with her familiar noises and I heard nothing more until some heavy steps went swiftly down the stairs. Just Bess being careless, I thought, or Catlin in his boots. Finally I left my chamber and looked into Bess's to see if she was there, but it was empty. I called her name down the stairs; there was no answer. Only then did I realize how queerly silent the house had become. I went to the floor below, called again, and heard naught. Belike she'd gone out with Catlin, yet an uneasiness scratched at me. I looked into the antler room and noticed a band of light at the foot of the closed library door. I crossed the room, went up, and lightly knocked. Though no one answered, I opened the door and stepped in.

Catlin was at his desk. All about him, along shelves and pushed to the edges of the table were thrown-open books, and sprawled before him were papers blackened with lines and stars and numbers and words. He had not heard the creaking door, nor did he see me enter. Instead he remained bent over his papers, his mind lost amidst their inky brambles.

"Catlin," I said softly.

His head jerked up. His body tightened as if to fend off a blow and his eyes stared with a glistering light. He saw then it was only me, caught in a breath of relief, and leaned back.

"I didn't mean to frighten you," I stammered.

He covered his face with his hands, then let them drop heavily.

"I was only looking for Bess," I said. "I wouldn't have disturbed you . . ." I intended to say, "with your studies," but paused at the sight of the circles and symbols of the horoscope.

He followed my glance. "I've been . . . casting away again. Casting and figuring."

"Yes, well, I hope it proves favorable to you." I shuffled backward. "Well then . . ."

"No, Sara—don't leave me yet. Stay."

Worried for him, I sat down in the chair opposite.

He stared again at the papers, too distracted to let his gaze settle on any particular one. "I've been, as you can see, casting away again," he repeated. "I know you don't approve of these things."

"Only when you carry the natural to an unnatural length. And, too, such stuff now reminds me of van Wouwere."

"Long gone to other places."

"And because you've always seemed to immerse yourself too much in it. You told me once before that you've read in your horoscope a terrible destiny. Then why cast you more still?"

"To learn if that unwanted future is still awaiting me. The months and years go by; the planets change their positions, so I must alter my calculations." A hastily drawn chart on one of the papers caught his attention. With a finger he traced out the circles within circles, the symbols for the planets and moon and sun, his scribbled notes and explanations. "A horoscope is a warning, a changing map of possibilities. By knowing something of those future possibilities, I might be able to avoid the most dire ones." He looked feverishly up at me. His eyes were sparked with such an obsessive glimmer that they seemed to illuminate the air. "It was Martin van den Bist who taught me astrology. I still have some of the horoscopes he cast for himself." He gestured to a closed standing-box by his elbow. For a moment I dreaded that he might open it for me, like a coffin. "A few years ago, know you what I found in them? Resemblances, too many resemblances betwixt his horoscope and mine, and both end with warnings of a violent death."

All he was saying split me in half. In part of me my heart was pounding; in the other I was thinking that this was all absurd, that he was a good man gone a little strange by being left too oft alone. I had felt much the same in me when my Jonathan died; I was left too solitary with mine own thoughts, and when as a result I began to nurture some eccentric notions, my friends set me right. But until Bess and I had come along, Catlin had no one.

"There are many common points 'mongst all men's lives," I said. " 'Tis only our pride that makes us see our lives as different from other's. And as for such a death . . ."

"Nay, I mean far more than that. Favorable times and unfavorable, times of poor health, danger, or fortune—too many fall together." A frenzy was shadowing him. "What know you, Sara, of van den Bist?"

"Not much, and then 'tis but hearsay."

"Know you he was murdered?"

"I do."

"He was stabbed twice." His voice tightened. "He was killed in his house and died at the foot of a table. What hour of the night he was set upon no one knew; none of the servants heard any noises. No evidence was found and no one pressed to have the murderer caught. My father did not even press for justice. Leave justice to God if we can wreak none, he said. I was in Amsterdam when I learned of his death and returned posthaste. Though I'd never much liked van den Bist, I had felt a deep loyalty to him since he sometimes settled fights between my father and me and would tell me I was for him the son he never had. Now I could only take his place as my father's partner.

"It was as a partner that I one day, some months later, had need to check my father's account book. Since he was just then away from our countinghouse I had to search for it and found it hidden within his desk. I skipped back through the old pages, all of them with matched columns of debts and payments, until I came to an entry that had only a debt and no payment. It read, 'Jean Carpette ought to give four pounds thirteen shillings English and is to pay the last day in July.' No 'so much received in cash' was recorded after it as with others. Only 'to van den Bist' was written in an angry hand by my father. There were many such entries, all recording loans the few months before and up till van den Bist's death; money was lent to people and none given back. Only, over and over, were the words 'to van den Bist' as if my father had written them all in the same day. The amounts weren't much, two or three English pounds or livres de gros de Flandres, twenty at the most. No reason was written in those columns to explain why van den Bist had been collecting on my father's loans. Then a memory came back to me. The day before I'd left for Amsterdam, I heard my father in a heated fit cursing van den Bist under his breath. This wasn't uncommon, yet still it was the first time my father called him a 'cheating bastard' and a 'lying knave.' And on that very night my father told me I was to leave for Amsterdam to handle business he had arranged just that day—an uncommon haste for him.

"Just then my father returned. He saw me with his account book, tore it out of my hands, and swore I'd no right to be looking in it. I told him what I had found. Had van den Bist been cheating him? I demanded. 'Aye, and he claimed he meant to repay me,' my father said, 'but already he'd spent the money.' My father raged on about the cheating, about van den Bist's sinful life, his whoring, his drinking, his heretical beliefs. My father was loyal to the Catholic church, though in his heart he was no Christian, whilst van den Bist was loyal to nothing and no one and delved into everything Protestant just to spite my father. He even began to unlawfully ship Lutheran writings; 'twas his way of biting his thumb at my father and at those he called 'holy hypocrites.' On all these things my father ranted till I shouted back at him, 'Then why did you not have him arrested? What forced you to kill him?'

"This struck him dumb. The shock on his face—not the shock of a man wrongly accused, but of one found out—in turn shocked me. For so long a time we only looked at each other. Then at last he spoke. 'Never speak of any of this again, not to anyone,' he said. 'I must trust in you, Bartholomew. Never betray me. You are my son.' "

A silence wrapped its shroud around us as Catlin fell wordless. So quiet did that small library become that I thought I could hear the mist gathering outside the window.

"And I never betrayed my father. For two years more I guiltily stayed by him and kept my silence. Then he died—alone in his countinghouse, hard at work o'er his books, and with too much drink in him. Still I kept my silence. Why shouldn't I? Though there was then no reason in keeping it, so there was no purpose in breaking it. I have kept it for fourteen years."

The coals in the stove sputtered. Catlin blinked as if the pain in him were at last ebbing away.

I took a deep breath. "And now the pressure of those years forces the story out."

"To one, I know, who can also keep silent. But you're not the first to hear the story. I've also told Bess of it and of more. After all these years, how strange it is to talk, as if in the confession there were absolution. Think you, Sara, that I've done a great evil in saying nothing about my father's guilt?"

"I cannot say." My mind stumbled over the question. "Certainly if so, you've done your penance, years of penance."

"Nay, not payment enow. Van den Bist isn't satisfied."

"But van den Bist is long dead and gone."

He shook his head and a "no" formed on his lips.

I felt my skin crawl. "He is dead," I insisted.

"But not gone. You know of his ghost; Bess has told you of how it haunts me."

I found myself swaying slightly. "Aye. And I heard steps once, Catlin. On the night you rode after van Wouwere. They were on the stairs and came up toward me. Up to my bedchamber door with me, and then down the hall. I could see nothing at all. But I heard those steps."

"Did you?" He seemed almost relieved at this, as if it were proof he wasn't mad. "Did you in sooth?"

"By God's holy blood, yes."

"And saw nothing. Aye, so he's been with me. I've sensed him, that came first. Then I heard him. I was sleeping in my bedchamber when something woke me. I felt an icy hand on my chest. My sheets were pushed down around my waist, but though the flames in my hearth threw off some light I saw nothing, and no one stood beside my bed." His eyes seemed to be gazing with horror into the darkness of his bedchamber. "And then I heard his voice in mine ear and felt no human breath. He said, 'You are not rid of me. You still must pay for your father's sin.' I tried to shout. I tried to push away the arm that belonged to that icy hand, but there was none. I leapt from my bed and ran from my chamber. No one followed. Five times since then I've heard his steps as he comes to me, as he came to you. I've kept his portrait and that damned account book as part of my penance, but that isn't enough for him. He's as unforgiving in death as he was in life."

I tucked my hands into mine elbows as if to ward off a cold touch. "Oh, Catlin! May God take that shade away from you!"

"God take him away? Would van den Bist's soul walk if God didn't want it to? Some men God punishes after death, some whilst they're still alive. Van den Bist is my punishment."

His stories were by then taking shape in my mind, and I noticed a pattern in them. "You say van den Bist whored and drank too much, held heretical beliefs, shipped Lutheran teachings. Forgive me, Catlin, but in that way you resemble him."

He mulled on this. "My father drank also. I spread Protestant doctrine to please God, van den Bist to spite my father. And as to van den Bist's whoring—too oft my desires haven't been in it, and I've felt a shame he never did. But too I've not my father's cold, chaste temperament."

"Yet you still believe your life and stars to be matching van den Bist's when in sooth you've chosen your acts and character to become like his, and so have taken on his life."

"To give me some peace! Aye, I sometimes act as he did. When I do, 'tis as if I were atoning for the murder by living out his wrongly ended life. I was making a payment on a debt. But then I discovered other parallels. I bedded a whore and found he too had bedded her. I shipped some pamphlets and was told by their writer that he had once sent the like amount and on the same ship through van den Bist. Later I was told the same again by another writer."

"The whore had most like slept with scores of men. The pamphlet writers could deal with only you few select men who chance unlawful shipping. These are mere hapless chances."

"I cannot believe that. For so many years now I've felt as though my fate has been cast by my father's sin." He gazed out the window at the half-hidden world beyond. " 'The sins of the father are visited upon the generations.' " He murmured the scriptural words like a prophecy fulfilled. "And I will, I fear, die for his."

"In God's name, don't say so!"

"And why not, Sara? I can be Christlike. I can die for the sins of others."

"Christ has already died for all men's sins."

"So that all men can be forgiven, amen."

"You sound blasphemous."

He grew harder. "Why not be like Christ? Mayhap my life is matching not only van den Bist's but Christ's passion. Remember you what happened at the Bourse. I was denied by those who once hailed me, save by you and Bess. Already van Wouwere has cast his lots and won."

"You're talking folly now." I put my hand on his and felt his cold sweat 'gainst my skin. "No man can truly know his fate or his end. He can know only his own will and trust in God's."

"Where does mine own will end and God's begin? Yet trust in Him who Himself keeps silent, that is all you have to tell me. Oh, and He keeps His own silence; He wraps Himself up in mystery. So I can vainly rail against a mystery or passively submit to the unknown. And when other men act upon me and I am a victim to their acts, then I must humbly declare, ' 'Tis God's will. God's will be done.' Yet I'm the one who's blasphemous? When all about me are Christians who generously give out as God's will the evil acts of man? Or is that the devil's will? I have it: The means are the devil's and the ends are God's. When a man commits a murder, he is submitting to the devil's will; and the murdered man is submitting, without choice, to God's will. There we have it.

"You talk to me of choosing, Sara, but you have your own Lutheran beliefs. Well, we have no free will, says Luther. We cannot choose goodness or evil. The human will, he says, is like a beast of burden; man is a captive, a servant, a bondslave either to the will of God or to the will of Satan. If God foreknew that Judas would be a traitor, Judas became a traitor of necessity, and Judas could not change what God had foreseen. Nay—don't argue with me. I've debated all this already with Bess. I quoted her Luther, she quoted me Erasmus and his arguments that we have a free will. I quoted Calvin, and she St. Augustine. It did the neither of us any good."

He looked about at all the figure- and word-filled papers and began to push them into a crooked pile. "With these poor things," he said with a sigh, "I try to look into God's mind."

"Catlin," said I tenderly, "you told me once that you shipped God's word to bribe Him for some peace, and before that you prayed. Don't you pray still?"

His voice was like a plainsong from a distant place. "Aye, till there's nothing left in me and all I feel around me is emptiness."

I was swaying again. "And yet you also try to evade God."

"Aye, and that Bess cannot understand."

"She'd be your opposite when it comes to that, wouldn't she? And I'm different from you both. What an odd lot the three of us make, almost a strange trinity. Bess, you, and I: defiance, evasion, and complacence."

Catlin didn't seem to hear me. He fell back against his chair, turned his face toward the stove, and stared at the twitching flames. I looked at him, wanting terribly to help him, ashamed that all I could offer was my poor presence and loving worry. Sadly, he moved his head, his aspect changed, and a haunted—and haunting—expression moved across his face. For a moment I thought I was looking at Bess, so alike was that expression to one I sometimes saw on her. A worry began riddling me. Suddenly I needed to search for her again.

"Catlin," said I, "know you where Bess is? I'd thought earlier she'd gone out with you."

He stirred. "Mayhap she went riding."

"On such a day? But what for?"

He stretched and came a little out of his melancholy fog. "She's gone riding several times of late. I've writ for her my permission to use my horse, and she shows it to the grooms at the stables. Then she most like pays for an escort."

"Still, for a young woman to go riding, and in such weather." I stood up. "I don't like the idea of her being out and walking alone to the stables. Belike I should go find her."

"The either of you are oft alone in the streets. But if you like, I'll help you look for her."

"Nay, Catlin, stay you here and rest—you need that. I'll to the stables and simply inquire if indeed she has gone riding. The place is but a few minutes' walk from here."

I moved toward Catlin and laid my hand on his shoulder, not knowing what else to do. "My dear friend," I said softly. He took my hand and kissed it. He was calmer now, and weary, no longer the frenzied eccentric but instead my familiar companion.

In minutes I had drawn on my warmest cloak, hat, and gloves—knowing I might be out of doors longer than I had led Catlin to think—and left the house. The streets had scant noise in them and few passersby, and the shops and countinghouses were all closed up in subdued observance of Sunday. Up beyond my head the mist hung, mixing with the smoke of endless chimneys.

No one was at the stables save one groom, a ruddy man kneeling beside an old mare whilst trimming her hooves. I described Bess to him, he was familiar with the sight of her, and I asked if she had been there that day.

"Nay, not today," he answered roughly, hoping I would go away.

"Then no one has taken out Mynheer Bartholomew Catlin's horse today? I trow she must have gone somewhere else." I was about to leave when the man stopped his trimming.

"Oh, his horse was taken out today. 'Tis out now."

I was a little surprised. "I didn't think anyone else had permission to ride it."

He became defensive. " 'Twas a young man, and he had permission. He showed me the bit o' paper, the one Mynheer Catlin has writ up. Didn't see the fellow's face too well—it was all covered up 'gainst the cold. But withal it looked familiar. He had permission. 'Tis none of my fault if he came by that paper wrongly. Said he'd have the horse back ere night."

Certes I was not about to challenge the groom's story; Catlin had merely given one of the apprentices or someone else the use of his horse. Still I hesitated to leave just yet. I had a feeling that Bess had indeed gone riding and had only rented a horse elsewhere, there being none here for her to have.

"Tell me, sirrah—have you a horse I might briefly use?"

" 'Twill cost you something."

"I mean to pay."

He grumbled and looked me up and down. "The only horse I can give you is this old mare. Won't much more than trot for you."

"She'll serve my purpose, but I must have her quickly."

With no great speed he readied the horse, helped me to mount, and thrust out his hand for payment ere letting go of the bridle. I paid him and was off.

I walked the mare out to the street and set her into a slow trot toward St. George's Gate. The sound of her iron-shod hooves upon the stones clattered in mine ears; I felt as though I were declaring mine unwise situation: a foolish woman riding alone out of the city, in pursuit of a niece she had only assumed was herself out riding. But I would ride only a short distance out, I told myself, and look over the land, that was all.

I came to the gate. Past its huge stone walls, through its open arch, I could see the guards moving, and at the far end a straight-standing one, his halberd stark before the open pale land beyond. Tied to the halberd was a scarlet ribbon that fluttered in the wind, its color sudden against the wintry distance. I rode under the arch, aware of the guards' curious glances toward me and of the echo of the horse's hooves as it struck the walls and returned upon my head too loudly. I passed out over the bridge spanning the moat. The bridge ended on a dirt road that led into a mist-shrouded country; I could not see very far at all, and certes I would have trouble finding Bess and her escort, even if they were close. I hurried the old mare into a trot that my ill-planned task would end the sooner.

I rode only a quarter of a mile, then stopped, for I thought I heard the neigh of another horse. I guided the mare off the road and over some of the frozen ground. It was bare, hard land, with threads of snow wrapping around tufts of shorn wheat. A dead weed, its stiff roots pulled from the earth, rolled along on its branches, past my horse's legs and down a hill as if on a pilgrimage into oblivion. I watched it till in the corner of mine eye I saw something move. Swiftly, I looked around. Not far from me, for only a moment, I saw a rider. But the mist drifted again and the image disappeared. I thought of Catlin; I knew not why that brief sight had evoked an image of him in me. Perchance it was the color of the horse or the figure of the man—and a man it had been. Whoever he might be, I told myself, I couldn't know, and he might well be a rogue or a brigand, thus it was best that I hied myself out of that place and back to the city. I drew my horse about and meant to hurry away, but a faint cry stopped me. Was that not Bess's voice? It had been a lone voice, crying out over that desolation, and had come from yonder, near where I had seen the rider. Disquieted, I carefully moved in that direction at a slow walk. Then I pulled up short.

A form was emerging from the sifting mist. The dull pound of a horse's hooves came sounding toward me. The mist folded back and a rider appeared. The same horse, the same rider that I had seen only in part before, appeared, like an unearthly wraith. The horse had been galloping but now the rider reined it in and let it walk forward, then turned it this way and that, as if he were looking for something or someone. In the turning, I saw the rider's arm hanging at his side, and clasped in its gloved hand was a long, thin sword. Again the rider turned around and at last I saw the face. My hand flew to my mouth. I gasped and tried not to cry out.

It was Bess. The rider was Bess, dressed in a man's clothing and straddling like a man Catlin's dun horse. The long dark cape that billowed around her was too Catlin's—that much I recognized; and when it blew away to her back I could see a rusty jerkin and a brown doublet, and on her legs, coming up over her knees, were heavy buskins. What I'd taken to be a hood was instead her hair, hanging black and loose down her back and entangled with itself. She had hastily dressed: She needed an e'en thicker doublet to keep her warm, and the jerkin wasn't laced all the way up so that the white shirt beneath it hung open at her throat. But the wintry chill seemed not to touch her, so fevered was she. I pulled farther back, dreading that she might see me, but her eyes were affixed on some distant sight.

She tipped back her head and it seemed she looked at nothing, or at some transfiguration born of her own heated soul. All at once, with a fierce thrust she stabbed the sword up into the hoary air, left it pointing, then slashed once and again let it and her arm hang at her side. She urged on her horse and the beast trotted onto higher ground and away from me, and there she reined it in again.

"Catlin!" she wailed. Her horse, frightened by its strange rider, stamped and treaded backward. She kicked its sides to control the snorting beast. "Catlin! You've made yourself my fate, then stay my fate! My God, I will not lose you!" Her voice flailed the air with savage determination.

Only God and I were her witnesses; no one else was near to deny or cheer her on. Yet she seemed ready to fight a denial that was ringing in her ears. All I could hear was a hollow wind in the distance. All I could understand was that what she had been dreading she had now seen happen. The storm had broken out in Catlin, and in it he was sailing away from her. She swung her sword this way and that, as if fighting hidden doubts. She found no satisfaction in the act and for some moments did not move. Suddenly she spurred her horse and it broke into a gallop, and she passed on and away and out of my sight.

I strained to look over the mounds and slopes of the landscape. Still I could not see her, nor could I hear her pounding horse. All about me there was only the sound of emptiness. I felt as if I had just beheld some terrible apparition, but now it was gone and I was alone on that dismal ground.

I jerked my horse, slapped it violently, and sped away back to the city.

XXV

The man Catlin had sent to Cologne, the nameless shadowy groom, spent but a short while there and returned home apace with all the information he had gathered. What he had uncovered he told Catlin and Catlin told us: Nicolas van Wouwere did indeed go to Cologne, and there stayed till the things he had shipped to himself arrived. Then he seemed to have disappeared; but the groom dug about incessantly and finally came upon a carter who worked for a different Italian transporting company than that van Wouwere had hired in Antwerp. For a price, and after enough drink had been poured into him, the carter revealed that van Wouwere had continued on to Rome under the name of Peter Heyns, and had thus shipped on his things in the care of this company. It was clear to the carter that van Wouwere meant to settle in Rome, and too that the doctor had on him and in all was worth far more than seven hundred Flemish pounds; having been in the transporting business for many years, the carter claimed to have become a formidable judge of a traveler's wealth, or the lack of it. For more money yet, the groom was able to obtain from him the name and location of an inn in Rome where the company's carters regularly stayed. Its innkeeper would for a price tell one the whereabouts of any newcomer to that city who e'en indirectly had aught to do with the business of his inn. After writing from Cologne to this innkeeper and asking for a reply to be sent to Catlin, the groom returned, his assigned task completed.

"Whatever the innkeeper can tell me," Catlin said with a sigh, "will do little good. Rome is too far for me to put my hold on van Wouwere, my stolen money, or his written lies of you."

"Send another man off after him," Bess urged.

"No, Bess. To pay for such a man's expenses of travel and his fee would only add all the more to the money I lost, should the task be unsuccessful. And I can't send him for your sake, which is more important, because there's too great a chance that it would be to no avail. By the time he reaches van Wouwere, the forged evidence 'gainst you will most like be on its way to Antwerp, or already here. 'Tis better to keep our forces here and intercept through bribery that evidence he sends to the magistrates."

" 'Twould not be better if the task does succeed, sith that way van Wouwere will pay for all our costs," said she. "Have of him your own money and what you spent to get it back. And I'll have from him a payment of mine own."

He smiled. "You yourself are e'en willing to go to Rome, aren't you?"

"You know I am."

They said no more on the matter, or if they did then not in my presence.

Catlin began to return to his customary habits and worked with other merchants and his apprentices. Bess too had let her work slacken but was again plunging into it with a determination fiercer even than his had ever been, as if she intended to finish with all her business and set aside as much profit as possible. Yet still, when a venture was completed or another day was done, then she and Catlin spent long hours at each other's side, or went off separately, feverish and unhappy. Ofttimes I would find Catlin in his library, reading deep into a book or bent again over his horoscopes, and sometimes I found him only sitting by the fire in the antler room, alone or with Bess. Where Bess went when she was in turn alone I never discovered, and knew it was fruitless to ask her. Once, whilst walking alone down a street, I thought I caught a glimpse of her, again in Catlin's clothes, her face distracted, her steps hurried, but ere I could confirm that it was indeed Bess, she—or whoever it was—had turned around a corner and was gone.

As for mine own and my sons' business in Antwerp, I could see the divers ventures finishing themselves, and with their completion close at hand was the ending of my need to remain there. I would soon be home, I knew, and was glad of it. Easter was coming upon us and with it the important Pask Mart at Bergen-op-Zoom, and to that fair my sons would be sending much English cloth to be sold. Therefore I planned with Bess and Catlin to attend it, and then to remain in Antwerp till after Pentecost when the bills for the fair were settled; but no longer, I promised myself.

I then received from home good news: Both my sons were at last free to be away from London for a little and would be accompanying to Bergen-op-Zoom the cloths they were sending over. Matthew and he would handle all the selling, Jeremy wrote; I need only enjoy myself and arrange the day to meet them in that town. I told Bess of this and she said she shared my joy, but I doubted her. Whether or no she would remain and marry Catlin or return to England with me after Pentecost, she never said, and, too, van Wouwere's forged papers that could send her fleeing from Antwerp had not yet been received at the Vierschare, so said the bribed clerk there. At another time, I decided, I would discuss or argue these things with her, but for the nonce I wanted nothing to spoil my present good cheer, so dear a feeling was it after all those gloomy winter months.

On the day after Easter Sunday we rode the thirty or so miles north to Bergen-op-Zoom. Riding through the sunshine, across the country greening with spring, I felt as if I were coming alive again, and I was windblown and free to do for a while exactly as I pleased, just as when I was young. I told Bess of how in my youth I had wanted to travel like this, to travel far and wide and to do so much. But things intervened—they always do—and dreams changed to practical plans, and years passed, and somehow what I had once wanted so intensely was forgotten.

Even the town, which I had been to a few times before, seemed a lovely sight when in the late afternoon we entered it. The ship-laden sea glimmered amber against the buildings, and all the colors of merchants' clothes and cloths and wares were crowded into bright reflections. The fair had begun on Good Friday, so already the town was filled with merchants and inns and houses were packed to bursting. Catlin had earlier written to his own favorite inn and thus saved us three rooms: one for Bess and me, the second for Jeremy and Matthew, and the last one for himself. We settled into them and quickly went out again to have a look about.

Merchant Adventurers were everywhere and I recognized several of them, chatted with a few, and examined this kersey or that broadcloth, content that at this mart I wouldn't have to be the busy merchant and barter and deal and buy and sell. Jeremy and Matthew would perform all such work, and Catlin was there to see not only to his own business but that of my other partners. I had scant trade with which to occupy myself, and my relief at this made me realize how truly tired of it all I was. Od's my life, I wondered, how many years now had I worked? More than six long years and hard since my Jonathan's death; those had been the roughest. Yet ere that too I had worked with him and for him, and for my sons. Oh, if to be idle is to be sinful then, I thought, Sweet Jesus forgive me, let me sin!

I slept well that night and rose betimes on the morrow. What time of the day Jeremy and Matthew's ship would arrive there was no telling, but most like it would dock in the forenoon. I was ready for it at dawn. Still I forced myself to wait, breakfasted with Bess and Catlin, and told them to go on about their work without me. Some time passed, and I headed down for the wharf.

Near to it, I caught sight of a familiar color. Ahead of me, disappearing behind other passing people, was a youth with sandy brown hair. I ran and called out and threw my arms around him and hugged him close ere finally pulling back to have a good look at him.

Matthew had dropped his bag to hold me and now stumbled over it as he too moved backward. "Ah yes—methought it was you." He grinned.

"Matthew, my dearest!" I patted and rubbed his shoulders. "It's been so long, so long."

"Eight months."

"Almost nine."

"And Jeremy you saw at September's end."

"When he was in Antwerp." I looked about me. "Where is your brother, then?"

"Somewhere hard by. I've just lost him."

"And your leg!" I bent down to examine it. "How is your leg?"

"Healed fast."

"Have you a limp from it?"

"Only when he wants sympathy" came Jeremy's voice, and then he appeared at my side.

I chattered on with them both till the traffic in the busy street forced us to be on our way. At the inn I helped them settle into their room, and all the while we gave each other our news and I studied them. Since I'd seen them last they had grown less boyish in their bodies, and still no unquiet shadows plagued their aspects; nothing about them was secret or melancholy, unlike Catlin. Matthew, as always, clowned in his easy fashion and threw back his head when he laughed and swaggered in a way that made women watch him. Jeremy, who was a little shorter than his brother, moved with much more restraint, as if distrusting the steadiness of his flapping feet or the appeal of his less handsome, bulbous-nosed face. Though they seemed as ever ready to bicker with each other, I sensed too a deepening bond betwixt them, strengthened no doubt by their having to rely all the more on each other whilst I was so long away. In mine absence, I had become less familiar, somewhat distant from them, and in turn had come to feel more at home with Bess. I have been away too long from England, I sighed.

"There's one thing, Mother, I've been meaning to ask you," Jeremy said. "And, in sooth, Meric Dugdale has been wondering the same, as have all our partners. About our factor, Bartholomew Catlin, and your living with him—all is well, isn't it?"

My answer came uneasily. "Of course all is well. Have you heard differently?"

"Nay. 'Tis only that in your letters you ofttimes seem to be leaving out or covering o'er something."

Matthew was blunter. "There be no problems with Catlin, or 'twixt him and you and Bess?"

"Nay, not at all." I lied so readily that I disliked myself.

"Well, good then. Good." Jeremy dug about for his looking glass so that he could better see the comb. "I suppose 'tis but the times that gave us the impression. There are growing disorders in England."

"There is more disorder here," Matthew reminded him. He sat down on the bed and sprawled his long legs out. "We've heard of all the Anabaptists and Lutherans who have been burned in the Lowlands."

" 'Tis true," I unhappily admitted.

Jeremy at last snapped the comb free from a few remaining hairs. "Such burnings have never before been as common in England. But twice now, whilst I was of late riding down to Berkshire to negotiate with our clothiers there, I pressed through villages where heretics were being burned at Queen Mary's order. And the people in such places are sickening at the bloodshed. There are e'en whispers of rebellion . . ."

Again, Matthew diminished his brother's opinion. "But there'll be none. Just more suspicion, more Protestants leaving England."

I wanted no suspicions on myself, or Bess, or Catlin. My loyalty to him was surging forward again, driving me to shield him even from my sons, who, though loving and loyal to me, could sometimes have loose tongues. "Not Catlin, nor Bess or I has aught to do with such troubles," said I, "and nothing is wrong among us."

After Jeremy and Matthew had settled and eaten a hardy meal, I walked with them to that part of town wherein Catlin said he would most likely be. When we found him, Jeremy greeted him and introduced Matthew.

"I pray all has fared well with you since last we met, Master Catlin?" asked Jeremy.

"Aye, all is well," Catlin said.

He talked with them for a little, and when he turned to me I could see the two exchange knowing glances, as if Matthew then understood what Jeremy had told him about our factor.

That afternoon my sons' cloths were unladed and readied for showing. On the morrow the cloths from our other partners arrived, and Catlin saw to them whilst Bess, busy with her own work, oft stayed near him. I myself did scant more at first than watch my sons, so hungry was I still for the sight of them. Matthew, ever handsome and full of charm, would flirt with what women he dealt with or caught his eye, thus annoying the earnest, awkward Jeremy who, when deep in work, could think only of that.

But mine ease ended: I was soon doing far more work than I'd thought I would or they had promised. My Flemish having been used daily for so long was fluent and better than theirs, thus Matthew wanted me present whenever he struck a deal in that language or e'en one in French. He asked me on occasion to negotiate a bargain or give him advice, and if he cared not for it, he gave me his own. Jeremy, in turn, ever the proud merchant, scorned his brother's dependence on me, yet relied on me withal to perform endless minor tasks for him. When, one day, I'd had enough of this and told Jeremy I wasn't his servant, Matthew took my side, the two of them bickered, then sided with each other against me, and not till we sat down over tankards of ale were we at peace again.

We had o'er the years become involved in many such arguments, as was normal for my family, I told myself; yet it seemed as though I'd forgotten as much. I had during all those foreign-spent months painted it with longings, till finally it became for me a picture of a little paradise. 'Twas better to be reminded of that paradise's faults and be disappointed now, rather than when I returned to it.

Certainly too I would have to work when I returned home; that was my least desired remembrance. I could only be returning to the busy routine I had followed ere leaving for Antwerp. My life at home would be as it always had been. Ah, but it was my home, where I had learned to find happiness in the small good things that marked my days. I felt old again.

All the cloths were soon sold, and cash was received for some of them and bills of exchange were drawn up for the rest. Catlin would be able to oversee the discharging of those bills after Pentecost, so I could return home before then. Only a little business yet held me in Antwerp. Jeremy and Matthew of course had to return to England presently and had not e'en the time to ride back to that city with us.

The evening before they were to sail, I walked along the wharf with my sons. Jeremy kept to my side and talked with me of small things, whilst Matthew drifted behind us, listening a little, saying less, and looking out across the waters. Only a curved chip of sun had not yet sunk into the sea, but still it shot purple and golden lights into the sky and dappled the air around us.

"I'll not be staying much longer with Catlin," I said. " 'Twill be sad to leave him after all this time. I believe I'll dearly miss him."

"Will Bess leave him at all?" Jeremy asked.

"So e'en you have noticed their friendship."

"Surely there must be more than that between them. Have they spoken of marriage?"

"They've touched on it." I searched for more to say. "I haven't yet wanted to talk with her of her plans. When we're in Antwerp again I must."

"Well, perchance they should marry, though by my troth I don't greatly like the man. I'm sorry to admit that, knowing of your own loving friendship with him. But truly, he is too . . ." Pausing to think, Jeremy pursed his lips.

Here Matthew caught up with us. "He acts as though there were something lurking in him that might get out, so he keeps himself in solitude, or with Cousin Bess."

"Aye, exactly that," said Jeremy.

We passed a fisherman whose net formed a spiral around him like a shell, and in its middle he sat and darned its broken joints.

The only thing that could force Bess from Catlin's side, I knew, was van Wouwere's damning forged "proof" with which he'd threatened her; that could indeed make her flee to England. "If Bess does return with me," said I, "I would wish her to live with us."

Jeremy shrugged. "As you wish."

Matthew ambled to the end of the wharf and there gazed down at several empty fishing boats that were knocking 'gainst each other, surrendering to each wave that rhythmically pushed them about. "She and Catlin should be left to each other" was all he said.

On the morrow I accompanied them to the ship on which they would sail home to London. Apprehending my wishes, Bess and Catlin left me alone whilst I bade good-bye to my sons and watched the ship sail away. I could not stop myself from wondering if I should have left with them.

The three of us remained in Bergen-op-Zoom for a sennight more, till our personal sales and purchases were completed, after which we returned to Antwerp. We rested only the evening of our arrival and in the morning went to the countinghouse.

A pile of letters awaited the each of us. Bess and I left Catlin to the privacy of his office and read our own letters in the chamber. The house was empty save for us, Michiel and Jan being elsewhere and the servant Dorothea off fetching food. We'd not been reading long when Catlin came out of his office with a letter in his hand, and half sat on our table's edge.

"This news I know will do the none of us any good," said he. "I've received a letter from Rome, from the innkeeper we were told of; I don't know his name, for he would not sign it and 'tis in poor French." He knew already so well what was in the letter that he had no need to consult it as he spoke on. "He writes that a Flemish doctor by the name of Nicolas van Wouwere has newly settled in Rome. Mine old friend is arrogantly certain of his safety, isn't he? Already he has dispensed with his disguise and false name. 'He must be a good doctor since he seems to be most wealthy,' this innkeeper says, and if he means to be sly I can't say. He says also that van Wouwere has already spent much money to furnish his new house—rented, of course—and is awaiting the arrival of other possessions from Cologne. How quickly he traveled."

Bess had listened eagerly to his every word. "Will you send someone to Rome?"

"I'm not certain. If a man can get to van Wouwere and take from him what is owed me and too enough to pay his own fee and the cost of his journey, and all with utmost stealth, then I would. I'll not have any authorities, even Roman ones, informed of this crime. I might lose or win in a court of law, but either way word would eventually get back here to Antwerp and I'd be humiliated. Now for your sake, Bess, I would send a man at once, but I think his task would be futile. We know the magistrates here have not yet received that forged proof from van Wouwere. Mayhap that was an empty threat, or mayhap he was traveling with such haste he had no time to compose carefully such papers. But now he's settled, hence now at any time those papers could arrive in Antwerp."

"And what of your own sake?" asked Bess.

"Mayhap I can quietly and firmly reclaim the tapestry bought by van Wouwere's friend in Cologne. I'll ask my agent there if this is possible."

"You'll do nothing more than that?"

His anger was sliding into frustration. "I might not be able to." Wanting no more to talk of it, closing into himself like a lock, he returned to his office.

I shook my head, mumbled, "Poor Catlin," and for long minutes could do no more than stare off into the air. Bess was doing the same, so I tried to stop this by talking of mundane things.

"Marry, Bess, we've only a few letters here, and if mine be like yours, the work they do charge us with is soon done. Methinks we might be able to return to England in a fortnight. Shall I book passage for us both?"

"No, for yourself only," she said.

So, already I was drawing from her what I wished to know. "Will you not be returning with me?"

"I will not."

I lowered my voice. "Well then, do you and Catlin mean to marry?"

Even now she wouldn't talk of it. Sharply, she shook her head. "I'm not talking about that. I say only that I will not leave Antwerp for England, but I will leave it for Rome."

I was astounded. "You are *not* going to Rome!" I sputtered. "You have no purpose that could take you there."

"I have mine own purposes, grave purposes." A hard resolve was sweeping o'er her. "I am going to Rome."

"You are not!" I retorted, far more incensed then than was she. "What madness can this be? Have you no idea how far away Rome is? Oh, I know, you think 'tis but a pleasant ride from one town to the next. You stubborn fool! Do you actually think you can hunt down van Wouwere, take back from him Catlin's money?"

" 'Tis not just his money!"

"Nor that false proof!" I spat. "Oh no, 'tis more than e'en that, isn't it, Bess? 'Tis those damn prophecies of van Wouwere—they're terrifying you! You believe them. So you have to hunt them down and prove van Wouwere is wrong."

She shot up and flung back her stool. "And I'll listen to you no more, not so long as you prate with this stupidity!"

At that moment Catlin hastened out of his office. "What is wrong here?" he demanded.

"Bess claims that she is going to trot off to Rome," I answered ere could she. "She stupidly believes she can pursue that pernicious van Wouwere."

"You'll not go there!" he snapped. "You must defend yourself against him here!"

"I cannot wait here endlessly, and I'll not just defend myself, I'll attack! And I will go despite what you say." She began to direct all her defiance against him, as if mine own protests mattered not at all. "I choose to go to Rome. I have more than enough money to do so. No business now holds me here, or anywhere. I must go. For mine own purposes, Catlin, I must go, and you know that."

"And know you why, Catlin?" I was by then nigh muffled with anger and frustration.

He only gazed at Bess. He was aware of her reasons, I now comprehended, and of her terror. The prophecies' effect on her he knew all about, and more, much more, just as he had told her more things than he had e'er told me. It was I who was ignorant.

"You do not have to," said he to her.

"Then say that I choose to." She made a bare, cunning smile. "Do not ascribe to my choice more importance than it deserves. I will go to Rome, and what of it? Do not hundreds, thousands of people travel to Rome every month? Pilgrims go, merchants go, hessemen driving carts from Antwerp to Italy leave every day. Certainly I will not go alone. Did you actually think I would madly dash off on a horse, Aunt?" she asked with facetious scorn. I knew her to be capable of doing just that, but did not say so. "I will go under the protection of a transporting company. There are several Italian companies that allow travelers, of course for a price, to accompany their trains, and give them protection." She began to think and plan aloud. "All of mine expenses—my horse, my stays at inns, my transportation on barges, the tolls on the Rhine—I must pay for, and as I have said, I can well afford them. Two months to travel to Rome, perchance, and less that back, since we'll return down the Rhine. I shall be traveling in the spring and summer months, the best possible time for a journey, the most agreeable time."

"Oh, this is folly!" I cried. "Of course, yes of course. You can go off to Rome with a group of hired men."

"And some female pilgrims, for whose company I will pay. Their own expenses they can pay for, since they are headed for Rome anyway."

"I've heard of these pilgrims," said I. "Some are not so very honest, nor holy. They might make sorry company for you, which you would richly deserve."

"Then come with me yourself, Aunt."

The mere suggestion, let alone the serious tone in which she made it, astonished me. "Why should I be as mad as you?"

"Because you have always wanted to travel, you've said so yourself. In your youth you would have gone everywhere, you've told me. Make this your pilgrimage then, though your feelings toward Rome are not very loyal. Or find your own purpose. But with you or without you, I am going." She spun about and strode into Catlin's office. We followed.

She was standing before the map that hung on the office wall. Her hand was at her mouth, rubbing away at worries. She stared at that map, smiled at mayhap the grandness of her plans, and a mirthless laugh escaped under her breath.

Catlin took her by the shoulders. "I'll send a man to Rome."

"Send him with me, since I'm going there myself," said she.

"By God, Sara is right!" he yelled, and shoved her away from the map. "You are mad and a fool if you think your pursuit of him will give you any peace."

"Do your pursuits give you any peace then?" she snapped. "You're the fool for thinking I should follow your means to peace!" As quickly as she had angered, she softened and touched his neck gently as if to soothe him and draw away the words she had just flung at him. Disturbed, not knowing now what to do or say, she hurried out of the room.

"Let me talk with her, Catlin," I said, with my hand around his arm to hold him back. Then I too went out.

Bess was standing at one of the windows in the front chamber as if lost and trying to think where next she should go. She heard me approaching but would not look behind her; instead she paced down the hall and to the back room. I found her in there, standing like a trapped creature. She turned sharply about, ready to fight more if need be, but I only went to rest tiredly against some boxes next to her.

"I'll not talk of your intention to go to Rome," I said quietly. "And I'll not fight you now. But tell me this: Can you be so willing to leave Catlin?"

"I am not willing to leave him. But for four, five months, for something I must do for mine own sake, not only for his . . . I must go."

She too now half rested upon the boxes, and they creaked under our weight. We were both silent for countless minutes; the only sounds in the house rolled in from the street.

"Do you still love him?" I asked finally.

For a long time she was mute, and when at last she spoke it was as if with battered emotions. "I can never stop loving him. I feel as if I have always loved him, even before I met him. As I have loved myself, so him, and as I have hated myself . . . so him."

Whilst she spoke, any lovely likeness she might have borne to other young women in passionate love fell away, and over her face a passion crept instead. "But for both our sakes, I have to go. Since van Wouwere defrauded him, since that day at the Bourse, Catlin has been drawing so far into himself that sometimes e'en I can't reach him. He is more terrified than ever that his life is following van den Bist's, and now too he fears that van Wouwere's prophecies for me may come true. So I have to go to Rome. I have to show Catlin what mine own will—and his—might do against any prophecy or horoscope or invented fate. We can give each other scant peace, we can scarce live long together, if I do nothing."

"But you love each other so much."

"That isn't enough."

I shook my head over and over, trying to wag away the turmoil she was imparting to me, and my sight grew bleary with tears of frustration. "I've too simple a nature for you. I do not know, I do not know at all what to do with you, if indeed I can do aught. Why must you be so very different from me that I cannot understand you? We are so oddly matched we can do each other little good."

"I have oft made you suffer," she said sadly.

I said nothing.

"Ah, I have then. And words of regret can little heal the pain. But you have done me much good. Far more have you given me than I you, and that too I regret."

"What have I done but taught you how to be a worthy Adventurer?"

"You took me with you to Antwerp."

"Let that be my regret."

She sighed. "You have been for me my only family and taken on, with charity and kindness and few complaints, though a thousand complaints be yours by right, all the hardships a mother must bear. And I have been your prodigal child."

My lips quivered. "Yet there is nothing of a child in you."

"I am old, am I not?" She sounded so distant. "So very old, I feel. And already I'm tired of life, though I cling so desperately to it. I do not wish for a long life. Let it be but a short one, and I would be content. For just a little peace that lasts, and some happiness, I would be content."

My frustration was mustering up into anger. "You need not go to Rome for that."

"Ah yes, Sara—I must indeed go."

What strength there was yet left in me broke, and noiselessly I began to cry. Helpless, I could not change her mind. Helpless, she could not comfort me.

The three of us returned home early that day, and there the fight over Bess's leaving for Rome continued. I myself retreated from the brawl, for she and Catlin clawed at each other with such word-stinging talons that I durst not come betwixt them or take either one's side. At one point Bess stormed out of the antler room and was about to go up the stairs to her bedchamber when Catlin dragged her back down off the steps.

" 'Tis reckless revenge, that's all!" he cried. "Van Wouwere assaulted you, in body and in words, and you wish your revenge!"

"Such revenge I've had already!" Bess wrenched her wrist away from his grasp. "When he grappled with me with his hands I more than paid him back in kind!"

"Then 'tis his prophecies you are pursuing! What a hypocrite you are. You've taunted me for my belief in his small foretellings, but you've the faith of a saint in his prophecies for you!"

They were by now circling about each other like two wild beasts. Catlin's violent despair seemed to be bristling out of his very skin. It terrified me, but Bess, her fingers hardening into steely hooks and her passions growling, was his undaunted match.

"I will hunt him down to prove his prophecies are false!" she declared. "I will not have a fate forced upon me. And I'll show you how false yours is!"

"I will not see you come to harm!"

"And no harm will come to me."

He grabbed her shoulders and held her fast. "God curse me for not hunting down van Wouwere when he left Antwerp! I gave up too easily.

I returned too soon. I should have pursued him to hell and back, that I may now keep you and not lose you."

"You can never lose me!" she whispered hotly.

They argued and fought and wrestled on, until hours later the house was at last vacant of those awful sounds. Then the night came and they found themselves lying on the rug before the fire, Catlin's head on a pillow, Bess's head on his chest, and their arms around each other. The very air about them seemed to be yawning with tender anguish. Yet nothing in either was truly transmuted, and nothing was resolved. They were but reposed, drowsing as if now destitute of strength and of dreams.

The days passed, and though I too battled and entreated Bess, eventually I surrendered. Neither I nor Catlin could dissuade her, and indeed there was a madness in being so obstinate against her, for as she had pointed out, thousands of people traveled hundreds of miles every year to Rome; all that set her apart from them was her purpose.

Catlin acknowledged how futile it was to oppose her ere I could. He investigated her initial preparations for the journey, found them lacking, and began to oversee every part. She would ride to Cologne in the company of several merchants and their servants and from Cologne would travel to Milan under the protection of a transporting company. In Milan she could find either more fellow merchants who were also headed for Rome and were willing to have her go along with them, or she could engage again the protection of a transporting company.

I was not annoyed when Catlin aided Bess for I knew he did so in order to assure as best he could her safety. An important element in the preparations was still missing, howe'er, and one afternoon I sought him out in his library and sat with him to talk of it.

He had before him a scattering of star-riddled papers, and when I saw them he pushed them aside with a trace of shame.

"I have been tormented with worry for Bess," said he, "and these stars be but poor assurances that she will fare well."

"God grant they be right," I feebly replied. It was an effort for me to carry on. "My work in Antwerp is finished. I may go home now, if I choose."

He nodded his awareness of this.

I contemplated the papers. "Have no female pilgrims been engaged to travel with Bess?"

"She has found none whose companionship she can tolerate for long."

"She should be more considerate and speculate if they could tolerate hers, which I doubt." I rose and paced about the small room. I'faith, she had conquered my resistance as she had intended to, I bethought me, and had so wearied me that all I could then feel was resignation. "Then, if you would, I pray you see to similar preparations for me, that I might accompany her."

He was less surprised by my words than I had anticipated. "Are you certain you want to go?"

"No, 'tis not what I want." I sighed. "But still I'll go."

And so there were no more arguments on the issue, only discussions concerning the preparations. I would after all be going with Bess. I could travel now the way I had once so dearly desired to, and I could see some great places, and even Rome, just as I had long ago dreamed of doing. That those youthful desires had much waned over the years I tried to disregard. Far more important to me was that she was mine only niece, in a way mine only daughter, whom I loved, and whether or no she needed my company, I felt the great need to protect her. I wrote to my sons and informed them of the journey and of my decision, which I nothing doubted astounded them, and promised to write home when possible. I was glad they were not present and so could not persuade me to sail instead straight back to London; and in their rushed letter sent in reply to mine they were too busy pointing out to me how ridiculous my intended journey was, and that I already well knew, to make enticing invitations to come back to them. I also could not help but be offended by their implication that it was better for me to be home working with them than to be for several months on mine own and idle.

Bess and I bought traveling clothes and divers provisions. We decided not to carry much with us but to travel lightly and buy along the way some of what we needed. Neither would we carry a great deal of money with us, but bills of exchange instead, so that in Cologne and Milan we would be able to obtain more if the need arose. Other details were seen to, and then we were ready to leave.

Early on the morning of our departure, Catlin went to the stables and came riding back on his dun horse whilst Arnout walked behind, holding the reins of two riderless ones. Onto those two horses, both of which had been fitted with women's palfreys, our bags were hung, and then Bess and I mounted. Lijsken and Maria bid us farewell and good fortune on our travels—so senseless to them—and watched us leave. Then Catlin rode on and we followed him. Bess kept her gaze upon his back but I twisted around to look at the house, and I looked still after we had turned the corner and I could no longer see it.

The merchants with whom we were going to Cologne had already through Catlin been introduced to us, and with them we had earlier discussed that part of our journey. Thus when we arrived at the meeting place, nothing was left to be said save the exchange of welcomes and the inevitable teasing they had from their friends and wives for "bounding off with two fair and wealthy widows."

Suddenly it was time to leave. They bade farewell to their friends and wives, and as they rode ahead and Catlin kept to our sides, we all headed for Kipdorp Gate. There the three of us stopped.

"Fare thee well." The words dropped out of Catlin as if he were struggling with the pain of his feelings.

"And you." Bess's voice was rusty with tears. "I worry more for you here than for myself where'er I am."

"Then return to me swiftly."

I bade him farewell, and he kissed me good-bye. "God keep you," said I. His face was so burdened with the desolation of coming loneliness that I could scarce stand to look upon him.

He turned to Bess. For sad moments they could only gaze upon each other. Then he leaned over to her and grasped her head with his hands, and he kissed her long and fervently, and when they finally parted he whispered to her and she to him, and with a sob she pulled away.

We urged on our horses and went through the gate to catch up with the others.

◆　◆　◆

Bess was dejected the rest of the morning, which in no way endeared her to our companions. Four servants rode behind us, and the four merchants with whom we rode—being good Flemings all—were spirited and eager to make wagers even as we traveled. Hazarding the odd groat and stiver, they bet on whatever trivial distraction we happened upon: whether the next person in the fields was a man or a maid, the number of carts we would pass in an hour, and so on. Now and then I joined in their wagers and so pocketed some coins.

Because of the many tolls along it, we were taking not the high road to Cologne, but instead were going through the sandy Campine. Still we passed a good number of villages and towns, and too as many inns. One of the men told me that on well-traveled roads everywhere such inns were every ten or fifteen miles. Our lodgings on Bess's and my trip, he told us, would give us few problems; 'twas the cheating innkeepers themselves we need guard against, said he, it being his expert opinion that not many were honest.

By the afternoon Bess had grown as merry as the others, and at the village inn wherein we stayed that night, and in the remaining days it took us to reach Cologne, merry she continued and I with her, and so much so that I considered myself foolish for nigh dreading this trip. Not that our traveling was easy: We changed horses several times a day, at several different posthouses, and by evening my back and muscles were full sore from the many hours I'd spent in the saddle. Natheless, I prayed, let us be this way, without problems, all the way to Rome.

Though I had never seen the city, Cologne was as I had pictured it to be: a sprawling crowd of buildings, proud dwarfs in the shadow of their giant cathedral. Our companions were familiar with the city, and ere departing from us they led us to the street and then the home of Catlin's factor.

The door was opened to us by Helmut Schorer himself, a graying, squinting man with a gentle manner who seated us in what seemed the best room of his house whilst his wife fetched us good beer and a servant carried our bags to the floor above. He was most willing to take us into his house for the two nights and three days we would be in the city, he said in excellent French. (English being such a minor language, I had decided that Bess and I would belike not hear it again till we were back in Antwerp.) When we were alone with him and our beer, he began to talk.

Through Catlin, he was aware in part of our purpose in coming to Cologne, and so was well prepared to defend the way in which he had conducted the tapestry's purchase. With fastidious care he related to us every detail of what had passed with van Wouwere and the purchase and how the payment had been turned over by himself, through what he had assumed were Catlin's instructions, to this doctor. When we did not doubt or challenge Schorer about these facts, he was much relieved.

"Catlin has steadfastly maintained that you are an honest man," said I, "and that I believe."

He had pulled out a handkerchief to wipe the damp edges of his brow. "I thank thee, madam. But even an honest man can be a fool. I did not see that rascal doctor for what he was. How clever he was. And sly and cunning. Too sly for my poor wits."

"He's fooled wiser than you," said Bess.

I put aside my beer. "And peradventure so has this man who now has the tapestry. What of him, Monsieur Schorer, be he also honest?"

"Oh, I can't say, I can't say. I've never met him, and I've heard about him only a little. His name is Mueller, Kurst Mueller. He's a disliked, wealthy man who keeps much to himself and is said to behave like a tyrant in his household. And he is the same to those who run afoul with him in business. I have tried to see him, but without success. When I learned from Catlin that this doctor had run off with all that money, I went to Mueller's house. Twice I went. But both times I was denied entrance and the servants were told to shut the door in my face. All I wanted was to ask him about his friend van Wouwere, where he went and so forth. That was all."

"What a rude knave!" said I.

"But he did send me a message in which he said (and in sooth I agree in part with him) that he had paid fairly for the tapestry and would hear no more on't. And it was none of his concern if a merchant in Antwerp had been cozened in this business."

I hated the logic in all this; I myself did not want to agree. "Well"—I stiffened my back—"well, he may yet still have to hear more on't. From us."

For a moment Schorer studied us, then his feet, then us again. "In Catlin's letter to me, wherein he wrote of your coming, he said he was considering the possibility of reclaiming the tapestry. That might be ill-advised, an ill-advised endeavor. Mueller is a powerful man. And he's in his own city, and country. Who do you think the courts and burgomasters would favor? Well, there you have it. Certes, Catlin may try. One never knows."

Through all this, Bess seemed to have been sinking deeper and deeper into ponderings. Now she emerged from them. "Mueller must have known more about van Wouwere's cozening than he claims. That is, if he is unlike you a dishonest man."

Schorer shrugged. "Indeed, he may be. People say things about him."

"Then I wish to see him."

"But why?"

"Because he may be more than a friend to van Wouwere. He may have conspired with him, and so may know more about van Wouwere's exact whereabouts in Rome and his plans and actions, let alone the money. And too, if I meet him I may better judge Catlin's chances in reclaiming the tapestry."

The webs of wrinkles in Schorer's cheeks drew together into deep lines as his mouth moved gloomily downward. "I fear I must be blunter. Catlin will never reclaim that tapestry. You will belike not e'en be allowed into Mueller's house."

"But if we do get into it and see him?"

"Then you will be in a very dangerous territory," said he, blunt yet again and now foreboding, "and I could no longer help you."

XXVII

That same afternoon, honoring our request 'spite his frowning upon it, Schorer led us to the street wherein was Kurst Mueller's house and then turned about and left, saying that if the servants there saw him with us, of a certainty they'd not let us in.

The house was a massive, elaborate brick thing that seemed all the more like a fortress when Bess knocked and not the door but only a small wooden window in its middle was opened to us. A man's face filled the small space.

"Herr Mueller?" asked Bess.

He said something in German, a tongue neither of us could speak, so Bess asked him in Flemish and then in French if Herr Mueller was in and that we had come to see him. He grumbled something to this, pulled his face away, and shut the window. For long moments we waited; we knew not if someone else were coming to speak to us or if we had been told to go away. We were about to knock again when the small window opened and a bearded man put his face to it.

"Bonjour, mesdames," said he.

"Bonjour, monsieur," replied Bess, and talked on with him in French. "We've come to see Monsieur Mueller. We must talk with him for but a few moments."

"Does he know you, mesdames?" He was polite but indifferent.

"I fear not. But it concerns a business matter."

"Business?" He wanted more facts.

I murmured to her that to begin our efforts with a lie could prove unwise. She nodded.

"Please tell Monsieur Mueller," said she, "that we are new-come from Antwerp and wish to ask him if he has any news of Doctor Nicolas van Wouwere."

"Van Wouwere?"

"Aye."

"And has this to do with a purchase made through him?"

Bess was so surprised that she could not answer. I too needed a moment ere I could step forward.

"The English merchant who sold Monsieur Mueller a particular item," said I, "only wishes us to . . ."

"Did he send you?"

"No, we came of our own accord, and whilst here wish to do him this favor."

" 'Twould take but a few minutes of Monsieur Mueller's time," Bess said.

"My master will see no one on the matter."

"Please you, sir . . ." I began.

"We've come from Antwerp for this!" Bess finished.

"Nay!" He solemnly shook his head. "Mine orders are clear."

He nigh shut the window, but Bess stopped him. Pulling herself up like the most noble of ladies, and curdling her voice with pride, she gave him her own orders.

"Please you, tell your master that my name is Bess Marwick and that I and mine aunt will return this afternoon. He will be so kind as to see us at that time. Now good day to you."

He was still watching us with appraising eyes as we went on our way. That we didn't know where we were going mattered not, I bethought me, so long as we went there regally.

Soon enow we did begin to find our way about, so we were able to spend the next several hours seeking out any shreds of news about van Wouwere. Our ignorance of German made this difficult, but with Flemish and French and a little silver we were able to confirm what the hired groom had found: that the man traveling to Rome and calling himself Peter Heyns was undeniably van Wouwere. We also discovered that whilst briefly in Cologne he had stayed at the house of Kurst Mueller.

"What does that tell us," said I, "save what we already know, that they were friends."

"Perchance good old friends," added Bess, "and thick as thieves."

Though we felt the act was bootless, we returned late that same day to Mueller's house. Again we knocked, and again the bearded man opened the small window within the door. But ere we said aught he opened the door itself and invited us to follow him. He led us through several long halls and small sets of stairs, as if guiding us into the very bowels of the fortress. And yet, though the place did seem curiously guarded, naught about it was stern or e'en masculine. Instead there were everywhere things of costly beauty—tapestries, the furniture, the objects on it, and the carpets beneath. Still more beautiful was the room wherein we were left alone, so that I saw the handsome desk ere I saw the man behind it.

My first instinct was to recoil. His face was a mass of lumps outlined by sparse reddish bristles on his crown and chin, and sunken amidst its tumid parts were slits for eyes that showed no whites, but only two stonelike things fixed upon us. He was, by God's holy truth, an ugly man, but what repulsed me was something more impalpable: an air of malice that hung over him, mayhap, or even a capacity for cruelty.

Like a live thing separate from the rest of him, his mouth moved. "I allowed you entrance for only one reason, to press upon you that I'll tolerate no more being persecuted about this, my legitimate purchase." His fat hand rose toward the wall at his right.

Spread wide upon it, in what scant sunlight was in the chamber, was the tapestry, more beautiful than I remembered it. And for the price of it alone I could buy my London house, warehouse, and counting-house thrice over. It seemed to be by far the finest tapestry in the house; hence even this man's purse was not bottomless.

"Monsieur Mueller," said Bess, "we have not come to persecute you. If you please, we wish only to ask after Nicolas van Wouwere."

He leaned his body toward her; it seemed but another mass of lumps beneath his velvet clothes. "It does not please me," he said.

"Then for that I am full sorry. But we've come the long distance from Antwerp . . ."

"To merely ask me a few questions?" His hand moved as if to strike his chest in mock humility. "I am honored."

"Sir, he told us you were his friend, and we've learned that he was a guest in this your house."

"To what are you leading?"

"We wish only to know . . ."

"If I were his partner in conspiracy? I was not, you know."

Though I myself had not seriously considered the possibility, in looking at him then, in listening to the way his voice oozed around us, I could not help but feel that he was as guilty of the fraud as had been van Wouwere.

"I paid the full seven hundred pounds to the agent Helmut Schorer. If he in turn handed over the money to my friend, that was his stupidity. I know nothing of it. The day van Wouwere was given the money was the day he left Cologne, and I've not seen him since. Nor have I seen a single coin of my payment, so presume not that he gave back to me aught. He was a liar and a thief." These last words he said only with a careless shrug. Then he grew darker. "And now I wish to be left alone."

Bess would not cower for him. "I cannot guarantee that you will be. We two are but representing the seller of this tapestry. What action the seller himself might take won't be the same."

"And the seller is Bartholomew Catlin."

"Aye, that you know well."

"And be you his good friend?"

"Aye."

Here Mueller smiled slowly as if she had just walked into a trap. "Then he may be most interested in this. Certes, Madame Marwick, you should be." He drew from out of his desk a thin paper package.

"And what is that?" Bess asked.

"Something van Wouwere thought he sent by post as he was leaving Cologne. I had a servant retrieve it from the post by putting silver in a hand or two. I knew what manner of papers were in it, you see. Van Wouwere had written them whilst he was my guest. He thought he had done so secretly, but there are no secrets in my house. Unbeknownst to him, I read his writings, and when I saw in them this Catlin's name, the man from whom I was buying a costly tapestry, then I thought that in time those papers might prove useful to me."

"Why? Are they meant for Bartholomew Catlin?" she asked.

"No. For the magistrates in the Vierschare of Antwerp."

My heart gave a jump. I looked to Bess. For a moment she was without voice, but she kept her wits about her and indifference on her face.

"If that package is meant for the magistrates, why are you showing it to me?"

His smile grew too knowing. "What a very good actress you are. Think you I cannot see how hungry you are for this small thing?" Teasingly he drew the package closer to him. "And what a good friend you are to Monsieur Catlin to travel all the way to Cologne for his sake, e'en though he has already sent his factor and a messenger to me. Oh no, madame. I can now see there is something else you are after—it is these papers."

Bess was challenging. "How can you know this?"

"Because I know what is in these papers—your name and your death and trouble for Monsieur Catlin."

Bess was struck dumb.

I myself was struggling with the riddle of his actions. "Why have you kept this thing and not sent it on? Ere today, the name Bess Marwick meant nothing to you, and when Monsieur Catlin began sending men to your door, you could have sent on that package and rendered him silent."

His eyes became yet sharper slits. "Indeed, I did consider doing so. But I knew these papers would make only Madame Marwick silent, and belike not him. He might be arrested and forced to pay a fine, but then he could buy his freedom with a bribe. So I bided my time. I am a patient man. I bethought me that a better situation might arise and it did—with you."

Bess's indifference was slipping, and only with difficulty could she now wrest her gaze from the package and raise it to his face. She held out her hand. "Then give me those papers now, and we'll not vex you again."

Mueller's cheeks swelled more as he smiled. "Think you I'm so easily satisfied? Ah no—I want a higher price than that."

"Master Catlin has lost a fortune through you already."

" 'Tis not money I want. Not at all."

I could feel Mueller's trap closing around us. "What is the price?" I blurted.

His rocklike eyes began to shift back and forth from Bess to me. "You must both sign a paper I have prepared. I wrote it myself this morning when my servant told me that a lady calling herself Bess Marwick pressed to see me. It is a statement in which you will swear to mine innocence in the crime perpetrated by van Wouwere. You will swear that because I am blameless you shall seek no more any repayment or satisfaction from me. And too, neither you nor Bartholomew Catlin himself nor any other man will ever again attempt to communicate with me. You claimed, Madame Marwick, to be representing Monsieur Catlin. You must therefore also sign for him."

We were speechless. The trap was closed. He laid the package square before him as if to tempt us the more and with smug triumph regarded us.

"Ah, mesdames," said he, "need you talk on this with each other? I beg you to do so." He gestured magnanimously to the corner behind us.

We went to it and huddled our shoulders together to block him out yet more.

"What shall we do?" I whispered.

Bess's lips were moving as if she were arguing with herself. "Forgive me, Catlin," she murmured, "for what I must now do for this package, because we have no choice."

"Aye. Catlin may not be able to intercept it if Mueller sends it to the Vierschare."

"And Mueller is cunning. Oh, he's cunning. And Catlin would urge me to take it. If the magistrates e'er see the papers in it, then I could stay no longer in Antwerp. Those papers could e'en mean my death and harm for Catlin."

"So we take the package. And perchance too whatever we sign can be declared void, and Catlin would still have a chance at reclaiming the tapestry."

She shook her head. "Catlin knows more than any of us that his legal efforts against Mueller would most like be futile. Remember you too that he'll not forbear a public trial or have any word on this get back to Antwerp."

"Then what of his great loss?"

"That money we can retrieve from van Wouwere."

"If we find him!" My lips were trembling. "But I know, Bess, I know what we must do."

"Aye."

I studied the pain in her face. "How feel you?"

"Like Judas."

We returned to the desk and looked down again on Mueller. He had made a steeple with his fingers and settled his chin on it. "You'll sign?"

Bess hid all emotion. "We will."

He pushed toward her a paper laid before him. Bess picked it up and read it, set it down, and as he was handing her a quill, gestured to the package. "I want it beside my hand when I sign."

As if accustomed to such distrust, he did as she requested. She signed and gave the paper to me. My mind was in a fog as I read the words, and as if my hand were something seen in the distance, I watched it take up the quill and sign also, and I heard the thin package crumple under Bess's grasp.

Mueller nodded. "I thank you, mesdames," said he.

◆　◆　◆

Not long after, we were many streets away and standing on a wharf. Some feet below were the fast brown waters of the Rhine River carrying away the cover of the package. The several papers it had held fluttered between Bess's fingers.

Save for a nameless note to the magistrates (written as we knew by van Wouwere), which mentioned Catlin and then denounced his friend Bess Marwick as a conjurer and witch and practitioner of the black arts, all the papers were written in Bess's supposed hand. A horoscope, incantations, prayers to Satan, profanities against God, odd symbols and cryptic words, spells and curses against the priests in Antwerp—"pox and piles on them"—these were the vile things that filled them. "I myself," said van Wouwere's nameless testimony, "have smelled brimstone when near her, and she did verily claim to me and others how she has talked familiarly with devils, heard and seen chimeras, owls, antics, great black dogs, and fiends." And the papers he offered as proof—so fragile, the sheets felt—could have burned Bess at the stake.

"We can write to Catlin tonight," said I, "and tell him of this—though in veiled words only he can grasp. 'Tis possible he is still being watched, or his letters read."

Bess was tearing the papers into strips and dropping them one by one into the waters.

"Well, we'll be going on to Rome after all," I said with a sigh.

"Hoped you we wouldn't?"

"Aye, a little."

The last strips drifted down and were caught by the current and swept away. If only what was now before us could be resolved as quickly as this grave problem had been, I bethought me. I had not been expecting at all such a rapid resolution to the danger hanging o'er Bess, yet I had been hoping for as much in finding van Wouwere and the stolen money. Now methought two such hopes could not be fulfilled. There was a fear growing in me that whatever I wanted or expected in the course of the rest of our journey would be confounded.

Whilst in Cologne we had made the final preparations for our trip to Italy. An agreement was reached betwixt us and the Italian transporting company Bess had earlier spoken with, and so on the following morning we were to leave with the company's carters and be under their protection all the way to Milan. Why we were going Helmut Schorer did not know; we only told him we were making a pilgrimage. He himself would never do the same, he said, and I sensed by the way he referred to the "holy city" that it was his anti-Catholic feelings that made him speak so. He was belike too dedicated a Lutheran to approve of any pilgrimage, but also too kind a man to censure or discourage us from making our own.

We left Cologne just after dawn. Schorer went with us down to the river, wished us God's protection, and saw to it that we were settled on the boat ere leaving us. It was only a small boat, but hitched to it was a long barge, and following them was another boat pulling another barge. Though not as swollen as it must have been earlier in the spring, the Rhine was still high and the carts, all packed tightly with wrapped merchandise, could be driven directly onto the barges. Once they were on and secured, then six horses on the riverbank were tied in pairs to each barge. That finished, the carters manned the boats and barges and horses, last instructions were shouted, and we floated off.

Our trip down the Rhine was not a rapid one, sometimes even sluggish, but with the horses pulling from the road along the river and two men on each barge pushing us the more forward with poles, we reached Mainz after several days, and there unloaded the barges and with the carts continued south by the main roads. Our journey until then had caused no great discomfort; Bess and I had little to do but sit on the boats, and the inns wherein we spent our nights were tolerable. Once past Mainz, howe'er, the difficulties began. We spent day after day in the saddle, growing tireder than the horses we rode, which at least could be exchanged at posthouses for other horses and did not like us have to continue ever onward. Each day we rode till we were sore, then walked till we were sore from that.

The only company we truly had was each other's, the carters being ill-bred, ignorant fellows who were either surly and silent or loud and vulgar. Though most of them spoke some Flemish, they talked always to one another in Italian and to us in the former tongue only when it was necessary. They'd little money with which to pay for their expenses, and since some of them were too fond of cheap wine and beer, they all sometimes chose to stay at the meanest of carters' inns, and there spend what they'd saved and drink till midnight. There were times when Bess and I would not stay at such inns, so filthy could those places be, but rather pressed on to a better one we saw not far down the road; sometimes she and I e'en rode alone, though at a safe gallop, one or two miles farther along, seeking out a better inn or posthouse we'd been told was close by. I was uneasy about staying at a large distance from the carters, but they were at least honest enow to meet us dutifully each morning and would not continue without us. Certes they provided us with needed protection, for though our train of carts and horses was never attacked, still there were hints that brigands and thieves were watching us. At such moments, each of the carters would brandish a knife or gun and quietly tell Bess and me to hie ourselves to the middle of the train, where we could more easily be kept safe.

During many of those long hours in the saddle, Bess and I read to each other from a Latin grammar book, trying to learn in part again the language we'd been familiar with but for years had little used. We also learned, by means of a book and from the carters, a smattering of Italian, that by the time we reached Rome we could be familiar with phrases we would need at inns and shops.

In this manner we traveled to Basel, and from there began to cross Switzerland. The Alps took my breath away. As we drew nearer them, as we climbed, I remained ever amazed. They were giants bigger than aught I could dream, with blue peaks piercing the sky and caps of clouds and eternal snow. I grew chilled, but didn't mind. I was glad when we stopped halfway up their sides and remained for a few days in a village. Whilst there, the carts were unloaded and fresh horses and mules had all the goods piled on their backs, and when that was finished we pressed on, going by long packtrain up and over the St. Gothard Pass. From the coldness of the mountains we descended again into the summer heat.

The empty carts were loaded again and on we went to the Po River, and Milan.

There Bess and I parted company from the carters with no regret and spent three days seeking out those merchants whose names Catlin had given us, and too some priests. We told them we were for Rome; knew they of anyone who was going also? Merchants or pilgrims who were mannerly and well-bred, we specified, fearing we might have to Rome the kind of company we had endured from Cologne. And, too, Bess added, we preferred a group that traveled rapidly. It had been a long two months since we had left Antwerp, and she was ready now to gallop the remaining distance.

'Twas at a convent that we were told of a suitable group. The good sisters arranged a meeting betwixt us and a Milanese signor whose sister and brother-in-law were leaving on the morrow for Rome. They and their servants would travel apace, he assured us, since they were supposed to have left the day before in order to reach Rome in time to attend a relative's wedding. As usual, the signor coughed, his sister was late in leaving.

And so, with the sister and brother-in-law and a small horde of servants, we went on to Rome. The woman was amiable and fat, and at first complained that two pilgrims were joining her. But when she found we were good gentlewomen and spoke better Latin than could she, then she welcomed us. Her kindness, howe'er, she gave to us like alms. Bess in turn treated her like a penance.

Eight days after leaving Milan, on the last day of July, we reached Rome. We came up over a hill and there amidst the fields the city lay, and whilst the others rode on Bess and I tarried to gaze at it. At last our destination was reached, I sighed happily; from Rome we would soon turn about and go home again.

Or so I hoped.

XXVIII

We rode up to the massive walls of Rome and passed through a gateway. Beyond it yawned a piazza but betwixt the two was a crowd of people and animals that moved back and forth like waves in the sea, making passage difficult. I was pushed away from my companions, and had scarce been thus separated when a young hand flew up from nowhere, grabbed the reins of my horse, and pulled the beast to a stop. I looked for the owner of the hand and found myself staring into the face of a boy, who was natheless quite strong for his few years, and who was smiling in humbleness and prating on in such rapid Italian that I could not understand a word he said.

Suddenly there was a smacking noise, he yowled in pain, and his red knuckles flew to his mouth in solace. I looked around and saw my benefactress, who was clenching her riding stick and holding it near my reins. She threw some angry words at the boy which I could not translate, and with her stick next smacked my horse's rump to force it forward. When we had joined the others and were again on our way, she explained in Italian mixed with poor Latin what the boy had been after. He was one of many boys hired by the best inns of the city to linger near the gates and urge travelers to stay at their hostelries. Bess and I had no need of such services, she assured us, for she knew of a good inn with fair prices that would suit our needs, one with the advantage of being run by a French family; under their roof at least we would have no problems with the language.

As we emerged from the edge of the crowd yet another hand flew up, but this one did not try to stop my horse. Rather it remained thrust up into the air, as if pleading. Then came its mate, grasping papers on which I could see drawn familiar designs of stars and lines. At last came the face of a hoary old man who was clad in robes once rich but now nigh threadbare. He spoke to me in Italian, perceived I comprehended little, and changed into the Latin tongue. He could cast the lady's stars, said he, with great precision and wisdom, and all for the smallest of payments. I gave him a determined no. Still he followed, shuffling alongside my horse, his hand still holding forth the papers, his bag for carrying the pen and ink and ephemerides and other necessary tools slapping at his side. I cried out to my benefactress for her stern aid, but at the sound of my raised voice the aged astrologer retreated swiftly into the crowd and there shrunk again into facelessness. I was surprised that he should feel such fear of having any attention drawn to him.

Though the inn she had chosen for us was out of the group's way, our benefactress kindly insisted on guiding us there and would not depart until Bess and I were certain that the lodgings were to our liking, or until she had bartered with the innkeeper and obtained for us what she thought was a fair price. The amount was still high, she let us know, but then what could one expect since everything in Rome was expensive. With a warning to us to look to our money and keep it safe, she bid us a hearty farewell and went on with the others, smiling benignly and content that her good duty to us poor pilgrims was completed.

The innkeeper's wife helped us to settle into our room. It was of average size, plain and clean, and had only one wide bed that Bess and I could share, but like the rest of the house it was sunny and cheerful. By that time, though, I little cared for anything but the water that stood ready in a basin, and I wanted only to wash the road's dust and the day's heat from me. Bess closed the shutters against the hot sunlight and lay down on the bed.

"Well traveled, well arrived, well settled," said she with a smile. "We can say that we've done well."

"And deserve a rest." I splashed cold water onto the back of my neck.

"I feel I deserve far more than that. Still we can have our rest now, though some of our business we must see to soon. We should this same afternoon at least go to the carters' inn and there hear what more that innkeeper might be able to tell us."

"We'll need a guide."

"Our innkeeper has a son; he'll suffice."

"You'd best have for him a reason for why we wish to go to such a place."

"I already have one."

I pulled off my kirtle. "Then we are also well prepared," said I.

I took off my other outer garments and splashed water onto my arms and face. The thin bars of sunlight that fell through the shutters and onto me seemed to dry my skin before I could wipe it with a towel, and they fell in stripes across my body when I lay down beside Bess. All about us, in the house, in the streets, drifted foreign voices, and all about us were the smells and sights and touch of things foreign. I was by then only too familiar with the like; for so many weeks had I been immersed in the alien and propelled by the constant urge to go ever onward. Always the purpose of our journey lay before us, though for days I had e'en forgotten about it, so concerned was I with the journey itself. But now, I needed to remind myself, we had reached Rome and somewhere near was van Wouwere, who was the cause for our being there and over whom Bess was determined, one way or another, to prevail. Now, at last, the time was upon us.

We rested only an hour, then Bess was up and seeing to it that fresh horses were saddled, and that the son could be engaged as our guide. The carters' inn that we sought was down near the Tiber, near the Jews' ghetto, not a very pleasant place, she was told by him, a beardless youth of mayhap fifteen. She said that a Cologne friend had asked us to there inquire after his brother, who was accompanying merchandise transported by carters; but the boy had no curiosity and was more concerned with the fee he should charge for his services.

I was able as we rode along to take my first good look at the city. There were towers everywhere and new buildings that rose beside the very old, and everywhere, too, ancient buildings and half ruins stood on the same ground since time out of mind. Little harmony existed amongst much of what I saw, and the dung-colored brick, the black and tan stones, and the blocks of granite and marble only added to the tumbled disorder. Yet for a famous city it was not particularly large, or at least there seemed to be fewer people than in Antwerp, and in scattered places were vacant grounds overgrown with weeds. The boy sometimes pointed out the finer houses, which oft belonged to cardinals, and gave us the name of this domed church or that and details of the relics they held. My eyes were soon tired with the bright heat,

262 • HELENA SOISTER

however, and I was nigh relieved when we drew near the Tiber where the houses became crowded and steep shadows were thrown along the narrow streets.

The cramped lane we went down ended at a broad corner, and there our guide stopped before one of the houses and announced that this was the carters' inn we were seeking. It was a square building with two or three uneven stories and only a handful of lean windows that broke through the flat walls, and its aged stones were encrusted with rotting, sun-bleached scum, a remembrance of the dangerous days when the nearby Tiber had flooded. He asked how long we would be within and Bess replied perchance five minutes, no more than a quarter of an hour, so he should wait there for us.

The first thing that greeted us as we stepped inside was a tangle of flies hovering above in the crook of the half-open door. We found ourselves in a murky, almost barren room. Whereas the outside of the house was like a stiff old skeleton, the interior was vaguely damp, the ceiling beams were warped and sagging, and edges and corners looked to be crumbling, holding in their decay a limp smell of waste and soured wine and old straw. Only after our eyes had adjusted to the dimness did we see a man sitting at the end of one of the long trestle tables. He was staring at us, blankly and silently.

Bess asked him in Italian if he spoke French or Flemish.

"Oui, je parle bien français," he answered.

Bess continued cautiously in French. We were seeking information on the whereabouts of a man whom we heard had recently arrived in Rome, she told him. He traveled with carters who had stayed at that inn, so perchance they or the innkeeper could help her, for carters were notorious gossips.

"I'm not here to give information to strangers," he rasped. "Not free. I don't give for free. I run an inn. This is mine inn."

Bess came a little nearer him. Feeling uneasy about the place and its keeper, I stayed close to her. Still the man did not rise, nor did he gesture for us to sit with him. Bess glanced superciliously down at the rough benches, as if to tell him silently that she preferred to stand and would not linger in his slovenly inn.

"The information need not be free, but neither is it worth much to us." Bess pulled out her capcase but did not yet open it.

The man grinned, and I saw his teeth glimmer yellow in his gaunt face. "This man cannot be important to you, then," said he.

"No, he is not. But he is a doctor who gave me good physic for a small illness whilst we were both in Cologne. I have heard that like me he is now in Rome, and since I am again ailing, I wish to see him."

"There are other doctors in Rome," he retorted.

"But I am not acquainted with any of them. I seldom trust doctors and am not willing to consult just any one of them. I would prefer to see him."

"Where is your doctor from?"

"I believe he is Flemish. He was new-come from the Lowlands when I met him in Cologne."

His grin turned hideous. He began to laugh and cough and his teeth rattled, making him take on the horrid appearance of a chattering death's-head. "What's he called? What's his name?" he demanded.

"Nicolas van Wouwere."

A thin shriek of delight cracked out of him. Clearly he knew something about van Wouwere that would interest us; clearly he would say nothing until he had been paid to talk.

Bess took out of her capcase a small gold coin and tossed it at him. It fell upon the table, rolled toward him, and was swiftly caught up in both his greedy hands. He looked up to her for more.

"If I give you aught else, then I shall pay you more than what I pay him for his physic." She put her capcase away. "The cure of my small ailment is not worth such a high price."

His grinning teeth bit again and again upon the edges of the coin. "You can't have his physic. Can't anyway. You can't see van Wouwere. Your doctor is arrested. Locked up." He was struggling with his French; he wanted now to prattle away with spiteful pleasure and tell Bess why she could not see the man she had paid to learn about.

"Arrested?" Bess had almost started at this, but she held herself still and carefully, with no especial show of interest, pressed him for more. "Jesu, that doth surprise me. I had thought him an honest doctor. How came you by this news?"

"The carters told me about the doctor. They said he was a rich man. I have a friend, and I told my friend about the doctor. My friend likes to meet rich people. They can be helpful to him. Then my friend said to me the doctor was arrested."

"But why?"

"I'm not sure. Not exactly. My friend said the doctor was an astrologer. He made predictions, false ones. Just to people who pay for them. So the Inquisition jumped on him. But you cannot ask the monks about him. They won't tell you anything in the Inquisition. It's not much safe anyway. Only if you want to tell them more things about a prisoner, like van Wouwere. Bad things. Things they can use against a prisoner. You show you worried about someone, you try to help and oomph!"—his eyes started from his head—"they jump on you too."

"And all for astrology?" I asked, feigning indifference though what he was saying made my hopes sink. "I had no idea astrology was against the law here."

"It is, it is!" He clattered his head up and down.

"How strange," said I. "Yet when we were coming in through the city gates today, an ancient astrologer tried to ply his trade with me. Of course I told him no."

He peered at me. "What gate you come through?"

"Methinks it was the Porta del Popolo."

"Ah, the old fool. He can be killed for that. In the old days, before this pope, astrologers were all around the Porta Romano. That's mostly where they went. New gate won't keep that fool safe."

"Well, that's all one." Bess shrugged. "So I cannot see van Wouwere. But what about his possessions? His physic, I mean. Perchance there is someone else who could sell me van Wouwere's physic."

"No. No one. The monks probably have all his things. If they burn him for heresy, they can keep all he has. The new pope made that law. It was an old law he made new again." He screwed up his face to think. "But they have not said he is a heretic. And my friend says the cardinal might take the doctor's money if he wants." He laughed again, delighted with the prospect of a rich man's downfall.

"The cardinal?" Bess sighed in frustration. "But there is a horde of cardinals in Rome. Only one wants his money?"

The innkeeper clicked his teeth, smoothed back his oily hair with one hand, and with the other scratched the coin across his scalp. "Only one cardinal runs Rome. Carafa. Damned Carafa family runs Rome. He's the pope's nephew. This pope is a holy bastard. Astrologers against the law. Actors and buffoons against the law. There used to be plenty of prostitutes here. Only a few now, and they all pay their respects to

Cardinal Carafa. He keeps them safe for money. He be the biggest sinner in Rome, and the old fool pope don't know. Everyone in Rome knows what is happening, everyone. But not the old pope. He starts up the Inquisition again, does the pope, so the monks can catch the doctor and fool heretics. But they can't catch the cardinal. He does what he wants. His fool uncle gave him power over all politics and law in Rome. He can use laws as he wants, the cardinal does. He uses them for or against criminals. Some of the prostitutes he likes to take to bed, so he won't arrest them." The death's-head looked from Bess to me, anxiously hoping he was shocking us.

I turned to leave. "If there is nothing more you can tell us about van Wouwere . . ."

"There is! If you don't mind prostitutes there is." He mumbled under his breath a joke to himself and cackled at it. "An old whore can tell you much."

Bess had grown rigid. The talk of the cardinal and the very word "whore" riveted her to the spot. "Why should I care anything about an old whore?" she asked too flatly. "I came here to ask about a doctor." She slapped suddenly at a fly that had landed on her arm, as if it were the familiar of van Wouwere.

"Your doctor visited her. My friend told me. I don't think he bedded her. No one wants to do that with her anymore. She's a courtesan. She calls herself Andreana Pescioni. She thinks she be special. She acts like a rich lady. She knows the cardinal too. Whatever happens to the doctor, Pescioni can tell you all about. She can try to get his money. Old whore grabbing for money, yes, she does that. She thinks she's a friend of the cardinal. She thinks she has his ear, and he trusts her. She thinks a lot of things. He uses her for information. Just like you come to me for information. She likes to get visits from foreign ladies. Only sometimes ladies visit her. The fools who think she's a lady and don't know she's just an old whore. She likes it when ladies think that, she talks and talks to them then." He was almost laughing at us now, so viciously gleeful was he. "Why don't you go see the old whore? She lives in a nice place, the Trastevere quarter. Near southern edge. She can tell you all about your doctor."

"He is not my doctor." Bess no longer hid her revulsion of the innkeeper. "And I will not ask after him at all now. I'll find a better one."

I myself was at last moved to speak. "Hold a moment, sirrah. Methinks you seem to know too many people. How know you too about this courtesan?"

"My friend is her bastard son."

Bess would say nothing more to the man, nor would I. Giving him only an expression of disgust, she turned about and we began to walk out of the place with even greater pride than when we had entered. Behind us we could hear his laugh again and the sound of the gold coin tapping the table like a stick tapping a drum.

"Go see Pescioni!" he crowed. "She be the best sight in Rome, now the buffoons are gone!"

♦   ♦   ♦

Bess and I did not talk at all of what the innkeeper had said until much later when the afternoon was ending and we were sitting in a piazza near our own inn. I was watching the dust from the cobblestones float up into the last rays of the sun, and Bess was looking at the people and houses. The city was now more foreign and stranger to us than when we had first entered it. I spoke of the churches I had seen that day; Bess complained of how hot the afternoon had been. I said that I would like to see St. Peter's on the morrow; that none of my friends had been to Rome and I wanted to tell them all about the holy city when I returned to Antwerp and England. I glanced through a book written in Latin that I had bought that day: *Marvels of the City of Rome.* "There are many things here I would like to see," I said.

"If naught else"—Bess smiled a little sadly—"we will at least be able to say that we saw Rome, and other places withal. We might as well see it, since this traveling of ours has cost us both much. But to see Rome will cost us too."

"And van Wouwere's money may be out of our grasp," said I. "Certes he himself is."

"I had not been expecting this."

"We should have expected it, for we knew the man enough to foresee—without any arts—what he would in time bring upon himself. Think you we should go to the monks at the Inquisition and tell them what van Wouwere has stolen from Catlin? It is unfavorable information they want about him."

"I'm too wary for that. If e'en some of what the innkeeper said be true, then we cannot trust the officials here. It would cost us nothing, though, to discover what this Pescioni could tell us."

A flock of starlings on black flickering wings swirled up over the roof and sped out of sight, their shrill twitterings echoing behind.

"There are whores everywhere, Bess," I quietly said, "and clerics to fit any prophecy."

"But this whore can tell us of our false prophet. We can perchance visit her in the morning, and after that we will go see your St. Peter's."

The starlings came back again, careened in a haphazard circle, then spun away and disappeared, again leaving behind their cries and the air ruffled by their beating wings.

XXIX

We knew the courtesan's name and we knew the area wherein she lived, but not which one of the houses was hers, a situation that rendered us some discomfort. I vainly hoped that in the southern part of the Trastevere we could ask after the woman's house and receive directions from strangers who had never heard of her reputation, or of her former occupation. This was not to be. Her reputation was clearly known to the two or three people we asked, for they looked Bess and me up and down as if wondering what in God's name we two respectable-seeming women would want with such a creature and leered upon hearing her name; and when we passed on they whispered it to their companions.

Andreana Pescioni's house was not a large one, but it boasted a rich and ornate exterior. We were let in by a maid, apparently not accustomed to seeing women like us at the door, who first sought permission from her mistress ere allowing us to pass any further than the entrance hall. We were shown upstairs and there left in a large chamber methought the finest and most elegantly decorated chamber I had ever seen. It was a sunny room, and the light lay shiny on the porcelain and crystal and on the polished wood of the dainty furniture, yet somehow it was as if the sunlight were allowed in only because it was a planned part of the room. 'Spite sunlight or no, there was no good cheer in that place, nor yet any melancholy; indeed there was no feeling save a coldness. Several costly chairs were about but I durst not sit as they looked uncomfortable and were there only to be admired, like beggars of flattery for their owner. So this is what a courtesan's house is like, I bethought me. I would have mistaken that chamber as one that belonged instead to a fastidious old maid.

In a few moments a woman glided into the chamber, and there could be no mistake that she was its mistress. Like the room, everything about her was stiffly in place and nothing was warm or natural, as if she too were on elegant show. I had been expecting an aging but beautiful woman, one who in her youth had charmed men out of their wealth, but I saw only an oval face that seemed brittly hard. When she was young she had belike been pretty, but now she was somewhere in her forties, her cheeks were sagging into jowls, her blond hair had an artificial hue, her eyebrows, made into thin pale lines, arched into a creased brow, her chest was thin, her hips plump, and her mouth vaguely pinched and dour.

Andreana Pescioni now bequeathed on us a practiced smile. She asked us something in Italian. Bess queried if she spoke French.

"Of course. What might I do for you?" Hers was a voice like hardening syrup.

We introduced ourselves and Bess told her that we were seeking a Doctor van Wouwere, of whom we had heard she was a friend, and gave her the same reasons she had given the innkeeper.

"Ah yes, I was acquainted with Nicolas," she replied. "But certainly I'll have naught to do with him now. You seem not to have heard that he had been arrested."

Bess grew wide-eyed with feigned amazement, claimed that indeed she had not heard the news, and asked why such a fate had befallen him.

"He has been charged with blasphemy and fortune-telling." She raised one hand and let it mark her sentences. It was a fair hand that looked at first glance like porcelain, but its age was beginning to show and veins were rippling through it like cracks. "I have also heard a rumor that he has since his arrest been charged with heresy. He was arrested only last week by the Inquisition, and any day now he will be tried and probably found guilty."

"Oh, that's dreadful." Bess clucked her tongue. "Marry, I can only say that I am full glad I little know him."

"But you intended to visit him?"

"Only as one would visit a doctor. I'll have to find another physician now." Bess displayed no concern. "Arrested by the Inquisition—I had no idea the man could be guilty of heinous crimes. They will punish him severely?"

"Beyond a doubt."

"And will he too be fined? I assume he will certes lose money over this misfortune."

"If he is found guilty of heresy, all his possessions and property will be confiscated by the Inquisition."

Bess blanched slightly. Perchance it was her change of color, or perchance her questions and curiosity, that made Signorina Pescioni pause and examine the both of us distrustfully.

"A bad ending for a bad man," said I, and crossed myself. Then I tried to talk for a little of only trivial things; I praised the chamber and the things that filled it, and she commented on this or that adornment. Each piece of flattery I gave her she accepted with a haughty nod, and with an expert finger she pointed out the room's details with which she was still unsatisfied. I found myself taken by her moving hands, arms, and head. They had only an echo of bygone vivacity; the substance had long since given way to her tight and guarded possession of herself.

The chamber's qualities having been discussed, Bess turned again to our former subject.

"Glad I am that we came to you, Signorina Pescioni, ere going elsewhere to ask about van Wouwere. You seem indeed to be well informed with Roman news. I nothing doubt that you have important friends who confide their affairs in you."

The woman acknowledged this with a nod. "Many important men have confided in me. Certainly I know some of Rome's prominent officials, but beyond all that, of course, is that I am actually a good friend of Cardinal Carlo Carafa."

Bess regarded her blankly, the innocent.

Signorina Pescioni asked aloud where were her manners and gestured at last for us to be seated. I lowered myself into an ornate chair that squealed upon receiving my full weight. Its mistress herself sat regally, as if she were holding court.

"You are clearly strangers in Rome," said she with a haughty air, "if you know not the Cardinal Carafa. It is he who controls Rome. He is a most powerful man, and I am fortunate to count myself amongst his friends. In sooth, he has told me that I won his friendship with my charms. He is the nephew of the pope and 'tis the pope who gave Carlo a power that seems without bounds. Carlo directs all of Rome's political business, all finance, all law, even the administration of the city and the states of the Church. His power is extraordinary, which it must be to enforce the many new laws his uncle has passed."

"I have heard," said Bess, "that the pope—who must be indeed a stern ascetic—has e'en banned buffoons in Rome."

"Buffoons, actors, usurers. Know you that one can be punished merely for breaking a fast? This is not now the Rome I used to know."

Bess continued innocently. "And prostitutes too are forbidden?"

"Of course. The pope has no affection for any sort of woman."

"Not e'en courtesans?"

Signorina Pescioni studied Bess's expression of naïveté. "Not even them," she finally replied. "The pope so hates women he will not allow so much as a nun near him. Therefore you can understand the more why my friendship with Carlo is very convenient. How sad, I sometimes think, how sad. Once I had been an honored guest in many of Rome's best houses. Many a cardinal and archbishop visited me, and not just to converse in Latin and French. Now I must remain in this my house too often, and few men feel safe enough to visit me."

I shifted uncomfortably in my chair. She paid me little mind but only looked about at her costly chamber.

"Of course, I have happily profited through some of the pope's acts." She let her fingers daintily arrange the lace at her throat. "He really cannot abide Jews, and so he's passed laws forbidding any Jew in Rome to own real estate; thus what land they owned ere his pontificate had to be sold to Christians within a fixed period. I was able to buy some Jew's land at half its true value in this manner. And they're no longer allowed to trade in any food save that for animals, so too then many a Jew's business had to be sold cheaply. Oh, and mark you, mesdames, if you wish to consult a physician he must be Christian; the Jewish ones are only for the Jews. Yes, all kinds of laws have been passed against the Jews here, but still you'll see them about. One can't help but see them, for they all must wear yellow caps. Really they stand out in a most gaudy fashion."

How different from Antwerp, I thought. There I had heard the Jewish merchants' rumors about the sad tales that were floating north from Rome, but I had not put much truth in them. Here now was the ugly confirmation of their tragic stories. I myself felt tainted by the cruelty and wanted to leave this room and this woman. The chair creaked as I shifted again and made ready to leave.

Signorina Pescioni glanced back at me. "It is too warm today. Would you care for some cool wine?"

"I thank ye, but no, signorina," I replied. "We must soon be going."

At this, her mouth curved down sadly and her jowls seemed to hang with dejection. Only then did I realize, though I should have ere then perceived it in her eagerness to talk away to us, how loneliness was tormenting her. It was more that gaping loneliness than her silly conceit that made her so falsely regal; yet still no warmth or pity could she evoke in me, only an uneasy fear.

"Not too soon, I hope." Her practiced smile was again displayed. "It has been so long sith I've been able to talk with English ladies. I prithee tell me, is there aught else I might tell you of Rome?"

"Perchance you might give us more news," said Bess. "This be stuff of little matter, but should I desire to ask after Nicolas van Wouwere at the Inquisition, merely to learn what in time becomes of him (I trow I be too curious for mine own good), to whom would I go?"

"No one." Her wrist wavered. "The Inquisition works in absolute secrecy. Whoever violates that secrecy is excommunicated. But mayhap I could learn of van Wouwere's fate from Carlo. If you like, I could even discover from him what passes for the prisoner."

Bess was wide-eyed with awe. "On such an insignificant matter— one that verily touches me not at all—you might approach the cardinal! Marry, he must be willing to grant you many favors!"

"He can be a most kind and generous friend."

"Ah, but too you must know well how to deal with men. Have you known many?"

Pescioni regarded her sideways, as if she were becoming too much Bess's superior to look directly at her. "In many ways. Some are best forgotten, some leave me with affectionate or comical memories, some prove to be convenient. And many of them loved me."

Though we were but strangers and she was revealing things most private, still she did not hush her voice with private tones, and though she seemed ready to say more, she paused. Slowly I understood that her words were rehearsed and that e'en the pause was part of her script, so that Bess felt obliged to ask her something.

"And loved you any of them?"

That line delivered, Pescioni continued. "Nay, nay. It was a cruel destiny God gave me: to be beautiful and lure men, yet be incapable of loving them in turn. And for this I feel no guilt. Why should I? As I was saying to Carlo but the other day, God must forgive me such transgressions, for by giving me my nature He forced me to commit them." She made her sins sound like baubles she had gathered.

"But how much of that is truly destiny?" Bess asked. "Surely you have more control than that over your life."

"God made me what I am, and without love. I am incapable of feeling it, and yet I am like a lodestar for men's love. To the best of them, though, I could give at least my"—she savored the word—"my passion."

Her voice fell away like a chip of crystal. She rose, glided to the window behind her chair, and there gazed out as if surveying her life. The sunlight fell across her form and for a moment she looked like another one of her adornments in a chamber meant only for show, where words and pretty objects could be moved about in perpetual search for satisfaction. 'Twas all just dramatic mummery, I thought, as unreal as her story.

Pescioni, having posed long enough, returned to her chair and smiled at us.

I tried to think of whatever was expected of me to say. "Most extraordinary, signorina."

"Indeed. An extraordinary destiny," Bess added.

With a slow blink and a nod, Pescioni accepted our offerings.

"Signorina," Bess said, "your story has moved me beyond words. I pray you, might we have the pleasure of visiting you again after you've next seen Cardinal Carafa?"

"I'd be most pleased to see you in two days' time."

"So swiftly will you be able to ask after van Wouwere?"

She raised her meager eyebrows and nodded. "And without any difficulty."

We thanked her for her generosity, and when the maid appeared to show us out, we bade her a farewell.

Standing but a few feet away from the closed door to Pescioni's chamber was a man looking hard at us. He directed the maid to leave, and as I had recognized the mistress of that place, so I suddenly recognized its master. This must be Pescioni's bastard son and the friend of the innkeeper.

He was soberly dressed, young, and with a soft face all thick about the jaws and neck, and his heavy-lidded eyes stayed unmoving upon us. He said nothing during the long moment that we looked upon one another, as if he would not bother speaking until he had finished his silent assessment of us. Already well disquieted by the courtesan's garrulity and her unexpected revelations, I had no wish to deal now with her equally strange son.

Bess and I continued on our way and the whoreson followed us, but not until we reached the stairs did he make a remark.

" 'Tis not often my mother has visitors. She will be seeing you again, mesdames?" He spoke in French.

Bess answered without looking back. "That is a question you may ask your mother, monsieur."

"Which I will have no need to do, as she will tell me all whether or no I ask."

"Then the question need not be asked by anyone."

We were by then descending the stairs.

"I do hope my mother's story amused you." His voice followed us like a hollow wind. "It always amuses me."

Bess now stopped and gazed coldly back at him. "What your mother told us she has apparently related to others before. Why bothered you to listen to her story again?"

"Oh, I had no need to. Of course she performed for you her passion play. She performs it for everyone who crosses her path. Tell me, did she also talk to you about Cardinal Carafa, her dear Carlo? Her dear friend is always making fun of her to me. That the two of them are friends is merely her illusion. Sometimes he can get a little information out of her—the old gossip—and so he doesn't arrest her. In sooth, he prefers the baser company of common whores."

Bess replied with caution. "There are people who spread such rumors about any cleric."

"But Carlo is no ordinary cleric. Know you he was not even a cardinal before the pope's election? He wasn't even a priest, and he still cannot read Latin. He had the reputation for being only a vile sinner.

But the pope, being a pious, detestable old knave, is convinced that his nephew has reformed. The cardinal can manipulate the pope the way a mother does a babe." There was no mirth in his voice or on his puffy face, nor yet any spite or anger or care. There was nothing natural.

"How do we know you are telling us truth or calumny?" Bess challenged him.

"You will find that out for yourselves." He smiled like a lizard. "I promise you that."

A shiver ran down my back and I was glad to leave this house. I had seldom heard a promise that so much sounded like a threat.

I was for a little a pilgrim whilst in Rome. I went to the churches, I knelt and prayed, I gave up my horse and walked from holy site to site. There were more churches than I could count and more pilgrims than I could apprehend, and many of those pilgrims were poor, and all the poor were walking, though not only out of piety but because they could afford nothing else. Near a few of the churches were butchers who took from their stalls the cattle skins and stretched them on the façades of the churches to dry and threw into the street the stinking guts and entrails of their slaughtered beasts. I avoided the messes as best I could, but such pilgrims did not; as they emerged from the sanctuaries and their prayers, they would there buy their foul dinners of pigs' trotters and tripe. Then from the paternostri who set up benches near the holiest places and from them hawked an array of religious goods, they would buy their rosaries and trinkets, and near the Vatican would pause again to buy straw, with which they would fill their mean pallets back at the taverns or inns wherein they slept. The kindest of the lowly priests oft looked after some of them and gave them shelter and washed their blistered feet, and when that was done turned to help the Roman beggars and aged and orphans and sick.

Riding on fine horses past all these scenes were insolent cardinals and other clerics and their servants, and government clerks and foreign officials. Ever and anon I saw a young girl or woman who was clearly a prostitute and bartering her wares until something told her that danger was drawing nigh, and then she would hurry back into a house or an alley like a mouse, or melt amongst the few Jews in the streets who in their yellow caps and clothes were more conspicuous than she. I saw whores find willing customers in some pilgrims. I saw the wealthy followed by their Nubian slaves and by vile vagabonds. I felt a hushed fear shared by common harmless people. This was the part of Rome I wanted nothing of. I wanted to belong to the other Rome of kindness and charity, but I felt irredeemably cut off from that, having already been drawn by mine own and Bess's acts into this crueler Rome, into this corruption.

Taking up our invitation, Bess and I returned to Andreana Pescioni's house two days after our first visit. We were admitted again by the maid, who showed us to the stairs. At the top stood the courtesan's son, again waiting for us.

"Ah, mesdames, you have come once more," he said as we ascended. A smile pushed into his fat cheeks. "Not to visit my mother, surely; no one visits her merely to have the pleasure of her company, there being no pleasure in it. No, you came because you wish to know more of Doctor van Wouwere."

I caught in my breath. Clearly his mother had talked about us with him, and that could only bode ill for us. He seemed so wily that with any sort of knowledge he could set mischief afoot. Still Bess and I walked on. We reached the landing and proceeded down the hall, but he blocked our way.

"Knew you that van Wouwere's wealth was great?" He was watching us both with grasping eyes, ready like claws to snatch up our responses. "He had a very large amount of money with him when he was arrested, and a small coffer filled with much more. Now it's all being safely kept in a room at the Inquisition. Of course my mother will tell you none of this, for she knows nothing of it. But do not mention it to her; she'll just deceive you into thinking that she was aware of it already. She's so greedy she may e'en try, through the cardinal, to get some of it for herself."

"And you are not greedy?" Bess asked. "Have you no intent to get for yourself this supposed wealth?"

He gave us his lizard smile, stepped out of our way, and opened for us the door to the chamber we had been in the day before.

We entered it and found ourselves facing not only Signorina Pescioni but a large bearded man with the stony eyes and fierce face of a weather-beaten gargoyle and attired in the blood-bright red robes of a cardinal. Both were sitting and both were annoyed for being interrupted. But when Signorina Pescioni saw that it was we who had entered, she lifted her chin proudly and greeted us. I stammered a reply, and my heart pounded with the fear that I knew the identity of her guest.

"You have met my son," she noted.

"No, signorina, not properly," Bess replied, as aware as I of his presence behind us.

"Then I shall introduce you. This is my son, Jacopo. And this"—she rose—"is His Eminence Cardinal Carlo Carafa."

Bess and I disregarded Jacopo but curtsied to the cardinal and approached him only close enough that we could kiss his ring. He in turn observed us with tired arrogance, yet still his glance was a scowl and I shuddered when it was upon us.

Signorina Pescioni introduced us to him as English ladies new-come from Germany, where we were living (Jacopo was right about her propensity to invent untruths rather than to admit ignorance); but I heeded her not. I had been told so much about the powers and malevolence of the man before us that I felt a fool for attracting his interest by asking after van Wouwere, and I prayed that Pescioni would not mention this. But I knew she would, and a sense of deep foreboding crept over me.

We sat down upon creaking chairs, all save for Jacopo, who stood off to one side as if he were there only to observe the lot of us. He half-faded into the scene like a piece of furniture, a feat rendered the easier by the bright hue of the cardinal's robe and the apricot and amber dress of Signorina Pescioni; next to them he was colorless and shapeless.

With ease and grace, Signorina Pescioni made small comments to begin the talk among us all. I dropped a flattering lie, like a shiny button, and said how pleasant it was to be again in that chamber. Then she mentioned van Wouwere, explaining to us that she had asked His Eminence the day before if he would do her the kindness of looking into the matter. My heart skipped a beat.

"I was"—her smile rose into a performer's sparkle—"able to inquire after the doctor with greater speed than could the Inquisition reach a decision. There is still no verdict on his guilt or innocence, but there should be one soon."

I was trying to imitate Cardinal Carafa's indifference. "Marry, howe'er they find him is truly no matter to me. Even if they find him innocent and release him, there are other and better physicians that we could consult whilst here in Rome."

"You will be in Rome for long?" Cardinal Carafa asked abruptly. These were the first words he had uttered to Bess or me, and I started upon hearing them.

Bess hurried to answer no, adding for only a few more days till we had finished our pilgrimage to the holy sites.

"The fate of a man being held by the Inquisition should not interest such transient visitors," said he. Still he kept his face full upon us.

"Indeed it should not," I hastened to agree, and apologized for our silly and weak female inquisitiveness.

Bess confirmed all that I said. "Oh, Your Eminence, I pray you, do forgive us if we have in any way imposed upon you. I must confess that I am now most abashed for giving rein to mine curiosity. It really is quite intolerable. I scarce know this doctor at all. I merely received from him some physic for a trifling pain in my hand—I burned it, you see"—she held out the back of her scarred hand to him—"and this was months and months ago in Cologne. Now I am in Rome and it is troubling me again, and when I learned this same doctor was here I asked after him in order to obtain again his balm for it. I should never have said a word about him as soon as I discovered he was in the Inquisition. But no, my curiosity I let rule my better judgment." She babbled on as if she were the soul of foolish femininity, repeating too oft all she said and blushing and stammering.

I worried that she was playing the role too broadly, but it seemed the cardinal, who appeared to be more credulous than I had anticipated, believed her explanations. Finally, being no longer intrigued but only bored with her, he halted her in midsentence with a stern wave of his hand.

"His Eminence is a generous man." Signorina Pescioni tipped her knobby fingers toward him. "He is generous to the point where he will use his great powers to fulfill my paltry requests."

His Eminence did not bother to flatter her in turn.

"Are his powers indeed so very great?" asked Bess in awe, still playing her role.

The question set Signorina Pescioni off again on another recounting of his official posts and abilities. This took some minutes, and in that time she became yet a shade more vain and haughty, as if because of the cardinal's presence and her friendship with him, his importance was reflected onto her.

As she talked about him, his indifference waned, his disposition changed, and he jested in Italian. Together they made an odd sight. Each was prouder than the other, each basked in vain importance, but the courtesan never faltered in her social graces, whereas I saw the cardinal had a countenance carved deep with ugly lines of anger and passion, and his gestures raked the air with speedy rashness. I felt like an idiot for being able to do naught but sit there and keep a benign smile upon my face. I glanced at Bess; despite herself her eyes were riveted upon them as if trying desperately to espy what they might eventually do with her or she with them.

Cardinal Carafa was at last becoming annoyed. He let go an exasperated sigh; Signorina Pescioni was quick to gather his meaning, and she turned to us.

"I pray you forgive me, but His Eminence must needs discuss divers private matters with me now," said she. "I pray too that we might meet again tomorrow."

For courtesy's sake I said we would be delighted to enjoy her company again. Then with curtsies to the cardinal and another kissing of his ring, we left.

Unfortunately, Jacopo accompanied us. As his mother had at length repeated herself in conversation, so now he repeated his behavior: He walked with us and observed us ere talking. I noticed, with a whisper of a shudder, that as his mother's chamber had been slightly altered, so too, at least for me, had his face. Its plump features were strangely malleable, each had nothing distinctive about it, and so each faded into the next. His was indeed the quintessence of a whoreson's face: Every man his mother had known could search in it for traces of himself and find that which he sought.

"So my mother is expecting you to come again tomorrow." His voice followed after us as we passed down the hall. "And it might be dear Carlo's pleasure too that you return. Of course he did not wish to be bothered with you in there, but natheless I could see that you struck his curiosity. Just as you want to find out about van Wouwere through her, so too will Carlo want to find out about you through her. She will be happy with such a situation. It makes her feel powerful."

"Our own curiosity, though," Bess replied coldly, "has been more than satisfied. Please you tender her our thanks and farewell."

"Ah, what a pity." He clucked his tongue in mock sadness. "Yours was the only company she had to look forward to. Yet why indeed would you see her again when you could find out van Wouwere's fate elsewhere? If he is found guilty—and that he will be, for the Inquisition seldom arrests anyone it does not eventually find guilty of something—then you may learn of his conviction and his punishment in a common posted notice. Only in two or three places can it be found. The one I know of is down near the Tiber, at the marketplace hard by the Ponte Quattro Capi. There is a chance that the verdict will be posted there today at about four of the clock. Carlo told my mother this but of course she would not tell you in turn, lest you need not return to her tomorrow."

That he was enjoying this petty revenge upon his mother I could perceive; he was already anticipating her unhappiness when she would comprehend, as the long, empty hours fell away, that we would not be coming again. It mattered little to me, I thought; let her and the evil cardinal wait in vain and her son play his bitter games; I myself would have naught to do with the lot of them again, especially since this whoreson shared our interest in van Wouwere.

"If you wish to read the notice," Jacopo continued, "then be there at its posting, or soon afterward, for in only a few hours it will be covered in mud and filth. You see, Romans really quite hate the Inquisition, and to smear accidentally its announcements and make them invisible is their timid way of fighting it. They're like little mice. Our dear Carlo is no more popular. Certes, if they could put their hands on him, they would do more than cover him with mud."

"Given a choice"—Bess smiled at him coldly—"what would you do with him?"

"Nothing myself. I will let others do the work for me," said he without feeling. "They can destroy him. That way the ends I desire will be achieved, but I shall be blameless and safe should there be repercussions."

"Clever," said Bess. "And now, monsieur, a most welcome and final adieu."

We left the house with the fears and suspicions that had gripped me all the stronger.

Jacopo's revelations sparked no hope in Bess. Sooth to say, since arriving in that city and making the first inquiries after van Wouwere, she did not once exhibit any faith in a successful ending to our task; and yet still she pressed relentlessly on, driven as ever by her obsession. Now she wanted to go to the marketplace and see if there was a posting. Like me, she was chary that there could be danger in doing so, yet still she would go, and sith I could not dissuade her I could not let her venture there alone.

At our inn the boy who had been our guide before told us where this Ponte Quattro Capi could be found. It was but a street or two away from the carters' inn we had visited and he offered to guide us to it, but Bess declined, saying that as we had been in the area before we could find it again. The fewer people who were there to watch what we were about, she told me later, the better. That was so, said I, yet Jacopo might well know we were there and that too was a danger.

At half after three we called for two horses to be saddled and brought around, and we changed into our plainest clothes that we might fade the better into the scene of a common market. Then we set off.

The marketplace was a humble area scarce broad enough at each end to allow the passage of a large wain. A handful of stalls and benches were set up along the high walls of the old buildings on either side. Several groups of noisy people were roaming about, and amongst all this we could mingle and not be paid much mind, so Bess and I dismounted and feigned to be shopping. Neither variety nor abundance marked what could be bought, and what was there was vaguely foul, consisting mostly of tallow, old copper pots and kettles, and thick maunds. Natheless we investigated these goods as if thinking to buy them, and it was in this perusing that we came upon a large pole with a few notices nailed to it, all appearing to be official pronouncements. The Latin headings we could read but of the Italian passages we could translate only an odd word or phrase. Nowhere in them did we see van Wouwere's name nor any that was Flemish, nor did we happen upon a reference to the Inquisition. Our reading, though, was made in haste, yet lest we be observed I gestured for Bess to move on. She wandered away to the other end of the marketplace and I in a different direction, and we continued our show of shopping whilst awaiting the arrival of anyone who would nail another notice to the pole.

It was then that I heard a strange wheezing and grumbling. The noise came from a small man who was examining the same papers we had, and then he turned and out of the dead color of his face burned bloodshot eyes that he set upon me. I smothered a scream. My knees buckled under me and I stumbled back. It was Damascus. He recognized me instantly as I had him, but he said not a word, only standing and holding those fearful eyes fixed on my face.

I tried to look elsewhere. I took several steps away and he did not follow. I forced myself to think that it was Catlin who had mattered to him; I meant nothing and so he would do nothing to me. I looked over my shoulder and saw the carters' inn where Bess and I had been, and bethought me of a sudden of the innkeeper who ruled its murky rooms. I had not liked the chance way that the inn and the marketplace were so close together. 'Twas not good, I said to myself; and now, e'en more foreboding, Damascus was here.

Suddenly the crowd at the other end of the marketplace parted and three guards stepped within. I had oft seen their liveries about the city, but to whom they belonged and what their function was I had never learned. The people around them went back to their bartering and buying, but I saw that they drew away from the guards, and all kept a wary eye cast in their direction.

The three guards came slowly forward, their sharp glances scanning the crowd. They were hunting for someone, I saw. There were a few people betwixt them and me and stealthily I moved farther back, hoping to be unseen. Bess too was watchful, for they were but some paces from her. One of them regarded her for a moment, seemed about to approach, then hesitated as like an ill-tempered peasant she busily examined an old black pot. Then he began to move toward another young woman.

Suddenly a hideous yowl cracked the air. Everyone stopped, held his breath. It had burst out of Damascus, and he was pointing a crooked finger, whether at the guard or at Bess I could not tell. His mouth was twisted and his red-burning eyes were wild, as like a maddened, damned prophet he thundered forth curses and cries of warning upon the guards. His howlings were in Italian, yet I could understand some of them, and they made my blood grow icy for they told all there that these were the men of Cardinal Carafa.

One guard threw himself at Damascus but he eluded the grasp and fled backward into the crowd, his skinny body slivering through the gaps and vanishing. 'Midst the shouts and cries and helter-skelter panic, another guard whirled about, saw the astonishment writ on Bess's face, and in Italian demanded something of her. She looked upon him blankly. He demanded again. She muttered something. He yelled at her and grasped her arms, and I heard her cry out in pain. Then the third guard took her roughly by the shoulders and the two started dragging her away.

I was set to jump out after Bess when a hand clasped my arm. I whipped about in fright and found myself staring into the gaunt face of the innkeeper. He was crouched betwixt two stalls and gesturing for me to keep quiet. I tried to pull away but he held me fast and his words froze me to the spot.

"They arrest you too," he rattled. "You can do your friend no good then. Get away now. Then you can help. You cannot help her if the cardinal gets you too."

The noise was dreadful. I could see the remaining guard, who still had not caught sight of me, drawing close to where I huddled. The innkeeper jerked hard on my arm and began to drag me after him. I stumbled, pulling back till panic at last struck me too and I hurried after him.

Like a crooked, half-lame spider, he ran through the crowd and up the street, bolted through the open door of his inn, and closed it after I had fallen in behind him. He did not pause. With a hand and arm swirling around and around, he gave a signal for me to follow him. Up the creaking stairs we went and into a room that overlooked the street. He peered out the window.

"The man is coming!" he cried. "Checking houses. Mayhap he saw us. Here!"

Like a rat he began to claw and dig through a pile of dirty clothes and rags that had been pushed into a corner; it was belike the inn's unwashed laundry. He pulled out an apron, a kirtle, and a kerchief and threw them at me, sputtering an order for me to put them on. I tore off my hood and tied on the kerchief, then rolled up my sleeves and over my clothes pulled on the kirtle and apron.

"He's coming! He's coming!" the innkeeper whispered. Again he pulled me after him and back down the stairs, and then he nigh swung me into the kitchen, just beyond the main room of the house, and told me to look busy. I found a tub of brown water and proceeded to scrub at the dishes piled within its murky depths. The innkeeper scuttled back into the other room, sat on a bench, leaned his elbows on the table, and looked idly out of the window.

The longest minutes passed and naught happened. Then we heard a noise, the front door opened, and the guard entered. He glanced about, wrinkling his nose at the stench. He saw me through the open door of the kitchen and demanded something of the innkeeper, who chattered away to him, scarce letting the guard say aught again himself. Whilst he talked, the man ambled about, coming finally into the kitchen. Remembering me how Bess had betrayed herself, I reached for an onion that lay beside the tub and took from it an enormous bite, chewing away with my cheeks puffed out like a squirrel's. The guard surveyed the kitchen and turned then to me, but saw that my mouth was too full to allow me to speak. With scorn he studied me. I looked back at him steadily and chewed still, insolent boredom writ on my face. All the while the innkeeper talked on and on, whilst my stomach was in a knot and I hid my sickness. At last the guard left the kitchen and went quickly up the stairs, the innkeeper following behind, and I heard their steps sound through the rooms above. Then they came back down, and without so much as a last glance around, the guard stalked from the house.

I felt weak. I grasped the edge of the tub to steady myself. "Gone now, gone now," the innkeeper was chattering like a cricket. I made to take off the filthy kerchief and apron but he stopped me. "Upstairs fast. Hide first." Again his arm swirled around and around to say that I should follow him, but ere I did I secretly slipped a knife out of the tub, slid it beneath the waist of my kirtle, and covered it with the apron. Then I hurried after him. We went up to the top of the house, through dark halls and gloomy rooms, until we arrived at a yet higher and smaller floor that I had not e'en known was there, and into a garret where the ceiling was low and slanted and what light there was fell through a narrow slice of window.

My hands were shaking and my knees could still scarce hold me up, so I sat upon a half-broken bench, the only piece of furniture in the room. The innkeeper closed the door, listened briefly at the crack, then turned back to me, his death's-head of a face glassy-eyed and grinning.

With fear and horrible suspicion, I studied my surprising benefactor. "Why did you help me?" I finally asked.

"Why did I help you?" he repeated.

"Why?"

He mumbled to me, "I do nothing for free. I help you, you pay me."

"But why didn't you help the guards? Then Cardinal Carafa could pay you. He could give you more money than e'er I could."

"Too dangerous. Dangerous man. I won't mix with him. And he does not give money to anyone. He would cut my throat first if he finds I cannot do more for him. People disappear all the time here in Rome. He arrests people. Throws their bodies in the Tiber. I've seen a few from my inn here, going down the Tiber."

"Bess!" I gasped.

"Won't hurt her." He shook his head like a clattering bag of bones. "Not yet. He has some reason. Will use her for something. And not while you still are free. Foreigners not safe to deal with. He knows that."

"Then I will pay you to help me. I have most of my money with me, but more back at the inn."

Again he shook his head. "Money there is no good to me. The cardinal will have it very soon."

My heart sank. The man was right; we had heard it was the Roman law that all innkeepers had to report the goods of their guests to the customs officials. As soon as Bess gave her name to her jailers, the cardinal or any other official would know where to go to confiscate her possessions—and mine. The clothes on my back and the money I had with me were all that were left.

"What possible cause had he to arrest us?" I wondered aloud.

"He needs no cause. But with you I think he has one."

"What is it?" I demanded.

He shrugged. "How can I know?"

"Can you discover it? And too where my niece is and what will happen to her?"

"There are ways. Secret ways. Money to a guard. Favors to repay. Give me money, I can find out."

He thrust out his oily hand and inched his way to me. In a trice I was on my feet and readying to strike him if he came nearer. He stopped.

"How can I trust you?" I demanded.

"No one else to trust, only me. I've done work like this before. Mine inn does not make enough money. Not for me."

I put my hand beneath mine apron and grasped the knife. I thought to ask him what there was to stop him from simply killing me and taking all my money, but did not lest the question might put an idea into his head.

"The cardinal takes my money, everybody's money." He waved his arms. "I can get some back now. Everybody hates him. I like to see him lose a prisoner."

I sighed and leaned against the wall; the damp plaster cracked and its powder stuck to my shoulder. He was right. There was no good choice left me but to trust him and stay there, or leave, and where could I go? I mourned our ill fortune. "Bess would have gotten away," I said aloud. "She would have easily walked out the other end of the market-place. But that vile, despicable man had to scream."

The innkeeper rattled his head and scratched the stubble on his cheeks. "Aye, I saw him. It was Damascus."

I was startled that e'en this innkeeper knew of Damascus. "Who is Damascus?" I asked, all innocent. "He seemed a madman to me."

"Mad indeed. I have seen him in the streets a week now, mayhap two. But not before."

"And what was he yelling at the guards? I made out but little of what he said."

"He was cursing them and the cardinal. Calling the pope the whore of Babylon. He hates the Church, hates Catholics. He be a heretic, a Protestant. The cardinal and Inquisition know about him and want to catch him. Mayhap he came here to curse the whore of Babylon, here to Rome, home of Catholics. No one knows where he's from. Some say he lives in Lowlands, near Antwerp. But I hear he wanders everywhere. He's ill. He has French disease. People say he caught it here in Rome years ago. He won't take any medicines for it. No *acqua del legno*, no *agnus castus*, nothing. There's a hospital here for men with *il mal francese*. He won't go near it. The disease has made him mad. But he yelled at guards. They know about him now. He must leave Rome. He might go back to Lowlands, or somewhere else. Mayhap Damascus thinks he has orders from God."

"He helped the cardinal today, and that I am certain was not the lack-brain's intent." I took off the filthy kerchief and threw it into a corner where it scattered the spiderwebs. "How quickly can you discover what has happened to my niece?"

288 • HELENA SOISTER

"I can ask around. I find out." He bended his shoulders, twisted his neck around as if it were a snake, and grinned up at me. Then he shoved out his hand.

I drew from my capcase two gold scudos and he took them eagerly. "You will have more when you prove to me your usefulness," said I. "I want information ere tonight. I have money enough to satisfy you, and too I have a great deal more in a bill of exchange that is on me, but it is worthless to you should you steal it. Help me to get Bess away from the cardinal, and help us to get out of Rome, and when I reach Milan—'tis in Milan I can draw on it—then I'll send you much more."

"How can I know you send money to me?" he rasped.

"How can I know that I can trust you?"

He laughed.

I spent hours in that wretched room, pacing and sitting help-
lessly, thinking and trying not to think. I reviewed furiously everything
Bess and I had said and done, everything we had heard and seen at
Pescioni's house, searching amidst subtleties for the cause for Bess's
arrest—and, had I not escaped, what would have been mine. I found
none. Only that we must have been betrayed by the whoreson Jacopo
and so were victims of the powerful cardinal. That seemed clear.

The late summer sunset had arrived, but by then the garret was
already dark. Noises drifted up from the rooms below; shouts and hard
laughter and scuffling and pounding echoing from a distance as carters
and common travelers returned to the inn for their suppers and their
beds. No one came near my room, not yet. I durst not open the door
and look out for fear that my secret place was being watched. I dreaded
the innkeeper, I suspected him of anything; still I waited impatiently for
his return. I did not e'en know his name, I bethought me, nor knew he
mine. Through my window I watched a speck of star reveal itself. If he
had lied to me I would not be surprised; certes I had lied to him: the
bill of exchange I had told him of was not on me but at my inn, and so
was now lost to the both of us. I had too less money in my capcase than
I had led him to believe.

At last quick padding footsteps approached, and threads of light
strayed in around the edges of the door. There was a mumbling, the rusty
door handle turned, and into the garret came the innkeeper, muttering
to himself and bearing two fat candles, one of which he gave to me.

"What of my niece?" I cried, nigh throwing myself at him.

He peered about the room and sniffed twice, careful that the
shadows hid none else save me.

"I asked around, I asked around." He coughed. "She's in jail, just another jail for criminals. Nothing said on what she's criminal of. No charges yet. Not in too much danger with Carafa, though. Word is he's giving her to the Inquisition tomorrow."

My heart stopped. "The Inquisition?" I whispered, refusing to believe him. I shook my head. I could not fight the panic that was grappling me.

The innkeeper grasped my arm, but I recoiled from his touch and stepped back. He was grinning with slyness and pushing a finger against his temple in a sign that he was craftily plotting.

"Be glad you have me, be glad, yes. For me the Inquisition is easier. Carafa is difficult, but the Inquisition—oh, I can get her out of that. I have friends. The Inquisition is secret. It is all locked up. But it's like any jail. It has servants who go in to clean. It has guards who watch the jails in it. Only one or two other people, maybe three, only two or three others let in. Those monks trust no one. But they're not there at night. And I can get in at night. I have a key to a door. And the guards are fools. I can trick them. You can go with me. I buy you clothes, and you look like servant. Tomorrow night."

"We can get her out? Are you certain?" I cried. "Sweet Jesus, let it be so! And you must get us safely out of Rome too."

He tapped his oily temple in thought. "A little difficult, that is. The monks might have gates watched."

"Then we must leave before they discover that Bess has escaped! We'll leave Rome tomorrow night too. Can we get by the night watches? Can we get by the guards at the gate? But they'll have the gates closed at night!"

"I think about it, I think about it. There are ways. Now"—he thrust out a bony hand—"give me more money. I get clothes for you and your friend."

I took a backward step, pulled out my capcase, and drew from it some coins, but I held them still until after I had given him special instructions. "Aye, get Bess clothes too, but I want you to get her man's clothing. Do you understand? They will be looking for two women, if there be any guards set out to look for us. But not the clothing of a manservant. Get those of a gentleman. The wealthier and more respectable at least one of us looks, the less likely we will be bothered by the guards."

He nodded. "Man's clothes. A gentleman's clothes."

"And we must have horses." My mind was whirling with a plot of its own. "It will not do to go walking up to the city gates. We must have two horses saddled and ready."

"That's not good, to bring horses near Inquisition."

"Then have them ready in a place away from there."

"Yes, yes." He turned to leave. "I can talk more later. I making plans. But I have mine inn to take care of now. I can bring you food and bedding soon."

A long time passed before he returned, and I could do naught but pace the small garret and fight my fears with the contemplation of how Bess and I might escape. I brooded too upon her arrest by the Inquisition and again who might have betrayed us—the cardinal or Jacopo, perchance. But why? I could render only wild speculations. When at last the innkeeper came back, he brought me bread and fatty meat and a bowl of sour wine, then was off again. In a few minutes he returned, dragging with him a mean pallet of straw that he flung into a corner and kicked to give it some shape. Though the food was without taste, I was natheless hungrily eating it as I bent over to inspect my bed. The cover over the straw was an old sheet that looked none too clean and more inviting to lice than mine own tired back. I stepped back to let the innkeeper finish his prodding and tripped on my kirtle. Swiftly I regained my balance, but not before there was a loud clatter.

The innkeeper flinched at the sudden noise, jumped about, and saw at the same time as I the knife that had been in my waist beneath my kirtle. It lay on the floor betwixt us and I was ready to dive for it, but he only bent down, picked it up, and examined it—of a surety recognizing it as one of his—and handed it back to me.

"You don't need this. Not till tomorrow night." He grinned. "If you are lucky, you will not need it then."

Then he left me, again not locking the door. I felt foolish and clumsy, but too a bit relieved: Only now was I beginning to have a faint trust in him.

I let the candle burn till morning. I did not want to be in darkness, and I stirred frequently and slept ill all the night long. Though the air was not especially warm and I had neither sheets nor blankets, still I was sweating and hot. I awoke finally at dawn and did not sleep again, rising only to watch from the thin window the sky as it grew pale with light, and to listen to the inn slowly break its silence as its sleepers and keepers rose and thumped about.

Not for another two hours, after the noise had grown and then died down and the place seemed once more nigh deserted, did the innkeeper come up with a small breakfast and some water with which I might wash myself. He spoke only to tell me that he was now going out to buy the clothes and arrange for the horses. More hours passed, each one warmer than the next. The heat in the close room was awful, and the damp walls seemed to swell and the slanting ceiling to sag yet more. The bells in the churches rang out the noon hour. Still I sat and paced and waited. More time dragged by, so much time it seemed, and at last the innkeeper came hurrying in with a large bundle.

"Got the clothes, got good clothes," he chattered. "Just the right clothes for you."

He dropped it onto the floor before me. I untied the torn sheet that held them all, and from the clothes that fell out of it pulled what looked to be only a common woman's petticoat and bodice. I held it up to me to judge its size and was surprised by the innkeeper's judgment, for it would fit very well. The man's clothes he had chosen for Bess looked as if they too would closely fit her, and though the jerkin and buskins were used and not at all costly, still they had a cheap shine that at night would pass for richness.

"Very good indeed," I said as I pulled the bodice over my clothes to check it. "And you have arranged for the horses?"

He gave a shrug. "I tried. I think there are two ready."

"You are not certain?"

"Stables want more money first."

I stopped adjusting my dress and peered at him. "I know of no stable that wants payment hours before the horses are ready. Whatever stable you are getting the horses from, tell the grooms you and I will stop by about half of an hour ere we fetch the horses, to be certain they are ready. But wait—no, we will not return to the stables after we bring Bess out of the Inquisition. We will tell them where to have the horses waiting, someplace where no one will see us, or at least pay us any mind. There are too many eyes and ears in a stable."

"Yes, yes. We can get horses then." Impatiently he rattled his head up and down.

I disliked his subtle avoidance on the matter, and the feeble trust I había había in him began to dwindle away.

had had in him began to dwindle away. "But you are certain Bess is in the Inquisition now?" I pressed him.

"I asked about, I asked about. She is there now. She went there this morning. The cardinal does not have her anymore."

Now he proceeded to give me instructions. Just after sunset, he said, we would leave for the Inquisition. He would be someone sent by the monks—he knew several of their names and could roll them off to the guard—who wanted a servant woman to examine the prisoner Bess Marwick and have her ready to face them in a short while. The monks had just been given evidence against her so they would be coming to interrogate her that same evening.

"That way we can get her out of jail and up to the room. Room where they first ask prisoners questions and charge them and judge them." He was grinning at his cleverness. "There are no guards there at night, just below. Get out of door from there, or window if there is trouble."

The innkeeper then padded out of the garret and returned in a little with another meal for me. I did not see him again till just past sunset. Hence I spent more wretched hours only waiting, alone too much with mine own thoughts, and pondering again every detail of our plans. I felt as if my brain were becoming numb from them and my heart unbearably heavy from too much worry. I was hot and dirty and moist with sweat, and I was panting air that seemed too thick to breathe, and murmuring prayers that I desperately hoped would help to make good our rescue of Bess and her and my escape.

When the evening's shadows were creeping through the garret, the innkeeper came in at last to tell me it was time to leave. He found me ready and anxious. I had long since changed into the servant's clothes and had tied beneath my petticoat some of Bess's disguise, and the remainder of it the innkeeper gathered up into a package. "I can bring it with me. No trouble. I can fool guard," he assured me. He himself had finally changed his foul clothes for ones that were a shade cleaner and more fitting for a cleric's official, and he had shaved the stubble off his sunken cheeks and smoothed back his oily hair. Then around and around his arm and hand went as he signaled for me to follow him. As we descended, we nigh encountered in the dark halls a few of the inn's lowly guests, but the innkeeper blew out his candle ere they could see our faces and we passed them unnoted. Unseen by anyone, we left the house and slipped outside.

Only a faint dusky light seeped through the night. Doors were already closed and windows shuttered, and the desiccated air floated about us like dust. During our long walk we passed but a handful of people, who did not look at us nor we at them. We padded down streets and along the edge of a piazza with a fire in its center, a smoky blaze with books for scarlet embers. About it were long, faceless figures, each of them throwing yet more books into the fire. Their movements were distorted by the dancing flames so that they looked like writhing contortions leaping up from hell.

We went on, over a bridge, down more streets, the innkeeper with his lame spider-walk and I following behind him. We came to the stables at last and there arranged for the horses; I told the groom the place—one familiar to me—I wished our mounts to be ready and waiting. Then we walked on and drew nigh St. Peter's; the scaffolding on the great half-built church loomed like a maze of gallows, black against the night-blue sky. At last I saw the home of the Inquisition. It was like a fortress, so impenetrable did it seem, so invincible. The innkeeper did not slacken his pace but went with confidence up to the front door—the only entrance I could see—and put a key into the lock. I heard the key rattle about and there was the hard noise of a bolt shifting.

Then the door swung wide and we were confronted by the guard who had been on the other side. He thrust a torch toward us that he might examine who was there, and his scowling face glared down upon us.

The innkeeper did not hesitate. Like a pompous petty official, he abruptly announced his name and purpose. The guard made to move, then first demanded more information, or so I gathered, for the innkeeper spoke impatiently to him and amongst his words I discerned the names of clerics and their titles. The guard stepped back, allowed us to enter, and locked the door behind us. More was said. The innkeeper now began to point to me, referred to the foreign woman Bess Marwick, and told a story convincing enough that the guard complied at last with his demands and led us on.

Down a long hall we went, dimly lit by scattered torches, and it hurled back at us the echoes of our intruding footsteps. The very sound of my forbidden presence in that dreaded place clanged in my ears and made my heart beat so loud within me that I feared the guard could hear it. I struggled to keep my aspect calm and hid my hands in the pockets of my petticoat lest he espy their shaking.

The guard unlocked a metal door and opened it. We followed him down stone steps into a fusty-smelling, dim and evil place. Everywhere were bars, and cold stone walls with only locked heavy doors to breach their solidity. Distant groans and crying whispers scraped weakly against the metal of the doors, and save for such pitiful sounds and the crackling of the torches, all was deathly still. I swore to myself that amidst the stench of human waste I could smell blood. And mine own blood drained away from me and I froze with horror. Heavenly God, have mercy on my Bess who is in this hell, I prayed.

We passed several cells wherein behind the bars there lay on damp straw solitary, unmoving lumps, one pathetic lump per cell, none of which I allowed myself to look at closely for fear I might be startled and cry out. At last the guard stopped at one of these cells and unlocked the bars.

A figure lay against the wall. I saw a familiar dress and long black hair in the dimness, and when we entered, a frightened face turned swiftly toward us, eyes wide, cheeks bruised and dirty. I choked down a cry. Bess said nothing; she only gasped, nigh cried out herself, and stared at me in wild confusion. The guard spoke roughly to her though he knew she understood him not, and went to wait outside the cell for us. Only then did the innkeeper speak to her, and in French.

"You must come with us. This woman can prepare you for an appearance. Before the Inquisition. Upstairs, fast. Not much time before they come."

Bess's confusion quickly waned; she took hold of herself and her courage, put on a worried face for the guard—of a surety her true feelings—and rose, her legs quivering in a spasm of pain. I nigh rushed to help her but a single glance from the innkeeper told me I should do naught that was suspicious; in that place any sign of compassion or ruth would cause doubts.

He walked busily out of the cell, then with a peremptory flip of his wrist gestured for the guard to lead us back upstairs. Bess looked about as we went, gazing into each barred cell and the mounds that lay in them. Her eyes were glazed with worry and her figure tense, and though her mind seemed to be apprehending the situation faster and faster and was most like already plotting, still flinders of it seemed to be elsewhere, chasing something removed from us.

The innkeeper gave the guard more directions, and we were led back to the main floor and into a large room that had in it only a long table and high-backed chairs along its far side. Apparently it was in this chamber and before this table that prisoners were brought for hearings. He ordered the guard to light the torches in preparation for the interrogation before he left us to return to his station.

Immediately the innkeeper closed the door. Bess flew to me and hugged me and all in one breath asked what was happening.

"God willing, we are getting you out of this place." I grabbed up my petticoat and pulled out the clothes hidden beneath.

The innkeeper lit another torch and tossed onto the table the package holding the remaining clothes. "Change in here. I can listen for guard." He slipped back into the hall.

Bess began to rip off her clothes whilst I threw the shirt and jerkin over her head and pulled her arms through sleeves and tied up the loose strings. Whilst she changed, we rapidly talked.

"Is not that the foul innkeeper we went to?"

"It is," I replied.

"But why is he helping us now? Surely not as a boon to strangers."

"No, for money, which I now have little of. It was he who saved me from being arrested. He got me out of that marketplace and hid me. I wanted to run after you, but he held me back."

"And thank God he did, else we both would be below in that nightmare of a place." She tied shut the jerkin. "Did you e'er discover why the cardinal had me arrested? Why he did so, and why he washed his hands of me by sending me here, I know not. I had thought his way of dispatching his enemies—real or imagined—was to have them killed, and not to give them to another power."

I wiped the dirt from her face. In the dim light her bruises looked almost like the shadow of a beard. "I don't know. Do your buskins fit well? Turn about, I'll fix your hair." I began to pin it up and shove it under a cap. "I'll secure this tightly, for we will be riding long this night. We are leaving Rome as soon as we are out of here. The innkeeper said we could pass ourselves off as messengers for the cardinal. He told me tonight that we need but cry 'Il messaggero del Cardinale Carafa' and we will be allowed to pass through the gates."

Bess frowned with doubt. "Can our getting through the gates be truly so simple?"

"We must hope so, though I've little trust in all our innkeeper tells us."

"Hold a moment, Sara. You say you have little money."

"Only what I had with me the day you were arrested less what I have given the innkeeper. Perchance I have enow to get us to Milan, but no farther. The cardinal, I believe, has confiscated everything else."

"I feared as much."

She was ready to go. She was stuffing her old clothes beneath a cupboard when the innkeeper appeared again.

"We wait a few minutes more," he whispered. "The guard is walking in hall now. Have money ready for horses. You pay for them fast, and you pay me fast. Pay me before you get to horses or you won't get out of Rome." His threat uttered, he hurried back out.

"I pray we can get to Milan with what I'll have left," I mumbled and took out my capcase to study the coins, quickly making my estimates.

"There is money *here!*" Bess whispered. "Or at least so Jacopo said. Van Wouwere's money, and others' too, I trow."

She looked about. At the far end of the room was another door. She hastened to it and looked into the room adjoining. "Naught," said she as she closed the door.

"What are you looking for?" I asked. "Not for van Wouwere's money!"

"Aye, or anyone's."

"Your brain must be fevered!"

"It is—from being in this place."

"Bess!"

But she seemed not to hear me as she took up the torch and rushed out into the empty hall. She ran soundlessly toward other doors, opened one and another and another, and shut them all. Then at last she let one stand open and disappeared into the chamber beyond. I sped in after her and closed the door.

This was a small chamber lined with cabinets and shelves, and what contents we could see were all of them papers. Bess went to the cabinets and began to tear them open, and I caught her fever and did the same. She found one locked, the others not, and in an unlocked one she uncovered a collection of weapons, likely confiscated from new prisoners. Whilst I slipped a dagger 'neath the waist of my skirt, she armed herself with a sword, and with another dagger stabbed at the locked cabinet. The door cracked. The noise this made was harsh, yet the innkeeper did not appear to see what was about.

Bess jerked open the broken door. A moment later she drew from within a small coffer with a key and a flat, cloth pouch of papers tied to it.

"The jackanapes at least did not lie about this chest." Bess laid it on a table and flourished the pouch. "This is van Wouwere's!"

Then Bess took the key and unlocked the coffer. When she lifted the lid, she gasped at what she saw. "I had not thought when I came to Rome that I would so desperately need this," she murmured.

I looked into the coffer. Filling it were masses of scudos and too a little bag which, when Bess opened it, proved to be holding a small pile of precious jewels. My body began to move faster than my mind. I had already pulled out Bess's skirt from beneath my petticoat and was ripping it up.

"We cannot carry a thing like that about with us. Tie the money into these rags," I ordered in a hushed voice.

We poured the coins onto them, then tied up the ends and muffled their clanging contents with more rags. I hung as many of the bags at my waist and 'neath my petticoat as I was able and Bess secured the remaining ones within her shirt.

We had been so busy that neither of us had heard the door open or noticed the innkeeper standing there.

"You have money for me?" He grinned.

"I have some money," said I. "But what if we take money or aught else from here? What of your safety? Can you be tracked down and caught? Will the guard point you out?"

"You give me money, lots of money, and I take risk. Now hurry. Only a minute, then we go." Again, he went out.

I checked myself and Bess to make certain we were ready, then made to go wait at the door, but Bess did not follow.

"What is it?" I asked.

"I want too those papers."

"What are you talking about? We cannot tarry."

But already she was at the table and opening the pouch that had been tied to the coffer. I watched her as she read the Latin words on the first paper she drew from it.

"What does it say?" I asked.

Still she was silent. She pulled another paper from the pouch, her lips moving silently as she read and her eyes filling with confusion.

"Van Wouwere was found guilty of blasphemy," she said at last. "But I do not understand. They have writ here his crimes; there are so many. He was condemned to be burned on the morrow. He was found guilty only today. But it says here he died today. He died after being tortured. He is gone."

Her hand was quivering as she laid down the paper. She reached into the pouch and drew forth a few more sheets, wrinkled and torn. I could see they were crossed with stars and lines and words that must have interpreted the stars, and they were blotted with astrologic symbols; but the edges had been burned and their ashes crumbled and fell betwixt her fingers.

"Van Wouwere was belike trying to destroy this evidence 'gainst him when they came to arrest him," I said. "But he must have been caught ere he could, and hence these papers destroyed him."

Bess gazed at the remnants of his prophecies, at the ashes that now lay atop the pouch.

My voice was taut with fear and frustration. "This is what has become of your obsessions! This is what all van Wouwere's prophecies have come to: ashes, no more! And you believed them, didn't you? They terrified you. So you pursued him all the way to Rome to prove him wrong and destroy that fate. The whore and the cleric—you nigh became their victim not through fate, but by your willful acts! You and Catlin . . ." I bit back mine anger. "Now, God help us, we have yet to get out of this hellish place and out of Rome!"

Bess was deathly white. She laid the papers back in the pouch and stepped away, her gaze ever upon it.

The innkeeper hissed at us from the hall. "We go now!"

At last Bess moved. She swung about, snatched up one paper from out of the pouch, and said, "The cardinal's seal might help us." The unfolded letter had indeed an unbroken seal at one end, which had by good fortune slipped off the other end when the paper was opened. Bess folded the sheet again so that only the seal showed and thrust it into her jerkin. Then we ran into the hall. There the innkeeper was signing us to hurry.

"I sent the guard downstairs," he said. "I said I forgot, the monks want her jail examined."

He sped away with Bess and me hard upon his heels. He unlocked the entrance door, locked it after us, looked about to see if anyone was about in the empty street, and with his crooked gait lurched along, hugging close to the buildings like a rat. The night had swallowed up the city and I squinted to see where we were going. We ran as noiselessly as we could, diving down narrow alleys, moving only in shadows. We saw a night-watch not far from us, his lantern a yellow atomy, but we slipped around a corner ere he could see the moving shades we cast. We crossed a bridge, crept down yet more streets, until at last I began to remember I had been near here but a little while before, and that our horses would be waiting for us close by.

The innkeeper turned another corner. We followed into an alley— but he had vanished. We hurried to the other end; he was not there. Fearful and hesitant, we started down a narrow passage that led from the alley. Then a dark figure stepped out before us, and I stumbled back in fright.

It was the whoreson Jacopo. His eyes were fastened unblinking upon us and he was smiling a limp smile. Frantic, we whipped about toward the alley whence we had come, but the yellow lantern of another night-watch floated by at the end of our passage and we pressed hard into a crevice to avoid being seen.

"Your guide has gone," said he in a voice that froze my bones, "so you may give me the money."

"We have no money!" Bess stammered.

"Oh, but you do."

"If that is what that vile innkeeper told you," said I, "then he was lying."

"He had no need to tell me, though tell me he did. He would not have led you out of the Inquisition until you had it. And you would not have been in there unless you were willing to steal the money."

"I went to save my niece," I whispered, "who had been arrested by your cardinal."

"Ah, but she would not have been arrested had not the both of you gone to the marketplace to discover your friend's fate—and so the fate of his possessions. And you, madame"—he nodded his head to me— "would not have escaped had I not willed it so."

So all that had happened in these terrible hours Jacopo had contrived. I grew dizzy to know this but for only a moment, so was again hard awake when a long blade of steel flashed before me. Jacopo was pointing a sword at us.

"So now, mesdames, you may give me the money."

The sound of metal against metal scraped beside me. Bess had whipped forth her own sword and was pointing it at him. He was startled enow to move out of the shadows and now I could see his face more clearly. 'Spite her sword, it wore a smug smile.

"Too late," said Bess. "You should have stolen it yourself, and ere tonight."

"So I meant to." Jacopo's voice was amused, as if he were indulging a child. "I was ready to have his money stolen and van Wouwere to disappear—through the cardinal, the Inquisition, there are so many ways—but the fool managed to have himself arrested ere I could."

"So you had your friend the cardinal help you," said Bess.

He inched backward, talking on as he gauged our positions. He seemed to be throwing out words as he would a lure that could trick us, or distract or overpower us. "He knew not that he was helping me. With him I could arrange the kind of arrest I desired; with the Inquisition it would have been more difficult. One of you was arrested; one of you, through the innkeeper, escaped. I could then convince our cardinal that sith you two were foreign travelers he might have some small difficulty after the arrest, for I had heard you had important merchant friends who would soon be joining you in Rome and they could make vexing inquiries about your disappearance. I suggested that the Inquisition should have the trouble instead. After he had confiscated your possessions, he agreed and sent his prisoner to the place I wanted her."

"Aye, for you had a key to that place and the innkeeper to help you." Secretly I clenched the dagger 'neath my waist. Only then did I feel too the heavy bags of money hanging on my hips and thighs and the bruises they had given me during our running. "Why did you not use it and fetch the money yourself?"

"There could have been danger in that. 'Twas best to have strangers do that for me."

"And had the cardinal no suspicions of you or your duplicity?" Bess asked. As I, so she too was tricking for time.

"He does indeed. But not the particulars. And with the money I can leave Rome and live in comfort till the old pope dies. Then Carlo will be overthrown, and I can return."

Bess shifted her weight. "And what have you planned for us now?"

Again the smile. "Think upon't. Would I have told you this much had I planned for you to survive this night?" Once more he held out a hand for the money whilst with the other he circled the point of his sword.

Swiftly I pulled out my knife, but Bess had already leapt forward and was pressing her own sword 'gainst his chest. He moved back a little and she leapt at him and swung. Their blades clashed. He slashed at her too broadly, she swung in turn, and they fought for only moments. Jacopo faltered back, watching for anyone else who might hear our battle. He was a clumsy swordsman and so was Bess, but she was fighting with a vicious rage. He moved farther down the passage and Bess followed. Suddenly he broke and ran and so too did we, whether after him or no mattered not to me, so long as we got out of that place and to our horses.

Bess ran too fast. When I reached the spot where the alley divided, I could not see her. Still I did not pause but hurried down one way, stumbling along until I reached the end and found myself in an open place. There, but a few yards away, stood Jacopo.

I had not time to do aught, for all at once there came a horrifying cry, and I jumped around as Bess hurled herself out from another street and rushed, face wild, sword ready, at the whoreson. For an eerie moment, I saw not Bess but Catlin and heard him in her cry and watched his movements in her body as she flung herself at Jacopo and fought him with an unleashed madness. He stumbled back, and for a frantic minute he fought her attack. Then her sword found its mark and stabbed him and he howled in pain and grasped his arm and the sword that was piercing it clear through. Scarce had she plucked back the bloody blade when he tore away into the shadows and disappeared.

I saw in the distance a yellow light hurrying nigh. "The nightwatch!" I cried to Bess.

Into its sheath flew her sword and we sped down a dark street. "This way!" I cried and now went down a way that seemed more familiar, and down another. Shop signs hung above us and pointed out the way. At last we came upon the place beside the Tiber where the horses were to be waiting for us. But they were not there. In a panic I looked all around us.

"Hold a moment!" Bess touched me and forced down her panting breaths that she might hear better. Far off there was the clatter of hooves.

We ran in their direction, up along the river. Soon we saw in the moonlight and in the light reflected by the river three horses, one ridden by the same groom I had talked to; with his free hand he was leading the others.

We called after him. He stopped. I drew out my purse, emptied its last scudos into my hand, and just as we caught up I held them out to him.

"We still have need of these horses. Here is your money!" In a trice I'd snatched from him the reins of the riderless horses, put in his same hand the coins, and was mounting one of the beasts.

I had cried at him in French, and baffled, he answered me in Italian. Neither Bess nor I heeded him but only galloped away.

We galloped at full speed down the streets, the horses' iron-shod hooves clamoring loudly 'gainst the stones. On we went, with lanterns of the night-watches sparking in and out of sight along the way and with shouts clamoring behind us. I knew vaguely what direction we were headed in, but I swore to myself that we were lost. The streets curved into a dangerous maze. Old ruins rose up to catch us. Then the city's walls rose ahead of us, and then the gate—the northern gate, I knew. Across the piazza we galloped and the guards at the gate yelled at us.

"Il messaggero del Cardinale Carafa!" Bess cried out to them, her voice nigh as deep as a man's. The guards began to raise the gate, but one took up a torch and stood before it as if waiting to receive from us more than those words.

When we reached him, Bess reined in her horse so abruptly that it nigh threw her, and she pulled from her jerkin and held out to him the letter with the cardinal's seal. He studied the imprint in the wax, handed the letter back, and signaled for the gate to be raised the more. He had scarce e'en glanced at Bess's face, which was deep in shadow.

The gate creaked and wheezed upward and was but halfway off the ground when Bess and I bent low over our horses and galloped under it and past the walls, and out of Rome at last.

XXXII

Endless miles passed away, and then days and weeks, and many a time we fell again into danger and hardships, and often our only comfort was the wealth we were carrying and the knowledge that we were for home. We were belike no longer hotly pursued; still as soon as the roofs of Antwerp rose before us on the flat horizon, Bess let fly a joyful whoop and I a laugh. Within the hour we were in the city, where she slapped her horse into a law-breaking gallop down the last streets to Catlin's house, and when the door was opened to us by Lijsken, Bess rushed into the woman's arms.

"Where's Master Catlin?" she nigh shouted.

"At the countinghouse!" Lijsken gasped.

In a trice Bess had mounted again and was off for the counting-house. I let her go on alone, that she and Catlin might have a private reunion. I talked with Lijsken and she helped me to settle our things into our bedchambers until an hour later, when there came the sound of Catlin's and Bess's voices below. I hurried downstairs, and scarce had I seen him when his arms were around me and we were swaying in a warm hug.

"Sara! 'Tis so good to have you back again!" he exclaimed. "So good! But you look tired."

"I'm well enow. Some weariness about the edges is part of my nature now. And you, Catlin, how have you fared all these months?"

"As well as I might without the two of you. Infinitely better now that you're back. Lijsken, why wait you there?" he cried to the woman, who had followed me down. "Fetch us some good food and wine that we may toast our friends' return!"

With happy oaths we went up to the antler room and there settled ourselves with wine and Lijsken's promises that food would be served as soon as she could cook it. The embers in the hearth had a log thrown on top of them and in a little the cold room was made warm again. It was in this light, and after the flurry had died down, that I saw Catlin the better. A haggardness was etched into his face and a redness stained his eyes, perchance because of too much drinking, and all his body sagged as if he had been fraught with disquiet. These things, as I became aware of them, seemed to grow yet more apparent, and then began to fade, as if Bess's very presence were making him well again.

She was sitting in loving closeness beside him, laughing and drinking, her arm draped over his shoulder and her eyes ever on him. That he was not yet informed of our misfortunes in Rome became evident when he told us he had not expected us to return so soon. At this, Bess and I let our talk stagger into silence.

"Ah, by the by," she said at last, "we have something to give you."

He grinned. "The prize you jested of to me?"

"You'll see soon enow." She rose and hurried out.

" 'Tis in your bedchamber, Bess," I called after her.

When she set before him a small bronze coffer, he said naught, only smiled and snapped back the latch, lifted the lid, and stared at the gold before him. He took her hand and kissed it, and too kissed mine. "You never needed to do this for me," he said.

"The desire sufficed, and mine own needs," Bess rejoined.

"But there are hundreds of scudos here."

"About three hundred, and in that bag I have set in the corner are divers jewels upon which a jeweler in Cologne gave us an estimate. Their worth and the coins should come to the approximate amount of seven hundred and fifty Flemish pounds."

He laughed to himself and shook his head in unbelief. Then a scowl crept across his brow and he lowered the lid. "I was such a damn fool for drawing that man into our lives. That you should atone for my wrongs . . ."

"I can swear to you, Catlin," said I, "that we are all fools, and that I alone have committed more errors than you. Oh, my holy pilgrimage is for me most memorable."

"Had you problems?"

Bess and I laughed at that.

"Of course you did." Catlin rested his hand on Bess's. "It must have been nigh impossible to get near this treasure. Sweet Jesus, how I wish I might have seen van Wouwere's foul face when he saw you both."

"We never saw him," said Bess.

"Then how came you by this?"

"The coffer we bought in Cologne; before that and until we reached there we carried this treasure in rags." Bess leaned against Catlin. "Those contents are all that remain of van Wouwere's wealth, or of him. There had been more, enough to pay for Sara's and my traveling there and back, and a modest reward to ourselves withal. Nothing else remains of him. He is dead."

Catlin caught in his breath, then drew his hands away from the coffer as if it were a malignant thing. "I will not rejoice in his death," he said, "but neither will I be a hypocrite and mourn his end. How did he die?"

"In the Inquisition, after being tortured." Bess was solemn.

Slowly, Catlin returned to his drink. "How easily doth forgiveness come now, after he has suffered." A thought made him pause. "How odd, now that I think on't. 'Twas he who suffered at the hands of the clerics, and he who lost all his wealth and too his life ere this year was three quarters done."

"Aye, I've thought that too," said I. "Mayhap he did tell his own fate in one of his prophecies, but the fool took it to be Bess's."

Bess played with her cup. "So what I pursued to Rome, Sara, was not mere ashes and paper, as you told me, but something real."

"His fate was real for him alone. For you it was unreal," said I. "It only became yours the day you left Antwerp for Rome, as had he."

"And what if I'd stayed in Antwerp?" she countered. "Think you I'd be safe still? Oh no. We would not have gotten from Mueller that damning evidence against me."

"Aye," said Catlin. "I was much glad to have your letter that you had intercepted and destroyed it."

"If I hadn't," Bess continued, "Mueller would belike have sent it on, and if it had slipped past the clerk you bribed, if it had reached the magistrates, then I might have indeed died the bloody death van Wouwere predicted. I would have been burnt as a witch."

I moaned. "And the price we paid for those papers forced us to go on to Rome."

"Whence we're now safely gone. Our wills prevailed over any fate."

"Our wills?" I scoffed. "Haven't you the wit to see you prevailed not just because of your acts, but because of forces beyond your control? And I mean not only God's will. Your life, your fate was for a little in my hands, and in Jacopo's and those faceless men's who run the Inquisition. You talk of free will and strike bravely at paper threats, but did it never occur to you that perchance it was your fate to go to Rome? God or the devil presented you with a temptation, and because of what you are and how you think—and your will is nigh a slave to those things—you fell to that temptation."

She winced, and the triumph slipped out of her. "Aye, Sara." She sighed. "Sometimes I've thought the same myself."

Catlin had been listening somewhat confused by our words. Now his voice moved between ours. "You've not yet told me what happened in Rome."

And so, weaving a narrative betwixt us, Bess and I began to tell him of our misfortunes in Rome and too of our encounter with Damascus, and of the rest. We were in the midst of the tale when mine eyes wandered to a window where I saw snow wheeling past. Letting Bess finish for me, I went to look out. The first snow of winter, I thought. I had never hoped to watch another winter's arrival in this house or in Antwerp. But time flies and plans go awry; that's a poor couplet I must need remember. Yet I felt no melancholy. I only gazed at the gathering beauty of the falling snow and was content.

Being very tired, I soon bid a good night to Bess and Catlin and went to bed. I awoke early in the morning, when the house was deep in rest and no one was yet stirring, and rose and dressed and went to see if Bess was awake. Her bed was empty, the covers untouched. I didn't think or wonder. I knew where she was. And 'tis good, I thought, 'tis good.

Since most of our business during our journey had been well supervised by Catlin, Bess and I had much idle time on our hands. She spent her time with him, whether or no he was working, and often when he himself was free and she was not near him, he would seek her out. I shall be paying passage for us soon, I said to her; in a week or so we'll be going home. She said naught, but I knew she would soon have an answer for me.

Some days after our return, whilst I was idly spending an afternoon in my bedchamber, Bess came in and for a little only observed me and waited for me to notice her presence. My back was to her and I didn't hear her enter; I was standing amidst clothes and my latest purchases, trying to decide what things to pack first. Finally I became aware of her.

" 'Tis a royal mess, isn't it, Bess?" said I. "And you've more to ship than I. Have you readied yourself at all?"

"I trust I'll soon be ready," she answered, "since I'm at home now."

I straightened up and looked at her. She was smiling, e'en nigh glowing, as if at last a darkness had fallen away from her. Not since she was much younger and innocent had I seen her like that. And yet, though she now had in her a contentment, a happiness, I sensed that not all of the disturbed emotions in her soul had been appeased.

"You'll be staying in Antwerp?" I asked.

"And in this house. Catlin and I have decided to marry."

My arms slackened and the pomander of sweet powders that had been in my hand fell onto my clothes, spilling the fine stuff. I'd been expecting such news since our return, and wanting it since long before that.

"Good Lord, so you're going to marry each other at last. God keep you both. God bless you. Well, I'm pleased. I'm pleased with this match. You'll give some peace to each other, perchance. Marriage—well, may it be a happier one for you this time, Bess." My thoughts were as disorderly as the things about me. I stumbled over them and went to hug her.

She was watching me closely. "Have you still your misgivings?"

"About the marriage?"

"And about Catlin."

Awkwardly I went back to my spilt powders and busied myself with scooping the grains back into the pomander. "I think I do. Aye, I confess I might indeed. But they're not so strong as my relief."

"How you've wanted me to stop sinning! Or at least not know about it."

I was quick to defend myself. "And I want to see the both of you happy, which the neither of you is when you're apart."

"And we were ofttimes not happy when together. But 'tis different now that van Wouwere is gone, now that I've shown Catlin I was not a victim to any fate. So at last he's put aside all his astrology. He still feels a little need to divine his future but can resist it. Can you understand what that means?"

My hands twisted around and around the pomander. This was too simple. All was not yet right, I feared. "And that is all it took? He's at peace with himself?"

She glanced away as if at an unwanted thought, and when she turned back to me that unearthly look was in her black eyes. "He has some peace."

"Well, please God you're right." I waxed cheerful again. "Certes you understand each other as much as anyone can. We can both see how ill he fared without you, and how he's better now you're back."

Feelings rumbled up in her. "He drank too much whilst we were gone, and still he drinks, but less now. I've mixed some tisane for him, and sometimes to please me he'll have that instead of wine. The herbs will do him good."

"And his shipping of pamphlets?"

"He'll no more of it. He stopped when his actions were being watched, and now he won't continue, as his life is his own again and not van den Bist's. That man is finally fast losing his hold o'er him."

"A dead man could never put a true hold on anyone. You should know that, and he. Catlin let himself be controlled by his own strange beliefs, and too by the guilt for his father's sin."

"Oh no, Sara." Bess stretched out her hand to me. "If I clasped you and you felt my flesh against yours, it would be to Catlin less real a hold than was van den Bist's on him. Now Catlin feels far more mine own touch."

I almost cracked the pomander in my squeezing hands. "Well, I pray that with you always near him, no room will be left for Martin van den Bist."

As Bess had been for me a daughter, so now I looked upon Catlin not only as a friend and factor, but a son-in-law. He was most welcome into my family, I told him, and with a smile added that he must see to Bess's needs and keep her well, for I'd oft be visiting them. I saw in him then what I'd seen in Bess: no great joy or peace, but some contentment and an inchoate happiness.

Since Bess would be remaining in Antwerp, she began again to invest her money in goods and shipped them to England, and also now to Catlin's factors in Amsterdam and Cologne. Again too she was working daily at the countinghouse with Michiel and Jan, both of whom seemed glad that she'd be their mistress. The bumbling Jan, I noted especially, might appreciate having about a kind of older sister like Bess. But only the day after he and Michiel had been given the news of the marriage, mine image of a harmless Jan was shattered.

I was sitting in the back room whilst Bess was examining the wrapping on some bolts of cloth she had bought that morning.

"Damn!" she muttered to herself.

"What is it?" I asked.

"The wrapping cloth on one of my bolts is torn. I examined them all ere buying them, and they'd not a spot on them. Now at least three ells of this bolt have been soiled. And this be fine linen."

"Did the carter tear it?"

"I'm not sure. Jan!" she called out.

He came down from above and asked her what she wanted.

"Three ells of my linen are stained because its wrapping was torn. Didn't you watch the carter unload these bolts? Or were you the one who handled them so carelessly?"

"I handled them passing well." He was all innocence. "It must have been the carter's fault."

"And your fault for not watching him closely."

He shrugged and looked about for an excuse. "Ah, now, Mistress Bess. Don't be harsh with me."

"I'll be as harsh as I please. Now what am I to do with this linen?"

He gave the bolt a glance. "Wash it. 'Tis only a little dirt, not a stain. The dirt'll come out."

"Then you'll have to wash it. I won't." She tossed the cloth back around the bolt. " 'Tis an apprentice's task."

She was already too tart and irritated, and he humiliated and insulted. Expectantly, she held out the bolt to him. As if this were now a battle of wills, he only turned around on his clumsy feet and headed back to the stairs.

"I want this washed now!" she demanded.

"Then wash it!" he snapped.

"What's this?"

He turned around and squared his shoulders. "Be you deaf?"

"You are the apprentice in this house, not I!"

"And you are not yet its mistress!"

The blow hit her, and she retreated. "I meant not to be rude to you, Jan," said she, "or accuse you of fumbling your tasks."

Her softer voice seemed only to stir his ire the more, as if he thought she was now teasing him. His cheeks flushed and on his boyish face the frightening aspect of a vicious man broke out like a rash.

"I care not a whit if you wish to play with me!" he barked. "You once feigned to be my sweetheart. You dallied with me. You stirred me hot and cold. But now I'm again only an apprentice, am I? And you too lofty for me? Well, you're not yet mistress of this house, if indeed you ever will be. Whilst you were gone Master Catlin had another mistress, and he'll never make her mistress of this countinghouse, either."

Bess stared at Jan in unbelief. Her legs weakened, and she grabbed at a box for balance. "There's no other woman for him. He has not lied to me."

"Is it lying to say nothing?" he shot back. "He's had a woman all these months you were gone. A common whore. He went to her all the time. She must have pleased him very much. She was a very pretty little thing, I've heard. Not like you at all. She's in a bawdy house over on Lepel Straat. Mayhap you and she could be friends."

At last he was finished. His face still burning, he hastened back upstairs, leaving Bess to gaze after him in blank pain.

"He's a cruel brat!" I exclaimed. "A cruel, spiteful boy who should be spanked like a common brat! Pay him no mind. Pay no mind to him or aught he said. He wanted to cut you to the quick, and like the devil he knew how to do it. So he devises a story he knows could only hurt you."

Still she didn't speak. Only when I put mine arm around her could she say, "And what if his story be true?"

"It couldn't be." I was adamant.

"Oh, Sara, you know as well as I that e'en when we lived with him, before we went to Rome, he went to whores."

"I know only what you've told me. And if he did so, weren't nigh all those times when van Wouwere was about? Then the doctor left, and Catlin was with you, and you were all he wanted."

Her head quivered a no. "Not all. He's not wholly satisfied with his life, just as I'm not with mine."

"And what will satisfy him he'll not find in a whore, and that he knows. For God's sake, Bess, you left him for nigh five months. He has no true friends save you and me. How horribly lonely he must have been. And what of van den Bist? With you gone, he took hold of Catlin again. Now you are returned, and that has changed."

She took mine arm off her. "I was lonely too."

"You had your traveling to keep you busy, and your obsession to keep you warm."

"Has he not his own obsessions?" A sob caught in her throat.

"Aye, and when they're upon him, then he does things he himself hates."

She began to pace the room. Catlin was still in his office, and several times she moved in its direction, only to veer away and go elsewhere until at last she announced to me that she would out of that place. I pulled on my cloak and went with her. We roved down streets, slipped into countless shops, and all the while she tried to talk about aught save Jan's revelation and struggled to keep from bursting out the pain in her. Two hours passed, and she began to head toward particular streets, as if heeding an inner voice. Not until she'd slowed her gait and I looked about did I perceive where she'd led me.

"Let's home now," said I. "My feet do ache most sorely."

"If you wish. We can go down this street and then have done with all this wandering."

"Bess, this is Lepel Straat."

"I know."

Fiercely, repeatedly, her eyes were skimming across each of the houses. Then one just ahead of us caught her attention. 'Twas a place someone had pointed out to us once as being one of the city's many bawdy houses. She glanced up at its windows, slowed more as we passed it, and walked on, her face saddened.

"Once more, Sara." She hooked her hand around mine arm and drew me back. "I want to see the place once more."

"Ah, Bess," I said with a sigh, "for what purpose? This walking past a certain spot again and again—what solace can that bring you?"

"None. Still I need to do this."

We turned and walked back down the way. We were just passing in front of the house when a window above opened and out of it leaned a very young woman. She'd a small, pretty face and hair the color of cowslips, which was gathered at the nape of her neck. She looked around, down at us, and for a second her eyes met Bess's. Then she withdrew, closing the window.

"One of many, and in that house alone," I said quietly to Bess.

We walked on, and said naught more.

Catlin arrived home just after dark. Bess was sitting in my bed-chamber, watching mine attempts to keep busy with a hem I was mending. When he called for her, she left me and went down to him. I waited for I knew not what to happen. Shouts and accusations I was expecting, some furious words at least, but a quarter of an hour passed, and still the house was peaceful. Not being able to sit any longer amidst my worries, I put away my sewing and went downstairs.

I stopped at the doorway of the antler room. Catlin was sitting on the table's edge and watching Bess as she came nearer him. She was holding something large and angular in her hands, and as I moved forward to see what it was, I realized it was the portrait of Martin van den Bist, and beneath it the aged account book that had always kept it dusty company.

Neither of them spoke. She stopped before the bright, high-scrambling flames on the hearth. Then she bent over and tossed onto them the book and beside it the portrait, frame and all, and took a step back and leaned against the table, and with Catlin watched them begin to burn.

I advanced till I too could watch the fire lick the hated objects. I shuddered, grew attentive to every crackle and spark, and then under-stood that I was expecting some dread manifestation to occur: the unearthly howl of a ghost or the appearance of a vengeful wraith or the rattling of the furniture—I knew not what. But nothing changed. There was only the burning. The brass buckle on the book was singed into blackness and the leather writhed, and the edges of hundreds of pages separated and hissed and began to crumble away, bit by bit, in tiny cinders. Flames smoldered beneath the portrait and the paints melted and cracked and the wood that held them was ruthlessly charred, and the horrid face of Martin van den Bist twisted within the embers. The hard mouth curled into a leer, the eyes glowed with mad sparks, the skin billowed with smoke, and for wretched moments the face was hellish and frightening. And then it was gone. The flames burst through from the back of the picture and devoured it until nothing at all was left.

And the three of us watched wordlessly.

Because Bess and Catlin were going to marry, I changed mine own plans and decided to stay in Antwerp for a little while longer than I had intended. Then Bess would return with me to London to arrange for the sale or continued leasing of her land and the transportation of her other possessions to Antwerp. Once these matters were seen to, she and I would sail for the Lowlands again, I would attend her wedding, and afterward I could at last truly go home.

During that same week, I accompanied Bess and Catlin to the English Quay, where he had a delivery to oversee. When the two of them were in the Custom House, I strolled about outside amongst the large bales sitting everywhere. Coming around one of them, I discovered my path was blocked and I would have to retreat, yet I did not then turn around. Something within me—a remembrance, a fear—was warning me not to. Then I recognized the foul stench and I heard the strange wheezing. I braced myself to turn at last.

Standing only arm's length away was Damascus. His death-pale face, his scarlet-veined eyes were staring at me, and his lips, deformed now by the crusted sores, were twisted into a frown. Dear Jesus, I whispered to myself, he was still pursuing us. We still had no peace.

"Thou wert in Rome!" His hoarse voice was like a beast's. "Thou wert with the idolators, and now thou art come back!"

My back was pressing hard against a table. I was suddenly so helpless I could not e'en cry out.

"But thou didst not go for the same reason as did I, didst thou!" In his mad mind he seemed to be compiling and distorting his scant knowledge of me. "I know why thou went! I know! And I know why thou art returned!" He leaned his body closer to mine.

His stench was sickening me. I feared he might attack me and could bear him no more. Ere he could blink I pushed myself off the bale and shoved him out of my way and went rushing onward, and when some distance away I looked over my shoulder, he had disappeared.

I arrived back at the Custom House just as Bess and Catlin were emerging from it.

"Catlin," I panted, "he's back! Damascus is back in Antwerp!"

He didn't want to believe me. "What? You've seen him?"

"Just now, here on the wharf." I told them of what had passed.

"What meant he, he knows why you were in Rome?" asked Bess.

With a shaking hand I waved away her question. "The devil knows."

"The devil indeed," Catlin moaned. "I've had naught to do with Brother Gerard all these months, nor with shipping pamphlets or e'en helping the Protestant exiles, so Damascus cannot be following me again."

"But he must have left Rome nigh the same time as did we," said I, "hence he's new-come here. Belike he doesn't yet know that you've forsaken those causes."

"I pray he discovers as much"—Catlin was anxious—"and soon finds another fool to guard."

Dear God, yes, I prayed, but in vain. On a morning soon thereafter, Damascus came to him.

I was sitting with Catlin in his countinghouse office and reviewing with him my partners' accounts. We were deep into our work and paid no attention to the sound of the entrance door opening, or to Michiel as he spoke with someone in the front chamber. Then there was a knock on the office door.

"I'm sorry to disturb you, Master Catlin, Mistress Lathbury," said Michiel, an exasperation wrinkling his freckled brow, "but there's a most ragged man here. He claims he has come to see you, sir. He claims to have some business with you."

"What is his name?" asked Catlin.

"He won't give it."

I became uneasy. "Has this stranger dun hair and sores about his mouth?"

"He does."

"I know the man, Michiel," Catlin quickly said. "He's a mad rogue. But be you careful with him. Tell him I'm not in and see that he leaves."

We could hear Michiel's voice and then a muffled reply. Michiel spoke louder, there was a scuffle of feet, and all at once the door to the office was flung open and in galloped Damascus. He hurled himself toward Catlin and up against the desk and grasped the edge, ready to hold fast if any man durst try to drag him away. Michiel rushed in after him, but looked first to Catlin for a signal of what next to do.

Damascus had only glanced at me afore nailing his wild eyes upon Catlin. His stinking breaths were rapid, his body exuded ferocity.

Catlin, at first stunned, swiftly regained his control and spoke stonily to him. "By what right do you force yourself in here?"

"By the right of the sanctified mission God hath given me!" Damascus rasped.

"You have no such mission. You only wish to torment me!"

"No! Long ago I guarded thee, I protected thee, but no longer. Now the torment shall begin!"

Anger exploded from Catlin. "Get out of my house or I will throw you out myself!"

"The hand of God shall not be stopped!" Damascus cried, and so ghastly was the screeching sound that Catlin clutched his desk and I my chair. "You are a defender of the scarlet whore of Babylon! You are an agent of the blasphemous pope! God's true Christians have come to you for help and you have forsaken them! They will write His words and spread His truth without you!"

"I know not what you are saying!" Catlin sputtered.

"This woman was in Rome!" His finger stabbed toward me. "Through her and the other woman who lives with thee thou receivest orders from Rome. They are spies for idolatrous priests, and so too art thou!"

"You're a madman and a liar!" Catlin shouted. "Get out!"

"Thou wilt have upon thee the wrath of God! The enemies of God's true faith shall inherit His vengeance!"

Catlin jumped up, his chair tumbling over with a crash. He seemed ready to strangle the howling man. "Get out!"

Damascus hurried backward out of the office, past a stunned Michiel, and was gone.

"Sweet Jesus!" I crossed myself.

Catlin cradled his head in his hands. "Aye, Sweet Jesus indeed."

"Michiel," said I, "bolt the door again, and look out in the street and make certain he's gone."

"I am sorry, sir!" Michiel stammered, wringing his hands. "I tried to stop him."

"I know, I know. Have Jan throttle him if he comes near this place again."

"Well," said I, when at last I could breathe again, "Damascus is no longer your unholy guardian."

Catlin lifted his head from his hands. "His guardianship alone put me in peril. Now that he is my sworn enemy and crying vengeance, what can that mean for me?"

"You'll no longer be suspected of heresy."

"That is scant solace. In truth, I had little to fear from the magistrates, unlike Bess with those charges of sorcery. Only the queen's agents and Brother Gerard were my concern."

"And Brother Gerard wants Damascus," I thought aloud. "And now that Damascus has denounced you, so making you appear the loyal Catholic, certes you are safe too from Brother Gerard."

"No, I am safe from neither. The friar will always suspect me, if not of heresy, then of other great offenses. This I have always known. He has cast me as his enemy, and there is no other role I can play for him."

"So it has begun again," said I.

"Aye, if e'er it was truly over. And I am caught between them. 'Tis as if each is planning a destiny for me, and no charts or star figuring can uncover what will happen."

"Well, surely there is still something we can do. We can have Damascus arrested for making threats 'gainst you. We can . . ."

"No, Sara. E'en Brother Gerard could not catch him."

"Then are you going to let him run freely about?"

"Nay, that's too dangerous." Of a sudden, he seemed to despair. "I will see what I can do," said he without meaning.

I reached out and laid my hand on his and smiled; what paltry comfort that was.

I knew that Catlin's resignation was but his first response to the shock of Damascus's wild appearance. But until then I could not bear being useless. I had to do something for him, and what seemed best kept haunting my mind. And so, whilst saying naught to him lest he react with anger, I set out on the morrow for a familiar place and arrived there at just the right hour of the clock.

I stood not at the well in the middle of the broad street, but near the doors of the monastery. They were open and in and out of the place went laborers carrying bundles or tools, and after a little, keeping apart from them like a celestial being from mortals, came Brother Gerard. We saw each other whilst still some distance apart, and he stopped before me.

More than half a year had passed since last I'd seen him. His face had grown gaunt, more stark and drawn, and his still-young flesh more bloodless.

I proceeded uneasily. "God give ye good den, Brother Gerard."

He nodded to me. "Mistress Lathbury."

"And I thank you for giving me this meeting."

" 'Tis only a small bother."

I knitted and unknitted my fingers. "I've been away from Antwerp for some months."

"I know."

"But now I am back. And so too is Damascus."

Something happened when I said that name. The corner of his eye twitched, his lips moved. His serenity was shaken, his hollow eyes peering around us as if looking for Damascus.

"Why have you come to me with this news?"

"Because Damascus is dangerous. Because you have sought him before, and now he is returned, bolder and madder than ever. Only yesterday he forced himself into Mynheer Catlin's presence and screamed insane falsehoods at him, that Catlin is against the Protestants, that he is a spy for Rome, and so too am I. I will not tolerate such abuse from a stranger."

"Then you want his ravings to be proof of Bartholomew Catlin's innocence of heresy."

"No. Damascus is too mad to be accepted as a witness against anyone. But you despise his heresy and wish to silence him. I too wish to have his abuse against us silenced. You want to capture him. Then do so now. Have the city's guards secretly follow Catlin about, for Damascus is following him. Or if you cannot catch him that way, then set another trap. We will go to that warehouse again or wherever you wish."

"You are asking for my help."

"You have given it before." I desperately searched for any hint in his unperturbed calm that would give me hope. I altered mine efforts by gentling my tone. "You warned Catlin, through me and my niece, of the impending investigation of Nicolas van Wouwere. Now I must again, Brother Gerard, rely on your goodness."

He did not respond to this, and I wondered if there was in fact no trace of goodness in him. Mayhap he had only been like a god bestowing a single and capricious mercy on a mortal. I made another attempt. "Damascus too seems wilier than ever, and even more an adversary you cannot control. I doubt nothing that he is plotting for violence against you."

Once more his eyes moved about, his head gave a small quick jerk as he looked behind him. I was right. Not knowing whether or no Damascus was near, not knowing when he would return or if he had e'en been long since back had worn him down. He had grown restless for his enemy.

"Indeed, Mevrouw Lathbury, he must be arrested." He was proper and formal. "I shall see what I can do. Good morrow to you."

With that, he nodded to me and walked on. I had wanted more from him. I had wanted assurance and even an immediate resolution, but he gave nothing. Mayhap he will send us word as he did the last time. Till then, I had to wait.

But some days passed, and no word was sent and no guards trailed distantly after Catlin. At least in that time we did not see Damascus again, nor did he try to approach Catlin. Yet somehow, in odd moments, in scattered places, he seemed to be near, cringing into his shadow, extinguishing his presence just as it was becoming perceptible. Once when Catlin and I were walking down a street, I thought I heard a wheezing creeping after us, and with it the shuffling of shoes. I peered urgently all about us and saw nothing. Still I sometimes apprehended flickers of movement that had been fastened upon Catlin; still I sensed that Damascus was wedged anxiously just out of reach, waiting and watching.

Then at last I saw him again, but only for a few moments. I was alone and walking down a busy street when again I felt his presence, this time drawing nigh most rapidly. A group of children pattered by, a ratcatcher ambled across their path, and scarce had they moved on when Damascus appeared on the other side of the street, galloping in the opposite direction from which I was headed. He was rolling up and down in a spindly gait, his scarecrow clothes flapping, his knuckles clenched, his arms held bent and rigid. He turned his head and saw me, and his face, which was strangely expressionless yet baleful, did not change. He turned forward again and galloped on, never slackening his pace. I was by then so fretted with worry from his unseen presence that now when I beheld him I was shaken, as if I had just witnessed something, however momentary, that was not meant to be seen.

XXXIV

'Twas on a Saturday that I had seen Damascus. I was at home by late afternoon, then at dusk Catlin too returned and we all sat down to supper. He said little whilst we ate, and only sank lower into a melancholy, and asked for wine and drank several glasses. Bess called for tisane and gently urged him to have it instead, but he would not listen to her. We had together a somber evening.

I rose early the next morning, dressed for mass, and went to Bess's chamber. Not only was she dressed, but she had a wakeful look as if she had been up for hours.

"Had you poor slumber?" I asked.

"What I had of it was poor."

"And you look ill for it, so nap awhile this afternoon."

"I still won't sleep," she said and shrugged. She reached for a missal lying on a chest beside her gloves, then realized she must put on her gloves first, and so laid the book back down and picked them up. Before pulling on her gloves, though, she glanced in a looking glass and fidgeted with her French hood, as if the familiar garb no longer fit. Through all these movements it seemed her mind was too strained to concentrate on anything. Then words began to slip out of her. "Last night, after you left us, Catlin told me what was weighing so heavily upon him. 'Tis news of his whore, or belike I should say the woman he was once wont to visit."

I did not know what to say.

She didn't look at me as she continued. "The woman died yesterday morning. Catlin was told by someone that unbeknownst to him she had for three months been with child. She miscarried two days ago and would not stop bleeding from it. And now she is dead." Bess spoke simply, as if she'd passed through much pain and was left weakened.

I crossed myself. "Alack the poor woman. God have mercy on her soul. Catlin had indeed good reason to be sad."

She pulled her cloak about her to ward off a chill I couldn't feel and went to stand beside the fireplace. "He fears the child might have been his."

Ah, my poor Bess, I thought, all the more pain for you is this. "But the child may not have been his at all," I argued, though this was scant consolation. "Of a surety she didn't sleep with him alone but with many men. I doubt nothing that even she could not have sworn which one of them was the father."

"And so I told Catlin. He isn't certain it was his child, but neither can he swear it wasn't, and so he feels that he might well have been the cause of her death."

"He should not feel so!"

"Tell him that and see what good it does." Finally she turned to me. "Another thing, Sara—does not this news remind you of something else?"

I shook my head.

"Strange, but when Catlin told me of her death, I did bethink me at once of what van Wouwere had said: that I would die a bloody woman's death. It was the second part of the prophecy he gave me, and if he had foretold aught, then again he told it wrongly. 'Twas another woman's death he saw, not mine."

Now I too felt the chill. "No more of this talk, Bess!" I demanded.

We had just descended the stairs when the front door opened and Catlin came in. His face was drawn and he looked as if he'd been out walking for hours in the wintry cold. I took one of his hands in the two of mine and murmured to him, "Bess told me. May God give you comfort."

He squeezed my hands. "Think not on't, Sara. I seldom saw her and never missed her. Still at least one man should mourn for her."

Bess did not move or speak nor did she betray any unseemly jealousy, and for that I was proud of her. Certes, I could now see, she had no reason to be so, for clearly what Catlin felt, beyond the guilt, was only a Christian pity.

He looked at Bess and me as if trying to recall what day of the week it was and where we might be going. "Are you for mass now?"

"Aye," I replied.

Again he looked long at us. "Might I come with you?"

"We'd be glad of your company." He had never gone with us to church before.

We arrived at Our Lady's just as the Kyrie Eleison of the mass was being recited and found a place in a quiet corner away from everyone, near hidden by a column. We sat in a grayness stained with colors, heard the familiar prayers passing betwixt priest and people, and knelt beneath the contemplative gazes of painted saints and glass-held angels. Ever and anon Catlin knitted his fingers together as if he were praying, but then they'd separate and hold his head, lie limply on his thighs, rub the back of the chair before him, knit again. Sometimes he murmured the responses, sometimes he seemed to have heard naught. During all this Bess just let him be, as if knowing that he desired only her warm presence. My heart ached for him; I knew he had come with us in hope of being granted a little peace. And there was indeed in him now a strand of it, perchance given to him by Bess and me by merely being close to him. Though the source of such a peace was mortal, still I felt that in its own way, it was holy.

On the morrow Catlin left to meet elsewhere yet another merchant. Having errands to run not far from where he would be, Bess and I accompanied him. He had his meeting, we finished our errands, and somehow we encountered him again in the same street where we had earlier parted. 'Twas a wide lane near the Bourse, and many merchants were walking there or standing in small groups. Whilst Catlin stood with such a group, Bess and I lingered a little away and waited for him.

Then a strange sight came up our dismal street. A sorry mule, led by a red-faced man, was pulling a cart in which was strapped a plain wooden coffin. This in itself was nothing to note; what made it strange was the sorry group of mourners straggling behind. There were only seven of them, all women and all common prostitutes. None wore any trumpery or jewels or lace, and no paint glowed on their cheeks. Yet still there was something slovenly about their dress, and their fair faces had a hardened boldness and their movements an easy indolence. All of them too, whilst tramping clumsily on their hard wooden pattens over the snow-slogged ground, of habit lifted too high their petticoats.

The merchants quieted their talking as the whores and the cart
moved past them. Some stared at the sight with contempt; some scarce
glanced the women's way. One man threw a taunt at them whilst two or
three mocked a solemn reverence for the procession.

Most of the whores were disdainful in turn and carried themselves
with as much haughty pride as they could muster. Some kept their eyes
cast down lest they draw more attention to themselves. The youngest
sniffed into her kerchief and watched the coffin before her with sadness.

The cart was now opposite Catlin. He had been silent since the first
sight of the procession and in his expression I could see his recognition
of the women. Then he stared at the coffin. A cruel jest muttered by a
man nearby made him stiffen. Other men, already weary of the spectacle, turned back to one another and talked again of business. By then
the coffin was passing Bess and me. She watched it and said naught. I
crossed myself, whispered a prayer, and looked around to see Catlin's
eyes still fixed upon the coffin.

He took a step forward, paused, then decided. He took off his hat
and held it low in his hands. Slowly, looking at no one, he moved
toward the whores and his steps fell in behind theirs. Up and down the
street the merchants quieted. His face was tense and his head bent,
though not to ward off the scorn brewing amongst the men, but to give
through this, his public mourning, a dignity to the dead whore in her
coffin.

For long moments a massing silence encompassed the merchants
and the only sounds were the clattering of the pattens and the mule's
hooves and the squeaking of the cart. Then there were mumblings.
Someone called to Catlin and asked if he was the husband of the blessed
dead. A few men laughed. Most were uncomfortable and held their
astonished objections to whispers. Through all, Catlin only walked
behind the coffin. At long last the cart reached the end of the street
and turned the corner. The whores followed it, so too did Catlin, and
then all were gone and out of our sight.

For some time more the conversations about us were strained.
There were expressions of disgust and laughter and the shaking of many
heads, and questions and answers flew, and everywhere was the name of
Bartholomew Catlin.

Bess was trembling. I linked mine arm through hers and whispered
that we should hie ourselves home.

"But Catlin?" she said, uncertain whether or no to go after him.

"He'll be home soon. Be waiting there for him."

For over an hour we waited, and then he returned. I smiled at him and asked if he'd like something warm to drink. Bess too made no mention of the funeral; indeed not then or ever did the three of us speak of it, as nothing needed to be said. Hours dwindled away, and we played at cards, talked, and drank. A calm was spreading over him, and as we slipped into good spirits I realized that since Bess's return from our journey to Rome Catlin had in truth lost the haunted look that had sometimes flickered in his eyes. Only when Damascus had burst into the countinghouse did it briefly return. Now that it was banished, once more the thin strand of peace I had seen in him the day before was e'en stronger, and for the first time since I had known him, Catlin seemed to have at last much peace of mind.

Word of Catlin's public mourning of a worthless whore spread within days to most of the merchants he knew, and thence to us. Their reactions were various, as had been those of the merchants at the scene, but all were similar in their reprehension of his action. Some considered it an incipient sign of madness. Though his character had not been admired, his professional integrity had ne'er been questioned; but no more. If even his public behavior was becoming gross and unseemly, the logic went, then too his business practices might be similar, and so it could be unwise to do business with him. I e'en saw once two Flemish merchants cross a street rather than pass by him. At the Bourse he was not censured or insulted, but a few men turned their backs on him and only those who owed him money were courteous.

Some of the Merchant Adventurers I met were not surprised by Catlin's action. A week after the funeral I went to the English House where an Adventurer told me he did not hold Catlin's "strange conduct" to be inexplicable. It was what one would expect of him, said he. With him and others I avoided the subject, but to no one would I deny my friendship with the man. I was instead proud of it.

Certes Catlin was hurt by all these acts and by the contempt thrown at him. As he had done before, so now again he pulled into himself and was at home more oft than at his countinghouse, and he kept closely to Bess. He was, too, displeased that his business was suffering: displeased, but not worried. Bess at last told him that he should look more to it and fight against any loss of his wealth. He was an important merchant, she averred; he should cling to what good reputation he had left. "No, Bess, let me be," he replied. "I'll be a good merchant still. But what you hold so important I no longer do."

On one of those days, when Bess was at the countinghouse and Catlin was at home, I found him in his library. He was sitting at the table and leaning against the window, watching the world outside shimmering in snowy quietude. I sat opposite him and watched too. From the stove came a glow and warmth that curled around us like a sleeping cat, and beyond our small room was a restful house, and on Catlin's face lay his glimmer of tranquility.

A long time passed, and at last he spoke. "Think you, Sara, that like Bess I should be at my work and not sitting idly about?"

"You know best your own work and when to attend to it, Catlin. And, too, if this is what you're like when idle, then I'd as lief have you idle than any other way."

"You were always a kind woman, Sara."

"No, not always. I've had to learn many things in my life, and kindness is one of them."

" 'Tis learned more easily when one has a good heart, and that you have." His breath had clouded a windowpane, and he wiped the film away. "I've not the same kind heart. I've learned too slowly." Though he seemed tired, his blue eyes were lucent as if, even whilst he was soothed, there was a part of him that ever smoldered, something that was always disturbed.

"Are there things in you Catlin," I asked, "that can never reach complete contentment?"

"God forbid they ever do. There's a passion in me, and it's as eternal as my soul. It *is* my soul. That's what I've learned, that life is given to us as a passion. Wise men and cold theologians have whispered of such before, and that this is why some sinners are so close to God, closer than those who are only tepidly good because they've not the passion to be aught else. And this much I've learned from my fellow merchants: We make God in our own image. I did the same, and stifled my soul's imagination by shaping God into a fastidious bookkeeper who records for each mortal an account of debits and credits and holds him to the strict payment for the smallest farthing of a sin."

I remembered me then what Catlin had once told me. "So you thought you might e'en be a bondslave to the will of God, or the devil's, and had not a will of your own. It seems then as though you've freed yourself from your own beliefs."

"Aye, that might be true."

"And now you can pray in peace?"

He smiled sadly. "I send up a few prayers, asking for forgiveness. I hope they're heard."

He fell silent again, and I with him. We watched once more the snow outside the window and gazed at the roofs and ledges that were covered in a luminous glow as if from a million white candles. I was content merely to sit there, in that room and with Catlin, and sit we did for a very long time.

That evening and a few more passed quietly by, until on one of
them I found myself alone in the emptying streets and yet some distance
from Catlin's house. The air was darkening with night; the moon and
stars, already risen, cast a wan light, and all along my way shutters were
closing against the cold, blinking out of sight candles being lit in the
rooms beyond. I crossed a snow-bordered marketplace where the stalls
and benches had been carried away, and only straw and muck and
slivers of garbage were left. Old women in black swept away at bits
of filth with twig brooms, toothlessly muttering prayers to God and
gossip to one another as they slowly, slowly wove about, sweeping
without stop. Their bony wrists, visible betwixt their black sleeves
and woolen mittens, looked like skeletons, thinner than their broom-
staffs.

I arrived on Catlin's doorstep and then paused—for what reason I
knew not—to glance up at the dark sky. I saw the stars and the horned
moon, but too I saw in the nightly depths flecks of cloud, or rather I
told myself they were clouds; they looked more like ghostly ships, sailing
this way and that across a vast ocean of sky. I watched them until I was
distracted by the tinkling of a distant bell. It sounded like the bell rung
for the Host during mass, I half thought, but then a memory stole
through me. No, 'twas the bell of a leper, mayhap the one at the church
that unhappy day. As if trying to escape the past, I knocked upon the
door and stepped swiftly inside when it was opened to me.

That evening too was restful. The three of us gathered in the antler
room and played at cards and told some stories and exchanged jests.
Always, Bess kept close to her Catlin, and with her near he was glad.
As the hours passed the room grew colder, and I threw more wood on

the fire. Bess complained that she was chilled and went to her bedchamber to change into something warmer. She had but left when, remembering that Lijsken had still my fresh-laundered pillowbere, which she was mending, I excused myself and went to fetch it.

Only Marie had gone to bed; Lijsken and Arnout were still up and sitting by the fire in the kitchen. The pillowbere was in her lap and she was putting final stitches in it, whilst Arnout had his head cocked toward the outside wall, as if listening to something. "What hear you?" I asked.

"Methinks I hear that dog again," he grumbled.

"Does one of the neighbors have a dog?"

"I trow it's no one's dog, 'tis such a mangy, vicious thing. Been coming around for a week now, sniffing for food and trying to get in. I'm surprised it's still alive. Any dogs roaming the streets are supposed to be killed, that's the new law. So many people starving this winter, isn't enow food for them, let alone for dogs."

Just then there came a scratching at the kitchen door, like a paw scraping away. Arnout grumbled and took up a poker from beside the hearth.

"I'm going to chase that dog away," he said, and unlocked the door and went out, shutting it behind him.

I took his place beside the fire and talked with Lijsken of household affairs. A creaking made me pause, for it sounded like the door opening, yet so familiar was I by then with all the squeaking doors in the house that I thought the noise too short for the door to have been opened and closed again. Still, to be certain I cast my glance into the shadowed recess beside the door where were hung large cleaning tools, but saw naught there.

Arnout soon returned, angry that he had not e'en seen the dog. "He is getting to be too clever," said he.

I took the pillowbere from Lijsken and thanked her, and we left the kitchen together, she and Arnout blowing out the candle and retiring for the night. I went along the hall and thought again I heard a noise, like a small creak or the sound of a breath. So I walked a little too heavily up the stairs, yet listened to naught more than the sound of mine own footsteps.

Catlin was alone at the table in the antler room as I passed, watching the fire and waiting for us to return, and I went on up to my bedchamber and restored my pillow to its cover. I could hear Bess moving about in her own chamber as I left mine.

I was only halfway back down the stairs when I started in horror. Out of the shadows at the bottom emerged the form of Damascus. He did not see me for he was staring with his wild eyes into the antler room, and his lips were pulled back from off his teeth and his shriveled body was ready to leap. In the second that he paused I glimpsed a knife clenched in his hand. In the next instant he ran into the antler room and I screamed out Catlin's name.

I fled down the stairs and into the room. Catlin had leapt up at my cry and spun around. Just as he turned, just as he saw me, he saw Damascus and threw out his arms. But Damascus was by then against him, with the hand holding the knife flung back. Ere Catlin could move, the hand swung with an animal strength and shoved the blade into him. I froze in horror. Catlin tried to cry out but I heard the sound fail in his throat. In a trice Damascus wrenched the knife out and Catlin grabbed at his belly and the blood spurting from it. Then a figure flew past me. It was Bess screaming to Catlin.

Damascus whipped about and ran back past me so quickly that he was gone in the blink of an eye. I did not look after him; Bess was already at Catlin's side and so too was I. He collapsed against the table, clutching still at his belly and gasping for air. Bess cried out at the sight of the blood pouring through his fingers.

I screamed for the servants. I ran to the stairs and screamed again. There were thumps and shouts and Lijsken and Arnout rushed up the stairs. I called to them that Catlin had been stabbed. Lijsken crossed herself and sped to him. Bess was holding him and had one hand pressed against his, as if to help him stop the deathly flow of blood.

Lijsken hastened away to fetch bandages and salves. With Bess's help Arnout carried Catlin up the stairs and laid him on his bed. Catlin gasped that he was cold, and I covered his legs with blankets. Then I ripped open his jerkin and shirt and with a kerchief wiped away as best I could the blood that surrounded the long wound gaping near the middle of his belly. Arnout raced away in search of a doctor, but already Lijsken was back. She dabbed at the wound with a wet warm cloth and smoothed a clear salve along the bloody edges. Then with strips of bandage she covered the wound and tightened it, but still it bled, and again she dabbed away the blood, again she smeared on more salve, again she covered his belly with bandages.

Bess knelt by Catlin's side and held his hand, and ever and anon squeezed it hard when he groaned from the pain. She stroked his face and murmured comforting words and tried not to betray the terror in her. Catlin had yet no voice and with his free hand he only gouged the bed beneath him.

The wound at last was wrapped tightly, but blood still seeped through the white bedclothes and spread, scarlet and bright, across them. I pulled the blankets over Catlin's shivering chest. Then I lit more candles and for a few moments there was only the sound of the fire in the hearth, the guttering of candles, and Catlin's labored breathing. A sweat peppered his brow. Before our eyes his face and hands paled to white against his black hair wet with sweat. He squeezed Bess's hand again, and in her face was alarm as she felt how much weaker was the movement now.

"Bess," said he. It was the faintest of whispers.

She whispered his name in turn. His pain seemed to fade and then to surge again. Bess drew so close to him that their faces were touching, and she kissed his temple.

The pain once again faded. "So it's done at last," he said. "But God has some kindness in Him." He rolled his head toward her. "He gave you to me in my last months, ere giving me my fate."

"No, Catlin!" I was choking on tears. "You'll be well yet. The bleeding is stopping." This I said though I could not know if it were so.

The chamber grew more hushed. I knelt down beside Bess. Lijsken stood on the opposite side of the bed, whispering prayers and silently weeping.

"Forgive me my sins," Catlin gasped. Then he smiled, as if something were being revealed to him. "I must have been forgiven, for I was given the both of you, and you've done me only good."

The effort of talking weakened him more. He sank lower into his bed, shutting his eyes against the pain. Then, as if he sensed something to be seen, he opened them slowly, looked into the vacant air at the foot of the bed as if someone were standing there gazing down at him, and his eyes grew large and then wild. He struggled to sit up with an awful strength that would not let us hold him down and put his weight on an elbow. He bent forward and raised his other arm, pointing hard as if at an unseen someone standing dreadfully visible before him.

"Look at me now!" he cried. "Aye, stare at me! 'Tis your last chance, because you've lost me!"

Then he fell back. The sweat had trickled down onto his cheeks and into his beard. His labored breathing melted away. He gazed at Bess, closed his eyes yet again against the pain, and called softly to her. She took his hand into both of hers and kissed it over and over. His fingers moved within hers. Then even as we listened unbelieving, his breathing stopped. Bess gazed stunned at his face. Her hand shaking violently, she touched his lips, his cheeks. She whispered his name and waited for him to answer.

I held her shoulders. A shudder raked through her body as if her life were being ripped out of her. Her head fell back and she wailed out for Catlin.

I could no longer control mine own sobs. Blinded by tears, I stumbled up and reached for strips of bandages to wipe them away. I looked down at Catlin's pale face, moved away, and could make only a few faltering steps to the end of the bed. A fearful coldness smote me in that place. The air was so icy that I shivered, and then I comprehended that I was shivering because I too felt evil in the spot at the foot of the bed. I stepped back, and as I did so the coldness and evil retreated also, passing away till it was no more.

Again I looked at Catlin. There was a peace in his face, as much as his poor body could show on this earth. He was indeed at peace, I felt, and only we were left in grief to mourn.

XXXVI

It has been a fortnight since his death, and still I weep for Catlin. I shall mourn him, I feel, for a long time yet to come. I shall always grievously miss him.

Bess wept for hours after his death, and then fell silent, and through the endless night kept motionless vigil beside his body. A cold dawn came and still she did not move, so I put my arms about her and led her away. But when his body had been laid within a coffin, she returned to him and through the day and another night she sat beside him and did not leave him again until the prayers had been said and the funeral rites were finished and he had been buried. During all that time and for days more, she scarcely touched food; she uttered no more than a few words, and then they were murmured to herself or as if to Catlin, rather than to anyone else. She tried to sleep, could not, and on at least one night drank herself into a stupor and finally was given some heavy slumber by the wine. She sat endlessly in the antler room or the library, lost in secret lamentation. She wandered through the house, oft in the middle of the night when she could not sleep, exhausted by her grief, her mind dragging behind her, and traveled deeper into the numbness that lay somewhere beyond the pain. I found her once at Catlin's desk in the countinghouse, looking at his ledgers, checking his sums, as if he would return soon and would wish the work done. I would not let her sit there nor look again into his books; I would not witness passively the raveling away of her sanity. Days more passed, and she began to return from whatever unmapped world her soul had gone to, bringing back with her an undivided sorrow.

Too soon, a lawyer appeared on one of those days, standing proudly at the house's front door and announcing when it was opened to him that he possessed Mynheer Catlin's will and that it was his own honor to be its executor. He was an elderly man about whom everything seemed to sag: his paunch, his jowls, his too-wide mouth. He expressed his sympathy, but it was given us as if in fulfillment of one of his many legal duties. I sat him in the dining room, then made certain that besides myself, Bess and Lijsken were present. He pulled out a few papers and began to read.

Having known Catlin so well by that time, and after having lived with him, I was not surprised when it was revealed in his will that Bess and I would receive most of his possessions. There had sadly been no one else in his life, no affectionate family or friends whom he felt deserved e'en to be mentioned in his will. I was given his countinghouse and what furniture it had, and Bess was to have his house and nigh all the things therein. She was not surprised by this fortune that had suddenly befallen her; rather she accepted the news with mute desolation. The apprentices, the lawyer read, shall have restored to them the full fee their parents had given Catlin some years before, and Jan and Michiel were themselves given each a modest sum of money and Catlin's praise for their loyalty and abilities. All the servants were also given money and too some household items; Lijsken, for that she was but a housekeeper, was given a considerable sum. After these gifts had been distributed, then the bulk of Catlin's wealth and too his business affairs were divided betwixt Bess and me. More details were read off, more matters that needed to be resolved and discussed.

The lawyer added that Catlin must have left cloths and other merchandise that had yet to be sold, and debts still to be collected from many people who had owed him money. He volunteered unctuously his services for this work but I declined his offer, knowing he would be expecting a fat fee for whatever work he did, and too because I did not want a stranger handling Catlin's business. I would do what I could, I said to him, and too my sons would aid me.

Whilst giving me the will to keep and putting away his own papers, the lawyer asked me what I planned to do with the countinghouse.

"I wot not, 'tis too early to decide," I replied. "Mayhap I shall keep it for our company's use. Mayhap rent it."

"I could find for you a worthy tenant," he said.

"If I rent it. Mayhap I shall sell it."

"Or a buyer," he was quick to say.

Bess, stunned at the mere mention of selling the building, shot unbelieving eyes at me. I retracted my words and added truthfully that not only would it be wiser and more profitable to keep it, but I could not part with the place precisely because it had been Catlin's.

"And you, mevrouw?" The lawyer bowed his head to Bess.

She glared at him. He clarified his meaning. "Will you be wishing to sell this house?"

"I will never sell it!" she muttered, as if cursing him.

I did not talk with her of her plans. When she later gave some indication that she would be remaining in the house, I talked carefully instead of the urgency with which we both had to return home. The matter of her land in England, I told her, could no longer be delayed, and she had her own purchases and sales to see to, and the more profits she had from them, the more easily she could maintain Catlin's house. Keep on Lijsken and Arnout, I told her; they could well look after the place whilst she was gone. Almost wordlessly, she conceded that she would return with me. I had by then already paid for passage on a ship for the both of us. I had too written my sons and partners informing them of the tragic news and that one of them must now come to Antwerp to hire another factor, for I'd not the heart to. Jeremy wrote that he would sail for Antwerp as soon as I was in London and had given him instructions regarding Catlin's business affairs. I was burdened with too much grief, he wrote, now to have put upon me such worries.

The day before we were to sail, Lijsken came to tell me what she had just heard at the market. A laundress who worked for the paupers' hospital near St. George's Gate had rattled on to her of some of the homeless poor who were looked after there. The newest arrival was a gravely ill man who, Lijsken swore, fit most closely the description I had given her of Damascus. She urged me to contact the authorities and tell them where Catlin's murderer lay, but I said I would myself go to the hospital and see if indeed it was Damascus; I would not hazard having an innocent pauper dragged from his sickbed.

The hospital was a plain building of a few narrow floors, all of them dismal and sparsely furnished. I invented an excuse for the black-robed nuns who were looking after the inhabitants and so was allowed entrance and a limited freedom to look for the someone I said was a former servant. I wended my way past the poor men and women and their babes, most of whom needed only food and a roof over their heads, and so whilst in the place could take care of themselves. There were too, however, the sickly indigent, who coughed and groaned upon pallets laid out in a few of the rooms and begged for attention from the patient nuns who were tending to them as best they could.

On the topmost floor, I came at last to a long room wherein, away from the others, lay, on a heap of old straw beneath the room's only window, a sticklike figure of a man. I saw the familiar shreds of hair and beard, more discolored than the straw, and the gaunt, sallow face spotted with sores. It was indeed Damascus. His eyes were open and staring up at the ceiling. I came closer still and crouched down beside him. His eyes did not move. He seemed unaware that I was there, or that anyone was near him. 'Twas clear he had no more than a few hours of life left in him.

I trembled as I looked down at his face and into his pale eyes, unmoving now yet still wild. I had heard, long ago, that there were men who were so evil that their souls descended into hell e'en before their bodies had died, and that devils ascended to take over their useless shells. Only devils, I felt, were keeping these wretched remains sputtering along. In a few hours his body would die, and a nun would come along and close his eyes, and Damascus would be forgotten and lost, somewhere in darkness, forever.

A wave of horror swept over me. I fled from him and from that awful place.

I wandered down endless streets. I paid no mind to where I was going until slowly I comprehended that there was one last visit I must make, one more man I must see. I turned my steps toward the Dominican monastery.

I knew at last the cruelty of this man. Brother Gerard had never e'en attempted to capture Damascus. Knowing his enemy well, he must have foreseen what the madman would do. So he had allowed to happen what they both wanted: the death of Catlin, heretic and sinner.

I waited a long time at the monastery's doors, watching friars come and go. When Brother Gerard emerged, he saw me and glided over. For a moment we only looked at each other. He had changed yet more. What few things in him that had been limp—his smile, his white hands—had given way to rigidity, as if he were now only a dry, dead leaf.

"I have heard of Mynheer Catlin's tragic death." His voice was hollow. "I grieved at the news."

I only gazed steadily at him and told myself I was a lady. I wished I could spit in his face. "Know you that 'twas Damascus who killed him?"

"I do."

I wanted to claw him till his own blood ran. "Know you where Damascus is?"

"No, not at all."

"I do."

He started and shot anxious glances about him.

I measured carefully what I now said. "He has left Antwerp again. He was again riding a donkey and was screaming to me that he will return, as he always does, and that once more he will wreak vengeance in God's name. He said—" I paused, espying that Brother Gerard was hanging hungrily onto my every word, as I wanted. "He shouted, 'The monk shall be next.' "

The blood was gone from his face. Beside one eye the skin began to quiver, all out of control.

"Did he mean you, Brother Gerard?" I innocently added.

His lips made an unwilling movement, but he said nothing.

"Slipping out of Antwerp, slipping back in, and even into locked houses and past secured walls." I gestured to the monastery as an example. "He is as impossible to catch as a shadow, isn't he?"

Nothing more need be said; I had dealt the final blow. Keeping my cold and angry gaze full upon him, aware that he knew why, I stepped away. "Good-bye, Brother Gerard."

I turned my back on him and walked away. Now, his waiting will begin, I reflected. As he had before, he will wait and wait for Damascus, but this time the waiting will be far more hellish. And I would be glad.

All the way home, I was lost in thought. Damascus and Brother Gerard had been so much like the devil and God in the doctrine Catlin had once believed in, and like a beast of burden they had ridden him. But now the devil was dead and the god had been pulled down. And above it all still was God, watching silently, untouched. I still didn't know if He had indeed given Catlin a fate. I could, as with a map, chart backward through the events leading to his death; many of them were the results of his own acts: It was he who sought friendship with van

Wouwere, and he who chose the secret shipping of pamphlets that attracted Damascus. Yet I could not help but blame God for what seemed indeed Catlin's cruel fate.

Still, I knew, I will in time forgive Him, as I wish to be forgiven.

Bess and I arrived at the English Quay betimes the next morning. Our coffers and trunks were laded onto our ship, and we put our lesser bags into our small cabin ere returning to the deck. The men were shouting and going to and fro, lading goods, checking supplies, rolling kilderkins along. The day was not especially good for sailing, but it was the best those sailors had seen for some weeks; December had thus far been so bitterly cold that for the first time in many years the Scheldt had frozen o'er, and only two days before did it melt enow for the braver ships to steer carefully through the crooked paths gaping amidst the ice.

Bess was quiet. She stood at the railing, watching the activity on the dock below, sometimes raising her head and gazing out over the city. She thought, I knew, that she would be soon returning, but she was wrong. For just as impediments had arisen whilst we were in Antwerp, delaying again and again my return to England, so now there will be delays for her. I will put impediments before her, I will complicate repeatedly her plans to leave until the weeks and months have passed, mayhap a year or more. I will delay her return until the wound in her is as healed as it can ever be, and England has again become her home, and Antwerp, without her Catlin, only a foreign place. When she will not haunt Catlin's house but live with some peace in it, then she will return.

As I stood with her and watched her, I bethought me of van Wouwere's prophecy. The first two parts, if they had ever held any truth in them, had concerned others and not her. But the third part of the prophecy, I sadly sensed, would indeed come true for her. Howe'er old she lives to be, whether she lives for one more year or fifty, she will die a lonely death for she will be without her Catlin.

The tide was growing strong. The sailors clambered about the deck, and the sails were unfurled and the ropes cast off. Then the ship moved. It creaked and swayed and floated away from the dock, and away from Antwerp.

May God, I thought, if He doth hear our prayers, make safe our journey home.